W9-BVF-866

NEW YORK TIMES BESTSELLING AUTHOR
JANET CHAPMAN
keeps the fire burning all year long. . . .

"Chapman is unmatched and unforgettable."
—*Romantic Times*

Praise for the charming Highlanders series

SECRETS OF THE HIGHLANDER

"Liberally spiced with mystery, this story has warmth and genuine love that make it the perfect antidote for stress."
—*Romantic Times*

ONLY WITH A HIGHLANDER

"A mystical, magical book if there ever was one. . . . A perfect 10!"
—Romance Reviews Today

"This time-traveling Highlander series has been a pure joy to read, and this book is no exception."
—*Romantic Times*

"An excellent addition to her entertaining Highlander series."
—*Booklist*

TEMPTING THE HIGHLANDER

"Chapman breathes such life and warmth into her characters, each story is impossible to put down."
—*Romantic Times*

WEDDING THE HIGHLANDER

"A series that just keeps getting better. . . . This is Chapman's most emotional, touching and powerful novel to date."

—*Romantic Times*

"Exciting . . . Janet Chapman writes a refreshingly entertaining novel."

—The Best Reviews

LOVING THE HIGHLANDER

"Janet Chapman has hit another home run with *Loving the Highlander*. It's a fresh take on time travel, with both humor and drama. She's a keeper."

—*New York Times* bestselling author Linda Howard

"The characters are lively, intriguing and full of passion."

—*Romantic Times*

CHARMING THE HIGHLANDER

"Splendid. We can expect great things from Janet Chapman."

—*The Oakland Press*

"Time travel, tragedy, temptation, along with desire, destiny, devotion, and, of course, true love, are all woven into Janet Chapman's romance."

—*Bangor Daily News*

"Terrific . . . A real gem of a story!"

—*Romantic Times*

. . . and for her captivating contemporary romances

THE MAN MUST MARRY

"Offbeat and charming. . . . Chapman's gift for creating characters you love spending time with is on full display."

—*Romantic Times*

"Ninety-percent laughter, ten-percent tears, and one-hundred-percent romance. Nobody writes a luscious romantic comedy like Janet Chapman. . . . Superb."

—ReadertoReader.com

THE STRANGER IN HER BED

"A thoroughly enjoyable tale of a modern-day knight and his feisty ladylove set in the rugged mountains of Maine."

—*Booklist*

THE SEDUCTION OF HIS WIFE

"A charming story of love, growth and trust."

—*Romantic Times*

"Chapman presents a cast of rugged characters in rural Maine who enact a surprisingly tender romance."

—*Booklist*

THE DANGEROUS PROTECTOR

"One thing that Chapman does so deftly is meld great characterization, sparkling humor and spicy adventure into a perfect blend."

—*Romantic Times*

Also by Janet Chapman

Moonlight Warrior

The Man Must Marry

Secrets of the Highlander

The Stranger in Her Bed

The Seduction of His Wife

Only with a Highlander

The Dangerous Protector

Tempting the Highlander

The Seductive Impostor

Wedding the Highlander

Loving the Highlander

Charming the Highlander

Available from Pocket Books

JANET CHAPMAN

A Highlander Christmas

POCKET **STAR** BOOKS

New York London Toronto Sydney

The sale of this book without its cover is unauthorized. If you purchased this book without a cover, you should be aware that it was reported to the publisher as "unsold and destroyed." Neither the author nor the publisher has received payment for the sale of this "stripped book."

Pocket Star Books
A Division of Simon & Schuster, Inc.
1230 Avenue of the Americas
New York, NY 10020

This book is a work of fiction. Names, characters, places, and incidents either are products of the author's imagination or are used fictitiously. Any resemblance to actual events or locales or persons, living or dead, is entirely coincidental.

Copyright © 2009 by Janet Chapman

All rights reserved, including the right to reproduce this book or portions thereof in any form whatsoever. For information address Pocket Books Subsidiary Rights Department, 1230 Avenue of the Americas, New York, NY 10020

This Pocket Star Books paperback edition November 2010

POCKET STAR BOOKS and colophon are registered trademarks of Simon & Schuster, Inc.

For information about special discounts for bulk purchases, please contact Simon & Schuster Special Sales at 1-866-506-1949 or business@simonandschuster.com

The Simon & Schuster Speakers Bureau can bring authors to your live event. For more information or to book an event contact the Simon & Schuster Speakers Bureau at 1-866-248-3049 or visit our website at www.simonspeakers.com.

Cover art by Alan Ayers
Cover design by Min Choi

Manufactured in the United States of America

10 9 8 7 6 5 4 3 2 1

ISBN: 978-1-4516-0941-7
ISBN: 978-1-4391-6684-0 (ebook)

*To those of you who don't believe in miracles, get ready,
because you're going to get them anyway!*

A Highlander
Christmas

Chapter One

The only thing stopping Grey from strangling the shivering man crouched in front of their hearth was that he didn't wish to upset Grace. And since his wife already looked pale enough to pass out, Greylen MacKeage contented himself with glaring at his son-in-law and chief of police, Jack Stone, who had *brought* the half-frozen man to them.

Apparently also stunned by the news, Jack merely shrugged.

"Would you mind repeating what you just said, Mr. Pascal?" Grace whispered, clutching the arms of her chair. "As I don't believe I heard you correctly the first time."

Luke Pascal turned from warming his hands at the fire, his worried glance darting to Grey before returning to Grace. "When I went to NASA and asked to see her a couple of months ago, I was told that Camry hasn't worked there since December of last year. Then when I went to her condo, I found out she had sold it sometime last spring. I'm sorry I've obviously shocked you, Dr. Sutter, but I assumed you knew. "

Honest to God, if Pascal didn't stop calling his wife Dr. *Sutter,* Grey really was going to strangle the bastard. "And how is it that ye know our daughter?" he asked.

Luke Pascal stood up from his crouched position and faced Grey. "I've been communicating with Camry by e-mail for quite some time." He shifted uncomfortably. "Or I had been up until this summer, when she suddenly stopped e-mailing me back."

Grace suddenly jumped to her feet, which made Pascal step back. "*You're* the Frenchman who was giving Camry fits?"

Pascal's chill-drawn face flushed. "I prefer to think we were engaged in a lively scientific discussion. It certainly wasn't my intention to give her fits." He winced. "Though judging from some of her e-mails, I can see that I may have hit a nerve or two."

"And you say she stopped e-mailing you last summer?"

"Right after I suggested that I should come to America so we could collaborate."

"My daughter didn't think that was a good idea?" Grey asked, drawing Pascal's attention again.

The man took another step back. "According to her last e-mail, I would have to say no, she didn't."

"But you came anyway."

Their slowly thawing guest looked at Grace, obviously knowing she was the scientist in the family and apparently deciding he'd rather deal with her. "I am this close to finally unlocking the secret to ion propulsion," he said, holding his thumb and index finger an inch apart. "And I was sure that if Camry and I tackled the problem together, we could have a working prototype within a year."

"And her reply was?"

"A rather succinct no," he muttered, edging back toward the fire. His navy blue eyes moved from Grace to Grey. "You haven't spoken with her at all in the last year?"

Jack snorted, and Grey shot him a glare, which he then turned on Pascal. "Camry's been home several times, but she always led us to believe she was returning to Florida whenever she left."

"And since she has a cell phone," Grace interjected, "we never bother calling her lab." She collapsed back in her chair, shaking her head. "I just spoke with her a few days ago, and she told me her work was going great." She lifted distressed eyes to Grey. "Why didn't she tell us she'd left NASA? And if she sold her condo, where is she living now?"

Not wanting to discuss family matters in front of a stranger, Grey headed toward the foyer. "Come, Pascal. I'll take you to our resort hotel and get ye a room."

"No," Grace said, jumping to her feet again. "Luke will stay here at Gù Brath."

"That isn't necessary," Pascal said, correctly reading Grey's desire that he get the hell out of their house. "I really don't wish to intrude. If I can just sleep in a warm bed for a couple of days to thaw out," he said with an involuntary shiver, "and get some hot food in my stomach, I will be good to go. I really should be heading back to France anyway, before I find myself out of a job."

"But I thought you came here to collaborate with Camry?"

"But Camry doesn't wish to collaborate with me, Dr. Sutter."

Grace waved that away, then suddenly looped her arm through his, walking him past Grey toward the stairs leading to the bedrooms. "Please call me Grace, Luke. I haven't been called 'Doctor' in years. Where are your belongings?"

"In my rental car, buried under three feet of snow someplace out there," he said, motioning with his hand. "I had no idea Maine got such fierce blizzards this early in the season. I thought February and March were your snowy months. I must have walked ten miles before Chief Stone came cruising by on his snowmobile."

Grace stopped at the bottom of the stairs and turned to the men. "Jack, could you find Luke's car and get his belongings for him?"

Jack nodded. "Not a problem, Mother Mac."

She started walking up the stairs, Luke still in tow. "In the meantime, I'll find you something to wear, and while you're taking a warm shower, I'll throw together a nice hot meal for you."

They walked along the balcony, and Pascal gave one last wary glance toward the foyer before disappearing down the hall.

Grey turned to his son-in-law, but Jack raised his hand. "Give me two hours, and I'll be able to tell you everything you want to know about Luke Pascal, right down to his birth weight."

"And you'll find out where the hell Camry is."

"Well, that might be a little harder," Jack told him. "If Cam's been lying to us for over a year about where she's working and living, she's certainly smart enough not to leave a paper trail."

"I'll call her, and you can trace her cell phone signal."

Jack shook his head. "That would require involving the feds, and I doubt they'd consider a father searching for his grown daughter to be a threat to homeland security."

"Then use your own skills for tracking down runaways."

"It often took me months to find those kids, Grey, and then most times it was sheer luck. Maybe Winter or Matt could help. Or Robbie."

"No, I don't wish to involve anyone else in this. Camry's been lying to them as well, and I would rather find out her reason first, and not embarrass her in front of the entire family."

Jack nodded. "I can respect that. I'll quietly track her down, but it might take a while. And anyway, the solstice birthday bash is only a little over two weeks away. You can ask her what's going on then."

"She's not coming this year. She claimed she couldn't get away from work."

"I'm sorry. It's got to be hard finding out from a stranger that your daughter's been lying to you. But what I can't figure out is why." Jack chuckled softly. "Of all your girls, Cam would be the one to throw us a curve, but outright lying?" He shook his head. "That's the last thing I'd expect from her."

Grey glanced up at the balcony. "She's not the only one lying to us. About the only thing Pascal said that I believe is that the blizzard caught him by surprise. By the looks of his beard and the condition of his clothes, he's been camping out for a while. Where, exactly, did ye find him?"

Jack stepped over to the door and put his hand on the knob. "About twenty miles north of town, on one of the tote roads leading to Springy Mountain."

"And what excuse did he give for being out in the middle of nowhere?"

"He said he was looking for an old camp that his grandfather used to own. But the moment I introduced myself, he mentioned Camry's name. That's when I knew he'd been searching for whatever fell out of the sky and crashed north of here last summer." Jack glanced up at the empty balcony, then back at Grey. "Are you really going to let him stay in the house?"

Grey found his first smile of the afternoon. "Keep your friends close and your enemies even closer, Stone."

"And Pascal is the enemy?"

"Until he proves otherwise, he is."

* * *

Luke stood under the blessedly hot shower spray, gritting his teeth against the pain of his toes thawing, and began shaving off his beard with the razor he'd found in the fully supplied bathroom. As the evidence of his last two months of living like a caveman slowly fell away, he wondered if he hadn't just jumped out of the proverbial frying pan and into the fire.

First and probably most surprisingly, Grace Sutter MacKeage wasn't at all what he'd been expecting. For a woman with enough academic degrees—two of which were doctorates—to wallpaper a house, she sure as hell didn't appear to have one nerdy bone in her body. Luke knew she was in her mid-sixties and was the mother of seven girls, but she didn't look a day over fifty.

Her husband, however, sent chills through Luke that had absolutely nothing to do with his state of near frostbite. Greylen MacKeage had to be closer to seventy, and every damn year of experience showed in his sharp, piercing green eyes. When Luke had innocently mentioned that Camry hadn't worked for NASA for over a year, Greylen had appeared ready to kill the messenger—as if somehow it was *his* fault that Camry had been lying to them.

When Luke had found out his rescuer was

Jack Stone, who he knew was married to Camry's sister, Megan, he'd thought his luck had finally changed. That is, until he'd come face-to-face with the woman whose life's work he had destroyed. It had been all he could do not to throw himself at Dr. Sutter's feet and beg her forgiveness for destroying Podly.

Although to be fair, he'd only been trying to eavesdrop on Podly's transmissions, not hijack the little satellite. And he sure as hell hadn't meant to make it fall out of orbit. But to have it crash so close to Pine Creek . . . that was just outright eerie.

Then to have his childhood idol welcome him into her home and treat him with nothing but kindness? Well, he definitely was going to hell for his deceptions.

Luke turned to let the hot spray cascade over his clean-shaven face and started washing his hair. Stone hadn't believed him about searching for an old family camp; Luke had read the suspicion in the quiet lawman's eyes before he'd even finished telling the lie. So he'd switched to the half-truth that he knew Camry MacKeage, and that he thought she lived in Pine Creek. Chief Stone had then loaded Luke onto his snowmobile and driven the machine right through town, into the TarStone Mountain Ski Resort, and right up to what he could only describe as a castle. Hell, they'd even had to walk across a drawbridge to reach the front door!

So now what was he supposed to do? He'd just spent the last five months searching for Podly: the first three going over trajectory data, and the last two scouring Springy Mountain. And he still didn't have a clue where that satellite was; the damn thing could be at the bottom of Pine Lake for all he knew.

Once again, Luke fought the overwhelming urge to throw himself at Grace's feet, beg her forgiveness, then ask her to help him find *her* satellite that *he* had lost. But then all he had to do was picture Greylen MacKeage's piercing green eyes, and remember the lethal-looking antique sword he'd seen hanging over the hearth. Confessing might be good for his soul, but getting skewered by an enraged husband was another matter entirely.

Which brought Luke's thinking around to their daughter; did Camry take after her mother or her father?

Her father, he would guess, judging by some of her more scathing e-mails—which had actually fired his desire to meet her in person.

That is, until today. Now he wasn't so sure he wanted to lock himself in a lab with Camry, because if she had inherited any of her daddy's highlander genes, one of them might not come out alive.

Maybe *Grace* was the MacKeage he should be trying to collaborate with. He certainly wouldn't mind fulfilling his childhood dream of working with the legendary woman. It was Grace Sutter MacKeage, after all, who had turned him on to space travel when, at the age of twelve, he'd come across an article she'd written in a science journal, where she'd talked about her ongoing search for a more efficient rocket fuel.

But she was probably on the phone to her daughter right now, telling Camry about his unexpected and decidedly unceremonious arrival. And Camry was probably telling her mother to kick him out on his frozen ass.

How had his altruistic endeavor turned into such a fiasco?

All he'd been trying to do was unlock the secret to ion propulsion, but he'd ended up destroying the final piece of the puzzle instead. Did Grace even know her forty-year-long experiment was scattered over several square miles of densely forested mountain terrain?

She had to. The entire civilized world knew something had crashed in these mountains; he just didn't know if Grace was aware it was her beloved Podly.

Finally able to feel his toes again, Luke shut off the water and dried off. He wrapped the towel around his waist, padded into the large, tastefully decorated bedroom he'd been given, and stopped dead in his tracks.

While he'd been in the shower, someone had set clean clothes on the bed, started a roaring fire in the hearth, and placed a tray of food on a table in front of it.

Oh, yeah. He definitely was going to hell.

Chapter Two

"I really don't care what Jack found out about Lucian Pascal Renoir," Grace said, dropping her robe and stepping into the shower. She popped her head out to glare at Grey in the bathroom mirror. "I'm more concerned where Camry is."

"How in hell can ye have lived with me for thirty-five years and not learned some sense of security?" Grey said, his razor stopped halfway to his face. "Ye welcomed a complete stranger into our home, and even showed him your lab today."

Grace closed the shower curtain, lathered her sponge with lilac soap, and stepped under the spray. "I don't need a sense of security—I have you." She smiled when she heard him snort. "And if you could have seen Luke when I took him down to my lab this morning, you'd understand why I don't need to know everything about him," she continued. "The man actually kept his hands in his pockets, as if he were afraid to touch anything, and spoke in reverent whispers. It took me nearly an hour to persuade him that he could spend the afternoon down there by himself, and even catch up on his e-mail if he wanted."

The shower curtain suddenly opened, and her husband's face—half covered with shaving cream—popped into view. "Ye left a rival scientist in your lab all by himself all afternoon?" He sighed heavily. "That's what I mean, Grace. You're too damn trusting for your own good sometimes."

She pushed him out and slid the curtain shut. "You're letting in a draft. And Luke's not a rival scientist because I am not competing with anyone. We are all working toward the same goal of seeing mankind travel to other planets."

The shower curtain opened again and Grey stepped in, stole the sponge from her, and started lathering his broad chest. "The man has been all but stalking our little girl for a year, and ye gave him complete access to her work right along with yours."

Grace didn't have the heart to point out that he was going to smell like lilacs all day tomorrow.

"And as soon as you and Jack figure out where Camry is," she said, "I intend to send Luke after her."

Grey dropped the sponge in surprise. "You will not! Ye may have talked me into not calling her yesterday and demanding she tell us where she is, but when we do find her, I'll be going to get her, not Pascal. I don't trust the bastard. He's been lying to us since he got here. He didn't even tell us his real name."

Grace wrapped her arms around his neck and leaned into him. "He told us most of his name," she whispered, running a finger over his clenched jaw. "And he wasn't lying about Camry getting fired. I called her former boss this morning, and he told me he had been forced to let Camry go because she was so harried and unfocused, she was disrupting everyone else's work. I know you think you should be the one to go get her," she said in a rush, placing her finger over his lips when he tried to speak. "But think about it, Grey. If you drag Camry back to Gù Brath before she's ready to come home on her own, it will alienate her even more."

"Then what makes ye think Pascal can accomplish what I can't? Camry got so angry at the man that she stopped e-mailing him."

Grace bent down and picked up the sponge, turned her husband around, and started washing his back. "Exactly. Luke must have hit a powerfully raw nerve for her to walk away from the rousing argument they were having. Don't you remember what Camry was like last winter, Grey? She was so excited about her work and so angry at Luke, she could have flown to the moon under her own power. But then everything suddenly stopped last summer."

"Because Pascal said he was coming to America."

"Exactly. Coming face-to-face with someone she was that passionately involved with obviously scared the hell out of her."

He turned around to glare at her. "Camry fears nothing."

"No? Then why has she been lying to us for over a year? And why hasn't she been home since the summer solstice? Why won't she meet Luke in person? And why is she hiding from us, and from him, and from the work she loves?"

Grey leaned his forehead against hers and closed his eyes. "I don't know. I thought there wasn't any problem our daughters couldn't come to us with."

Grace wrapped her arms around his waist. "This isn't something you can fix, Grey. Camry has to fix herself." She smiled up at him. "And I honestly believe that Lucian Pascal Renoir is just the catalyst to get her roaring back into life again."

"Ye believe sending one liar after another will get us our little girl back?"

"No, I believe that two people, each of whom appears to be in desperate need of a miracle, can get themselves back. And I also believe that the next time we see our 'little girl,' she'll be a fully realized, self-empowered woman, and Luke Pascal will have that same dazed look on his face that all you men get when you suddenly realize you've met your match."

"And Camry is Pascal's match?"

"Aye, MacKeage," Grace said, mimicking his burr as she slid her hands up over his ribs. "I think those two lying young fools absolutely deserve each other. I need you tonight, husband," she whispered.

His arms around her tightened, and Grace felt the evidence of his own need pushing into her belly. He suddenly reached behind her and shut off the water, swept her up in his strong arms, and carried her into the bedroom.

"Do ye honestly believe that in all our years together, I haven't known what you're up to when you get all soft and pliable in my arms during one of our little discussions?" he asked, setting her down on the bed, then quickly covering her damp body with his.

She trailed a finger over his smile. "I prefer to

believe that I merely point out a reasonable course of action and, being the wise man that you are, you simply see things my way."

"And you've taught this trick to our daughters?"

"All seven of them," she said with a delighted laugh.

"May God have mercy on your soul, woman," he muttered, covering her mouth with his.

Grace looked up from the beautiful Christmas card she was holding and smiled at Grey sitting across the breakfast table. "You can tell Jack to stop searching for Camry," she said, pushing an envelope toward him. "Because we just found her."

Grey picked up the envelope, saw there wasn't a return address, and frowned.

"Read the postmark," she instructed.

"Go Back Cove, Maine?" He held out his hand to her. "Camry sent us a Christmas card?"

Grace handed him the card, which had an enchanting angel on the front, floating in a small forest clearing surrounded by fir trees dusted with snow. "Before you read the inside, take a moment to study the picture," she told him. "Besides the angel, what do you see?"

"I see a crow hiding in the trees," he said, his frown deepening.

Grace arched a brow. "Do we know any crows?"

His frown turned to an outright scowl, and he flipped open the card. "Your *unborn* great-grandson did not send us a Christmas card. See," he said, tapping the bottom of the card, "it's not signed *Tom*, it's signed only with an *F*."

His frown returned. "What does this F person mean by thanking us for raising such a wonderful daughter?" He turned the card to see if there was anything written on the back, just as Grace had done earlier. Finding nothing, he reread the short note. "That's it? Just 'thank ye for raising such a wonderful daughter'? He or she doesn't even say *which* daughter." He tossed the card on the table between them. "It could be any one of our wonderful girls."

"F is referring to Camry," Grace insisted, picking up the card and smiling at the beautiful angel. She stood up and walked to the map of Maine hanging beside the back door over the row of coat pegs. "I've never heard of Go Back Cove, have you?"

Grey came over and also studied the map. "No. But *cove* implies water, so it must be on the coast."

"Or on any one of Maine's six thousand lakes and ponds." She went over to the computer on the counter next to the fridge, opened Google Earth, and typed in "Go Back Cove, Maine." "You're right, it is on the coast," she said, pointing at the map on the screen. "It's about thirty miles north of Portland."

Luke Pascal walked into the kitchen but stopped in the doorway when Grey turned and frowned at him. "Luke," Grace said, going over and holding out the card. "We found Camry. She's living in Go Back Cove, Maine." As soon as he took the card, she led him over to the computer. "It's a small town on the coast, north of Portland."

Luke moved his gaze from the computer screen to the open card in his hand, then turned it to see if there was anything written on the back. "Who is F?" he asked.

Grace waved his question away, rushing to the table to get the envelope. "We don't know, other than that it's obviously someone who knows Camry."

"But he or she doesn't even mention her by name," Luke said, taking the envelope and reading the postmark. He glanced uncertainly at Grey, then at Grace. "So how do you know it's Camry this F person is talking about?"

"Of course it is. All of our daughters are wonderful, but Camry's the only one who's missing right now."

"This handwriting looks feminine," he said, closing the card to study the angel on the front. He turned sympathetic eyes on Grace. "I realize it's distressing not knowing where Camry is, Dr. Sutt—I mean Grace," he quickly corrected, darting a frantic look at Grey.

Grace had finally had to explain to Luke that her husband preferred *MacKeage* to Sutter, before the younger scientist had finally started calling her by her first name.

"But what I don't understand," he continued, "is how you can conclude that a half-signed Christmas card, that doesn't even mention her name, tells you Camry is living in Go Back Cove."

"Do you believe in magic, Luke?" she asked, ignoring her husband's not-so-subtle growl.

"Magic?" Luke repeated with a frown.

"How about serendipitous coincidence, then?"

"Excuse me?"

Grace sighed and took the card and envelope from him. "Okay then, let's just call it *mother's intuition,* shall we?" She waved the card between Luke and Grey. "You will both simply have to trust me when I say that Camry is living in Go Back Cove." She looked at her watch, then at Luke. "It's only nine. If you leave right after lunch, you should be there in plenty of time to settle into your hotel."

"Excuse me?" he repeated, looking even more confused.

Grey sighed, only much more heavily than Grace had. "You're going to Go Back Cove, Pascal, to talk our daughter into coming home."

Luke's eyes widened and he took a step back. "I am?"

"But you only have two weeks to make it happen," Grace interjected. "We want her home by the winter solstice."

Luke took another step back, his alarm evident. "Considering Camry's last e-mail to me, I am probably the last person she wants to see. And this really is a family matter, don't you think? Shouldn't the two of you go after her?"

"We can't," Grace told him.

"But why?" he asked, tugging on the sleeve of his shirt.

"Because she can't know that we know she was fired from NASA, much less that we know she's been lying to us," Grace explained. "She has to *want* to come home, and she needs to tell us in person what she's been doing for the last year."

"Then how am I supposed to persuade her to come home if I can't reveal how worried you are about her?"

"That should be easy for you, Renoir," Grey said. "Ye just elaborate on the lies you've been telling *us*."

Luke dropped his gaze to Grace's feet, but then he suddenly stiffened, as if fighting some urge, and looked at Grey. "My full name is Lucian Pascal Renoir, but I go by Luke Pascal . . . sometimes." He tugged on his sleeve again, as if the borrowed shirt irritated him. "And because Camry knew me as Lucian Renoir from my e-mails, and I thought she might be here when Jack Stone found me, I told him my name was Pascal so I wouldn't get thrown back out in the snow on my as—on my ear."

"Then when you arrive in Go Back Cove," Grace said, pulling out a chair at the table and urging him to sit down, "I suggest you continue using 'Luke Pascal.' "

"But . . ."

She patted his shoulder. "It'll be okay, Luke," she assured him, going to the oven and getting the plate of eggs and toast she'd kept warming for him. "As soon as you're done with breakfast, you can sort through your belongings and give me what clothes need to be washed. Then we'll get on the Internet and find you a hotel in Go Back Cove. It's a small town, so it shouldn't take you too long to find Camry."

"My car was recovered?"

Grace set the plate down in front of him. "Jack and his deputy brought it back just this morning.

It's parked in the upper driveway behind the kitchen."

"Really, Dr. Sutter, I don't think I'm the one to go after your daughter."

"Of course you are, Luke. Because if I know Camry, the moment you work up the nerve to tell her that Podly is scattered over half of Springy Mountain, she'll drag you back here so fast your head will be spinning."

Luke snapped his navy blue eyes to hers, his face draining of color. "Y-you know about Podly?" he whispered, glancing at Grey before looking back at her. "You *know* it was your satellite that crashed here last summer?"

Grace went to the fridge to get him some juice, giving her equally stunned husband a smug smile as she walked by. "Do you honestly believe I wouldn't know someone was eavesdropping on Podly's transmissions?" she asked, bringing the juice back to Luke. "All the time you and Camry were burning up the Internet with your e-mails, I was watching you watching Podly."

"Did Camry know?" he asked, absently taking the juice she handed him.

"I never told her. But if she'd bothered to check, she's certainly smart enough to have found out. But then, I doubt she would have been looking for an eavesdropper."

"But you were?"

Grace shrugged. "An old habit from my days working for StarShip Spaceline."

He looked down at his plate. "Then you also know that I caused the satellite to malfunction." He looked up at her, his eyes filled with sincere remorse. "I'm sorry. I really don't know what I did to make it crash. I spent three months going over the data in my own lab, and the last two months scouring the mountain, hoping I could find enough salvageable parts to figure out what went wrong." He turned in his seat to face her fully and took her hand in both of his. "You have my word, Dr. Sutter, I was going to bring whatever I found directly to you. I-I'm sorry," he repeated.

Grace patted his shoulder. "I believe you, Luke." She nudged him around to his plate of rapidly cooling food. "Now eat, so we can get you packed up and headed to Go Back Cove. The sooner you find Camry, the sooner you can talk her into helping you find our satellite. Podly had heat shields in case something like this happened, so there's a good chance the data bank survived reentry. Camry knows these mountains quite well, and between your trajectory data and her love of a good challenge, I'm sure you'll both be locked in my lab with Podly by the winter solstice. Eat," she repeated, pointing at his food when he tried to say something else.

He snapped his mouth shut with a frown and picked up his fork.

Grace took hold of her also frowning husband and led him up the back stairway.

"That's it?" Grey asked as soon as they reached the upstairs hall. "The man destroys your life's work, and ye not only hand it over to him, you practically hand him our daughter as well?"

"Luke didn't destroy anything," she said, pulling him into their bedroom and closing the door. "He just told ye he crashed Podly."

"No, he told me he *thinks* he caused Podly to crash." She stepped into his arms and started toying with one of the buttons on his shirt. "And I merely let him believe that he did," she said softly.

Grey's hands went to her shoulders. "Did *you* crash the satellite?"

"I was rather busy right about then, Grey. If you remember correctly, our baby girl was giving birth to our granddaughter at that precise moment."

"Then if you didn't make it crash, and Pascal didn't, who did?"

"I have no idea." She started toying with his buttons again, undoing the top one. "Maybe the same person who sent us that Christmas card?

Because what are the chances that my satellite would crash so close to my home?" She looked up. "The odds of that happening are astronomical, Grey. It *has* to be the magic."

He reached up and stilled her hand just as she undid the next button. "I find myself growing worried about ye, wife."

"How's that?" she asked, still managing to undo the next button.

"You've been acting far too much like *me* lately."

Grace went perfectly still. Oh God, he was right! She'd turned into a *warrior,* only instead of wielding a sword, her weapon was deceit.

She headed for the door. "I'm going to go tell Luke everything."

"Oh, no you're not," he said, sweeping her up in his arms with a laugh and striding to their bed. "If ye confess to Pascal, then *I'll* be forced to go get Camry, and I agree it would turn out badly for all of us."

He opened his arms and dropped her on their bed, then quickly settled on top of her. "I'm not upset ye guilted Pascal into going after Camry, only that I hadn't thought of it myself." He started undoing the buttons on her blouse. "But then, I didn't have all the pieces of the puzzle, did I? So when were ye going to tell me your little satellite is scattered over half of Springy Mountain? I would have found it for ye, Grace."

"I know you would have, and I love you for that. But Podly really isn't mine anymore, Grey. It's Camry's future. And I need for her to *want* to go find it herself."

"And is the secret to ion propulsion sitting under three feet of snow right now?"

"Yes."

He stopped undressing her. "Ye solved the puzzle? Then we have to go get it!"

He started to get up, but Grace pulled him back. "No, we don't. Podly's been holding the secret for twenty years; I think it can wait another couple of weeks."

"Twenty years! Ye solved the problem twenty years ago, and you've been letting it orbit the Earth all this time? Grace, that's been your life's work!"

"Don't get so excited," she soothed, cupping his cheeks and setting her thumbs over his lips. "I didn't find the answer, *Camry* did—when she was twelve."

He tried to sit up, but she held him over her. "One day when Camry was twelve, she was down in the lab with me, working on a project for her school science fair. But then she started looking over my shoulder and asking me one question after another about what I was doing. And when I told her the particular problem I was having, she merely pointed at the screen and asked why I simply didn't transpose two seemingly disconnected integers in the equation I was working on."

She gently patted his cheeks when he frowned, and gave a soft laugh. "Don't ask me to explain it right now, or we'll still be in this bed come spring. Anyway, it might have been a question from an unschooled child, but it was pure genius. I reversed the numbers, which forced me to change several more, and within an hour I knew I could make ion propulsion work."

"And why didn't ye shout it to the world?"

"Because unlocking the code actually created a whole new set of problems. I couldn't really claim I had mastered ion propulsion, because I hadn't figured out how to actually *control* it." She sighed. "Ions can be used for more than just propulsion, Grey; they can also be used as a weapon. I wasn't ready to go there, because I wasn't sure the world was ready to go there."

"And now?" he asked. "If Camry and Pascal find Podly like ye hope, and they discover the secret, is the world ready now?"

"Don't you think I've been asking myself that question all this time?"

He reared up slightly. "So that's what you've

been doing for the last twenty years, when ye locked yourself in your lab? Instead of trying to figure out how to make ion propulsion viable, you've been working on how you can keep it from being used as a weapon?" He frowned again. "Have ye succeeded?"

"Almost. But I'm sure that if Camry, Luke, and I put our heads together, we can hand the world a propulsion system that can be used for space travel." She cupped his cheeks again. "And if some other scientist takes our work and turns it into a weapon . . . well, I've finally made peace with the fact that all I can control is *my* contribution to mankind, which will be a more efficient propulsion system."

"And if Pascal doesn't feel the same way?"

"Then he will have to live with his decision, as every scientist must." She smiled. "But sometimes we simply have to trust the magic, don't we, when it starts messing with us? If you look at all the coincidences that brought Luke to our door, you have to realize there's no such thing as a coincidence."

Grey groaned, laying his forehead on her. "If you're trying to tell me that Winter or Matt had anything to do with any of this, I swear I'll—"

Grace placed her finger over his mouth. "Not them," she said with a laugh. "I believe it's someone even more magical."

"Who?"

"On the winter solstice, when my house is overflowing with *all* my children and grandchildren, then I will tell you who I think it is. Make love to me, husband. Take me traveling beyond the stars under *your* power."

Chapter Three

At about the same time a half-frozen Lucian Pascal Renoir was walking across the drawbridge of Gù Brath, Camry MacKeage was being dragged toward the beach of Go Back Cove by three massive dogs and one clueless dachshund that thought it was God's gift to the world. As soon as she saw that the beach was completely deserted—which wasn't surprising, considering it was only a few degrees above freezing—Camry unsnapped all four leashes and released her charges.

"Go on!" she shouted, racing after them with a laugh. "Run until you drop so we can get home and take a nap. I have to tend bar tonight!"

She ran along behind them for maybe a mile,

until a stitch in her side forced her to stop. It was as she was bent over with her hands on her knees, watching her panting breath condense in the cold air, that she heard what sounded like someone sobbing.

Camry straightened and looked around but saw only the dogs racing back toward her, their having discovered she was no longer following. She headed toward the dead grass and dormant rugosa rose bushes separating the beach from the old county road, her ear chocked in the direction the sound was coming from. She suddenly stopped at the sight of a girl, huddled shivering inside a totally inadequate jacket, her face buried in her knees.

"Hey, there," Cam said, slowly approaching.

The girl snapped her head up, her crystal blue eyes huge with surprise.

Cam stopped several yards away when the girl frantically looked around, as if searching for an escape route. "Hey, it's okay," she said gently, shoving her hands in her pockets. She shrugged, smiling at the girl. "I'm sorry if I startled you. I thought the beach was deserted."

The three large dogs descended on Camry, kicking up sand as they screeched to a halt and started wrestling with one another at her feet. The dachshund, its tongue whipping its cheek as it panted to catch up, suddenly changed direction.

"Tigger!" Camry cried just as the dachshund launched itself at the girl.

The previously sobbing young woman caught the small dog with a gasp, then gave a strangled giggle when Tigger started washing her face.

The three other dogs, suddenly realizing there was a new toy on their beach, took off. Camry lunged after them, but was able to grab only one by the collar. The other two plowed into the girl, sending her onto her back and forcing her to cover her face to protect herself from their slobbering tongues.

"Max! Ruffles! Get off her!" Cam shouted, her lone captive dragging her to the girl's rescue. She finally had to let go of the whining German shepherd in order to deal with the black Lab and golden retriever. She pushed the two larger dogs off the girl and scooped Tigger up in her arms, then had to use her knee to shove away the shepherd, who was determined to get in a few slobbers of its own.

Desperate to save the girl from getting licked to death, Camry set Tigger down, grabbed the hysterically giggling young woman, and hauled her to her feet. "Jeesh, I'm sorry," she said, trying to push away the excited dogs. "They won't hurt you, I promise."

The girl instantly sobered and blinked at her.

"They're really just four-legged cupcakes," Cam said, grabbing Max's collar when the Lab knocked the girl back a step. Cam shoved the dog away, then picked up a short piece of driftwood. "Fetch!" she shouted, flinging it toward the beach.

The three large dogs immediately shot after it, but Tigger sat down and started whining, staring up at the girl. The young woman picked up the dachshund and hugged it to her chest.

"I'm Camry. And that bundle of ecstasy you're holding is Tigger."

The girl said nothing, merely rubbed her cheek against Tigger's fur.

"Do you live around here?" Cam asked, scanning the road behind the low dunes for signs of a car—although she wasn't even sure the girl was old enough to drive.

"No," the girl whispered, her beautiful blue eyes wary.

"Do you have a name?"

"Fiona."

Cam didn't even try to hide her surprise. "Really? Fiona?" She smiled broadly. "I have a five-and-a-half-month-old niece named Fiona. Um . . . Fiona what?"

The girl didn't answer, but merely rubbed her cheek over Tigger's fur again.

Cam sighed. Judging by the condition of her clothes, and the fact that she was reluctant to give her full name, Camry figured the girl was a runaway. Another contributing factor was that Fiona looked as if she hadn't seen a bar of soap or hot water for a week, or a decent meal in days. She was pale and shivering, and looked so vulnerable, Cam just wanted to pull her into her arms and hug her senseless.

"If you don't live around here, then you must just be passing through. Do you have a place to stay tonight?"

"I was told there's a shelter down in Portland."

Camry fought to keep her horror from showing. Surely the girl wasn't hitchhiking! "Portland's thirty miles from here. I tell you what," she said, backing onto the beach. "I live close by, and have a spare bed at my place. And I have this really huge fireplace we could build a roaring fire in, and a hot-water supply that will let you take an hour-long shower if you want." She canted her head with a lopsided grin. "And it just so happens I was planning to drive into Portland tomorrow, so I could give you a ride."

That is, assuming she couldn't talk her into going home instead.

When she saw that Fiona was following—albeit hesitantly—Cam turned and slowly started walking up the beach toward her house. "I have to go to work tonight," she continued conversationally, "but the pub where I tend bar has some of the best food this side of Portland." She smiled over at Fiona, who had fallen into step beside her, still hugging Tigger tightly, apparently enjoying the warmth.

But then Fiona suddenly ran inland, and Cam's heart sank at the sight of the girl bolting, until she realized she was taking off with Tigger!

"Hey, my dog!" she shouted, giving chase.

Fiona just as suddenly stopped in the grass and set Tigger down, reached behind a bush, and straightened with a large backpack in her hand.

Cam sighed in relief. "Oh, good," she said, starting down the beach again as if nothing had happened. "I also have a washer and dryer, if you need to do laundry."

"What will your husband say about your letting me stay the night?" Fiona asked, rushing to catch up, the pack slung over her shoulders and Tigger back in her arms.

"I don't have a husband."

"Oh. You're divorced, then?"

Camry gave her a sidelong glance. "No. I've never been married."

Fiona stopped to blink at her. "How old are you?"

Camry blinked back. "Almost thirty-two. Why?"

"And you've *never* been married?"

She started walking again. "Last I knew, it wasn't a crime to be thirty-two and single. How about you? You married?"

"I'm only sixteen!"

Cam smiled. "I don't believe it's a crime to be single at sixteen, either. So Fiona, what's so exciting about staying in a shelter in Portland?"

The girl didn't answer for several heartbeats, then quietly said, "It's got to be better than living at home."

"I see. Pretty bad, is it?"

"My father is impossible. It seems as if every time I turn around, he's lecturing me about something."

Cam snorted. "Tell me about it. What is it between fathers and daughters, anyway? It's like the minute we're born, a man's lecturing gene kicks into high gear."

Fiona stopped again. "Your father lectured you, too?"

"Are you kidding? He's *still* lecturing me."

"At thirty-two?" She hugged Tigger closer. "Sometimes my dad treats me like I don't have the sense to come in out of the rain. He doesn't like most of my friends, especially the boys, and he doesn't like how I dress."

Camry grabbed the stick from the shepherd's mouth and threw it down the beach, sending the three dogs scurrying after it. She started walking again. "Oh, yeah? Just wait until you're two years out of college and still unmarried. Then the lectures change from warnings that 'all men are wolves,' to 'how come you can't find a man?' And by the time you're thirty, they change again to 'ye can't give me grandchildren if ye don't find yourself a husband,' " she said, mimicking her father's highland brogue.

Fiona giggled at the stern expression Camry gave along with the accent and covered her mouth with her hand. "Are you serious?" she asked, her big blue eyes widening. "The lectures are *never* going to stop?"

"Nope. And you know why?"

"Why?"

"Because we daughters scare the hell out of our daddies. They love us to death, and worry about us so much, that they can't stand our not having a husband to take care of us."

"We *scare* our fathers?" Fiona snorted. "I don't think anything scares my dad."

Camry saw the girl hug Tigger on a shiver, and started walking again. "*You* scare him, because he loves you. That's my house, right there," she said, pointing to the small cottage sitting on the bluff.

"Wow, you live right on the beach. Are you rich?"

Camry laughed. "Not exactly. I'm just renting. How about you? Are you rich?"

Fiona snorted. "Money isn't everything, you know."

"But it sure helps buy designer jeans, expensive backpacks, and fancy watches, doesn't it?" she said, nodding at the watch on the girl's wrist.

"I can't help it if my parents are rich," Fiona said defensively.

"No, just like you can't help that they're probably so worried right now, they've got every law enforcement official in the state looking for you. How long have you been on the run, Fiona?"

"Not long enough," she snapped, spinning around and heading for the house.

Cam gave a sharp whistle and the three dogs bounded up to her. "Come on, let's get the sand off you before your loving masters come pick you up," she told them, running to catch up with Fiona. "Hey, I wouldn't be a responsible adult if I didn't at least *try* to point out that your family is worried sick about you."

"They probably don't even realize I'm missing."

"Trust me, any father who loves you enough to lecture you definitely knows when you're not sleeping in your bed. I swear I couldn't sneak out of our house after dark without running into my father at the end of the driveway." She opened the door and motioned for Fiona to precede her onto the enclosed porch. "Don't let the dogs in the house. I have to wipe the sand off them first. Just set Tigger down and go warm up. I'll be right along."

"I'll help."

Camry handed her an old towel. "Okay. The Lab's name is Max, the golden is Ruffles, and the shepherd is Suki. I've got to get them spit-shined before their parents pick them up in an hour."

"They're not yours?"

"Good Lord, no. What would I want with this pack of overgrown babies? I just dog-sit them while their owners work to keep them in kibble. You know, sort of like a doggie day care."

"That's it? That's what you do for a living?"

"It pays the bills. And I also bartend at a pub Friday and Saturday nights."

Fiona gaped at her.

"What?"

"But you said you're almost *thirty-two*. How come you don't have a real career?"

"You mean like Suzy Homemaker or president of the United States? Or maybe a rocket scientist or something?"

The young woman flushed to the roots of her

dirty-blond hair. "I'm sorry. I didn't mean you had to be something as brilliant as a rocket scientist. It's just that . . . well, you seem so smart and everything." She motioned toward the dogs. "I mean, is this all you're going to do for the rest of your life, babysit other people's dogs and serve drinks on weekends?"

Camry grabbed Max and started brushing the sand off his legs. "Rocket science isn't all you think it's cracked up to be," she muttered. "You going to stand out here shivering all afternoon, or help me clean up these mutts?"

Camry spent the next two days trying to persuade Fiona to call her parents, all the while making sure she didn't *sound* like a parent for fear the girl would take off on her own again. But all her efforts got her was a roommate who suddenly didn't seem in any hurry to leave.

She'd been stunned speechless the first night, when Fiona had emerged from the shower wearing the clothes she'd lent her. The girl was breathtakingly beautiful; her wavy, waist-length hair was actually strawberry blonde, her complexion was flawless, and in clothes that fit her far better than they did Cam, her figure would have made a dead man sit up and take notice.

Hell, if she was Fiona's daddy, she wouldn't

waste her time lecturing the girl, she'd lock her in her room until she was thirty!

She'd had second thoughts about taking Fiona to the Go Back Grill that first night, but since she had only three eggs and some outdated mayonnaise in the fridge, Cam had been forced to take her to work. So she'd sat the girl at the end of the bar to keep an eye on her, then stuffed her full of greasy, fattening food.

By the second night, she'd talked Dave Bean—who owned the Go Back Grill—into letting Fiona bus a few tables to pay for all the greasy, fattening food she'd been wolfing down as if she had a hollow leg.

But it was Sunday afternoon, and Camry was feeling more like a worried parent than a roommate as Fiona got ready for work. That's why she had Dave on the phone, giving him hell for giving the girl a permanent job!

"You can't have a sixteen-year-old on staff at a bar, Dave," Cam growled into her cell phone. "Child Services is going to come after you for hiring a minor."

"That's not what you said last night, when you kindly pointed out that her busing tables was perfectly legal," Dave growled back. "Make up your mind, Cam."

"It's only legal when *I'm* working there. Hey,

wait. If you hired her, what name did she put on the W-2 form?"

"Fiona Smith."

Camry snorted. "She had to give you a Social Security number. What is it?"

"Now, Cam, you know I can't give that out to anyone."

Camry looked around to make sure Fiona was still in the spare bedroom getting dressed, and turned her back and lowered her voice. "But she's a runaway, Dave. I called the police Friday, but they don't have any missing teens fitting her description. I need that number to find out who she really is so I can call her parents."

A heavy sigh came over the phone. "I know. But you're putting me between a rock and a hard place here. I promise, first thing tomorrow morning I'll turn Fiona's W-2 over to my accountant and ask him look into it. But it's probably a bogus number, just like Smith is obviously fake."

"Yet you hired her anyway."

"Because I'm desperate to find bus staff. Kids today don't want to work for an honest wage; they want Mommy and Daddy to just hand them money. And besides," he said, lowering his own voice. "I didn't dare say no when she asked me for a job, because like you, I want her hanging around long enough for us to find her parents."

Cam sighed in defeat. "At least it'll buy us time. But how am I supposed to keep an eye on her when I'm not scheduled to work? She'll be running around your bar, being watched by every single *and* married male in the joint."

"It's Sunday night, and I have nearly every table reserved up until nine," Dave countered. "And you know why? Because all the flyers I've been passing out have let everyone know that I've classed the place up and hired new staff."

"Then I want to come to work tonight, too."

"Betty's covering the bar tonight."

"Then I'll wait tables."

"I'm still recovering from the last time you waited tables. You're a good bartender, MacKeage, but you suck as a waitress."

"I promise, I won't dump anything on anyone."

A pained sigh came over the phone. "I'll keep an eye on your kid. She's just busing tables."

"She can bus on Fridays and Saturdays."

"But I've never had more than two reservations on a Sunday night."

"Which must mean you need extra staff."

He sighed again. "You promise you won't get smart-mouthed with my patrons, or dump any food on them?"

"Scout's honor."

"And you'll wear one of my new waitress uniforms?"

"Those . . . *things* hanging in the back room are uniforms?" She snorted. "I thought you wanted to turn the place into a *family* pub, not some pseudo-colonial bar with waitresses dressed like wenches. "

"Go Back Cove was supposed to have been a hideout for pirates back in the 1800s, and I'm simply playing up the old legend. I spent all last night and this morning redecorating the place."

"Fiona is *not* wearing a low-cut blouse and one of those leather bustier thingies. I swear I'll call Child Services myself if you put her in one of those sexist costumes."

"I have mostly bus *boys,* Cam. Fiona can wear jeans and a T-shirt, just like they do. But," he said before she could say anything, "you can wait tables tonight if you're willing to wear the new uniform."

Dammit, dammit, dammit. She didn't want to dress up like a wench!

Then again, she didn't want Fiona going to work without her, either.

But if she tried to talk the girl out of going to her new job, that made her no better than Fiona's parents. And she'd be damned if she was going to mother the child.

"What'll it be, Cam? You coming to work or not?"

"I'll be there," she snapped, hitting the End button when she heard Dave chuckle and slinging the phone at the couch.

"Are you going to stay and have supper when you drive me in?" Fiona asked, walking into the room. "Because there's still nothing in the fridge."

Camry closed her eyes and counted to ten, suddenly having a whole new appreciation for her own mother, who had managed to raise seven girls without losing her sanity. She opened her eyes, and, yup, her roommate was still dressed like a prostitute. "Um . . . is that one of the outfits your father objected to?"

Fiona looked down at herself, then smiled at Cam. "Yeah. He asked me if I'd stolen it off some hooker the last time he took me to New York City."

"Well . . . at the risk of sounding like your father," Camry said with a crooked grin, choosing her words carefully, "is there any chance I could get you to wear an oversize T-shirt and a pair of *my* jeans tonight?"

Camry held up her hand to forestall the objection forming on Fiona's lips, took a deep breath, and jumped right into the quagmire. "It's not that I don't think that's a fabulous outfit, but you're working in a *bar,* Fiona. And you're certainly old enough to realize that some men, when they've had a little more beer than they should, forget this is the twenty-first century and that women were not put on this Earth merely for their entertainment." She shrugged. "I know it's archaic, but I also know that you're bright enough to realize that sometimes we women are better off downplaying our assets instead of . . . accentuating them."

Oh God, those words could have come straight out of *her* mother's mouth!

Fiona stared at her for the longest time, saying nothing, then suddenly smiled. "Okay," she said, spinning around and heading back into the bedroom. "Can I wear your black jeans?"

"Yeah, go ahead," Cam said, closing her eyes in relief, suddenly remembering why the mere thought of having kids scared the hell out of her.

Chapter Four

Luke slid into the booth at the Go Back Grill, the smell of greasy food all but making him salivate. Though he was still trying to recover from two months of living on nothing but trail mix and rehydrated soup, he had to admit the results felt pretty damn good.

When he'd seen himself naked in the bathroom mirror at Gù Brath that first night, he'd been stunned to realize that he'd lost over twenty-five pounds of fat. But he'd probably added ten pounds of lean, hard muscle, and for the first time in years, Luke was more than casually aware of the six-foot-two, broad-shouldered body that housed his brain. He really had been spending too much time in the lab, and once he got back to work, he'd have to remind himself to get more exercise.

"Beer?" the waitress asked just as he opened the menu.

"What do you have for imported wine?" he asked absently, scanning the various food offerings that were thoughtfully accompanied by pictures.

"Red, white, or blush."

"What do you have for imported red?"

"That's it. Red house wine, white house wine, or blush," she said dryly. "You want anything fancier, you have to drive to Portland. We serve forty-two different beers, mixed drinks, and house wines."

Luke finally looked up with a frown, only to come face to . . . chest with a set of creamy white breasts being pushed out of an indecently low-cut blouse by an impossibly tight black leather corset.

The woman belonging to the breasts lifted his chin with the end of her pencil, forcing his gaze up to her scowling face. "Red, white, or blush," she repeated through gritted teeth.

"I'll have a Guinness," he said, carefully lifting his chin off her pencil and looking back at his menu. "And your largest steak, a baked potato—loaded—and coleslaw. *And,*" he said a bit more forcefully when she started to leave, "a large salad, no onions, with blue cheese dressing."

As she stomped away, Luke heard a soft giggle over the din of patrons. The young woman clearing the table across the aisle continued to laugh behind her hand as she watched his waitress leaving, then looked back at him.

Luke glanced around to make sure he was the one causing her amusement, then smiled at her. "Do you think I should give her a bigger tip for that stunt, or not leave her anything?" he asked.

The young girl tossed her rag in the bucket on her cart of dirty dishes, and walked over. "It took an act of Congress to get her into that uniform tonight," she said. "Add to that how uncomfortable that leather bustier is, and you're lucky she only used that pencil to close your mouth, instead of using it to poke out your eyes." She suddenly held out her hand. "Hello, I'm Fiona."

Surprised but utterly charmed by the beautiful young woman's straightforwardness, Luke took her offered hand and gently shook it. "Luke Pascal."

"Do you live here in Go Back Cove, Luke?" she asked. "Or are you just passing through?"

"I checked into the hotel across the street just a few minutes ago, but I plan to hang around awhile. I'm on sabbatical from work, and I thought I'd spend some time at the coast while I'm visiting Maine."

"The winter ocean is so desolate and lonely-looking, don't you think?" she asked. "Sometimes it's just a bleak gray that softly ebbs and flows, as if it were waiting for its true love to appear, and sometimes it's churning and angry, mad because that love is taking so long to show up," she said dreamily, her sad smile and crystalline blue eyes making her face practically glow.

Luke decided she wasn't charming, she was enchanting. She was beautiful, poised, and well spoken, and she reminded him of his baby half sister, Kate, who had a dramatic streak a mile wide and a romantic imagination to go with it.

"Table three needs clearing," his waitress told Fiona as she thunked Luke's bottle of Guinness—and no glass—down on the table without even looking at him. "If you don't want to get fired your first night, you better keep moving."

Completely unruffled by the waitress's stern handling, Fiona reached in her apron pocket and handed her some money. "Here. This is from table three."

"A buck?" the waitress growled, staring at the single dollar bill in her hand.

Fiona softly snorted. "I saw the man leave you a

ten, but when he went to pay the bill, the woman with him stuffed it in her purse and replaced it with a one."

The waitress turned her back on Luke to whisper to the girl. "I told Dave these stupid costumes would backfire on us. Go on, you better get hustling." She started walking away with her, still whispering. "You have to stop fraternizing with the customers, Fiona. This is a pub, not a social club."

"I'm sorry, Camry. I keep forgetting because I like meeting new people."

Luke didn't hear any more of their conversation as they moved away, but he did turn to stare after them.

Camry? As in Camry MacKeage? What in hell was a physicist doing working in a bar, dressed like an eighteenth-century wench?

Naw, it couldn't be her. The probability of stumbling across Dr. MacKeage after being in town less than an hour had to be a million to one.

Not that Go Back Cove was a thriving metropolis or anything. And *Fiona* could even be the F person who had sent the Christmas card.

What had Grace called it? Magic? Serendipitous coincidence?

Luke picked up his beer and took a long

swallow. Naw. He didn't believe in anything but cold hard facts, and then only if he could back them up with numbers.

Still, if he found out Miss Congeniality had piercing green eyes—assuming he could keep his gaze on her face long enough to find out—then the numbers had just turned a bit more in his favor, hadn't they?

"Here," Camry snapped, slapping the dollar bill on the counter in front of Dave. "Put this toward the damages."

"What damages?" her boss asked, frantically looking around.

"The damages I'm going to cause the next time one of your precious patrons stiffs me. I swear if I'd seen that woman swap my tip, I'd have chased her right out the door and stuffed that stupid dollar bill down her throat." She tugged on the bustier, which wasn't only cutting into her boobs but cutting off her breath, and glowered at Dave. "I told you these stupid uniforms would backfire on us. The men are leaving us nice tips, but the women with them are scoffing them up as soon as the men turn their backs. For someone who claims he's trying to run a family pub, you seem to be moving in exactly the opposite direction. Women patrons do *not* like being served by wenches with escaping anatomy, and mothers do *not* like their children staring up their waitress's skirt."

Dave sighed. "Doris told me she had a similar problem with the tipping, but she also said that the unaccompanied males are leaving double what they usually do." He grinned, shoving the dollar bill back across the counter. "So that evens things out."

"I've nearly dropped three trays of food because of these stupid heels," she muttered, shifting her weight to give her left foot a rest. "It has to be against insurance codes or something for wait-resses to serve in heels. If we don't kill someone with a falling tray, at the very least we could pop a tendon."

"It's not like they're stilettos or anything; they're only two inches high."

"Doris is nearly sixty, Dave. She's *limping*."

He sighed again. "I already told her to change back into her sneakers, even if they do look silly."

"You mean sillier than a grandmother show-ing enough cleavage to make a saint drool and enough leg to make a thoroughbred envious?"

He held up his hand. "Okay. Okay. The heels were a bad idea, and maybe the skirts are a bit short." He shrugged. "But hey, the rest of my new theme seems to be a hit. The kids really like the eye patches and swords I've been handing out, and I think we burned up a blender tonight making Jolly Roger Zingers."

He leaned over the counter toward her. "And I saw you prodding Fiona along a couple of times when she got chatty with the customers. Don't. They like talking to her, and she's giving the place a homey, friendly feel."

"Did you also see that guy try to slip a twenty-dollar bill in her apron pocket?"

Dave straightened with a frown. "I thought she handled that quite well. Unlike your little stunt last month, she didn't *accidentally* dump his drink over his head. She merely waggled her finger at him and scampered away."

"My guy wasn't trying to stuff money in my *apron*."

Dave sighed louder and harder. "Tell me again why you work here?"

Camry tapped her chin with her finger. "Gee, let me think. Maybe because on Columbus Day they rolled up the sidewalks and closed the town when the tourists left?"

"Portland's just down the road."

"I prefer the peace and quiet of this place."

"That's right, *Dr.* MacKeage, I forgot you came here from Florida." He snorted. "The problem with you brainy types is that you think we working stiffs don't know how to run our own businesses."

Camry gaped at him. "I am not an academic snob. The only reason you even know I hold a doctorate is because your stupid employment application asked me to list all my schooling."

"To which you had to add an entire page for all your degrees." He suddenly stared over her shoulder for several seconds, then glanced down the bar. "Betty," he said, motioning the bartender closer. "No more drinks for booth nine, okay? All four of those guys have had enough. And if they give Wanda any trouble, you have her come see me and I'll handle them."

"Okay, Dave," Betty said, returning to the blender she'd left running.

"And your point is?" Cam asked Dave the minute she had his attention again.

"What were we talking about?"

"I believe you had just implied I'm a snob."

"Oh, come on, MacKeage," he said with a sudden smile. "You need to lighten up. It doesn't look good in front of the staff when you give the boss grief. And I don't want to have to fire you, because"—he leaned closer—"I actually like you," he whispered, his smile widening as he straightened back up. "You sort of remind me of a Jack Russell terrier I used to have that was always growling at me, as if she needed a good fight to keep herself entertained."

"I remind you of your *dog*?"

"I loved that dog, God rest Pip's soul," he said with a laugh. He arched his bushy eyebrows at her. "You want to know what finally settled her down?"

"Not really."

"I got her a boyfriend, which in turn got her a litter of babies. Mellowed my little darling right out, those pups did."

Cam just gaped at him.

"So the moral of this little story," he had the audacity to continue, "is that instead of scowling at your customers, maybe you should trying smiling at them."

She snapped her mouth shut and scowled at *him*.

He sighed. "You've been living in Go Back Cove and eating here for what . . . seven or eight months? And working for me for two? And in all that time, I have never once seen you with a date."

"Maybe I'm gay," she snapped.

Dave chuckled. "Nope. It's not the girls I see you watching, it's the men. Oh, you're interested, all right. You're just too scared to actually play with the big boys."

Camry made a point of visually searching the wall behind the counter, even going on tiptoe to look down the length of the back wall of the bar.

"What are you looking for?"

"Your degree in psychology."

His laughter came straight from the belly as he took the slip and money from a customer who'd walked up to pay his bill. "My degree is from the school of hard knocks, kiddo, and it took me thirty years of tending bar to earn it." He hit some buttons on the register, then shot her a wink. "You watch Fiona working the room tonight, Cam, and maybe you'll learn something. That girl's got a gift for making people smile. How was your dining experience?" he asked the man, handing him his change.

"Delightful," the customer said, glancing over at Camry—specifically at her chest. "I've heard the food here is good, but I especially like the uniforms." He cleared his throat. "Except maybe they don't work so well on all your waitresses." He leaned closer to Dave and lowered his voice so Camry wouldn't hear.

But of course she did.

"That older waitress," he continued in a whisper. "I kept expecting the laces on her corset to pop and maim someone, and she tripped and nearly spilled beer on me."

"We're rethinking the uniforms."

"Or you could just hire younger waitresses," the lech suggested.

"Doris is the prettiest woman here," Camry growled at him. "And the best damn waitress we have!"

The man stepped away in alarm, and all but ran for the door.

Dave sighed again. "Will you lighten up?"

"Will you get real?" she said, spinning away and heading for the kitchen.

Honest to God, she really didn't know why she worked here.

Other than that it might be entertaining.

And she was *not* like some stupid old Jack Russell terrier!

She was a *happy* person, dammit, right down to her blistered toes.

Chapter Five

"Good Lord, what's wrong?" Fiona asked, pushing her busing cart into the kitchen and stopping beside Camry.

"What? Nothing. Why?"

"Because you look like you want to punch someone."

Camry took a deep breath—at least as deep as her stupid corset would allow—and forcibly shook off her foul mood. "Sorry. I was just wondering why I work here."

"Because you love people."

"I do?"

"Of course you do, silly," Fiona said with a laugh, giving her a playful punch on the arm.

"You spend all week with a bunch of dogs, so you need to work here on the weekends to remind yourself that you're human."

"My dogs are better behaved than some of the customers."

"You'd be bored to tears if you spent all your time around well-behaved people. That's what I like best about you, Cam. You say what you think, and you back up what you say with action."

"I do?"

"Sure. Take me, for instance. I know you've been wanting to browbeat my name out of me so you can call my parents, but you've been treating me like an adult even though I'm not one. That's why you can't bring yourself to go through my backpack to find my ID."

"How do you know I haven't?"

"Because I'm still here, aren't I? And you know why? Because I remind you of *yourself* when you were my age, and that's why you're so determined that I'll call my parents on my own."

Camry shot her a lopsided grin. "Did you say you were sixteen, or sixty?"

"MacKeage! Your order for table ten is getting cold," the cook shouted from the serving station. "Where in hell's your pager? I've been beeping you for ten minutes."

Cam felt at the back of her waist. "Damn, it

must have fallen off. It's probably kicking around under some table," she muttered, heading to the heat lamps to pick up her order. "Or more likely in some four-year-old's pocket."

"I'll help you look for it," Fiona said, abandoning her cart to follow her into the dining room. "I'll start searching the floor while you take Luke his food."

"Luke?" Cam repeated, weaving her way through the crowded pub.

"The big dreamy guy at table ten," Fiona explained, stepping around her to run interference when a young child bolted past them, waving a plastic sword and wearing an eye patch. She redirected the toddler back to his parents, then looked at Cam. "You don't think he's dreamy? His eyes are a really deep navy blue, and his hair's almost long enough to tie back. I love long hair on a man, don't you?"

Cam glanced toward table ten. "He's old enough to be your father."

The girl made an exasperated sound. "I don't think he's dreamy for *me,* silly, I think he's perfect for *you*. But he's only going to be in town a short while because he's on sabbatical, so you need to work fast. You should give him your phone number when you bring him his bill."

Camry nearly dropped the heavy tray she was holding. "What?"

Apparently thinking that was a rhetorical question, Fiona started running interference again, occasionally bending over to search under the tables. Deciding she better have a talk with her roommate on their ride home from work, Cam followed her toward the sidewall of booths. But just as Fiona walked past table ten, a hand suddenly snaked out from table nine, grabbed the young girl's arm, and pulled her into the booth of drunken men.

Fiona's yelp of surprise was also laced with pain when she hit the corner of the table. Without skipping a beat, Cam rushed forward with every intention of cleaning the jerk's clock. Only it was at that exact moment that table ten's Dream Guy shot out of his own booth and also launched himself at the jerk—his shoulder knocking the tray full of food out of Camry's hands and sending it crashing to the floor.

Pandemonium ensued when two of the jerk's drunken buddies scrambled out to go after Dream Guy at the same time that Camry also headed into the fray. Only her damn heels got tangled up in the broken dishes and food, and she ended up *falling* into the fight instead.

Her head exploded in pain when her cheek slammed into one man's elbow, which was cocked back to take a swing at Dream Guy. The force of the backward punch threw her into a nearby table, scattering dishes and food over people trying to scramble out of the way.

Camry straightened and spun around, frantically searching for Fiona in the tangle of bodies. She spotted the girl preparing to drive a fork into the arm of the jerk who was trying to pull her out from under the table by her hair. Cam screamed the girl's name at the top of her lungs, hoping Fiona could hear her over the sound of crashing dishes and the growls and grunts of the fighting men.

But it was too late. Even though Fiona tried to halt her downward swing as her eyes snapped to Camry, the fork still found its target. The ensuing shout of pain came just as another one of the drunken men flew backward, sending Camry to the floor with her own cry of pain as her ankle twisted under the weight of his landing on top of her.

Almost as quickly as it had begun, the pandemonium ceased when Dave, along with several of the grill's regular male patrons, started grabbing men by the scruffs of their necks and pulling them off Dream Guy and Camry.

Fiona immediately crawled over and lifted Cam into a sitting position, wrapping her arms around her protectively. Cam snatched the fork out of her fist just as Dave came over and crouched down in front of them.

"Damn, are you girls okay?" he asked, brushing hair back off Camry's face.

Cam jerked away when his fingers touched her throbbing cheek. "I just want to sit here a minute, okay?" she said shakily, carefully straightening her right leg.

"I've been stabbed!" a man shouted. "I'm bleeding! That bitch stabbed me!"

Dave looked down at the fork in her hand, which Camry immediately tossed under a nearby table. "You stay put until the ambulance gets here," he said, getting to his feet and going over to the loudly complaining victim.

Fiona knelt behind Camry and pulled her against her for support. "Other than that shiner that's already starting to swell," Fiona said, "what else hurts?"

"My ankle is throbbing like hell," Camry whispered. She turned to look up at Fiona. "Mind telling me what possessed you to stab that guy with a fork? You don't think that was a little . . . extreme?"

Fiona shrugged. "My dad always told me that if I'm ever accosted, I'm supposed to see everything as a weapon, and not hesitate to use it."

"Your father actually said that?"

She nodded soberly. "He said that I better not think like a woman, but like a warrior." She suddenly smiled. "And that a woman's greatest weapon is surprise, because men don't expect us to fight back."

Camry blinked up at her. "Your dad and my dad must have read the same book on raising daughters. Oh, God, I can't breathe," she groaned, twisting to face forward, trying to get air in her lungs as she frantically tugged on the laces of her bustier. "Help me get this stupid thing off."

Fiona tried to untie the lacing on the front but couldn't work the knotted bow free. "Luke," she cried as he sat down next to them, holding a napkin up to his temple. "Help me. Camry can't breathe."

"Cut this damn thing off," Cam panted, trying to find a position that allowed her to breathe. "Ow! My ankle!"

"Stop thrashing around. You're making it worse," Luke said. He dropped the napkin so he could hold her down, then unsnapped a pouch on his belt with his other hand. He pulled out a multitool and opened it to expose the blade. "Help me, Fiona," he instructed, tugging on the knotted bow. "Hold her chest out of the way."

Camry covered her own breasts. "You can't see what you're doing with blood in your eye," she said, worried he might cut more than just the laces.

While she covered her precious anatomy with her hands, Fiona used her own hands to block Cam's view of what he was doing. "He won't cut you, I promise," the girl said with all the bravado of someone whose boobs weren't inches from a sharp blade.

Camry felt several tugs on her torso, a very welcome release of pressure, and all of a sudden she could breathe again! She tried to roll to her side, but discovered that Luke was straddling her hips. His weight suddenly disappeared, but instead of standing up, he rolled to lie flat on the floor beside her.

"Slow down your breathing or you'll hyperventilate," he instructed, also taking labored breaths. "Damn, I think I have a couple of cracked ribs."

Fiona lifted Camry into a sitting position again, wedging herself behind her for support as Luke rolled toward her with a groan, then rose to his knees.

"Where else are you hurt?" he asked.

"She twisted her ankle," Fiona answered for her.

Luke sidled down to her legs and very gently slid her shoe off her right foot. It was as he went to look up at her that his gaze suddenly stopped, and Camry realized he could look right down her unconfined blouse! But when she slapped her hand to her chest and his gaze lowered, she realized he could also look right up her skirt! She started wiggling as she tugged on the hem, trying to pull her skirt down as she also tried to hold up the front of her blouse.

"What *is* your problem?" he snapped, falling back when her flailing left foot kicked his thigh—apparently quite close to his groin.

"Nothing!"

"I'm pressing charges against whoever stabbed me," Fiona's victim cried from three tables down.

Still holding her blouse to her chest, Camry dropped her head to her knees with a groan. "Honest to God, I am *never* stepping foot in another bar," she muttered, remembering the last time someone had wanted to press charges against her, after a barroom brawl in Pine Creek last summer.

Fiona patted her back. "I'll tell Dave I was the one who stabbed that jerk."

Camry straightened. "You will not. If the authorities find out your age, then *Dave* will get in trouble." She suddenly smiled. "Unless you want your parents to get a call from the police, telling them their missing daughter is sitting in jail. Just think of the lecture dear old Daddy's going to give you then. You won't see daylight for years."

"What do you mean, *missing daughter*?" Luke asked, his gaze darting between Cam and Fiona. He finally settled on Fiona. "Did you run away from home or something?"

"Or something," Fiona said.

Luke's gaze snapped to Camry. "You *know* she's a runaway, and you haven't done anything about it?"

"I suppose I could have left her on the beach. Or let her hitchhike to Portland so she could stay at a homeless shelter."

Luke reached in his pocket, pulled out his cell phone, and handed it to Fiona. "You have to call your parents right this minute, young lady. They must be worried sick about you!"

Camry couldn't believe how dense the guy was.

But even more, she couldn't believe that Fiona actually took the phone, flipped it open, and started pushing buttons.

Her mouth gaping in shock, Cam blinked at Luke.

He shot her a smug smile. "Apparently she responds to *male* authority."

Fiona suddenly handed the phone back to Luke.

"You didn't call them!"

"I will. Eventually." She gave him an equally

smug smile. "But I did add Camry's number to your phone list. Just in case you want to call her, seeing as how you're going to be here for a while and don't know anyone."

Luke looked down at his phone. He started pushing buttons with his thumb, his eyes suddenly widened, and he snapped his gaze back to Camry.

Cam held out her hand. "Give me that."

He flipped the phone closed and shoved it in his pocket.

"I'm changing my number first thing tomorrow."

"Okay, the cops and the ambulance are here," Dave said, walking over. "Folks," he said to the dining room of stunned patrons. "I'm sorry for the disturbance. If you stop at the counter on your way out, my staff will give you vouchers for a free meal. First, though, I believe the police wish to speak with each of you before you leave. You all come visit the Go Back Grill again, okay? And bring your friends!"

He crouched down in front of Camry. "Christ, Cam, that's one hell of a shiner you got there." He scowled at her ankle. "And you need to get that foot X-rayed. The ambulance will take you in, and you just tell them to bill me."

"All I need is an ice pack, because it's only

sprained. And I am not riding in an ambulance. They're for people having heart attacks or bleeding to death."

His scowl darkened. "Don't make me use my boss voice," he said, dismissing her by turning to Luke and holding out his hand. "Dave Bean, Mr. . . . ?"

"Pascal," Luke said, taking his hand. "Luke Pascal."

"I'm sorry, Luke, that you got caught up in this mess. But I did see you come to our little girl's rescue," he said, nodding toward Fiona, "and I thank you. Most people aren't so quick to get involved in other people's business."

Luke shrugged. "I have a kid sister about the same age as Fiona."

"Food's on the house for as long as you're in town, Luke." Dave looked at Luke's bleeding cut, and the way he was cradling his ribs. "You go with Cam in the ambulance and let them check you out at the hospital. That cut might need stitches, and you might have some cracked ribs. I'll cover the medical bills."

He turned back to Camry. "You did good, kiddo. Don't worry about anyone pressing any charges. By the time I'm done with those four, they'll wish they'd driven straight through town." He flushed and awkwardly patted her shoulder.

"You take as much time off as you need to get back on your feet. You want me to call anyone? Your family, maybe?"

"No!" Camry said a bit more emphatically than she'd meant to, causing Dave to flinch. "I mean, thanks, but I'm really not hurt that badly." She smiled over at Fiona. "And I happen to have a roommate at the moment, who can wait on me hand and foot for a few days."

Two EMTs came over, wheeling a gurney. One of the men crouched down in front of Luke and pointed a tiny flashlight in his eyes. The other one did the same to Camry. He must have decided she was going to live, because he grinned at her. "Can you hop up on the gurney yourself, or are you willing to risk being dropped if I go weak in the knees when I pick you up?"

"I want to change into my jeans and sweater before I go anywhere."

"Why? They're just going to take everything back off you at the hospital." He scanned his gaze over her costume, then grinned at her again. "What you're wearing is just lovely. And anyway, Doc Griswell's working the ER tonight, and he's got a thing for legs—I mean ankles. I bet he puts you ahead of the stab wound and facial cut."

Camry made an effort to stand, but the ruggedly built EMT suddenly lifted her in his arms, stood up, and set her on the gurney. "It's a good thing you didn't crack a smile," he said dryly, spreading a blanket over her, "or I really would have gone weak in the knees."

"Fiona, why don't you go get Camry's purse and clothes," Luke suggested as soon as his EMT helped him to his feet. "And you can ride in the ambulance with her. I'll follow in my car so I can bring you both home after."

"We'll take a taxi back," Camry told him, holding the blanket up to her chest. She looked at Luke's EMT. "He shouldn't be driving, should he?"

"No."

Camry finally found her smile, and she made sure it was damn smug. Fiona might have put the idea in Luke's head that she might welcome his attention by giving him her number, but she'd be damned if she was entertaining some bored tourist on sabbatical.

"I'd offer to drive you home from the hospital," Dave said, walking over to the gurney. He waved toward the police talking to people lined up to get their vouchers. "But I'm afraid I'm going to be tied up here until the wee hours." He stepped closer. "Wipe that smirk off your face, MacKeage. The guy did rescue our little girl, after all," he whispered.

"I don't like pushy men," she whispered back. "And I sure as hell don't want to encourage them by being nice."

Dave snorted. "I can see that's been working well for you."

Chapter Six

Camry woke up to a wet tongue slobbering in her ear, but wasn't alarmed because she recognized Max's doggie breath. She rolled away with a groan, unwilling to open her eyes for fear of increasing the throbbing in her temple.

That is, until she rolled into a body that wasn't canine. She sat up with a start, grabbed her head to keep it from splitting wide open, and fell back against the pillow with an even louder groan.

"What is licking my face?" Luke Pascal rasped from beside her. "I know it's not your tongue, MacKeage, because it's way too friendly."

"That's Ruffles," she muttered. "And she's a

shameless hussy. Is there a reason you're in my bed, Pascal? Not that it matters, because if you're not out of it in two seconds, I'm going to blacken your other eye."

"Give me a minute, would you? My head is killing me, and I'm afraid a rib will pierce my lung if I move right now."

"What are you doing here?"

"I heard you whimpering in the night, so I came in and checked on you. I must have fallen asleep before I could leave."

"That's a flat-out lie, because I never whimper."

"What in hell did they give us at the hospital?"

"Obviously some very powerful pain pills. Um . . . you don't happen to have any spare ones in your pocket, do you?"

"Boxers don't have pockets."

"I have some for both of you. Max, get down," Fiona said, walking up to Camry's side of the bed. "You, too, Ruffles. Go on, shoo!"

Camry felt the bed dip and cracked open her one good eye to see Fiona holding a pill and a glass of water. Cam opened her mouth and the girl popped in the pill, then lifted her head to give her a drink. As soon as she was done, Fiona got up and headed around the bed to do the same for Luke.

"The doctor warned me that you'd both be

pretty sore this morning. Max! I told you to go in the living room!"

"Whisper," Cam whispered.

"Sorry."

"Why is Luke here?" Cam asked.

"The nice EMT from the ambulance called his wife, and they both hung out in the waiting room with me. Then they gave us a ride home and helped me get you both settled in for the night. John put Luke in my bed, and his wife, Glenna, helped me put you in yours. I slept on the couch, so I don't know how you two ended up in bed together," she finished, sounding way too delighted.

"No, I mean why is Luke in my *house*?"

"Oh, that. When the doctor gave me instructions for both of you, I figured Luke should come stay with us for a few days." She smiled at Cam's one-eyed glare. "After he so gallantly came to my rescue last night, I thought it was the least we could do."

"*He* doesn't care to be talked about as if *he* isn't here," Luke said. "And thank you," he muttered, only to groan when Tigger jumped up on the bed, jostling them both. "How the hell many dogs do you own, anyway?"

"None," Cam told him. "But I babysit four."

"You babysit dogs? Why?"

"To pay the bills."

Camry heard Fiona sigh. "She's still trying to decide what she wants to be when she grows up."

"Excuse me?" Luke said.

"Right now she's torn between being Suzy Homemaker or president of the United States. I told her she's smart enough to be a rocket scientist if she wanted, but she doesn't think that would be all that exciting."

Apparently Luke was so impressed, he couldn't comment.

Cam felt her arm being patted, and found Fiona standing beside her again. "Don't worry about the dogs. I'll take them for their runs for the next few days. The doctor said you need to stay off that ankle."

She looked over at Luke, then back at Cam. "And Luke's got some badly bruised ribs, and Doctor Griswell said they'll probably hurt worse than if they were broken." She grinned. "But don't worry; he sent you both home with plenty of pain pills."

"Can he at least walk back to his own bed?" Cam asked.

"*He* can, just as soon as Fiona leaves," Luke said. "Because *he* is only wearing boxer shorts."

Fiona swept Tigger into her arms, spun around with a giggle, and left.

Luke still didn't move.

"She's gone."

"I know. How about giving me enough time for the pill to kick in?"

"You get five minutes, Pascal."

"So, you babysit dogs and wait tables for a living?"

"No, I babysit dogs through the week and tend bar on the weekends. I was just waiting tables last night so I could keep an eye on Fiona."

"How long has she been . . . missing?"

"I found her on the beach this past Friday. She told me she'd run away from home four days prior to that."

"And you can't get her to tell you anything about her family?"

"No. And I don't dare push her, because I'm afraid she'll run away from *me*."

"Christ, her parents must be going out of their minds. Did you at least call the police to see if they have a missing child reported?"

"First thing Friday, while she was taking a shower. They said no one fitting Fiona's description had been reported missing. Um . . . thank you for rescuing her last night. Dave's right, a lot of men wouldn't have gotten involved, especially considering there were four of those drunken jerks. Hell, there were plenty of other men sitting right there last night, but I didn't see any of them jump out of their seats."

"I have a half sister about Fiona's age."

"Fiona said you're on sabbatical. From what?"

He was silent for several heartbeats, then softly chuckled. "Would you believe rocket science?"

Camry went perfectly still, not even daring to breathe as she tried to calculate the odds of two physicists getting into a barroom brawl and winding up in the same bed the next morning.

"And you know what?" he continued. "Contrary to what you told Fiona, I happen to believe it's an exciting profession."

"How can crunching numbers until your eyes cross be exciting? Especially if those numbers suddenly stop making a lick of sense?"

"You know something about mathematical physics, do you?"

"I know it must be frustrating as hell."

"And babysitting other people's dogs is exciting?"

"The dogs don't question every damn thing I say in an e-mail, or *kindly* point out my mistakes."

"I didn't know dogs used e-mail," he said, amusement lacing his voice.

Camry gave him a shove. "The pill's obviously working now."

"Ow, my ribs! It definitely *isn't* working yet."

"Sorry."

She felt the bed jostle and cracked open her eye just enough to see that he'd rolled toward her, propping his head on his hand. "So you babysit dogs because they think you're the smartest thing since sliced bread, is that it? You don't care to have an engaging argument with a worthy opponent once in a while?"

Camry pulled the blanket up to her chin and tucked it down between them. "I like a good argument when the person I'm arguing with isn't so full of himself that he insists on coming to America to set me straight in person."

"Hmm, I'm a little lost here. I thought we were talking about arguing in general, but you seem to be talking about something a bit more specific. Mind elaborating?"

"No. Go away, Pascal."

He eased back onto his pillow and sighed. "I'm hungry. I never did get supper last night."

"There's some mayonnaise in the fridge. You're welcome to it."

"That's it? You don't cook?"

"Why bother, when I can just go to the Go Back Grill?"

"Maybe you should lean more toward being president when you grow up, instead of Suzy

Homemaker." He sighed again. "I don't suppose anyone delivers in this half-deserted town. Maybe Dave or one of his waitresses could bring something over to us."

"Dave brought Cam's SUV home last night," Fiona said, walking back into the bedroom carrying a tray of food and setting it down between them.

Cam slowly sat up, the smell making her mouth water. "He brought food, too?"

"No, I drove to the grocery store this morning and was able to get back before the mutts arrived," Fiona told her, placing the pillow behind her against the headboard.

"You have a driver's license?"

"Almost," Fiona said, going around to set Luke's pillow in place. "And since those pills will knock both of you out soon, I'll wait until then to run to Luke's hotel and get his stuff. Is your room key in your pants, Luke? What's your room number?"

"You can't drive with *almost* a license," Cam told her. "You're supposed to have an adult with you."

"Don't worry that I'll crash your truck, Cam. I've been driving on tote roads since I was ten," the girl said. "I'll take Suki with me and put your sunglasses on her. She's big enough to look like an adult."

"Tote roads?" Camry said, perking up. "That means you live in western Maine."

"They have tote roads in Aroostook and Washington Counties, too." Fiona caught Tigger in midleap when the dachshund tried to jump on the bed, then headed back out of the room with the dog. She stopped at the door. "I'm going to leave Max and Ruffles here, and I'll take Suki and Tigger with me. Luke, your room number?"

"He's going back to his hotel this morning," Camry told her.

"It's room seven," he said, picking up a piece of toast. "And I haven't unpacked, so you'll find my suitcase on the bed."

"You are *not* moving in here with us."

"You heard what the doctor told Fiona. I'm going to be in a lot of pain for the next few days, and it's not safe to take powerful drugs if there's no one around to make sure I don't maim myself. I need supervision, and since you do, too, we might as well be supervised together."

"That makes perfect sense to me," Fiona said from the doorway. "And I certainly don't mind taking care of the both of you. In fact, it will let me know if I want to be a nurse when I grow up." The young girl, who appeared to be enjoying herself way too much, arched her brows at Camry. "Unlike *someone* around here, I want it all: a career *and* a husband *and* children before my biological clock starts ticking down."

Camry grabbed an orange off the tray to fling at her. "You little brat!"

Luke snatched it out of her hand before she could throw it. "Not the food!"

Camry pointed at Fiona. "You just wait until your daddy gets hold of you, young lady. I intend to be standing right beside him, helping him lecture you. And as soon as I can walk, I'm going through all your belongings to find out his name."

"Too late. I burned everything with my name on it in the fireplace this morning."

Camry gasped, sincerely hurt. "You don't trust me?"

Fiona stepped closer. "Of course I do, Camry. It's Luke I don't trust," she said, rolling her eyes. "I mean, really, he *is* a man."

Luke started to hurl the orange at her, but Camry snatched it out of his hand and began peeling it. Fiona spun away with a laugh, shooed the three other dogs out ahead of her, and closed the bedroom door.

"She's been living with you only a few days, and you've already corrupted her opinion of men," Luke accused, just before taking a bite of his toast.

"I'm pretty sure Fiona had you men figured out long before I found her. She told me she left home because her father wouldn't stop lecturing her."

"Because he loves her."

She stopped ripping into the orange and looked at him. "Why can't men love their wives and daughters without lecturing them to death?"

"How in hell should I know? I've never had a wife or a daughter."

"How about a girlfriend? You got one of those?"

"Not at the moment," he said, staring down at his toast. "I don't seem to have any problem *getting* a girlfriend, I just can't seem to keep one."

"Because you lecture them to death."

"No, that's not it." He picked up the plate of eggs and started eating, talking between bites. "They never stick around long enough for me to reach the lecture stage." He looked over at her. "Assuming there even is one," he said, returning to wolfing down his food.

Camry found herself quite intrigued. She could see why Luke Pascal didn't have trouble getting girlfriends, since Fiona had been dead-on about his being dreamy. He had the body of an athlete—which really didn't go with the physicist thing—and his eyes were a beautiful deep blue. As for his hair, well, she had to admit she did like it long; it gave him a rugged, rebellious look, which also didn't match his profession.

His chest wasn't anything to scoff at, either. His shoulders were broad and his well-defined pecs, liberally sprinkled with soft-looking hair, certainly rang *her* bell.

"So why can't you keep a girlfriend?" she asked, wondering if maybe he bombed in the bedroom. He was a nerd, after all, even if he did have a good deal of brawn.

"According to the women who were still speaking to me when they packed up their toothbrushes, I'm boring. Apparently you ladies need a guy's undivided attention," he said, sounding more confounded than resigned.

Camry almost burst out laughing, but caught herself when she realized he was serious. "So you spent all your time working instead of with your girlfriends?"

"If they wanted to be with me, why didn't they come hang out at my lab?"

Okay, the guy truly was clueless. "Maybe you should try dating other physicists. You know, another scientist who would understand being ignored?"

"Have you *met* many women scientists?" He actually shivered. "They scare the hell out of me."

"They do? How?"

"I can name you three right off the top of my head who pull their hair back so tight, they look like they have botched face-lifts." He shivered again. "And two women come to mind who could probably knock me on my ass in three seconds flat." He snorted. "And a lot of female scientists have the personality of lab rats."

Camry didn't know why, but she found that hilariously funny. "And most of the *male* scientists I've met," she said through her laughter, "couldn't dance their way out of a wet paper bag!"

"Hey, *I* can dance."

"And I've met fish with more personality than most of them have."

Luke started laughing, too. "Okay, you've got me there. So have I."

Camry threw back the covers and started to swing her legs off the bed.

"Hey, where are you going?" he asked, grabbing her arm. "You can't walk."

"I have to use the bathroom."

He grinned. "Me, too. Okay, here's what we'll do. You wait right there, and I'll walk around and help you since I don't have a bum ankle."

"Okay, but I get the bathroom first."

Luke set his plate on the tray between them, then walked around to her side.

Camry nearly fell over, tilting her head to look at him. "You're a lot bigger when you're half naked." Her eyes stopped halfway up, and she reached out and touched his ribs. "Wow, that's one hell of a bruise." Her gaze finally made it to his battered face. "Are you sure you're a physicist? You certainly held your own last night."

"I've been working out," he said, puffing up his chest, only to let it sink with a groan as he cradled his ribs. "Okay. Give me your hand, and don't put any weight on your nakle."

Camry giggled. "I think your pill's working."

"Nope. I can still feel my ribs."

She pulled herself out of bed—thankful that Fiona had put her in flannel pajamas—then clutched his arm as she balanced on her good leg. "My pill isn't working, either. Both my head and nankle hurt. Don't let me fall."

"I won't. You know why, MacKeage?" he asked, leading her to the bathroom.

"Why?"

"Because you're downright pretty when you smile."

She smiled up at him. "You're not so bad your-self, for a physy-ist."

They reached the bathroom, and Camry trans-ferred her weight from his arm to the sink. "Okay. Go away."

"You won't take forever, will you? I really have to go, too," he said.

She waved toward the bedroom. "Pee out the window or something. I don't have any neighbors."

He walked out and Cam closed the door, locked it, and hobbled over to the toilet.

"You know what I think?" Luke called through the bathroom door.

"Gee, I don't have a clue. What?"

"You know that guy you were having the e-mail argument with? I think you should meet him in person."

"So I can punch him in the nose?"

He didn't answer right away. "Did you really think he was full of himself?"

"He was a know-it-all, holier-than-thou, arrogant son of a bitch."

Luke said nothing to that.

"And if I ever do meet him in person, I will cram his laptop down his throat." She snorted. "He's probably five feet three and four hundred pounds, bald as an eagle, and wears Coke bottles for glasses."

"He really pissed you off, didn't he?" Luke said softly.

Done taking care of business, Camry hobbled to the sink, looked in the mirror, and screamed.

The doorknob rattled. "What's wrong? Did you fall?"

"No, I just looked in the mirror," she said with a slightly hysterical laugh, carefully touching her swollen eye.

It sounded like Luke thunked his head against the door. "Dammit, you just scared the hell out of me!"

"I just scared the hell out of myself." She washed and dried her hands, quickly ran her fingers through her rumpled hair, and unlocked the door.

Luke stumbled into the room when she opened it.

"Your turn," she said.

"I just need to wash my hands and throw some water on my face."

"Why?"

He grinned crookedly. "I peed out the window."

"I was *kidding*."

"You were taking too long," he said, stepping around her to use the sink.

She'd give him credit, he didn't scream when he looked in the mirror, but he did gasp.

"Aren't we a pair?" she asked, smiling at him in the mirror. "At least we've got two good eyes between us, and you can walk and I can . . . I can . . ."

She hung her head. "I can never go into another bar. Every time I get into trouble, it's in a bar."

He lifted her chin with his finger. "You can go with me. I won't let you get into trouble."

"Said the spider to the fly."

"Smile again."

"No. It hurts my face."

"Because of your shiner, or just when you're around men in general?"

"Hey, I am a *happy* person, dammit."

"Wow, that pill sure wore off fast. Should I ask Fiona to give you another one?"

Camry reached up and grabbed his ears, pulled down his head, then kissed him full on the mouth. "There!" she snapped. "Is *that* happy enough for you?"

He pulled her into his arms, cradled her head against his shoulder, and kissed her back—a bit more forcefully, quite a bit longer, and definitely . . .

Okay, he didn't keep losing girlfriends because he bombed in the bedroom. This guy could *kiss*.

But then, so could she. As a matter of fact, she had perfected kissing.

Camry went weak in the knees—especially the one holding her weight—and sagged against him when his tongue started doing delicious things to hers. She nearly burst into tears when he suddenly pulled away.

"Christ, you're scary," he rasped, his blue eyes locked on hers.

Her head spun in confusion. "Scary?" she repeated, running her fingertip over his jaw. "How's that?"

He tilted her head back again and started kissing her cheek, then trailed soft, shivering kisses down her neck.

Camry trembled with blossoming passion. Yup, he *definitely* rang her bell.

No, wait, there was a *real* bell ringing somewhere.

She pulled away. "Oh my God, what time is it? That's my mother!"

"You have a mother?" Luke muttered, trying to kiss her again, the evidence of his own blossoming passion poking her belly. "She'll call back."

Camry untangled herself from his embrace and hobbled toward her bed. "But if I don't answer, she'll call my lab." She suddenly changed directions when she realized her cell phone wasn't on her nightstand. "Come on, where in hell are you?" She looked around the room, honed in on the bureau, and snatched up her purse.

"Hi, Mom," she said as soon as she flipped open her cell phone. "Gee, is it Monday already? I've been so involved in my work, I don't even know what day it is."

She jumped when Luke took hold of her arm, then let him help her to the bed so she could sit down. "Really?" she said into the phone as she waved him away. "Three feet? It's early for that much snow, isn't it? But it's good for the ski business."

She frowned at Luke when, instead of leaving, he walked around and sat down on his side of the bed and started eating her orange.

"Um, Mom? Could you hold on a minute? Someone just walked in. Stay on the line—this will only take a minute."

She found the Mute button and held it down with her thumb, then snatched her orange from him. "Can't you see I'm having a personal conversation here? Go back to your own bed."

"But it's small. And the damn thing's too short for me." He picked up the toast on her plate of scrambled eggs and dismissed her with a wave. "Don't let me stop you. I'm just going to finish my breakfast and have a nap."

"You are not sleeping in my bed."

"It'll be easier for Fiona if we're both in the same room."

She arched a brow. "So you wouldn't mind if *your* baby sister took care of two virtual strangers sharing the same bed?"

He scowled at her, then stuffed his mouth full of toast.

Camry released the Mute button and held the phone back to her ear. "Can I call you back later, Mom? There's something going on here that needs my undivided attention. What?" She sighed. "Yeah, I'm afraid I still can't make it home for the solstice. I know, but better than anyone, you should understand how this work goes. I really don't dare lose my focus for that long. And I can't work at home during the holidays because of all the chaos. Okay, I'll talk to you later. Yes, I love you, too. Bye, Mom. Tell Daddy I love him," she said in a rush, just before hitting the End button.

"You're not going home for Christmas?" Luke asked, taking another bite of toast.

Camry stuffed what was left of her orange in her mouth.

"Wait, you said if you didn't answer, your mom would call your *lab*. You have a lab?" He made a production of looking at all the doors in the room, then pointed at the closet door. "Is it in there? What kind of lab is it?" He gasped dramatically. "Not a *meth* lab!" He shook his head. "And you're worried about what impression our being in the same bed will have on Fiona."

"Will you get real? Better yet, get out of here."

"What kind of lab were you talking about, MacKeage?"

She settled back against the headboard with a sigh, and pushed around her eggs with a fork. "I used to be a rocket propulsion physicist."

"You're a rocket scientist? For real? Wait, you said used to be. As in you're *not* a physicist anymore?" He grinned. "What happened, did you suddenly forget how to count past ten without undressing your feet?"

She glared over at him. "No, I got stuck."

"Stuck?" He snorted. "Real scientists don't get stuck, MacKeage. We hit brick walls sometimes, but we either find a way around them or start digging through them. Wait," he said, snapping his fingers. "Did your brick wall have anything to do with that guy you were having the e-mail argument with?"

"The arrogant bastard sent me an equation that completely contradicted three years of my work," she growled, throwing the fork across the room, where it hit the wall and clattered to the floor. "And then he had the audacity to suggest we should work on the problem *together*."

"So, are you angry because a fellow scientist wants to work with you, or because the equation he sent you was correct?"

"His name is Lucian Renoir. God, even his name sounds arrogant. But I'm the one who's going to give the world a viable ion propulsion system," she said, slapping her chest, "whereas he just wants to come here and steal my work."

"Um, there's a bit of a flaw in your theory, MacKeage. He can't steal what doesn't exist. You walked away, remember?" He suddenly smiled at her. "But if you think this Renoir fellow is five feet three and weighs four hundred pounds, maybe you're expecting him to croak any minute, and then you'll start working again?"

Since she'd thrown the fork, Camry used her fingers to eat some of the scrambled eggs. "I can't start up again if I can't figure out how to get unstuck." She glanced at him, then looked back at the tray. "He . . . the equation he sent me was correct. I had to retrace nearly two years of work before I found where I'd shot off on a tangent." She looked over at him. "But even though I found the problem, I still can't figure out how to fix it."

"Maybe Renoir could help you."

"But if he can make it work, then I should be able to, too." She actually smiled. "But I doubt he can do it on his own, because he's really not all that bright."

"He's not?"

"He can't even figure out that my mother is Dr. Grace Sutter."

"*The* Dr. Sutter, who used to work for StarShip Spaceline? Hell, I've read all her papers. She's the one who turned me on to space science when I was twelve."

Cam snorted. "She turned me on to it in her womb."

"So why aren't you collaborating with her?"

She looked back down at the tray and frowned. "I've tried, but she refuses. She just suddenly walked away from ion propulsion when I was a kid, and started locking herself in her lab to work on something else." She snorted. "Probably cookie recipes. Having seven daughters seems to have taken the edge off her passion for science." She looked over at him. "You men don't have to worry about pregnancies messing you up with nurturing hormones, so you never lose your edge."

His navy blue eyes studied her for several heartbeats. "Is that what you think happened to your mother?"

"What else could it be? She was really close to perfecting ion propulsion when she met my father and started having babies, and, thirty-five years later, we *still* don't have a viable system."

"But the paper I read was written . . ." He looked away in thought. "I was around twelve then, and I'm thirty-three now." He looked back at her. "Your mother was still publishing just twenty years ago. And I believe she's published as recently as six years ago, though not on ion propulsion. She's still in the game, Camry. At least *she* didn't just suddenly walk away to start bartending and babysitting dogs."

Cam said nothing as she looked down at the tray again.

"What really made you walk away, MacKeage?" His eyes suddenly widened. "Does it have something to do with what Fiona said just a minute ago? Maybe you're not standing in front of a brick wall, but are smack in the middle of a midlife crisis." He pointed at the bedroom door. "When you were Fiona's age, didn't you want it all, too: a career *and* a husband *and* children? But where you had one out of the three, now you have none." He suddenly smiled. "Or are you really on sabbatical, working on goals two and three?"

"I don't ever intend to get married and have children."

"Not ever? That's a hell of a long time."

"I don't see you rushing out to get yourself a wife and children."

He let out a huge yawn and suddenly scooted down in the bed. "I would probably be married right now if I could keep a girlfriend long enough to propose to her. I just can't seem to find one who gets turned on by what I do."

Camry glared at him, even though his eyes were closed. But then she also let out a yawn.

She started to shove the tray toward him to make room for herself, only to suddenly remember his bruised ribs. She set the tray on the floor beside the bed, slid down under the blankets, and turned her back to him.

Maybe instead of ion propulsion, she should work on the science of *men* having babies, so Mother Nature could screw with their hormones for a change.

Chapter Seven

*L*uke sat sprawled on the couch four days later, watching the infomercial explaining how mineral-based makeup would make his skin feel like he wasn't wearing anything, so bored out of his skull he was damn close to tears.

How in hell did Camry do this five days a week, week after week?

Granted, the dogs were entertaining—for all of ten minutes—but how did she just hang around this house all day, doing virtually nothing? How does anyone with even half a brain not justify the air they breathe by at least trying to be productive?

When she'd mentioned her e-mail argument

that first morning, Luke had felt guilty that he might have been responsible for Camry's walking away from her work. But as he'd gotten to know her over the last four days, he'd come to realize that her little midlife crisis had more to do with her mother—and her concept of family in general—than it had to do with him or her work.

He now believed that Camry was afraid of being just like her mother instead of wanting to emulate her, afraid that falling in love with a man and having babies would addle her brain, and afraid of losing her passion for the sciences—which she readily admitted she'd acquired in the womb—just like she believed her mother had.

And Luke was pretty sure that being afraid of anything was as mind-boggling to Camry Mac-Keage as doing nothing all day was to him.

That's why he'd spent the last four days trying to figure out how he might jump-start Camry—not only back into her work, but also back to her family. Admitting he was Lucian Renoir certainly might do the trick, but he wasn't convinced it wouldn't just as easily push her in the opposite direction.

Unless he also confessed that he'd destroyed her mother's satellite. Because if that didn't make her want to kill him in his sleep, maybe she'd at least try to kill him in the scientific arena.

Not that it mattered, considering he'd committed professional suicide the moment he'd started eavesdropping on Podly.

Luke drove his hand into the cellophane bag Fiona had given him before she'd gone to help Camry take a shower, and pulled out a fistful of corn chips. Four heads lifted and eight ears perked up. Four drooling tongues appeared, and eight hopeful brown eyes locked on his hand moving toward his mouth.

Luke suddenly lifted his hand over his head, then darted it to the side, then quickly shot it over to his other side—all the while watching the canine eating machines track his movements with the intensity of a guided missile locked on its target.

"You are such uncomplicated beasts," he muttered, tossing the chips to the floor.

While they were occupied chomping down the junk food and inhaling stray crumbs up their noses, Luke quietly reached into the bag again and quickly filled his own mouth as he absently watched the magical transformation as a woman's face went from blotchy red to visibly flawless.

Camry MacKeage certainly didn't need this product; she hadn't been wearing any makeup that first morning he'd awakened beside her, and her skin had looked damned flawless to him—except for the bruise on her left cheek and around her eye, which was only now starting to fade.

She'd felt pretty damn good in his arms, too, when she had recklessly kissed him right there in the bathroom, and he had just as recklessly kissed her back.

When he'd decided to come to America, Luke had known Camry was somewhere around five feet three, but had hoped *her* weight had blossomed to four hundred pounds. And it wouldn't have hurt, either, if she'd sprouted horns soon after the photo had been taken that he'd found of her on the Internet. Considering his track record with women, he'd have preferred that Dr. MacKeage be anything but gorgeous, because he hadn't wanted even a hint of sexual tension to creep into their work.

So much for that pipe dream. Hell, if they both hadn't been so beaten up that first morning, he wouldn't be bored to tears right now because he would have spent the last four days making love to her.

Not that he hadn't tried.

It had become somewhat of a game between them—or maybe *challenge* was a better word— where they flirted right up to the edge of full-blown passion, then withdrew into what Luke could only describe as salacious hell. He was so sexually frustrated, and so damned *in lust* with Camry MacKeage, that the next time she kissed him he wasn't going to care if the dogs watched, he intended to take her right here on the couch.

Hell, he'd nearly nailed her this morning, when he'd awakened to find *her* in *his* bed. Looking him straight in the face with the same piercing green eyes as her father, she'd had the nerve to say she'd heard him whimpering in his sleep but had fallen asleep before she could return to her bed.

Fiona, apparently not the least bit impressionable, had breezed in, popped a pill in each of their mouths, and told them she was running out to buy groceries. Beginning to suspect the romantically inclined teenager was keeping them drugged so they would keep playing musical beds, Luke had started hiding his pill in his cheek, then slipping it behind the headboard the moment the girl turned her back.

If Camry had a mouse problem, they were certainly happy rodents now.

In an attempt to distract himself from his raging lust, Luke had tried focusing on Fiona instead, specifically on finding out her last name so he could locate her parents. But apparently teens today were much sharper than he had been, because when *he* had run away from home, he hadn't made it ten miles before his stepfather had found him. André had dragged Luke home, handed him a crosscut saw and ax, and made him cut, chop, and stack eight cords of firewood by hand while he contemplated the hell he had put his mother through.

Luke hadn't run away from home again until age twenty-four.

He heard the bedroom door open and knew that Camry—likely armored in lilac-scented soap for another one of their salacious battles—was heading over to sit down beside him while Fiona took the dogs out for their morning walk. The winter solstice was only a week away, and Luke figured he had only one or two days left to talk Camry into going home before she claimed he was fully recovered and kicked him out on his sexually frustrated ass.

He sighed, scooting over to make room for her on the couch as he patted his pocket to make sure he'd remembered the condoms. It was time, he'd decided this morning while shaving, to launch a full frontal attack: first on Camry's body—because he really, painfully wanted her—and then on her conscience.

"I'm heading out to walk the mutts," Fiona said as she put on her jacket. "Is there anything either of you need before I go?"

"A beer would be nice," Luke said, not caring if it was only ten in the morning, because he was so damned bored. Dave had brought him a six-pack, but Fiona had hidden it, claiming he couldn't mix beer with the drugs she thought he was still taking.

"If you don't take your afternoon pill, you can have one tonight with supper," she promised, snapping leashes on the four tail-wagging dogs and heading outside.

"You seem to be getting around quite well," Luke said when Camry swiped his bag of corn chips. "How's the ankle feeling?"

"Ready to run a marathon," she said, stuffing her mouth with chips.

"Are you going to waste time eating, or can we go straight to the necking part of this morning's entertainment? They'll only be gone an hour."

She looked over at him, blinking her pretty green eyes, and Luke realized there had been an edge in his voice. He grinned. "Or we can skip the necking and just kick things up a notch. But I suggest we use your bed, because the spare really isn't large enough for the two of us—as you found out this morning, when I gallantly saved you from falling out on your sexy little . . . behind."

She blinked at him again.

Okay, so maybe *direct* wasn't the best approach after all. He threw his arm over the back of the couch behind her, drove his other hand into the bag of chips, and munched away while he waited for her to make the first move.

Assuming she made it in five minutes. He figured he needed at least forty-five minutes in the bedroom, and that gave him only ten minutes' leeway in case Fiona walked fast today.

Camry attacked him in three.

The bag of junk food suddenly went flying and she scrambled onto his lap; before he'd even finishing swallowing, she cupped his face in her delicate hands and kissed him. Quickly recovering from the surprising assault, Luke wrapped his arms around her and let her have her wicked way with him, because . . .

Well, because just as soon as she got herself worked into a really good frenzy, he was hopefully going to use two of the three condoms in his pocket.

And once she was so exhausted she couldn't speak, and hopefully too mellow to care, then he would casually mention who he actually was.

Then he'd tell her what he'd done to Podly.

And then he would very nicely ask her to help him find the little satellite so they could bring it back to her mother, and the three of them could lock themselves in Gù Brath's lab until they had a viable propulsion system to present to the world.

Realizing he was about to pop the zipper on his jeans, and seeing how Camry had his shirt unbuttoned and was doing wickedly delightful things to his nipples with her tongue, Luke cupped her backside, stood up, and headed toward her bedroom.

She didn't even notice the sudden change of venue, she was so busy working herself into a frenzy. And when he laid her on the bed, settled his sexually frustrated body beside her, and started undoing her blouse, she very kindly helped.

Surprised he even had the sense of mind to glance at the clock on the nightstand, Luke gave himself five minutes to get her naked.

Only she had him naked in two. And herself naked in one.

Luke began to wonder who was seducing whom.

"Beautiful," he murmured, his mouth trailing down her throat on its way to her lovely breasts, and his hands . . . hell, he simply touched her everywhere, since every damn square inch of her turned him on.

Though he thought she had already worked herself into quite a frenzy, Luke discovered she was only getting started. Camry turned so suddenly wild and urgently aggressive, she reminded him of the blizzard that had all but immobilized him for two entire days with its intensity.

She didn't waste time exploring any parts of his body that didn't seem immensely interesting. Her hands went straight to his groin, and Luke pretty near bucked them off the bed when she wrapped her fingers around him.

Where in hell had she thrown his pants with the condoms?

Alarmed to see her head dipping in the same direction as her hands, and fearing four days of building frustration would be over in three seconds if he didn't get her under control, Luke took hold of her shoulders and hauled her up beside him.

But then he had to pin her hands over her head and throw his leg over hers to keep *her* from bucking them off the bed.

"Slow down," he rasped, trying to catch his breath.

She was also panting, as if she really had run a marathon, and Luke worried that if just getting naked left them both winded, full-blown sex might actually kill them.

He slid his free hand down her ribs to her pelvis, and found her moist and hot and definitely ready for him.

Where in hell were his pants!

She made a ragged sound of pleasure and arched into his touch. Luke increased the pressure and slid a finger inside her, retreated, and repeated the intoxicating dance. She tightened around him, her body humming with building tension as she strained against his hold on her wrists. Her climax was as sudden and gloriously breathtaking as an exploding nova.

And it didn't slow her down one damn bit.

So caught up in the wave of pleasure he was witnessing, Luke didn't realize he'd slackened his grip. And before he knew it, Camry's hands were back at his groin, doing gloriously breathtaking things to him.

And just as suddenly as she had, he made an utter disgrace of himself.

He flopped back on the bed beside her with a groan and stared up at the ceiling, trying to catch his breath as he wondered what had just happened.

Little Miss Exploding Nova, also panting raggedly, rolled over and snuggled against him with a sigh. She patted his chest. "Thanks. I really needed that."

Chapter Eight

$\mathcal{L}$uke pulled the unused condoms out of his pants pocket two mornings later and tossed them in his ditty bag with a derisive snort. He'd just experienced two days of the best sex of his life, and he hadn't even gotten to use one of the damn things. He still couldn't figure out how he could be so sexually sated without technically having sex, or how Camry MacKeage had managed to fool him into believing he *was*.

Dammit, what sort of perverted game was she playing? They'd done it every way but standing on their heads, but they hadn't actually done it!

Luke suddenly reached in the ditty bag, pulled out one of the condoms, and stuffed it back in his pocket. He was on to her now, by God, and he'd be damned if he was going to be used as some convenient boy toy to stave off *her* boredom.

The very next time they got naked together he was calling her bluff, and either she could put out for real, or he was taking the next flight back to France. To hell with her and this whole damn mess. He'd been deluding himself long enough, holding out hope there was anything left of that damn satellite worth salvaging. And being in lust with a woman was one thing, but deliberately being used by her was . . . it was . . .

Dammit, he actually felt violated!

Fired up with righteous indignation and no small amount of wounded pride, Luke stormed out of the bathroom in search of the green-eyed siren.

Only finding the house was empty, he stood in the living room, nonplussed. Fiona must have taken the dogs out for their walk early, and Camry must have gone with her. Dammit to hell! Had she grown bored with him already?

But wait. She couldn't stay out the entire hour; her ankle still wasn't that strong. Luke grabbed his jacket, fully intending to sit on the steps and ambush her when she returned. Only he nearly fell over her when he rushed out the porch door, because Camry was sitting on the top step. She didn't even bother looking up when he bumped into her, but simply continued to stare down at something in her hand.

Immediately sensing something was wrong, Luke silently sat down beside her. It was then he noticed she was holding open a card. And though he couldn't quite read it, the handwriting looked eerily familiar. When Camry still didn't acknowledge he was there, he glanced around for Fiona, even standing up to see the beach, looking in both directions for the girl.

"She's gone," Camry said, her voice lacking any emotion.

Luke sat back down. "She took all the dogs to the grocery store?"

"The dogs don't come on Saturdays."

He glanced at Camry with growing alarm. "Will she be back soon?"

"She's not coming back."

The hair on his neck stood up, his gut tightened painfully, and every muscle in his body tensed. "She ran off?" he whispered. He stood up again. "Come on then, we have to go find her. I don't care how mature she seems, we can't let her wander around alone!"

Camry still didn't move. "She's okay. She's gone . . . home."

Luke took a deep breath in an attempt to control

his pounding heart and sat back down beside her with a disheartened sigh. "All she left us was a card? She couldn't even say good-bye in person?"

Camry reached down between her knees, her hand returning with an envelope, and Luke finally noticed the small box sitting on the step below her, between her feet.

"Fiona left you this," she said, handing him the envelope.

His heart started pounding again when he saw his name—*Lucian Pascal Renoir*—in flourished handwriting that was definitely familiar. He glanced over at Camry, but she continued to stare out at the ocean. He slid his finger under the sealed flap and pulled out a card exactly like the one Grace and Greylen MacKeage had received over a week ago.

He opened it. *Please don't give up on her,* Luke silently read, *because everyone needs a miracle once in a while, and you are hers.* She'd drawn a little smiley face, then continued. *And though you might find it hard to believe right now, she is your miracle. Have a great adventure together, you two. I'll see you again . . . sooner than you think.* She'd drawn another smiley face, before signing, *All my love, Fiona Gregor.*

Luke lifted his gaze to the ocean. *Gregor.* Why did that name sound familiar?

Fiona Gregor.

"Don't you have a brother-in-law named Gregor?" he asked.

"Matt. He's married to my sister Winter," Camry said, still looking out to sea. "Fiona's their daughter. And my niece."

He frowned at her. "You didn't recognize your own niece?"

She dropped her gaze to the card in her hand. "I didn't recognize her because right now she's only five and a half months old."

Luke's heart started trying to pound out of his chest again. He didn't know which alarmed him more: what Camry was saying, or her utter lack of emotion. She had obviously read his name on the envelope she'd handed him, so she knew exactly who he was. Why wasn't she going for his jugular, or at least screaming her head off?

And what in hell did she mean, Fiona was only five months old?

This had to be some sort of bizarre joke.

And how had Fiona found out his full name, anyway?

He snorted. "Apparently our respecting the little brat enough not to go through her belongings wasn't reciprocated. She obviously went through my briefcase when she picked it up for me."

He held the envelope with his name on it in

front of Camry, but when she still didn't respond, he dropped his hand back on his thigh. "I know you probably won't believe me, but I was going to tell you today." He shifted uncomfortably, disguising the action by sliding the card back in its envelope. "In fact, I've spent all week trying to figure out how to tell you. I . . . you should also know that your mother asked me to come here and talk you into going home for Christmas."

She finally looked at him, her eyes filled with horror. "Mom *knows* I'm living in Maine?" she whispered. "D-does Daddy know, too?"

Luke nodded.

She was on her feet and off the steps so fast, it took him a moment to realize she was bolting. The colorfully wrapped box clattered down the steps after her, the card she'd been holding trailing behind it.

Luke jumped to his feet and ran after her. "Camry!" he shouted, tearing onto the beach, amazed she could run so fast on her ankle. "Wait! Let me explain! Dammit, will you stop! You're going to hurt your ankle again!"

It took him an amazingly long time to catch her, and then he had to tackle her to get her to stop, twisting so he took the brunt of their fall. But then he was forced to protect himself from her pummeling fists, his heart nearly stopping when he realized she was sobbing as she lashed out at him.

He finally just hugged her so tightly that her blows became ineffective, and cupped her head to his cheek. "Shhh," he crooned, wrapping his legs around hers to stop her struggles. "It's okay. Everything's going to be okay."

She suddenly went limp. "Let me go."

He chuckled humorlessly. "Not a chance, lady. Just listen to me, will you?" he said in a rush when she started struggling again. "I just spent the last two months searching Springy Mountain for your mother's satellite, which crashed there last summer."

She went still again, only this time she remained guardedly tense.

"But I got caught in a blizzard, and your brother-in-law Jack Stone found me and brought me to your parents," he quickly continued. "I told them who I was. Well, I told them I was Luke Pascal, but I did say I was the man you'd been corresponding with all last winter. Anyway, I wasn't aware they didn't know you no longer worked for NASA, so you can blame that one on me. But it was Fiona who sent them a Christmas card, which led them to believe you were living here in Go Back Cove."

He shrugged, shrugging her with him. "I don't

know why they refused to come get you themselves. But your mother said something about their needing you to *want* to come home. So she asked me to come get you."

He sighed, pressing his face into her hair. "I don't know if any of this is making any sense, Camry, or even getting through to you. I only know that your parents love you immensely, and they're . . . aw hell, they're hurt and confused and probably scared sick that you've been keeping your secret from them for so long."

She went completely limp again, and this time Luke knew she wasn't faking. It might have had something to do with her silent sobs, or the fact that instead of pushing him away, she was now clutching him with wrenching desperation.

He slid his fingers through her hair. "I'm sorry," he murmured. "I am so damned sorry for not telling you up front who I was, and I'm sorry for letting your parents talk me into coming after you in the first place. This was none of my business, really, but since I'm rather invested now, I have to ask: Why couldn't you tell your mother what was going on with your work?"

He slackened his hold just enough to lift her chin, and his heart nearly stopped again at the pain he saw in her eyes. He brushed a tear off her cheek and smiled tenderly. "You have my word,

MacKeage: I won't run home to your mama and tattle. That's completely between you and her. But having met Grace, and seeing how much she loves you, I can't figure out why you couldn't go to her with your problem." He widened his smile. "As for your father, that man scares the hell out of me almost as much as you do."

She blinked at him, and Luke took a relieved breath, figuring he'd gotten them past the worst part. He slackened his hold even more, and when she didn't start swinging at him, he released her totally, gently rolled her off him, and sat up. But when she tried to stand, he took hold of her wrist and held her sitting beside him.

"Just a minute. There's a bit more you need to hear."

She didn't try to break his grip, but simply stared out at the ocean.

Luke took a deep breath. "I had been eavesdropping on your mother's satellite for several months before I started corresponding with you. I was fascinated with what your mother was doing, and have been working on the same problem myself for nearly ten years. I know what I did was unconscionable, but I was getting so frustrated and so damned desperate, I simply didn't care anymore."

He looked over at her. "I swear, it wasn't my

intention to steal your mother's work; I just wanted to find something—anything—that would move my own work along. But last summer something went terribly wrong, and Podly suddenly fell out of orbit and crashed just north of Pine Creek. I've spent the last two months searching for it on Springy Mountain, hoping I could take it to Grace so she could salvage some part of her work."

"You don't find it strange that Podly crashed so close to Pine Creek?" she asked, her voice raspy with lingering sobs.

He frowned. "Well, I admit it's more than a little perplexing." He turned to face her fully, and lifted her hand so he could hold it in both of his. "But what I'm trying to tell you is, I am truly, profoundly sorry for what I did. And I'm asking for another chance. Please, let me prove to you that even though nothing could ever justify what I've done, my intentions have always been honorable."

She pulled free, folded her hands on her lap, and stared out at the ocean again.

"Please don't shut me out, Camry. Let me prove my sincerity. Help me find Podly and bring it back to your mother."

"I can't ever go home again," she whispered. She hugged her knees to her chest, huge tears spilling down her cheeks as she continued staring out at the ocean. "I can't face either of them. I've been lying for what seems like forever. I've been lying to my entire family." She dropped her head to her knees. "They'll never forgive me."

Luke leaned down and brushed away a tear with his thumb. "So you're saying that if one of your sisters had a bit of a midlife crisis, then tried to cover it up and deal with it herself, you wouldn't forgive her?"

"You don't understand. This wouldn't happen to one of my sisters. MacKeage women don't have midlife crises, because we're too damn busy being brilliant, successful, and happy."

Luke snorted, then smiled when she glared at him. "Nobody goes through life avoiding brick walls. I'd bet my last dollar that every one of your sisters has hit at least one, if not several, walls." He took hold of her hand again and held it in his. "You may be standing in front of one right now, but it's not the end of the road. If you can't go around it, then you just have to find a way through it. And your mother," he said, giving her a squeeze, "is desperate to help you. And your father . . . well, I bet he'd give his right arm to help you through this." He leaned forward to look her in the eyes. "And so would I, Camry."

She said nothing, pulling her hand away to hug her knees again as she stared out at the ocean.

Luke turned to watch the waves gently lapping toward them. "I sold my soul trying to unlock the secret of ion propulsion, but over the course of this last week, I've decided that I don't give a flying damn about it anymore." He looked over at her and took a deep breath. "Tell me how to help you fix this," he softly petitioned. "I'll do whatever you want . . . except walk away. I'll go home and face your parents with you, or if you prefer, I'll go get them and bring them here. Or I can take you home to my mother in British Columbia and wait until you're ready to go home to yours."

She remained silent, then suddenly got to her feet. "I need to think."

He also scrambled to his feet. "I don't have a problem with that," he offered, falling in step beside her as they headed toward the house. "As long as you understand that I'm not leaving."

Chapter Nine

Camry walked down the beach at a brisk pace, her head feeling like it was going to explode from the tears she desperately fought to hold back. So much had happened this morning, she wasn't sure she'd ever recover. She'd been hit with so many lies and half-truths about so many things— not the least of which was silently walking beside her.

He was *Lucian Renoir,* the man of her dreams and nightmares of over a year.

In her dreams, she had worked side by side with a fantasy version of the handsome physicist, sharing their scientific passions by day and in- dulging their sexual passions at night.

But she'd also had a recurring nightmare involving an equally handsome Dr. Renoir, where he was standing at a podium as she sat cowered before him wearing nothing but her underwear. He was lecturing her in front of an assembly of their peers, expounding at length on her inability to solve even the simplest equation. Her mother and father, and all her brilliant, successful sisters sat in the front row, their heads hung in shame.

But all her dreams and nightmares combined were nothing compared to Lucian Renoir in the flesh. He was even more handsome than she'd imagined: definitely taller, a heck of a lot leaner, and more rugged-looking than the man in the grainy photo she'd found on the Internet. It was the long hair and ripped body, she guessed, that had prevented her from being suspicious of having bumped into a fellow physicist in the unlikely town of Go Back Cove.

That's why it felt as though she'd taken a punch in the gut this morning, when she had read the name on the card Fiona had left him. Having grown quite fond of Luke as they'd recuperated together, and finding herself more and more sexually attracted to him with each passing day, she had actually started weaving fantasies of following him home at the end of his sabbatical. She better than anyone could handle being ignored when he got involved at his lab, and she had hoped his passion for his work might actually rub off on her, and maybe even nudge her back into the game.

But he wasn't good old Luke Pascal, was he?

He was *Lucian Renoir*. Which brought her right back to her nightmare of sitting cowering on a stage instead of realizing her dream of spending her days in his lab and her nights in his bed.

They reached the porch steps, and Luke picked up the gaily wrapped box that Fiona had left with the cards on the kitchen table, before the girl had vanished as mysteriously as she had appeared only a week ago.

He held the gift out to her, but Camry shoved her hands in her pockets. "It's addressed to both of us," she said. "You open it."

He tucked it under his arm, gathered up the cards that had blown into the tall grass, then walked up the stairs and held open the door. Camry preceded him inside and went directly to her bedroom, closed and locked the door, then threw herself down on the bed and burst into tears.

Luke stood leaning against the kitchen counter, sipping his third beer from the six-pack he'd found in the fridge, and stared at the box he'd placed on the table along with Fiona's two cards.

He just didn't feel right opening the gift without Camry.

He hadn't felt right about reading the note Fiona had left her, either, but since he was already flying down the slippery slope of deceit, he'd read it anyway. He'd actually chuckled, despite feeling like hell, when he discovered the romantic teenager had left Camry a note almost identical to his.

Just as short and idealistic, the young girl's note had asked Camry not to give up on *him,* and she'd echoed that they were each other's miracle. The only deviation had been that Fiona had finished Camry's note by saying that she'd see her favorite *auntie* next week, on the winter solstice.

Luke twisted off the cap on another beer and took a long swig. Christ, the house felt empty without the brat and the mutts. The gut-wrenching sobs coming from the bedroom—which hadn't stopped until he'd heard the shower turn on twenty minutes ago—were the only reminder he wasn't alone.

He honest to God didn't know what to do. His heart ached to see Camry happy, but he couldn't figure out how to make that happen. And he didn't have a clue what he could say to help her find the courage to face her parents. Hell, he was about as much help as were the cryptic notes that Fiona had left them.

A miracle? What in hell did the girl mean, they were each other's miracle? They'd screwed up their own lives so badly, he questioned if they were even competent to babysit the dogs.

Luke straightened when he heard the bedroom door open. He quickly shoved his empty beer bottles back in the holder and put everything back in the fridge except the one he was drinking. But then he grabbed one of the full bottles and set it on the table, and had just made it back to lean against the counter when Camry walked into the kitchen.

She sat down, folded her hands on the table, took a deep breath, and looked at him. "Okay, I'm ready. You can begin," she said, her voice husky. She suddenly held up her hand when he tried to speak. "Only I wish you'd keep it under an hour, because I still have some thinking to do."

"Um . . . begin what?"

"The lecture you've been dying to give me ever since you arrived in Go Back Cove," she said, her tone implying he was a bit dense for making her state the obvious.

"I've been dying to give you a lecture?" he repeated, *feeling* dense. "About what?" He suddenly stiffened. "You want me to lecture you about the mistake in your equation? Camry, I told you, I don't give a flying damn about that anymore."

She gaped at him.

He sighed. "Okay, look. If you want to talk about it we can, but some other time. Right now I'd rather hear from you." He took a swig of liquid courage, then looked back at her. "I really need to know how things stand between us, because I really need for you not to shut me out."

She snapped her mouth closed, opened it several times, as if she were searching for words, then finally whispered, "Are you for real?"

Luke shifted uneasily, then suddenly flinched when she shot out of her chair and rushed up to him. He sucked in his breath when she just as suddenly shoved on his belly at the same time as she pulled out his belt and looked down his pants!

He sidestepped away in alarm. "What *are* you doing?"

"I'm looking to see if you still have your balls."

"My what!" he yelped, stepping even farther away.

She walked back to her chair, sat down, and folded her hands on the table again. "Don't worry, they're still there. So let's get on with it, okay? I told you, I still have some thinking to do."

"Get on with *what*?" he growled, tugging one pants leg.

"Your lecture."

Luke sighed, long and loud and heartfelt. "Will

you please tell me what I'm supposed to be lecturing you on?"

"On what a selfish, inconsiderate daughter I am. While you're expounding on what a no-good rotten liar I am, you might as well get in a few licks on my cowardice."

The lightbulb finally clicked on, and Luke went utterly still, then collapsed into the chair opposite her. "Camry," he said softly. "There is nothing I can or would say to you that you can't or haven't already said to yourself."

She was back to gaping at him.

He shook his head. "You've obviously been beating yourself up over this for an entire year; I'm not about to beat up on you, too." He covered her hands with one of his. "But I can be a damn good team player. You do as much thinking as you need to, but while you're at it, try to think of how I can help you. Whatever course of action you decide on, I'm with you one hundred percent."

"Why?"

He reared back, not having seen that particular question coming.

"Why don't you just walk away?" she elaborated. "Because you said it yourself, this really is none of your business."

"Well, it isn't," he agreed, choosing his words

carefully. "Or it wasn't until . . . sometime around Tuesday, I figure."

"What happened on Tuesday?"

"I fell head over heels in lust with you."

It was her turn to rear back, and, yup, she was gaping at him again.

Luke reached in his pants pocket, pulled out the condom, and set it on the table. "Do you know what this is?"

"It's a condom."

"And do you know what it's used for?"

"Preventing unwanted pregnancies and venereal diseases."

He nodded. "Not bad for a used-to-be scientist. Tell me, have you ever actually seen one out of its packet?" he asked, ripping open the foil.

She leaned back in her chair even farther.

"I only ask because while you were in the bedroom this past hour *thinking*, I was doing a bit of thinking myself. And you know what I was thinking about?" He slid the condom out of its package, then lifted a brow, waiting for her answer.

"N-no," she whispered, her gaze dropping to the condom again.

Luke rolled it open, then left it sitting on the table between them as he picked up the unopened bottle of beer, twisted off the cap, and leaned back in his chair. "I was thinking about how you've perfected the art of satisfying a man in bed so well, he doesn't even realize he's not having intercourse."

She paled to the roots of her beautiful red hair.

He leaned forward to rest his arms on the table. "I think you should know," he continued softly, "that this morning when I realized what had actually been going on the last two days, I wanted to wring your pretty little neck. But sometime in the last hour," he said, motioning toward the bedroom, "everything suddenly made sense."

He leaned even closer, looking her directly in the eyes. "You're a virgin," he said, stating a fact, not asking a question. "You've been so afraid that having a child will steal your passion for your work, you've never been able to go all the way."

"I really don't think that's any of your business."

"You are such a passionate woman, Camry, in and out of bed. Everything you do is full speed ahead, no holds barred, one hundred and ten percent." He leaned back in his chair again. "So to answer your question as to why I don't simply walk away, it's because I can't. For the first time in my adult life, I'm letting my lower brain make my decisions. I'm in lust with you, Camry, and I'm asking you to do what Fiona also asked, and that's for you not to give up on me. Let's solve our problems together."

"I-I don't do commitment well," she whispered, her gaze back on the condom.

"Sure you do," he contradicted, which certainly brought her eyes up to his. "You commit yourself completely, just not long-term. You hit hard and fast, and then you take off before a guy realizes what's happening . . . or rather, what *isn't* happening."

That got the paleness out of her cheeks. She set her hands on the table and stood up, presumably the better to glare down at him. "If you think I'm going to let you blackmail me into having sex, think again, buster."

"Blackmail you!" he said on a strangled laugh. "With what? Hell, *I'm* the one who should worry about being blackmailed. You and your mother have enough dirt on me not only to ruin my career, but to get me thrown in jail for destroying a multimillion-dollar satellite."

She collapsed back in her chair. "My mother knows you were eavesdropping on Podly?"

"From the beginning, apparently," he admitted. "And she also knows that I caused it to crash. Hell, *she's* the blackmailer. She guilted me into coming after you."

Camry buried her face in her hands and

thunked her head down on the table. "What are we going to do?" she muttered. "How am I ever going to face her again?"

Luke nearly jumped up with a shout, he was so happy to hear her speaking in terms of *we*. He did stand up, though, and went to the fridge, pulled out the last bottle of beer, and waited until she'd finally sat up before he handed it to her.

"I have no idea what we're going to do," he said, sitting down again. He slid the gaily wrapped box toward her. "But maybe we should start by opening Fiona's gift. It's possible the meddling little brat left us another cryptic clue. I mean, seeing as how she's so *magical* that she can be five months old and sixteen at the same time."

Camry spit her mouthful of beer all over the gift, the table, and Luke. "Oh God, don't tell me *you* believe in the magic!" she cried, her horrified gaze locked on his.

Luke wiped his cheek with the back of his hand. "What in hell are you talking about? I was kidding, Camry. Fiona—if that's even her real name—obviously found out you had a niece named Fiona Gregor, and decided to mess with your head. She's a *teenager*; it's her job to drive adults crazy. Believe in the magic," he muttered. "What is it with you MacKeages, anyway? I don't believe in magic, serendipitous coincidences, mother's intuition, or miracles. I'm a scientist, and I only believe in what I can back up with cold, hard facts."

Camry absently toyed with the ribbon on the gift as she watched him out the corner of her eye. "So you don't believe it's astronomically impossible that my mother's satellite crashed near her home, or that you arrived at Gù Brath at about the same time Fiona was mailing her card to my parents? And it doesn't seem like a strange coincidence to you that you ran into me within minutes of arriving in Go Back Cove? Or that we ended up in bed together your very first night here, or—"

He held his hand up to stop her. "The odds of all those things happening are huge, I'll admit, but not impossible."

"Okay. Then how about calculating the odds of Podly's crashing into Springy Mountain at the exact time of the summer solstice? Which also happens to be the exact moment—right down to the second, I feel compelled to point out—that Fiona Gregor was born."

He frowned. "That's pushing things a bit much, I think."

She slipped the ribbon off the box, carefully unwrapped the gift, then lifted the cardboard lid just enough to look inside. At first she frowned, then her eyes suddenly widened. She looked up at Luke, spun the box around, and pushed it across the table. "Okay, then explain *that* to me using cold, hard facts."

Luke lifted the flap on the box and also frowned, not quite sure what he was looking at. But then his eyes widened just as Camry's had. He reached in and, as carefully as if he were handling the Holy Grail, he lifted out the slightly charred, fist-sized instrument . . . that actually had the words STARSHIP SPACELINE etched in tiny letters on its side.

"Come on," Camry said smugly, "explain what that piece of Podly is doing in my kitchen, or how a five-month-old *teenager* got her hands on it in the first place, when it should be buried under three feet of snow somewhere on Springy Mountain."

His hands trembling because he was afraid to drop it, Luke carefully set what appeared to be the satellite's transmitter down on the table. "Please tell me I'm dreaming."

"I'm sorry, Luke, I wish I could," she said just as softly. She reached over and picked up the transmitter, which caused him to flinch. She chuckled. "It's already survived a rather long fall," she drawled. "I think it can survive my handling."

She turned it over to study it, and the tiny instrument suddenly chirped.

Camry threw it down as they both jumped in surprise.

The transmitter rolled off the table, and Luke made a lunge for it at the same time she did. But they fell into each other trying to catch it, and the precious instrument clattered to the floor. It rolled across the linoleum, smacked up against the stove, and softly chirped.

Sprawled on their bellies, they both stared at it, utterly speechless.

The damn thing chirped again.

"It's still functioning?" Luke whispered. He looked at her. "Do you suppose there's . . . could more of the satellite have survived, do you think?"

She didn't respond right away, apparently unable to tear her gaze from the transmitter. She finally looked at him, her eyes shining intensely—quite like they did when she was about to rip off his clothes. "I think we're going to have to go to Springy Mountain to answer that question."

"Excuse me?" he whispered, not daring to hope—but hoping anyway.

She straightened to her knees, grabbed their bottles of beer off the table, and handed one to Luke once he sat up to lean against the cupboards. She settled down on the floor beside him and took a long chug of her beer—swallowing this time—then suddenly grinned. "The way I see it, we have three choices. We can break into my family's ski-resort maintenance garage and steal one of the snowcats; we can steal some horses from my cousin Robbie; or we can snowshoe the forty miles to Springy Mountain. Your choice, Dr. Renoir."

She was going home!

And she was taking him with her!

"I have a fourth choice," he carefully offered, not wanting to dampen her spirit—or get himself thrown off her team. "You can go home and tell your parents how much you love them, then *ask* them if we could *borrow* a snowcat. I'm sure they'll be so happy to see you, they will gladly lend us one."

She glared at him.

"What?" he asked, his hopes waning.

"I thought you said you'd do anything to help me."

"I will. I *am*." He ran his hand through his hair, wondering if his lower brain wasn't going to be the death of him. "It's just that I'm pretty sure you and I have both deceived your parents quite enough already. Stealing from them is more or less adding insult to injury, don't you think?"

"Okay then, we'll steal from Robbie," she said, rolling onto her hands and knees and crawling toward the transmitter. "Riding horses into Springy will be colder, but it beats the hell out of snowshoeing."

He grabbed her arm to stop her, then urged her to turn to face him. "Camry, you're going to have to deal with your parents eventually."

"I will, just as soon as we find Podly."

He tightened his grip. "You think you can't go home unless you're bearing gifts?" He shook his head, his eyes never leaving hers. "Take it from a world-class ass of a son and stepson—parents don't want anything from their children but love. And the lesson it took me six stubborn years to learn is that loving them means trusting them."

She blinked at him, then suddenly threw herself at his chest, knocking him back against the cupboards. Luke quickly set down his beer to wrap his arms around her just as she buried her face in his shirt.

He cupped her head to his chest. "It'll be okay, I promise."

"They're never going to forgive me."

"Of course they will. They already have." He lifted her chin. "They're just waiting for you to forgive yourself."

"But you don't understand," she whispered, burying her face again.

"Then explain it to me," he petitioned, holding her tightly against him.

She quietly sighed, saying nothing.

Luke contented himself with just holding her as he stared at the tiny transmitter sitting next to the stove . . . and resigned himself to the fact that he was about to add stealing a snowcat to his growing list of crimes.

Chapter Ten

It had taken Luke less than twenty minutes to throw his belongings in his suitcase, so he'd spent the rest of the afternoon studying Podly's transmitter—which for some reason had stopped chirping. Camry had stayed in her bedroom, supposedly packing, but Luke suspected she'd taken a nap. It was early evening, and they were sitting across the table from each other, eating the only thing he knew how to cook: scrambled eggs and toast.

Or rather, Camry was eating. He was getting one hell of a lesson on letting his lower brain call the shots. "What do you mean, I have to go stay at the hotel?" he repeated. "I thought we were leaving for Pine Creek in the morning?"

"I've decided not to leave until Wednesday." She shoved her fork into her eggs. "Or maybe Tuesday evening, so we'll arrive in Pine Creek around midnight. It'll be easier to steal the snowcat then."

Dammit, she was ditching him! "Then let's leave tonight," he offered, careful to keep his frustration from showing. "The sooner we get going, the sooner we'll find the rest of Podly. I had the Weather Channel on all afternoon, and they're talking about another snowstorm heading north by Thursday or Friday. With any luck, we can be on and off the mountain before it hits."

She shot him a confounded look. "You said you spent *two months* searching for Podly. You expect that because I'll be with you this time, we're going to drive directly up to the satellite, load it in the snowcat, and be off the mountain in a matter of days? It will probably take us weeks to find where it crashed."

"Then all the more reason to leave now."

"I can't," she muttered, poking her eggs a bit more forcefully. "I have a couple of commitments here I have to deal with first."

"What commitments?"

"I babysit four dogs, remember? I can't just take off all of a sudden and leave my clients without day care."

"They're dogs, Camry, not kids. They can stay home while their masters work, like normal dogs do."

"But I promised Tigger's and Max's owners that I would keep them over the holidays. The Hemples are leaving for England tomorrow, and I'm supposed to have Tigger for an entire month. And Max's mother is leaving on Tuesday for Wisconsin, and she won't be back until after New Year's."

"Call and tell them you have a family emergency or something."

"You want me to *lie* to them?"

Luke very kindly refrained from pointing out that she'd been lying to her parents for almost a year. "Then let's get on the phone and find alternative accommodations for their pets. Surely there are kennels around here."

"Tigger can't stay in a kennel! She'd be scarred for life. And so would Max. Why do you think these people have me babysit them? They're not dogs, they're *family*."

Luke sighed, not wanting to ask his next question, but seeing how his lower brain was in charge, he asked it anyway. "So what's your plan, then?"

She looked back down at her eggs. "We're going to have to take Tigger and Max with us," she said, so quietly that Luke had to lean forward to hear her.

He reared back. "You expect to take two dogs to Springy Mountain in the middle of the winter? Camry, the snow's deeper than Tigger is tall. And the snowcat's going to be crowded enough with the two of us and our gear. Where are you planning to put Max? He's the size of person."

"We can carry most of our gear on the roof, and we'll steal one of the resort's larger groomers. That way we can even sleep in it if we have to."

Luke dropped his head in his hands to stare down at his plate. Had she changed her mind about his going with her, or did she intend to go home at all?

She touched his arm, and he lifted his head. "You have my word, I'm not trying to ditch you," she said, apparently reading his mind. "It's just that while I was packing this afternoon, I suddenly remembered I'd committed myself for the next month." She smiled crookedly. "We'll find Podly, I promise. And who knows, maybe Max and Tigger will come in handy. They're both hunting breeds; they can sniff out the satellite for us."

Luke laced his fingers through hers. "If you're really not trying to ditch me, then why do I have to go back to the hotel until Tuesday?"

Her cheeks turned a lovely pink, and her gaze dropped. She tried to pull away, but Luke actually tossed her hand away with a snort. "You're out of here ten minutes after I leave. Only you're not going home, you're running away again."

"That's not true! It's just that . . . I don't want . . . Dammit, I'm not going to be fit company for the next two days! I just want to be left alone, okay? Come back Tuesday afternoon, and we'll leave after supper."

"Not fit . . . What in hell are you talking about?"

Her cheeks turned blistering red. "Look, I started my period today, okay? And for the next two days, I'm going to be a miserable, achy grump."

He was so relieved, he started laughing.

Camry jumped up and ran out of the room.

Luke instantly sobered. "Hey, wait! I'm sorry!" he called, scrambling after her.

Her bedroom door nearly hit him when she slammed it shut, and she managed to get it locked before he could open it.

He thunked his head against it with a groan. "Camry, I'm sorry. I wasn't laughing at you. I mean, not really. Dammit, don't shut me out."

"Go away," she said, her voice coming through the wood only inches from his. "I'll be right here come Tuesday, I promise."

God, he was an idiot. For a man who'd managed to earn several degrees, he didn't seem to have a clue when it came to women. Which was surprising, considering he'd spent the first thirteen years of his life in an all-female household.

"Have I mentioned that I was raised by my single mother, my grandmother, and my aunt?" he asked, his head still resting on the door.

"No," she whispered after several heartbeats.

"And I can certainly attest the old myth is true, that when women live together their menses gravitate to the same schedule." He chuckled.

"What's so funny about that?" she growled.

"I just thought of your poor father, living in a household of eight women."

"That's a sexist remark!"

"It's not sexist if it's a scientific fact."

"Go away, Luke."

He straightened away from the door, running his fingers through his hair. Dammit to hell. He didn't want to leave. "The only reason I pointed out my having been raised by women was to let you know that I don't care how grumpy you get. I can pretty much handle anything you dish out." He hesitated. "Except being told to get lost."

When she didn't respond, Luke walked to the living room, threw himself down on the couch, and glared at the transmitter sitting on the coffee table. He leaned forward and picked up the stubbornly silent instrument. "You are obviously the design of a feminine mind," he muttered: "Why in hell do women have to be so complicated?"

"Because it's our job."

Luke jumped, fumbling to hold on to the transmitter, but it still went flying when Camry plopped down on the couch beside him.

"Because men are such simple creatures, women need to be complicated to balance things out," she continued, preventing him from going after the transmitter by snuggling against his chest.

Luke wrapped his arms around her and sighed heavily.

"Did your mother really tell you to get lost all the time?"

"No, my aunt did. She was a grumpy woman every day, but it wasn't until I was nine or ten that I realized she was downright mean a few days each month." He softly snorted. "The day we moved out of Gram's house and in with my new stepfather, my mother actually apologized for making me live with Aunt Faith for thirteen years."

"Why was Aunt Faith so grumpy?"

"Who knows. My guess is she was bitter. Even though my biological father took off the day he found out about me, I think Faith was jealous that Mom had even had a passionate affair." He shrugged. "Faith didn't have much luck with men, and I finally decided she was lonely."

"Maybe she would have had better luck if she wasn't so grumpy."

Luke chuckled humorlessly. "I actually told her that once. It was around the time my mother met André Renoir. I was eleven. Aunt Faith went from grumpy to openly hostile the deeper in love Mom fell with André."

Camry popped her head up. "André Renoir became your stepfather?"

Luke nodded. "When I was thirteen. And he legally adopted me the day they got married." He nudged her head to his chest so she'd quit looking at him. "I hadn't minded André up until then, since he made Mom happy. But I didn't see why I suddenly had to change my name, too, as well as let him have any say over my life."

She popped her head up again. "Was he mean to you?"

"Oh no. André is a good man, and he was sincerely interested in me," he said, pulling her back against him. "But for the first thirteen years of my life, I pretty much did what I wanted without receiving much flack. I'd lock myself in my room for days with my books and computer, and nobody bothered me. But after we moved in with André, the man kept dragging me outdoors, saying I needed to get the stink blown off me."

Luke laughed. "He tried to teach me to play baseball, but I kept striking out on purpose. So he took me hunting with him, and I made enough noise stomping through the woods to scare off all the game. But God bless the patient man, no matter how much I sabotaged his good intentions, he just kept trying . . . until the day I ran away from home."

"You ran away from home? How old were you?"

"Fourteen. My mother and André told me I was going to have a baby sister." He chuckled. "Even though I knew all about the birds and bees, I was horrified to suddenly realize they'd been having *sex*. I waited until they went to bed that night, then took off."

"Where'd you go?" she asked with a giggle.

"I decided to go back and live with Gram and Aunt Faith, so I started walking to Vancouver, which was a little over a hundred miles away. But I didn't care. I just wanted my old self-centered life back, grumpy aunt and all."

"And? Did they take you back?"

"I didn't make it ten miles. It was the dead of winter, and André found me half frozen to death, stubbornly trudging along the side of the road.

He never said a word the entire ride back home. But when we drove into our dooryard, instead of letting me go inside and warm up, he dragged me out to the woodshed, and—"

"He *beat* you?" she gasped as she straightened.

Luke grinned at her fierce expression. "No. But it was the first time I'd ever seen him angry. He handed me a crosscut saw and axe, and told me to start working up next year's firewood. And that while I did, I was to contemplate one simple question, and give him the answer when I was done."

"And that question was?"

"He asked me the definition of love."

Camry's eyes grew huge with anticipation. "And what did you tell him love was?"

Luke snorted. "I was fourteen—what in hell did I know about love?"

She scrambled off the couch and stood glaring at him. "But you had to have told him something! You obviously didn't freeze to death in the wood-shed."

Luke stood, then walked over and picked up the transmitter before looking at her again. "Oh, I came up with an answer that at least got me back in the house—though it didn't get me out of working up eight cords of firewood. André told me what I'd come up with was only a start, but that he would know I had figured out the rest when I finally apologized to my mother."

"And did you?"

He nodded. "When I was twenty."

"So, what's the definition of love?" she asked, her expression eager again.

Luke eyed her speculatively, wondering how far he could push her. "If you let me stay, I'll tell you on the drive to Pine Creek."

She actually stomped her foot in frustration, then immediately grabbed her leg and hopped back to the couch. "Now look what you made me do," she muttered, lifting her foot onto the coffee table as she glared up at him. "That's blackmail."

"You can thank your mother for teaching me that one." He sat down on the table, tossed the transmitter on her lap, and set her foot on his thigh so he could take off her sock and rub her ankle. "When I came out of the woodshed, I told André that love meant not hurting someone who loved me."

She leaned back and started toying with the transmitter. "That was a good answer for a fourteen-year-old kid."

"But incomplete, according to André."

"Why didn't he just tell you the whole answer?"

"Don't think I didn't ask him to. But he said it's

not something one person can explain to another; I had to *feel* love to know it."

She suddenly smiled. "Then you can't tell me, either, which means you just gave up your chance to blackmail me into staying."

He arched a brow. "Or I just made you curious enough to let me stay."

"How do you figure that?"

"I told you that I apologized to my mother when I was twenty. Aren't you even a little bit curious as to why then?"

She looked down at the transmitter, shrugging indifferently. "Maybe."

But Luke knew she was dying to know—likely wondering if some girl had broken his heart. "Can I stay?" he asked softly.

She looked up, the gleam of challenge in her eyes. "Only if you give me a hint as to what happened when you were twenty that led you to have your great epiphany."

Oh yeah, he had her now—he just had to reel her in. Luke stared off over her head as if considering her offer, then finally locked his gaze on hers. "I died."

Chapter Eleven

Camry pulled out of the L.L.Bean parking lot in Freeport late Tuesday afternoon, her partner in crime sitting beside her, two dogs and all their paraphernalia in the rear seat, and the back of her SUV crammed full of cold-weather camping equipment and supplies.

Luke immediately became engrossed in the new and supposedly improved GPS tracking device he'd just purchased, and Camry turned north onto Interstate 95 with a smile of anticipation. As much as she loved her doggie friends and tending bar at Dave's, she realized there was nothing like a winter camping trip to blow off the cobwebs—and a dream guy who just happened to be in lust with her to add a bit of interest.

Cam thought back to all the boyfriends she'd had over the years, and tried to decide if she had spent time with any of them that even came close to the weekend she'd just spent with Luke. The last three days had been amazingly intimate—which Cam found rather interesting, since she had always equated intimacy with lovemaking. But she'd shared her bed with Luke for three wonderfully celibate nights, and she couldn't remember the last time she'd slept so soundly.

Cam merged into traffic with a silent giggle, remembering what had happened Sunday morning. Since Fiona had blown his cover, Lucian Renoir the physicist had suddenly emerged, and Luke had risen long before sunrise, dug out his laptop, and started crunching numbers. When she'd run into the living room in her pajamas, frantic that *he* had suddenly decided to ditch *her,* she'd found him writing on one of her walls.

Apparently so engrossed in his work that he wasn't even aware he was using her wall as a whiteboard, Luke had appeared confused when she'd shouted. He'd apologized profusely as he went to the kitchen to get a wet rag, but then *he* had shouted when he'd returned to find her overwriting one of his equations. They'd spent the rest of the day covering two more walls with equations as they retraced Podly's solstice descent—a trajectory that defied every law of physics. And not only had Camry not bothered to change out of her pajamas, she had completely forgotten to be grumpy and miserable.

She was still a bit shaken by how quickly Luke had figured out her little game of letting her boyfriends think they were having mind-blowing sex. Hell, she'd gotten so good at it, she had practically convinced herself that she was utterly, totally fulfilled.

The men certainly had never complained.

Except Luke: after only two days, he'd wanted to wring her neck. She still couldn't believe he'd actually pulled out a condom, opened the damn thing, and then asked if she knew what it was. She should have been outraged, but instead she had found herself wondering what he planned to do about her . . . virginity. Would he continue their lusty little affair on her terms, or did he see her as a challenge now? Did he have hopes of taking things to the next level?

She wasn't worried he'd push her into going all the way; Luke didn't seem to have a pushy bone in his body. Camry smiled at the road ahead. He certainly would try nudging her, though, because for all of his civilized trappings, he was still a perfectly functioning male.

But then, she also loved a good challenge.

"According to my GPS, we're going seventy-six miles per hour," he said into the silence, glancing over at the odometer.

Camry kept her foot steady on the accelerator. "I'm just keeping up with what little traffic there is."

A moan came from the backseat, and Luke glanced over his shoulder. "Um . . . Max doesn't look so good. He's drooling, and his eyes are watery."

"He gets carsick. The pill I gave him in Freeport will kick in soon."

"You intend to keep him drugged the entire trip?"

"Max won't need his medicine once he gets in the snowcat; he'll be too excited about being on an adventure. He only gets sick in cars because he worries he might be going to the vet."

Luke started pushing buttons on his GPS again.

Camry swiped it out of his hand and set it on the dash on her side of the truck, out of his reach. "Okay. I didn't make you go back to your hotel, and we're on the road. So pony up, Dr. Renoir. If you died when you were twenty, how come you're still breathing?"

"Because the raging river that killed me also slammed me into a rock and knocked the air back into my lungs."

She scowled over at him. "From the beginning, Luke. And your intriguing little story had better explain what made you apologize to your mother."

He started repacking everything that had come with the GPS. "You already know I have a kid sister named Kate. Well, when she was five, Mom and André and I took her to the pound on Christmas Eve, and she picked out a monster of a dog that appeared to be eight or nine years old. He was coal black with wiry hair, half of one of his ears was missing, and his eyes were clouded with developing cataracts. I tried to get her to choose one of the puppies, or at least something less pathetic-looking, but Kate claimed she wanted that one because it was the beautifulest dog in the world and she was going to love it forever."

He shrugged. "She insisted on naming it Maxine, even though I explained it was a male dog. But on Christmas morning, when Kate took Maxine out to play, almost two hours went by before anyone realized they weren't in the yard."

"Two hours?"

"It was one of those 'I thought she was with you' things. Mom thought Kate had ridden over to check on our neighbor with André, and André had driven away thinking she was in the house playing with the toys Santa had brought her."

He leaned his head back and closed his eyes, and Camry realized that even though he'd promised to tell her his story, it obviously wasn't going to be easy for him.

"When André got back and Mom realized Kate wasn't with him, we all started looking for her. When we hadn't found her an hour later, we went back to the house and Mom called our local conservation officer to start an organized search. André and I put on snowshoes and split up, and started searching in opposite directions."

"But if you needed snowshoes, didn't Kate and the dog leave tracks you could follow?" Cam whispered, suddenly afraid this wasn't going to be any easier for her to hear than it was for him to tell.

He glanced over at her, then looked out his side window at the darkened woods passing by. "We'd had an ice storm two days before, and Kate and Maxine were light enough that they could walk on the crust, whereas André and I kept breaking through. We eventually moved far enough away from each other that I could no longer hear him calling for Kate. But I could hear the distant roar of the river." He hesitated, then said softly, "That's when I stepped under a giant spruce tree that had sheltered the snow from the rain, and found the tracks of a small child and dog."

He looked out the windshield, but Cam knew he wasn't seeing the road. "I started running in the direction the tracks went, which was straight toward the river."

Camry tightened her grip on the steering wheel. "I know Kate survived, because you said she's Fiona's age. So I don't want to hear any more of this story, Luke."

"Yes, you do." He reached over and patted her thigh. "Because this is when I learned exactly what I had put my mother through when I'd run away six years earlier." He took a deep breath, but left his hand on her leg. "I had never before and have never since been so scared. I broke into a cold sweat, having horrific images of Kate being swept away by the river. I hated that damn dog for luring her into the woods, and swore that when I found them I would wring his ugly black neck."

His hand on her thigh tightened, then was suddenly gone. "I still have nightmares about what I saw when I reached the river. Kate was dangling on the edge of the ice only a few feet above the rushing water. She was utterly motionless, and

that dog—that beautiful, mangy pound mutt—
had his teeth clamped on her coat, holding her
back from falling in." Luke looked over at her. "I
have no idea how long Maxine had been holding
her like that, but I swear that if Kate fell, he had
every intention of going with her."

Camry checked her mirror and guided her
truck to the side of the interstate, braking to a
stop all the way over on the grass before shutting
off the engine. She closed her eyes and buried her
face in her hands on the steering wheel.

"Hey, it's okay," he said, cupping her head in
his broad palm. "I stripped off my snowshoes and
carefully made my way to them. Maxine was quivering uncontrollably, and his mouth was bloody
from the strain on his teeth. His feet were bloody,
too, and I could see where he'd been gouging the
crust, trying to pull Kate up over the lip of ice."

Picturing the scene all too vividly in her mind,
and fearing what was coming, Camry scrambled
over the console and into his arms.

Luke cradled her against his chest and quietly
continued. "As I approached them, I felt the ice
shelf start to buckle. Just then I heard several
shouts, and realized that André and some other
men had spotted us. But it was too late. I grabbed
Kate's coat and pulled her up, yanking her out of
Maxine's mouth, then flung her as far as I could

back across the crust just as the shelf gave way. The dog and I fell into the river."

"Oh, God," Camry whispered. "The water must have been freezing."

"It literally took my breath away. The force of the rapids slammed me into boulders and held me under until I thought my lungs were going to burst."

"And y-you died."

His arms around her tightened. "I suddenly wasn't cold anymore, and everything went . . . peaceful."

"But then you came back."

"The current must have slammed me into another rock, and I broke the surface and sucked air back into my lungs. But I was completely disoriented. Then something snagged the shoulder of my jacket, and I felt clawing on my legs."

"Maxine."

"Just like with Kate, that damn dog latched on to me and started swimming across the current. There was enough light left that I could see the river was frozen solid where it turned to flat water up ahead, and I knew that if we didn't make it to shore, we were going to be swept under the ice."

"You both made it."

"I did."

"A-and Maxine?"

"I spent the next three weeks searching for his body, but I never found him."

"He died!" Cam wailed, burying her face in his shirt. She punched his arm. "I said I didn't want to hear this story!"

"I've never told anyone what happened after I fell in the river; not about my drowning, nor what Maxine had done," Luke murmured into her hair.

That surprised her. "But why? Wouldn't you at least want Kate to know that Maxine died saving your life?"

"It seemed too personal to share with anyone. Or maybe . . . sacred is a better word. So I just let everyone be thankful that Maxine had saved Kate's life." He sighed heavily. "The dog hadn't lured her into the woods; he had followed her."

Cam relaxed against him. She was still upset that Maxine hadn't survived, but damned glad that Luke had. "Did you find out why Kate had left the dooryard?"

"She told us she was looking for a special rock in the pool of pretty pebbles she remembered seeing that summer, when she and André had been fishing in the river."

"What made her think she could find it with snow on the ground?"

"Five-year-olds don't think about silly details like that; they just go after what they want." His lips touched her hair again. "All Kate was focused on was finding a special rock so she could give it to me for Christmas. Because, she told me that night when she came to my room after we got back from the hospital, she didn't want me returning to college without something to remind me of home . . . and of her."

He took a ragged breath. "I came unglued. She'd nearly died trying to find some stupid rock for me, and I started yelling at her. But instead of bursting into tears like a normal kid, you know what she did?"

Camry said nothing, because she couldn't.

"She wrapped her tiny arms around my legs and told me that she loved me so much, her heart hurt when she thought of my missing her the way she missed me." He took another shuddering breath. "And then she explained that she could sit in my room whenever she missed me, but that I didn't have anything to remind me of her when I was away at college."

"My knees buckled," he continued, his voice raspy, "and I knelt down to hug her. But before I could, Kate held up her tiny fist and opened her fingers to reveal a black-and-white speckled pebble in her palm. She told me it was a lot smaller than the rock she'd wanted to find for me, but that she'd been forced to grab the beautifulest one she could reach in the pool of open water, because Maxine had kept pulling on her coat."

Luke ducked his head to press his cheek against hers. "You know what love really is, Camry? It's uncompromising, unpretentious, and unconditional, and sometimes it makes your heart hurt. I apologized to Kate for yelling at her, and she patted my cheek and said that she knew I was angry because I loved her—just like Maxine had growled at her when she'd climbed down to the water. Kate said, and I quote, 'Maxine didn't let me fall in the river because he knew I was going to love him forever.' "

Luke rested his chin on her head with a sigh. "I had never paid much attention to Kate for the first five years of her life. I didn't have a clue what to do with an infant, and by the time she was a toddler, I was away at college most of the year or working in town and hanging out with my friends all summer. But that didn't stop her from loving me so much that her heart hurt when I was gone."

He lifted Cam's chin to make her look at him, his smile tender in the glow of the dash lights. "I tucked Kate in bed, then went downstairs to the living room, got down on my knees, and apologized to my mother for running away when I was fourteen. Then I apologized to André for being such a self-centered bastard, and thanked him for not giving up on me."

He shifted beneath her without breaking his embrace, then pressed something into the palm of her hand. "Here. If you try real hard, I bet you can feel the love, too," he whispered, folding her fingers over the tiny, smooth object. "The next summer, just before I headed off to college again, I took Kate down to the river and we built a huge rock cairn in honor of Maxine. Then I searched until I found a very special rock, and gave it to Kate. She hugged it to her heart and said it was the beautifulest rock she'd ever seen." He squeezed Cam's fist. "I've carried this pebble since that Christmas. No matter where I am in the world, or what I'm doing, I just have to reach in my pocket to know that I am uncompromisingly, unpretentiously, and unconditionally loved."

He lifted her hand to his mouth and kissed it. "And the moral of my story, I've since realized, is that sometimes our most profound lessons come from a five-year-old child, and sometimes they show up as a mangy old dog."

"Or as a fellow scientist who for some reason has clamped his teeth into me, and refuses to let go until I go home and apologize to my mother?"

He suddenly stiffened. "No," he said with a growl. He set her back over the console and into her seat. "*Don't* compare me to Maxine. That dog was a gutsy, selfless hero, whereas I'm a self-serving bastard who didn't think twice about stealing someone's life's work."

She gasped softly. "Is that how you see yourself?"

He looked over at her, the dash lights accentuating the harsh planes of his face. "Fiona had it wrong, Camry. I'm nobody's miracle."

"But you didn't mean to destroy Podly."

"I sure as hell meant to use the data I was trying to download," he said, turning away to look out his side window.

Camry stared out the windshield, desperately wanting to tell Luke that *he* hadn't caused Podly to crash, Fiona had. But even though she knew they would have to talk about it eventually, she simply didn't have the courage to open that particular Pandora's box quite yet.

She started the truck, checked for oncoming traffic, and accelerated back onto the interstate. Maybe Fiona did have it wrong. Miracles were the stuff of magic, after all, and the magic wasn't known for rewarding hijackers and no-good, rotten liars. It was more prone to toying with them the way a cat toyed with a mouse—or the way an impish niece with a thing for satellites did—just before sending down some seriously bad karma.

Yeah, well . . . if she and Luke had some dues to pay, Camry couldn't think of a better person to pay them with. Because contrary to what he might think of himself, she knew that, just like Maxine, Lucian Renoir had no intention of letting the raging river sweep her away.

Chapter Twelve

They arrived in Pine Creek shortly after midnight, but it took them another two hours to get their hands on a snowcat—which they virtually stole out from under the noses of the TarStone Mountain Ski Resort night-grooming crew. It was nearly three in the morning before they got back to the truck they'd hidden several miles from the resort, and Luke couldn't decide if Camry had a death wish or if she just got her jollies from skulking around in the shadows.

He did learn some interesting things about himself, however. One, he probably should stick to physics, as he'd likely starve to death if he had to steal for a living; and two, even if he had spent the entire night in a cold sweat, he rather liked performing any number of illegal acts with Camry. At one point he'd even been tempted to look down the front of *her* pants to see what equipment *she* was packing; the woman appeared to have nerves of steel, the focus of a Navy Seal, and the mind of a master criminal.

She also had a rather perverse sense of timing; like when they'd been hiding in the maintenance garage while they'd waited for one of the workers to kindly refuel the groomer they intended to . . . borrow. Apparently having grown bored, Camry had gone after *Luke's* package. But just as he'd been trying to wrestle her hands away from his belt buckle, the garage lights had suddenly gone out and the man had left.

Camry had immediately returned to criminal mode, leaving Luke—and his bewildered lower brain—sprawled in the corner, in total darkness, wondering when exactly he had lost his mind.

Camry finally pulled the snowcat to a stop beside her SUV and shut off the engine, snapped on the interior lights, and shot him a smug smile.

Luke pried his fingers off the handle he'd been

clutching in a death grip. "Would you care to explain what your intentions were back there in the garage?"

"I intended to steal us transportation. Which I did."

"No, I mean when we were stuck hiding behind that equipment. It wasn't exactly the time or place for slap and tickle. And besides, I thought you were . . . um, off the market for a few days."

Her smile turned downright cheeky. "Hey, just because the Ferris wheel isn't running doesn't mean the *entire* amusement park is shut down," she said with a laugh, opening her door and hopping out.

Luke stared after her, nonplussed.

He suddenly gave a bark of laughter and scrambled after her, happy to realize their little affair was still on—which made him glad he'd snuck out to the drugstore yesterday and purchased a whole box of condoms.

Camry opened the back door of the truck to let the dogs out as Luke approached her, still chuckling. "What's so funny?" she asked.

"Oh, nothing. I was just thinking how this excursion into the wilderness is going to be a lot more interesting than my last one."

Tigger bounded out of the truck behind

Max, only to give a yelp of surprise when she suddenly disappeared. Luke fished the dachshund out of the snow and set her back on the seat. "Yes, Tigger," he said, brushing off the shivering dog. "I'll bet this is exactly how you pictured your Christmas sleepover with Auntie Cam, isn't it?"

"Her sweater is in the green backpack," Camry said. She opened the rear hatch and started transferring their gear to the snowcat. "Just stomp down a circle in the snow so she can go pee."

Luke dug through the backpack, found what looked like a doll's sweater, and started dressing Tigger. Or he tried to, realizing he should have paid better attention when Kate had conned him into playing house with her dolls. "At least it's bright pink, so we'll be able to find you," he muttered, pushing what he hoped was the neck down over Tigger's head. "What are we going to do for fuel?" he called back to Camry. "I don't remember seeing any gas stations on Springy when I was there."

"I stole this particular groomer because it burns diesel. And Megan and Jack are building a camp on the lake at the base of the mountain, which means they would have lugged up a drum of fuel last summer that we can use."

"Did you hear that, Tig? We're going to teach you to steal, too. That way we can all share a jail cell so you won't be scarred for life."

Luke finally sighed in defeat, scooped Tigger up, and carried her to the back of the truck. "Here," he said, holding the dog out to Camry. "You figure this contraption out and I'll load our gear."

She tucked her hands behind her back. "You need the practice for when you have kids," she said, her eyes shining with amusement.

Luke hugged the half-dressed dachshund to his chest. "I've decided not to have children, because I'm afraid they might addle my brain."

Camry instantly sobered, spun around, grabbed their sleeping bags, and headed to the snowcat.

Luke smiled at her stomping away, and rubbed Tigger's head with the short beard he'd started growing three days ago for their camping trip.

Oh yeah, it was going to be a very interesting adventure.

Camry gritted her teeth as she grabbed the handle to keep herself from flying into the windshield, rethinking her brilliant idea of teaching Luke how to drive the snowcat. "Are you *aiming* for every damn rock and fallen log?"

"It's not like they're marked with BUMP signs." He shoved Max into the backseat. "I can't see them because Max keeps breathing on the glass and fogging it up."

"Wait. Stop here," she said. "I think this is the turnoff we need to take."

"You *think*?"

Cam scowled over at him. "It's been years since I've been this far north. I'll get my bearings once the sun rises." She reached over and shut off the engine, opened her door, then nearly fell out when Max shoved past her. "Okay, you overgrown brat, it's time we set down some rules," she said, lunging after the dog. She took hold of the lab's head and held him facing her, her nose only inches from his. "One, you wait until I tell you it's okay to get out. And two, you stay in the backseat with Tigger. You try to crawl in the front with us again, and you're riding on the roof with our gear."

"That put the fear of God in him," Luke said, walking around the snowcat with Tigger in his arms. He stopped to look at their surroundings in the stingy light of the breaking dawn. "It might have been years since you've been up here, but I just spent two months scouring these woods. This tote road leads up the south side of Springy." He pointed in the other direction.

"And that way will take us closer to the lake, and eventually around to the north side of the mountain."

"Then we should go that way," she said. "Since your trajectory data points to the satellite's having come in from the north."

"Except that it couldn't have," he contradicted. "Based on its orbit at the time it malfunctioned, Podly should have crashed into the south side of Springy."

Cam stopped packing down the snow to make a spot for Tigger and looked at him. "So are you suggesting we search the same woods you already spent two months searching, or do you want to look where the satellite really is? Because I happen to know it's on the north side of the mountain."

He narrowed his eyes at her. "How?"

"Because I watched its entire descent."

"You actually *saw* it?"

Cam took Tigger out of his arms and set the dachshund in the circle she'd stomped down. "Winter was having her baby right then, and my other sisters and I were sitting down on the dock in front of her home, waiting for the big arrival. That's when we noticed what we thought was a meteor streaking through the sky, heading right toward Springy Mountain. It was coming from the north, traveling south. We all saw it, but just then Mom came out of the house and shouted to us that we had a brand-new baby niece." She shrugged. "I completely forgot about it until Saturday, when you told me Podly had crashed north of Pine Creek last June."

Luke stared at her, his jaw slack. "Then I guess we head north, don't we? Wait. You said you were at Winter's house. She had her baby at home?"

Cam nodded. "My mother and all my sisters had their babies at home. It's sort of a MacKeage tradition."

His jaw went slack again.

"What's so odd about that?" she asked. "Women have been having babies at home since we lived in caves."

"But what if something went wrong? You're miles from the nearest hospital."

Seeing that Tigger was done with her business, Cam set her in the snowcat, then turned back to Luke. "I guess you could say that it's also our tradition to have relatively easy births."

Luke's expression turned unreadable. "So if you were to have a baby . . . would you be expected to have it at home, too?"

"Expected? No. Each of my sisters chose to have her babies at home with a midwife, but they weren't *expected* to. In fact, Daddy practically begged them to go to the hospital." She started looking around for Max. "But if I ever do decide to have children, I would likely follow tradition."

Luke took hold of her sleeve and turned her to face him. "Does that scare you?"

"It's a moot point, since I'm not having kids."

"Because they'll steal your passion for science?" he asked softly.

"And because I want it to be my choice, not the universe's."

"Excuse me?"

Camry eyed him for several heartbeats, then sat down on the track of the snowcat with a sigh. "Okay, since you're madly in lust with me, I suppose you have a right to know why I've been . . . reluctant to have intercourse."

He snorted, but then held up his hand when she shot him a scowl. "Okay, we'll go with *reluctant*." He sat down beside her. "So what's the universe got to do with your having sex?"

Cam hesitated, wondering just how much of her family background she should disclose. But the more time she spent with Luke, the more she realized he wasn't at all like any of the men she'd dated. He was . . .

Hell. For the first time in her life, she was tempted to risk it all on a man.

And since he would be risking it all, too, he

certainly deserved to know what he was getting himself into, didn't he?

She pivoted to face him, made several attempts to start, then finally said, "Have you ever heard the saying that the seventh son of a seventh son is gifted?"

He arched a brow. "I believe I've heard something to that effect."

"Well, my mother was supposed to be the seventh son of a seventh son, but when she was born a *girl,* everyone thought that was the end of that. But instead of the end, Grace Sutter's birth was actually the beginning of an even stranger axiom. You see, Mom and her six brothers, and her sister Mary, were all born on the summer solstice."

He leaned away, both eyebrows raised in disbelief. "All eight kids?"

She nodded. "But here's where it gets even more improbable. Mom had seven daughters, and all of us were born on the *winter* solstice."

Luke snorted. "Now you're just messing with me."

Cam took hold of his sleeve and looked him directly in the eye, letting him see she was deadly serious. "My sisters' children have been born on random dates throughout the years, all except for Fiona, who was born on this summer's solstice. And Winter is Mom's seventh daughter."

"It's just a date on a calendar, Camry. Millions of kids have been born on one of the solstices. But what does any of that have to do with your reluctance to have sex?"

"Well, there's another tradition in our family," she said, dropping her gaze and letting go of his sleeve. "It seems that all six of my sisters got pregnant the very first time they made love to their husbands," she whispered.

He said nothing for several heartbeats, then softly asked, "And were they all virgins when they met their husbands?"

"No. Or at least several of them weren't." She stared off into the woods. "I believe Winter was. Heather got married when she was eighteen, so she might have been, too. But I'm pretty sure Megan, Sarah, Chelsea, and Elizabeth weren't." She looked over at Luke. "But their virginity is not the issue. Every one of them got pregnant the very first time they made love to the man they eventually *married*."

"And so you've never gone all the way because you've been afraid that . . . what? That you might get pregnant and then have to marry the father? But birth control is very reliable today."

"That's what Megan and Sarah and Elizabeth thought. I know that Sarah was on birth control pills, and Megan told me Jack used a condom. But don't you see? It's like the *universe* picked out their husbands for them."

"They didn't have to marry those men, Camry. That was their choice."

"But they loved them."

"Then what's the problem? Everything worked out for the best."

She stood up, crossing her arms to hug herself as she faced the woods. "But what if I want to love someone and not have babies with him?" She spun around to face him. "Where is it written that I can't have one without the other?"

He walked over and cupped her face, rubbing his thumbs across her cheek, and Cam was startled to realize she was crying.

He pressed his lips to her forehead, then pulled her into his arms and held her against his chest. "It isn't written anywhere, Camry. If you ever decide to get married, it will be to the man *you* choose, not who the universe chooses. And if you have a baby with him, it will be the choice of both of you."

"But I want to make love to you," she whispered.

He tilted her head back and looked down at her in surprise. "You do?" He grinned somewhat drunkenly. "You've fallen in lust with me?"

She buried her face in his chest again. "I don't know what I'm feeling," she growled. "Other than confused. What if we make love and I get pregnant?"

"You won't. We'll take precautions."

Cam melted against him with a heavy sigh. "Father Daar says that if a baby's wanting to be born, no contraceptive will stop it."

"Father Daar?"

She looked up at him. "He's an old priest who used to live in a cabin up on TarStone, but now he lives on the coast with Matt's brother, Kenzie Gregor. Daar's been around forever, and presided over my parents' and all of my sisters' weddings. And he's always told us girls that if a child is wanting to be born, it will be, and that we just have to accept what *Providence* decides."

Luke gave her a crooked smile. "Please don't take this the wrong way, but for a scientist, you have some really strange notions."

She nestled back against him. "I can't help it," she said with another sigh. "I was born into a really strange family." She looked up at him. "So . . . are you still in lust with me? Or have I managed to scare you off?"

He arched a brow. "That would depend on if your father is going to come after me with a shotgun. Greylen strikes me as rather old-fashioned." He grinned. "Is that the real reason your sisters married the men who got them pregnant?"

Cam toyed with the zipper on his jacket. "And if Daddy did come after you with a shotgun," she asked, finally looking up into his eyes, "would you make an honest woman of me, or jump on the first plane back to France?"

"Hmmm . . . I don't know."

Cam squirmed to break free, but Luke pulled her back against him with a laugh, and tucked her head under his chin. "Give me a minute here, MacKeage. On the one hand, I'm no more ready than you are to think about having a baby, but . . ." He ducked his head to look her in the eye. "But the more time we spend together, the more in lust with you I get. And I do have a whole box of condoms that I'd hate to see go to waste. But then . . ." He suddenly set her away, shaking his head. "Nope, I'm too tired right now to know what I'd do. So let's head north, find a place to set up camp, and have a nap." He spun around and headed into the woods in the direction Max had gone. "Don't worry, you'll be the first to know what I decide," he said over his shoulder.

Cam stood gaping at him walking away. Of all the . . .

Wait. Had he been *teasing* her?

But nobody teased her. Ever. They didn't dare, because they knew that though she occasionally got mad, she *always* got even.

Cam suddenly smiled. So he wanted to have a nap, did he?

She just as suddenly scowled.

He'd brought a *whole box* of condoms?

Chapter Thirteen

$\mathscr{B}$y the time they finished setting up camp halfway up the north side of Springy Mountain—after stopping at Megan and Jack's building lot to refuel the snowcat—Camry was so exhausted that she didn't care if she *died* a virgin; she simply didn't have the energy to get even with Luke.

The dogs cooperated, and immediately settled down on their new doggie bed inside the large tent she and Luke had just pitched. Getting Luke to cooperate, however, was another matter entirely, as the man appeared jumpier than a cat in a room full of rocking chairs.

"I told you those PowerBars were loaded with

sugar and caffeine," she muttered, stripping off her outer clothes.

He looked up from unlacing his boots. "We'd be camping in a snowbank right now if I hadn't eaten them," he said, waving at the tent they were in. "I've been awake for over thirty hours."

Stripped down to her long johns, Cam crawled into the sleeping bags she'd zipped together. "If you'd taken a nap like I did yesterday, instead of sneaking out to buy condoms, you wouldn't have needed to eat them. Now you won't be able to sleep."

"Oh, I'll sleep, all right," he said, crawling in beside her.

Luke then let out a yawn—which made her yawn—and folded his hands on his stomach. But instead of falling asleep, Camry noticed he started twiddling his thumbs as he stared up at the tent roof. "You do realize that as soon as your father discovers one of his groomers is missing, he's going to know you're the one who stole it."

"I know."

"Which will lead your mother to believe that you'll be home for Christmas."

"Go to sleep, Luke."

He stayed silent for all of sixty seconds. "Only Grace didn't seem to be worried about Christmas," he murmured, apparently talking to himself as much as to her. "She asked me to have you home by the *solstice*."

Even though her eyes were closed, she could tell that his thumbs had stopped twiddling and that he was looking at her. "I thought it was strange at the time, but now I know it's because it's your birthday." He snorted. "As well as all your sisters' birthday."

"Go to *sleep*, Luke."

A full ninety seconds went by before she felt him roll toward her. "And since your big day is December twentieth, I've been thinking maybe we could hop on a plane after your birthday party and spend Christmas with my family in British Columbia."

That got her eyes open. "What?"

Propping his head on his hand as he faced her, he rested his other hand across her belly to cup her opposite hip. "It'll be fun," he said with an eager smile. "Mom and André are dying to meet you, and Kate is beside herself with curiosity. She's been sending me at least ten text messages a day for the last week, asking about you."

"You *told* your family about me?"

"Of course. And I promised that I'd bring you home to meet them."

"But why?" Cam whispered, horrified at the thought of meeting his family, considering she couldn't even face her own. "What did you tell them about me?"

He suddenly flopped onto his back, folded his hands on his belly, and stared up at the tent roof again. "I told them that just as soon as I worked up the nerve, I was going to ask you to marry me."

Camry bolted upright. "You *what!*" she attempted to shout—only it came out as a squeak.

He hadn't really just mentioned the *M*-word, had he?

He also sat up, and took her suddenly trembling hands in his. "I was going to wait until after we found Podly and you made up with your parents to ask you." Two flags of red rose into his shadowy beard. "In fact, I even planned to buy a ring and get down on one knee, but . . ." He lifted her hands to his mouth and kissed them. "But when you told me about your strange family traditions yet admitted you wanted to make love to me anyway, I started thinking that maybe I should take blatant advantage of your confusion and propose *before* we made love."

He let go of her hands to close her gaping mouth, then immediately placed his finger over her lips to keep her from saying anything.

Not that she could have.

"I realize this is rather sudden for you, so I really don't want you to give me an answer right now."

"But you're only in *lust* with me," Cam managed to whisper behind his finger.

He reached down and took hold of her hands again. "Oh, I'm definitely in lust with you. But while we were hiding in the maintenance garage, I realized that lust doesn't hold a candle to the intimacy we've shared this past week." He took what appeared to be a fortifying breath and held her hands to his chest, over his solidly beating heart. "So, Camry MacKeage, would you do me the honor of *considering* spending the rest of your life being intimate with me?"

She dropped her gaze to her hands clasped in his. "I-I have to think about it."

He released what sounded like a relieved sigh and flopped back on the air mattress, pulling her with him and snuggling her up against his side. "Thank you. But while you're thinking, I'd like you to consider one more thing." He tilted her chin up for her to look at him. "Marrying me just might be your chance to trump the universe."

"How?"

"By your getting married *before* you make love to your husband. That way you can't ever question that you're the one doing the choosing, not Providence."

Cam tucked her head into his shoulder and stared across his chest. "But what if I marry you, then we make love, and I *don't* get pregnant?" she whispered, clutching his shirt in her fist. "That would mean you're *not* the man I'm supposed to marry."

His chest fell on a heavy sigh. "Camry, sweetheart, you have to stop letting your fear that something might or might not occur dictate your life. Your only basis for assuming that what happened to your sisters has any bearing on what will happen to you is your belief that *tradition* is even a tangible integer. But the very fact that your sisters loved the men they married precludes any direct correlation to their getting pregnant. If you were to develop a matrix, with tradition being X and seemingly related occurrences being Y, I believe you would see how rarely they actually intersect. In fact, I'd be surprised if such an equation could even be written, because—"

Camry stifled a yawn and melted bonelessly against him with deep and utter contentment. Because honest to God, the very fact that he was *lecturing* her made Cam's heart swell with the realization that he truly loved her!

And seeing how her ears weren't wanting to fall off, well . . . could that mean she just might love him back?

Chapter Fourteen

Somewhere in the far reaches of sleep, Luke heard Max and Tigger stirring—only seconds before he heard the zipper on the tent slide open. The realization that it wasn't Camry doing the zipping, because she was snuggled tightly against him, made Luke bolt up in adrenaline-laced alarm.

"You people are trespassing," said the man holding the shotgun only inches from his chest, his voice a menacing growl.

Luke cut off Camry's yelp of surprise by shoving her behind his back when she also sprang upright. "We're not looking for trouble," he told the white-bearded, wild-haired old man. "We're just doing a little winter camping."

Camry peeked past Luke's arm. "You're the one trespassing," she said. "This mountain belongs to Jack and Megan Stone."

"You look like land developers to me," the man snarled, though he did lower the shotgun barrel slightly.

Which still disconcerted Luke, as now it was aimed at his groin. "We're not land developers," he said, leaning sideways to put himself in front of Camry again. He eyed Max and Tigger, wondering why neither dog seemed particularly worried. In fact, they looked downright pleased to have company. "We're on sabbatical from work, getting some fresh mountain air before we go home to our families for Christmas."

"I'm Camry MacKeage," Camry said, leaning around him again. "My family lives in Pine Creek. We own TarStone Mountain Ski Resort."

The gun barrel lowered several more inches as the man arched his bushy brows in surprise. "*Camry* MacKeage, you say?" His eyes narrowed again on Luke. "You Lucian Renoir?"

Luke stiffened. "Yes."

Their uninvited guest's expression suddenly turned eager. "Well okay, then!" he said, backing out of the tent—and taking his shotgun with him. Tigger and Max bounded after him. "I've been waiting weeks for you people to show up!" he continued from outside. "Dag-nab-it, it took you two long enough to get here!"

Luke turned to Camry with an inquisitive arch of his brow.

When she merely shrugged, they both scrambled to put on their boots. They slid their jackets on over their long johns and rushed for the tent door, but Luke pulled Camry to a stop. "Let me go first."

"It's obvious he's only a harmless old hermit."

"Who just happens to know our names? I spent two months on this mountain, and I never saw a trace of him. So just humor me, would you, and let me go out first?"

She stared into his eyes for what seemed like forever, then suddenly smiled and motioned toward the tent flap. "Be my guest, Maxine."

Luke shot her a warning scowl, then poked his head through the flap to find the man sitting on the ground, laughing uncontrollably as Tigger attacked his face with her tongue. Max was flopped on his back with all four paws in the air, his tail thumping the snow as the guy rubbed his belly. Luke looked around for the shotgun and saw it leaning against the track of the snowcat, beside the . . . next to the . . .

He scrambled out of the tent, pulling Camry with him. The moment she stood up, Luke surreptitiously motioned toward the cat. "Is that what I think it is?"

"Oh my God," she softly gasped. "That looks like Podly. Or at least its outer housing." She glanced briefly at the man, who seemed to have completely forgotten them in favor of playing with the dogs. "He's using our satellite as a *sled*?"

"You go check it out," Luke whispered, heading toward the man. He stopped and held his hand down to him. "You can call me Luke, Mr. . . . ?"

The still-laughing man took hold of Luke's hand, but instead of shaking it, he used it to pull himself to his feet. "Dag-nab-it, I seem to be getting older instead of younger," he chortled, finally shaking Luke's hand. "Name's Roger AuClair. You like that sled, Missy MacKeage? I'd be willing to sell it to you," he called to Camry. "Or if'n you want, I can custom make you one just like it, only out of wood scraps."

He walked over to her. "A wooden one would cost you less than this one, 'cause this stuff don't fall out of the sky every day, you know," he said, running his gnarled hand over the charred metal. "I still got to polish it up some. You got any sweets in your fancy snow machine?" he asked, peering in through the window of the snowcat. He looked back at Camry. "I'm open to bartering. Pound for pound, anything I build for you in exchange for anything you got that's sweet, be it home-baked or store-bought."

"I believe we have some sweet granola bars," Camry offered with obvious amusement. She glanced toward Luke, then down at the sled, then back at Roger. "But instead of trading me this beautiful piece, would you happen to have other parts of whatever fell out of the sky that we might barter for?"

"Something about this big, maybe?" Luke added, holding his hands not quite a foot apart. "Sort of square, and rather heavy for its size?"

"I might," Roger said, scratching his beard as his gaze moved to Luke. "You know anything about satellite dishes? 'Cause this thing," he muttered, kicking the sled, "knocked my television dish clean off my roof last June, just before it smashed into the trees behind my cabin. I fashioned another dish from the blasted thing's parts, but I only get half the channels I used to." His gaze narrowed. "I *might* be able to find something about the size you want, if'n you get all my channels to come in. As well as those sweet bar thingies your missy just mentioned."

"I know a little something about satellite dishes," Luke offered.

Roger snatched up his shotgun, grabbed the rope handle on his sled, and started off up the tote road they were camped beside. "Then come on, people! We only got two hours of daylight left. And today's Wednesday, and *Survivorman* is on tonight. I already missed nearly six months of episodes."

Luke stood beside Camry, both of them watching the man disappear around a curve, Max hot on his heels. Tigger, getting mired in the deep snow, rushed back to them and started whining.

Luke scooped up the dog. "Does AuClair look familiar to you?" he asked, still staring up the road. "Those green eyes of his, maybe?"

"I can't say," Camry murmured, "what with all that wild hair covering everything." She glanced up at Luke. "How does he know our names? And what did he mean, he's been waiting for us to show up for weeks?"

"I suppose we're going to have to ask him." Luke opened the door of the snowcat and set Tigger inside, then headed back to the tent. "Let's get dressed and secure everything here so we can catch up with him."

Luke crawled inside the tent, sat on the sleeping bag, and slipped off his boots to pull on his pants. "You know anything about television dishes?" he asked. "Because short of tying the old hermit up and ransacking his place—which, despite my actions to date, is one crime I refuse to consider—it looks as if we're going to have to repair his dish if we want Podly's data banks."

Camry fastened her pants, then slipped back into her boots. She reached over and shut off their catalytic heater, then quickly straightened their sleeping bags before heading back outside. "How many rocket scientists does it take to repair a television antenna?" she asked with a giggle.

"Two," Luke said, crawling out behind her. He pulled her into his arms and kissed the tip of her nose. "One to stand on the roof holding the aluminum foil, and the other one to tell him which direction to turn." He kissed her again, then hugged her so tightly she squeaked. "We just found Podly," he whispered.

"Let's not start celebrating just yet," she warned. "For all we know, Roger AuClair dismantled the data bank and is using it for a tea tin."

Luke dragged her to the snowcat. "Don't even think it!"

Camry sat at the rickety old table in the ramshackle old cabin, sipping the peppermint tea Roger had made her before he'd taken Max and Tigger outside to supervise Luke as he repaired the dish.

The cabin sported two rooms, the dividing wall fashioned from mismatched snowshoes;

several broken skis; and a large number of crooked sticks—some with the bark carefully removed to expose beautiful knots. An assortment of dishes and dented pots were neatly stacked on shelves beneath a sagging counter holding a pock-marked enamel sink and hand pump that looked more rusty than solid. The large wood cookstove sitting in the center of the sidewall, radiating the heat of a sauna, was covered with cast-iron pots wafting up steam that smelled of citrus and cloves.

Basically, Cam might have thought she was sitting smack in the middle of the nineteenth century but for the giant flat-screened television hanging on the opposite wall. On each side of it, rising from floor to rafter, were shelves crammed full of books. Sitting just a few feet in front of the television was a fine-grained leather recliner that looked as if it belonged in a New York penthouse. And tucked into every available nook and cranny scattered around the cabin were what appeared to be pieces of Podly—some the size of a gum stick, some as big as a basketball.

She did not, however, see anything that resembled a data bank.

Hearing Luke's footsteps on the roof—which creaked threateningly under his weight—Cam reached into her coat and pulled Podly's transmitter out of the pocket. She stood up to glance out the window and saw Roger sitting on the ground, fighting back two ecstatic dogs as he called instructions up to Luke.

Cam looked down at the transmitter. "I don't know what you're up to, Fiona," she whispered as she started walking around the cabin, holding the tiny instrument out in front of her. "But if this is about that bib I gave you that said *Shamans Rock,* you're a smart enough girl to know that I was only trying to piss off your daddy. You're going to grow up to be a wonderful drùidh just like your parents, probably even more powerful. And really, I truly enjoyed spending time with you this past week—even if you were only messing with me. But please, Fiona, don't mess with Luke. He's such a good man, and he's trying so hard to make up for eavesdropping on Podly. Help me help him find the data bank . . . in one piece," she tacked on as she continued around the cabin.

"A-and while you're at it, could you help me figure out if this ache in my chest is because I love Luke more than I fear the magic? Because if that's what's making my heart hurt, then I'm afraid you're also going to have to help me find the courage to do something about it."

The little transmitter suddenly chirped, and Cam stilled on an indrawn breath. "Where?" she whispered, moving the instrument left and then right.

It chirped again when she started walking toward the front of the cabin, giving a series of beeps that increased in frequency. As she waved it back and forth like a homing device, it eventually led her to the front wall, then started vibrating when she passed it near a dusty old frame hanging at eye level.

It took Cam a moment to realize she was looking at some sort of certificate. She pulled down the sleeve of her sweater, rubbed away the dust, and suddenly frowned.

Roger AuClair was a justice of the peace?

She squinted to read the date, but the ink was smudged by what appeared to be a thumbprint. June something, the year two thousand and . . . something.

She held the transmitter next to the frame, and it started vibrating excitedly again. Cam's heart thumped madly, and a flurry of butterflies took flight in her belly. "What are you saying?" she whispered.

The cabin door beside her suddenly opened, startling Cam into tossing the transmitter into the air with a gasp of surprise. It bounced off an equally startled Roger, causing Luke to bump into him when the old hermit stopped in midstep. All three of them watched as the transmitter clattered to the floor, rolled up against the leather recliner, and loudly chirped.

Roger walked over and picked it up just as Max tried to grab it. "Dag-nab-it, what are you doing back here, you infernal thing?" he asked the instrument. He held it toward Camry. "You make it stop that blasted noise, Missy MacKeage, or I swear I'm going to take my shotgun to it."

When Cam only gaped at him, he thrust the transmitter toward Luke. "I thought I'd seen the last of this blasted thing when I gave it to Fiona."

Luke stopped in midreach. "Did you say *Fiona*? She was here?"

"Of course she was here." Roger slapped the transmitter into Luke's hand. "Who do you think told me to expect you?"

"Fiona *Gregor*?" Luke glanced uncertainly at Camry. "How old is she?"

Roger's eyebrows drew together. "Yes, Gregor. And I never know how old she's going to be when she shows up." He held his arm out at eye level. "But this time she was in her teens, about yea-high, with long blond hair and big blue eyes." He kissed his fingers with a loud smack. "And she bakes the sweetest pies this side of heaven."

"When was Fiona here?" Camry asked.

"Well, let me see," Roger murmured, smoothing

down his shaggy white beard, then tapping his fingers against it as if counting. "Last time, it was almost three weeks ago." He nodded toward the transmitter. "I bartered her six apple pies for that thing. But what she didn't know was that I would have given it to her for free." He suddenly scowled, pointing at them. "But don't you go telling her that when you see her, you hear? It would hurt her feelings," he said with a nod. "She was beside herself happy, thinking she was getting the best end of the bargain, 'cause I didn't tell her it suddenly starts squawking for no reason. I spent the good part of last summer tearing this cabin apart looking for a mouse before I realized it was *that* thing making those little noises."

Camry inched closer to Luke and slipped her hand into his, taking a fortifying breath when he quietly squeezed it. "I noticed you're a justice of the peace, Mr. AuClair, and I was wondering if you perform weddings?" she asked, squeezing Luke's hand in return when he stiffened. "And what you might charge for your services."

"Well now," Roger said, his eyes glinting in the setting sunlight coming through the open door. "That would depend on what you might have that I'd want." He arched one bushy brow. "I'd be willing to barter for that big dog of yours, seeing as how I lost my own faithful black friend almost thirteen years ago. He wasn't half as handsome as your Max, what with his missing part of one ear and his eyes being foggy, but he was all heart, I tell you." He nodded. "I'd marry you two up for Max, but you can keep Tigger. She's friendly enough, but she don't seem all that practical, what with having almost no legs and needing to wear that prissy sweater."

"I'm sorry, but Max is—"

"Will you please excuse us, Mr. AuClair?" Luke said, cutting Cam off by dragging her out the door. "We'll just be a moment."

Luke led her a fair distance from the cabin, then spun around to face her. "Mind telling me what you're up to?" he asked, a distinct edge in his voice.

"I'm accepting your proposal."

"Now? You want some crazy old hermit to marry us?" He took hold of her shoulders. "Camry, this isn't the time or the place. I asked you to marry me only hours ago, and that's not enough time for you to make that kind of decision."

Cam's heart started pounding so hard that her ribs actually hurt. "A-are you having second thoughts?"

"No!" His hands on her shoulders tightened. "But if we're not legally married, then you won't believe you're trumping the universe."

"But he's a real justice of the peace. I saw his certificate hanging on the wall."

"That certificate is probably as old as the cabin."

"No, it was issued to Roger AuClair by the state of Maine in the year two thousand and something. It's real. It even has the Maine seal on it."

"But we don't have a license. Or witnesses. And I'm not an American citizen. This isn't a decision you can make in a few hours and then do in two minutes."

"You young folks needn't worry about the paperwork," Roger said, waving some papers as he walked toward them. "You'll be legally wed. Fiona brought me your license," Roger continued when Luke spun around in surprise. He handed the papers to him. "She filled out all your information, and she even signed as your witness."

"That's impossible." Luke scanned the page, then flipped over to the next page. "Who in hell is this other witness, Thomas Gregor Smythe?" he asked, turning to Cam when she gasped.

"H-he's an old hermit who used to live in Pine Creek. And he's also Winter's . . . grandson," she whispered, her heartache turning to dread when Luke took a step back.

She glanced briefly at Roger AuClair, then back at Luke. Only instead of calmly explaining what she finally realized was going on, Cam suddenly threw herself into his arms. "I've spent my whole life running from the magic!" she cried. "And instead of hating me for it, the magic gave me you!" She looked up, blinking back tears as she clutched his jacket. "Please, Luke, I need you to love me uncompromisingly, unpretentiously, and . . . and unconditionally," she ended in a desperate whisper.

Luke took hold of her shoulders and held her away from him. "But the real Fiona Gregor is only five months old. And her mother is younger than you are. Thomas Smythe can't be Winter's grandson, because he isn't even been born yet," he growled. "None of this is making any sense, Camry."

"Miracles don't have to make sense," Roger interjected, drawing Luke's attention. "That's the *unconditional* part of love, Renoir. It's what causes a mangy old pound mutt to hold on to a child who would love him forever for nearly an hour, and compels a mother to wait twenty years," he said, looking at Cam, "letting the secret to ion propulsion orbit the world until her daughter is ready to take ownership of her destiny." He nodded toward the papers Luke held crushed in his fist. "And it's opportunities given to those courageous enough to look deep inside themselves, and accept what they see—flaws and all—as the miracles they are.

"It's not the magic you've been running from, Camry," he continued gently. "It's your extraordinary passion for life. Your baby sister's powers have always seemed so overwhelming that you assumed you had none of your own. But the magic works for everyone, including those who won't accept it, and those who don't understand it." He shot her a wink, gesturing toward Luke. "*Especially* those who don't understand it."

"Wh-who are you, really?" she whispered.

He smoothed down the front of his tattered coat with a shrug. "Let's just say I'm a very old distant relative, shall we?" He puffed out his chest. "But I assure you both, I have the authority—and the means—to make your marriage legal and binding. That is, if you're both brave enough to follow your hearts."

He held up his hand when she tried to ask him another question. "As for your little worry about getting pregnant, let me assure you that the choice has *always* been yours. And now Luke's, too, of course," he added with a nod. "Your sisters knew they wanted children, so Providence simply granted each of them their wish—though maybe not quite *when* they wished," he added with a chuckle.

He held his arms out to encompass their surroundings. "To put this in terms you folks *can* understand, life is really nothing more than an infinite, interconnected matrix. It runs on a rather simple equation for the most part, only appearing complex when you factor in *free will*. And free will always trumps Providence," he said, giving Camry another wink. "So just take having a child out of the equation, both of you, as you look deep inside yourselves and acknowledge the miracle Fiona has asked you to be for each other."

He dropped his hands to his sides with a shrug. "You can't make a mistake if you follow your heart. Not if you have the courage to go where it leads you. There are no wrong decisions, only the consequence of not making any decision at all by running away from life instead of toward it," he ended gently, his eyes warm and his smile encouraging.

Absolute silence settled around them.

Roger AuClair suddenly rubbed his hands together, his expression turning expectant. "So, people, are we having a wedding or not? 'Cause if'n I can't have the dog, then it's gonna cost you that fancy snow machine you drove up in, and that's my final offer," he declared, his old hermit persona suddenly returning.

He frowned when Cam and Luke continued standing silently, staring at him.

"Okay then," he said, holding his hands up,

palms toward them. "I can see you need to think on it some. I'll leave you to discuss it between you then, 'cause I know you two people are intelligent enough not to take marriage lightly—seeing as how you each hold a handful of fancy school degrees." He spun around and headed to the cabin, Max and Tigger bounding after him. "Just don't take too long, 'cause if you're not hitched before *Survivorman* comes on, you'll be unzipping those sleeping bags and finding yourselves camped at opposite ends of my cabin." He stopped at the door and looked back at them, his sharp green eyes gleaming with amusement. " 'Cause until I give my blessing, the *entire* amusement park is shut down."

Chapter Fifteen

"When did you tell him about Maxine?" Luke quietly asked when Roger disappeared inside the cabin.

"I didn't."

"Then how did he know what happened to Kate thirteen years ago?" He held the papers toward her. "And this license; how could Fiona have given it to him three weeks ago, before she even met me? Every bit of information on here is correct, right down to my biological father's name."

Camry said nothing, staring at the papers in his hand.

Luke lifted her chin to make her look at him. "How can Roger AuClair possibly know so much about us?" he asked, fighting the alarm tightening his gut. "Even your amusement park comment. It's almost as if he's been listening to our conversations for the past week."

Luke suddenly drove his hand into his pocket and pulled out the transmitter. "This," he growled, holding it up between them. "It's not a transmitter, it's some sort of listening device!" He wound his arm back and threw it, watching it shatter into pieces against a tree, then took hold of Camry's hand and started toward the snowcat. "I can't explain what's going on, much less why, but we are getting the hell off this mountain."

He opened the door and tried to lift her inside, but Camry pulled free and took several steps back.

"Oh, right. The dogs." He headed toward the cabin.

"No, Luke!" she cried, grabbing his arm and spinning around. "Wait. I can explain," she said, her eyes searching his. "I-it's the magic," she whispered. "I know you don't believe in anything but cold hard facts," she rushed on, clutching his arms to follow him when he took a step back. "But the very energy that powers *you and me* is the exact same energy that powers the universe. From the cradle, I've been taught that it's *the magic* that powers life—quietly, benevolently, and . . . and unpretentious in its desire to see each of us reach our full potential."

She dropped her gaze to his chest. "And I've spent my entire adult life running from it." She looked up, smiling sadly. "Until I woke up one morning to find a handsome, sexy, unassuming rocket scientist in my bed, who didn't seem to take me anywhere near as seriously as I took myself."

"I've always taken you seriously," Luke barely managed to say.

She let go of him and hugged herself, her smile turning self-abasing as she shook her head in denial. "I've been so full of myself, it's a wonder my head fits through doors. I've blamed all my problems on everyone but myself; my mother wouldn't collaborate with me, some jerk in France was trying to steal my work, all my sisters were so damned happy I wanted to kick them, and . . ." She reached up and clasped his face in her shaking hands. "And then *you* magically appeared. And for the first time in a very long time, I wanted to be damned happy, too. With you."

She wrapped her arms around his waist and pressed her cheek to his pounding heart. "Over this past week, I found myself falling in love with a man who sees brick walls as opportunities, a belligerent colleague as a challenge, and a grumpy roommate as an intimate partner."

She tilted her head back to look up at him, and Luke's knees turned to jelly at the raw, unadulterated truth he saw in her tear-filled eyes.

"I want to spend forever with you, Luke, seeing life the way you see it. I didn't need a few hours to consider your proposal; I only needed the courage to admit to myself that I love you so much, my heart hurts when I think about a future that doesn't include you. I've never felt this alive, Luke. Normally that would scare the hell out of me, but *you* make me brave."

She covered his mouth with her fingers when he tried to speak. "There's more," she whispered. "A-and it's important that you hear it from me." She stepped out of his arms—making Luke's knees nearly buckle—and squared her shoulders on a shuddering breath. "Roger AuClair's eyes look familiar to you because they're the mirror image of my father's eyes, and mine, and those of every other MacKeage born since the beginning of time. Only Winter has blue eyes, like my mother. And Fiona." She gestured toward the cabin. "If I had to guess, I would say Roger is one of my original ancestors, born in a time when the magic was honored instead of held suspect like it is today. Which is why he's appeared to you—to *us*—as a harmless old hermit."

She held her arms out from her sides. "I am

of the highland clan MacKeage, and loving me means accepting the magic that rules our science." She swiped away a tear running down her cheek, her beautiful green eyes locked on his, her vulnerability fully exposed. "So if you still want to spend the rest of your life with me after all you've seen today, and can wrap your mind around the notion that it's only the tip of the iceberg, then I would ask that you let Roger marry us—right now, in this magical place."

Luke's legs finally buckled and he dropped to his knees, holding his arms out to her. Camry threw herself at him with a cry of relief, and hugged him so tight he grunted.

"Right now, right here," he said into her hair. He tilted her head back. "But only because I happen to be insanely in love with you," he growled, covering her mouth with his.

"Okay, then!" Roger AuClair called out as he walked to them. "Let's get these vows said before you folks set these poor dogs to blushing!"

Luke forced himself to stop making delicious love to Camry's mouth and looked up, only to blink at the man dressed in . . . wearing a . . .

Camry covered his gaping mouth with her hand. "Don't ask, Luke, just accept," she said, leaning her forehead against his with a giggle. "It's a drùidh thing."

"It'll be a first for me," Roger said, "but if you two want to give your vows on your knees, I don't mind none."

Luke scrambled to his feet, pulling Camry with him and immediately tucking her up against his side as he faced what he could only describe as . . . honest to God, the man looked like a fairy-tale *wizard*. Roger AuClair was wearing a black-and-gold spun robe that billowed to the ground, a thick leather belt encrusted with enough jewels to ransom a nation, and a pointed hat that looked an awful lot like the one Mickey Mouse wore in the Disney movie *Fantasia*—which Luke must have watched a hundred times with Kate.

"Would you folks be wanting the *short* version, or the really, really long one that will probably run over into my *Survivorman* show?" Roger asked. He suddenly shot Luke a broad smile. "I see your fancy degrees *are* worth the paper they're printed on, Renoir. I'm getting all my channels now."

"Thank you," Luke said. "And we'd like the short version, please."

The old hermit started patting himself down, until his hand suddenly disappeared inside his robe, only to reappear holding a book that had to weigh fifteen pounds if it weighed an ounce. He started leafing through the pages, murmuring to himself.

Luke glanced down at Camry tucked under his

arm, and found her smiling up at him. She patted his chest. "Don't worry, the amusement park will be open all night."

"I might be old, missy, but I'm not deaf," Roger muttered, still leafing through his tome. "Okay then," he said, his voice booming with authority as he launched into a guttural litany that sounded more spat than spoken.

"Excuse me," Luke interrupted. "That's not Latin."

Roger shot him a dark look. "It's Gaelic." He looked back down at his book with a heavy sigh. "Now I have to start all over."

Which he did.

"But how am I supposed to know what I'm vowing?" Luke asked.

Roger stopped in midsputter with a fuming glare aimed at Camry. "Shut him up, missy, or you're going to find yourself married to a toad."

Camry bumped Luke's hip. "Quit interrupting him."

Luke leaned down to whisper in her ear. "Can he really turn me into a toad?"

Roger sighed heavily again. "You have the whole rest of your lives for her to explain the magic, Renoir. Can we *please* get this done?" He looked up at the sky, then back at Luke. "My show starts in twenty minutes."

Luke suddenly realized the sun had set, and it was completely dark out. Except that the three of them seemed to be standing in some sort of glowing light, which appeared to be emanating from Roger. Luke wiped a trembling hand over his face.

The magic that rules our science, Camry had called it.

Whereas he was thinking *insanity* might be more accurate.

Roger launched into his litany again for what sounded like a sum total of eight or ten sentences, then suddenly stopped and looked at Camry expectantly.

"I do," she said.

Roger turned his expectant look on Luke.

Oh, what the hell. "I do," he firmly echoed.

Roger closed his book with a snap. "You may exchange your rings now," he said with a regal nod.

Luke felt Camry's shoulders slump. "We don't have rings," she said.

"We didn't exactly plan to get married today," Luke drawled, giving Camry a bolstering squeeze. "We'll go straight to a jeweler when we get to Pine Creek."

"You should wear the rings Fiona gave you," Roger said. "They're her wedding present to you. She went to a lot of trouble to find just the right stone to make them."

"Fiona never gave us any rings," Camry said.

Roger's eyebrows lifted into the rim of his pointed hat. "She didn't? But she said she intended to present them in a container that had very special meaning to both of you. She even showed me the paper she was going to wrap it up in. It was deep blue, covered with glittering gold stars."

Luke stiffened.

"The transmitter!" Camry said with a gasp. She bolted out of Luke's embrace and ran toward the tree where he'd thrown it.

"Come on, AuClair," Luke said, falling in behind the dogs bounding after her. "We need your light."

Luke immediately got down on his knees beside Camry and started searching the snow. "Don't worry, we'll find them," he assured her, picking up and discarding tiny pieces of metal debris.

"Here! I found one!" Camry cried, holding something up. She suddenly tossed it away. "No, it's just a rubber O-ring."

Luke shoved Max out of the way, then snatched something out of Tigger's mouth. He held it up to the light Roger was emanating. "This could be one of them." He handed it to Camry. "It seems to be made out of some sort of stone."

She also held it up to Roger's light, then looked

at Luke. "It's black-and-white-speckled rock, just like the stone Kate gave you. Where's your pebble, Luke?"

"In my pocket," he said, reaching into his pants pocket. Only when he didn't find it, he reached into his other pocket. When he still didn't find it, he stood up and started shoving his hands into every pocket he had. He suddenly stilled, looking down at her. "I lost it."

"No, *this* is the special rock Kate gave you," she said, holding it up to him.

Luke took the smooth stone circle from her, which certainly appeared to have been cut from the tiny rock Kate had given him. "But that's impossible. I distinctly remember it was in my pocket this morning."

Roger snorted, looking at Camry. "You sure you want to marry a man who doesn't believe in anything but cold hard facts? The deed's not fully done, missy; I haven't given my blessing yet. You can still back out."

Camry dropped down onto all fours and started searching the snow again. "I'm not backing out," she muttered. "Luke, help me find your ring. That one must be mine, because it's too small for your finger."

By God, he wasn't backing out, either! He didn't care if he *was* losing his mind, as long as he lost it with Camry. Luke got down beside her and resumed searching.

"What I can't figure out," Roger said, peering over their shoulders—his light actually helping them—"is how Fiona's thoughtful gift ended up over here in the first place, all smashed to pieces."

Luke straightened to his knees, lifting a brow. "Don't you have some sort of crystal ball you can look into that will tell you?"

Roger shot him a threatening scowl. "From what I hear, women aren't all that fond of kissing toads."

Camry grabbed Luke's sleeve and tugged him back down. "Leave him alone and help me find your ring."

The light suddenly started to fade, and Luke realized that Roger was heading down the mountain. "Where are you going?" he called out.

"To unzip your sleeping bags," the old hermit muttered. "'Cause in ten minutes, I intend to be sitting in my chair, watching an all-night *Survivorman* marathon."

"I found it!" Camry cried, scrambling to her feet. She grabbed Luke's hand and ran to Roger. "Okay, we've said 'I do,' so now what?"

"Well, now you slide the rings on each other's fingers, and pledge your troths in your own words."

"But we didn't have time to write our own

vows. Wait!" she yelped when Roger turned away again. She took hold of Luke's hands and looked directly into his eyes. "I promise to love you forever, Lucian Pascal Renoir," she whispered, slipping the smooth stone ring onto his finger, "uncompromisingly, unpretentiously, and unconditionally." She shot him a crooked smile. "And I promise never to lie to you, or send you any more unladylike e-mails, or imagine ten different ways to make you beg for mercy, or—"

Luke covered her mouth with a laugh. "Let's at least keep our *vows* in the realm of reality." He lifted her hand and slid the smooth stone ring onto her finger. "And I promise you, Camry MacKeage, to love and honor you with every breath I take, forever. And I promise never to steal your work," he added with his own crooked smile. "Or lecture you until your ears fall off. And if you decide to go on any more crime sprees, I will definitely have your back."

Roger snorted. "Okay then. I guess you two do deserve each other—seeing as how you won't find anyone else willing to put up with either of you." He held his hands up, encompassing them both. "So I give my blessing to this union and pronounce you husband and wife—may God have mercy on *all* our souls," he finished with a mutter, heading toward his cabin.

"Wait. Don't I get to kiss my bride now?" Luke asked.

Roger turned and shot him a scowl. "Not until you get back to your tent." He spun back around and headed to the cabin again, patting his leg to call the dogs to him. He opened the door to let them inside, then turned back. "I'll be keeping Max and Tigger with me tonight, so the poor beasts aren't scarred for life." He pointed at the snowcat. "And you'll be walking to your tent. That fancy snow machine is now mine."

"But you can't actually *keep* it," Camry said. "We really only borrowed it from my father. We have to bring it back."

"Oh no, you don't. A deal's a deal, Missy MacKeage." He suddenly gave Luke an apologetic nod. "Excuse me, I meant *Missus Renoir*. Which means she's your problem now." He looked back at Camry. "For which your papa will be so grateful, I'm sure he would want me to have the machine for my role in getting you off his hands."

When Camry started toward the old man, Luke spun her around and started down the mountain. "Come on, *Missus* Renoir," he said with a laugh. "Before he turns *you* into a toad."

Chapter Sixteen

$\mathcal{W}$ith the rising, nearly full moon lighting their way and the crunch of the cold snow keeping rhythm with their breathing, their mile walk to the tent was made in silence. Cam assumed Luke was trying to assimilate all that had happened. And though she would have loved to explain Roger to him, and Fiona, and the seemingly unre-lated chain of events that had brought them to be walking hand in hand tonight toward the rest of their lives together, she honestly didn't know how to explain something she barely comprehended herself. The only thing she did know for sure was that she loved Luke more than she loved anything else in the world—even her beloved science.

She suddenly stopped walking.

"What is it?" Luke asked, stepping around to take hold of her shoulders. "Are you getting cold feet?" He chuckled softly. "Figuratively speaking, I mean?"

She looked up at him in wonder. "No. I suddenly just realized that the only thing more powerful than my mother's love for her work is her love for Daddy. Because if I had to choose between you and my work, I'd choose you."

"Ahh, sweetheart," Luke said, hugging her to him, then squeezing her tightly. "Grace never had to choose between anything, because she knew she could have it all." He leaned back to smile down at her. "I only spent a few days with your parents, but it was long enough for me to see that your father doesn't have to be a scientist to understand your mother's passion for her work. He appears to be her biggest fan, supporting her a hundred and ten percent. Didn't he build her that beautiful lab?"

"Yes."

"He didn't steal anything from your mother, Camry, he *empowered* her. And I bet he also encouraged all you girls to go after your own dreams, didn't he?"

"Sometimes to the point that we wanted to scream."

"And hasn't your mother always supported your *father's* passion? TarStone Mountain Ski Resort couldn't have become a world-class destination on its own."

She smiled up at him. "I guess that's another thing we can add to our definition of love: its ability to expand exponentially. It's not at all constraining, it's *unlimiting*."

He kissed the tip of her nose with a delighted laugh. "And are you ready to add one more passion to your expanding list, Mrs. Renoir? Say . . . something that involves our getting naked together?"

She toyed with the zipper on his jacket. "I-I've heard that when a person gets on a Ferris wheel the first time, the ride can be somewhat scary."

He kissed the top of her head, then took her hand and led her toward the tent. "Naw, it's only scary for the faint of heart. With your highlander genes, it's more likely the person you're riding with who'll be scared."

Cam stopped just as she was about to unzip the tent flap and looked up.

Luke was scared?

Well, damn. She'd been so focused on her own worry about finally going all the way, she hadn't even thought about what he must be feeling. Hell, what man wanted the responsibility of introducing a thirty-two-year-old virgin to lovemaking?

She unzipped the tent and crawled inside, then poked her head out to stop him from following. "Can you give me a few minutes?" she asked. "I'll start the heater and warm up the tent."

"Oh, sure. I'm sorry. Of course," he said, jumping up and quickly stepping away. He shoved his hands in his pockets. "You take as long as you need."

Luke stood in the middle of the tote road, staring up at the night sky, and fingered the perfectly sized stone ring on his left hand as he thought about all that had happened this afternoon.

Or had it really started long before today? Could finding himself on this mountain, married to the woman of his dreams, have actually begun over a year ago, when he'd tapped the key on his computer that had put him in contact with Podly? At the time, he had assumed the sheer magnitude of what he'd just done was what had caused that spark to run up his arm, jolting him to his very core. Only now he wasn't so sure it had been guilt making his heart pound wildly, but rather the distinct feeling that some tiny, unseen hand had *pushed* his hovering finger down on that button.

Was it truly possible that an imp of a girl, with piercing blue eyes and a contagious smile, could already have been working her magic?

Luke looked over at the tent glowing in the cold dark night, the lantern inside casting the movements of a faint but decidedly feminine silhouette. After today, he had to believe that anything was possible, the undeniable proof being that he had just married the most remarkable, most outrageous, sexiest woman he'd ever met.

The true miracle here, as far as he was concerned, was that Camry loved *him*.

"You must be freezing, Luke. Come in here and let me warm you up."

"I'll be right along," he called back.

Luke sucked in a deep breath of cold air, hoping to free the knot that had started forming in his gut during their walk down the mountain. For as focused as he'd been these last few days on actually getting to use one of his condoms . . . well, everything had changed in the maintenance garage, when he had realized that he wasn't just in lust with Camry: he was in love with her.

But even in his wildest dreams, he hadn't expected his honeymoon suite to be a tent, his wedding bed a sleeping bag, or his marriage to be blessed by a . . . wizard.

And he sure as hell hadn't expected his bride to be a virgin.

"Vroom! Vroom!"

Luke snapped his gaze to the tent.

"Oh my God, Luke, did you hear that? The Ferris wheel is starting without you! Get in here before you miss the ride!"

Luke dropped his chin to his chest, the knot in his gut unraveling on a strangled laugh. What was he doing standing out here worrying about his lovemaking living up to Camry's expectations, when he should be worried about surviving *hers*?

He unzipped his jacket and ran to the tent. "You keep your hands away from those controls, lady!" he barked out, dropping to his knees in front of the tent. "It takes an experienced operator who knows what he's doing to start up that Ferris wheel." He pulled his sweater and long-john top over his head, then unbuckled his belt and shoved down his pants. "If you push the wrong button, it could take me all night to get it running correctly."

"Vroom, vroom," she purred with a giggle. "Oh! I think I found it, Luke. Quick, get in here and tell me if this is the right button."

He had to sit on his jacket to unlace his boots, but instead of undoing them, he ended up with a handful of knots. "Stop playing with the equipment!" He tugged on the mess he'd made of his laces, which only served to tighten them. "That's my job!"

When her purr turned to a lusty moan, Luke

pulled his multitool out of its pouch and cut the laces on both boots. He shoved off his pants and long-john bottoms, then turned and crawled into the tent. "Do you have any idea what the penalty is for messing with such delicate equip—" Luke snapped his mouth shut on an indrawn breath. "My God, you're beautiful," he whispered.

"You're not so bad yourself," she whispered back, opening her arms to him.

But instead of covering her body with his, he settled beside her, propped his head on his hand, and let his gaze travel over her beautiful, naked, inviting body. "Exactly which button did you push that made that wonderful noise?" he asked.

"The 'vroom, vroom'?"

"No, that sweet little lusty moan."

"Oh, that noise." She pointed down at her belly. "You could try pressing here and see what happens."

Luke dipped his finger into her belly button, and she gasped loudly.

"Nope, that's not it," he muttered, walking his fingers toward her breasts.

She immediately stopped him. "Your hands are cold."

Luke flopped onto his back and folded his cold hands behind his head. "Then I guess the amusement park's shut down until they warm up."

"Maybe I can hurry the process along," she murmured, rolling over and crawling on top of him. She walked her warm fingers up his chest to his shoulders, and leaned down and touched her lips to his. "I wonder what buttons you have," she said into his mouth. "And what sort of noises I can get *you* to make."

She certainly got a groan out of him when she wiggled her hips up the length of his shaft just as her mouth took possession of his. And while she made delicious love to his mouth, Luke tried to think where he'd put his ditty bag.

He suddenly bolted upright, wrapping his arms around her to keep her from falling. "Dammit, the condoms are in the snowcat!"

She leaned away to see his eyes. "We don't really need them . . . do we?"

"That is one decision we are not making today."

She shot him a smug smile. "Then we'll just have to use the condoms I brought."

Luke reared back. "*You* brought condoms?"

"Don't brilliant minds think alike? You're not the only horny toad in this tent."

Luke shuddered. "Let's not refer to ourselves as toads, okay?"

"Ohhhh, do that again," she said on a moan, wiggling intimately against him. "I think you just found one of my buttons."

Luke held himself perfectly still. "The condoms."

"Under my pillow," she murmured, pulling his face toward hers so she could attack his mouth again.

Luke blindly felt behind him for her pillow while she conveniently worked herself into a really good frenzy, kissing him senseless and running her hands over his shoulders, her nails sending shivers coursing through him. But he suddenly stilled again when he found the condoms and counted out three sleeves.

Three packs per sleeve equaled nine.

Holy hell, did she think he was Superman?

He snatched up one of the sleeves, wrestled his mouth from hers, and set her away. She immediately snatched the packs out of his hand, tore one open, then scooted down his legs and started to roll the condom down over him.

Luke gritted his teeth against the explosion of sensation—both visual and tactile—that shot through every cell in his body as she awkwardly attempted to sheath him. The lantern cast its glow on her beautiful breasts, her movements making her peaked nipples brush his thighs. Her hands caressed his scrotum as her fingers slowly slid down the length of his shaft, and Luke felt beads of sweat break out on his forehead. Which was why just as soon as she was done, he snatched her hands away and rolled on top of her.

"My turn to drive you insane," he growled, settling between her thighs.

She immediately lifted her hips, her hands clutching his shoulders. "Yes, make me insane," she pleaded with ragged urgency. "I want to feel you inside me, Luke. Deep, where I ache."

Her tension was palpable, her desire desperate. Searching for any sign of discomfort, Luke eased himself down until he was poised to enter her, then reached between them and caressed her intimately. She was surprisingly moist and slick and ready for him—except that she seemed to be holding her breath.

"If you pass out, you're going to miss the best part," he said with a forced laugh, feeling somewhat desperate himself. He kissed the tip of her nose, then locked his gaze back onto hers. "Close your eyes and picture yourself opening up for me. Feel me sliding into you this first time, Camry, and savor each little rippling sensation."

He lowered more of his weight and pressed into her, feeling her stretch to accommodate him as he brushed his lips over her eyelids, then trailed tiny kisses across her cheek. "Lift your hips," he said into her ear. "And meet me halfway."

He felt her heels press into the sleeping bag

beside his thighs, and Luke slipped deeper as she lifted toward him. "Feel yourself surrounding me, making me yours," he continued soothingly when her breath caught on a gasp.

He seated himself fully, capturing her sound of distress in his mouth, then immediately stilled, lifting his head to smile into her wondrous eyes. "Hello, wife."

She hesitantly smiled back. "H-hello, husband."

"Are you okay?"

She thought about that, then nodded. "I'm okay. S-so that's it? This is what I've been missing all these years?"

Luke arched a brow. "What exactly were you expecting?"

"Well," she said, the corners of her mouth turning up, "I guess I expected fireworks or something. Or at the very least, some moaning and shouting."

He raised his other brow. "I heard moaning."

Two flags of red appeared in her cheeks. "I meant from you."

"Oh. Well, Mrs. Renoir, just as soon as you give me the nod that it's okay to move, I'll see if I can't scare up some moaning and shouting."

"So that's what's wrong with this Ferris wheel? It's not *moving*?" She made a tsking sound. "And you said you were an experienced operator. Um . . . why are you trembling?" she asked, her hands flexing on his shoulders.

"Because you are so damn hot and tight and beautiful, it's taking every ounce of strength I possess not to drive into you like a mindless idiot."

Her eyes widened, her mouth forming a perfect O.

Feeling his restraint slipping, Luke forced a smile. "Here's an idea: Why don't you move first?"

The second she tentatively squirmed—which sent rockets of pleasure shooting through him—Luke realized that had been a really bad idea. He dropped his forehead to hers with a groan. "No, don't move."

"I'm sorry. Am I *too* damn hot and tight and beautiful for you?"

He snapped his head up to stare down at her, and found her smiling at him.

"Vroom-vroom, husband," she whispered.

The last thread of his restraint broke on a bark of laughter. Luke dropped to his elbows to lace his fingers through her hair, and attacked her mouth as he lifted his hips just enough to push into her again. Swallowing her moan of pleasure, he repeated the action, rising back up so he could watch the play of emotions on her face.

Her hands moved from his shoulders to his

chest, her fingers kneading into him, her encouraging mewls growing demanding. Her breathing turned ragged as he increased his rhythm, and Luke felt her tightening with building energy as she rose up to meet his thrusts. He reached between them and caressed her, watching her eyes glass over as she arched up into his touch.

"Come with me, Luke!" she cried, her breathing growing more ragged as she moved restlessly, straining toward her release.

Luke rose to his knees, grasped her hips, and pulled her into his thrusts. He wanted to whisper encouragement but found he was beyond speech, every fiber of his being completely focused on the explosion building inside her.

He suddenly stilled, holding her high on his thighs, and reached down and caressed her again. Her climax broke with a cry of utter abandon, and she tightened around him in pulsing waves of molten heat.

His own climax hit hard and fast, tearing a shout from his throat as her wild convulsions pulled him into the maelstrom, his mind emptying of all thoughts save one: that *miracles* packed one hell of a powerful wallop.

Chapter Seventeen

"*I* am *so* going to kill my sisters," Cam muttered as soon as she could speak, her racing heart threatening to crack her ribs.

"Why?"

"For neglecting to mention how mind-blowing sex really is."

Luke rolled toward her and propped his head on his hand. "Mind-blowing, huh?"

Silently thanking her very wise mother for teaching all her daughters about the delicate subtleties of the male ego, Cam reached over and patted Luke's heaving chest. "I'm sure it was because I had such an experienced operator at the controls."

He grunted agreement, then flopped onto his back. "So long as you realize that it wouldn't have been mind-blowing with any of your old boyfriends. If they were so dumb they didn't even realize they weren't having sex, they sure as hell wouldn't have known which buttons to push, much less *when*."

Cam snuggled against him with a sigh of utter contentment, her amused smile turning into a yawn. "You better get some sleep," she murmured, resting her cheek on his thumping heart. "Because just as soon as I get my strength back, I'm going to start pushing *your* buttons."

Luke was reluctant to open his eyes, worried that if Camry knew he was awake she might attack him again. The insatiable woman had somehow managed to keep the Ferris wheel running all night, at times so fast that he'd gotten dizzy. She'd also managed to put a healthy dent in her stash of condoms, and Luke decided he was buying himself a red cape and a T-shirt with a large *S* on the front of it.

"Are you awake?" she asked from the depths of the sleeping bag, where her cold nose was pressed into his ribs.

"No."

"Is the sun up?"

"It must be, since I can see my breath."

The edge of the sleeping bag folded back, and two sleepy green eyes blinked up at him. "I suppose we're going to have to get dressed and go rescue Max and Tigger before Roger spoils them rotten."

"That sounds like a plan," Luke said, not moving. "You trudge right up there and save them while I stay here and pack up camp."

"Oh no." She threw off the sleeping bag and immediately started scrambling into her clothes. "You're coming with me."

"He's *your* long-lost relative. You should spend some quality time alone with him before we leave," he said, sitting up and looking around for his long johns. Finally remembering he'd undressed outside, he pulled the sleeping bag back up around his shoulders. "Can you reach outside and get my clothes?" he asked, seeing as how she was already mostly dressed. "The heater must have run out of fuel."

"Hours ago." She poked her head out the tent flap—giving him a really nice view of her really nice backside—then reappeared with his clothes and boots. "It looks like it's been snowing quite a while," she said, shaking the snow off his long johns before handing them to him. "And you have to go to Roger's with me so you can help me steal the snowcat back."

"Well, why not," he said with a snort, slipping into his cold clothes. "What could possibly go wrong stealing from a man who can turn us into toads? At least we're keeping our crimes in the family."

"And while we're at it, I'll distract him so you can find the data bank," she said, handing Luke his boots. "Hey, what happened to your laces?"

He put on the boots and tied what was left of the laces. "I seem to remember something about you starting the honeymoon without me."

She blinked at him, her cheeks flushing a dull red.

Luke cupped her face in his hands. "Good morning, wife."

"We're really married, aren't we?" she whispered back.

"After last night, I certainly hope so."

"Any second thoughts?"

"Only that our honeymoon suite was a tent instead of a five-star room in Tahiti."

"Oh no! I love that our wedding night was out here in the wilderness." She pulled his hands down to hold them in hers. "The tent was cozy and intimate, and I swear it was like we were the only two people on Earth." Her eyes sparkled with humor. "And there's also the added bonus that only the animals heard you shouting for mercy."

"Okay, that does it," he growled, pushing her onto her back to pin her down with his body. "There's one more secret little button that I didn't push last night," he said, having to raise his voice over her laughter, "because I didn't want you fainting from passion overload. But now I—"

A fiberglass support suddenly snapped overhead, and the tent collapsed, billowing down around them.

"Dammit, I told you this wasn't a four-season tent." He pushed up to his hands and knees, using his body as a new tent support. "But oh no, you wanted the larger one so there would be room for the dogs. Just as soon as you stop laughing, could you maybe find the zipper and crawl out?"

He grunted when her elbow rammed his chest, then jackknifed his hips when her head butted his groin, and she fell back with a giggle. "Anytime today," he ground out, pushing at the tent to shake off some of the heavy snow. "We need to get down off the mountain before the storm intensifies."

She finally crawled outside, then held the flap open for him. Luke gave one last push at the tent, then dove for the opening just as the rest of the snow slid off the outer storm fly and down the back of his neck.

"Lovely," he said, standing up and digging the

snow out of his collar. He looked around to find that visibility was less than a quarter mile. "We've already gotten six or seven inches of heavy wet snow, but if the temperature drops and the wind kicks up, we won't be able to see past our noses."

"Roger won't really keep our snowcat, will he?" she asked, brushing more snow off his shoulders.

"If he doesn't give it back when we ask nicely, we'll just threaten to break his satellite dish so that he doesn't get *any* channels."

Camry started dismantling what was left of the tent. "I love your criminal mind."

While she rolled up the storm fly and collapsed the rest of the supports, Luke pulled everything out from inside and started making a pile of their gear to pick up on their way back. In twenty minutes they were entirely packed up, and half an hour after that, they arrived at the cabin.

Or rather, they arrived at where the cabin *should* have been.

"It's gone!" Camry cried in dismay.

"That's impossible. We must have walked right past it. The wind's picked up, making visibility worse."

"No, this is the right spot." She pointed to their right. "I distinctly remember that pine tree with the burn scar where Podly crashed. The cabin should be right here!"

"An entire building can't just suddenly vanish overnight."

She looked up at him with a gasp. "And he took Tigger and Max!"

Luke wiped a gloved hand over his face, attempting to wipe away his disbelief along with the snowflakes catching on his beard. "Okay, let's think about this. There has to be a perfectly logical explanation for why we can't find the cabin, or Roger, or the dogs." He shot her a scowl when she snorted. "An explanation *other* than magic."

"I know! A spaceship swooped down and took Roger and Tigger and Max back to Mars to add to their zoo."

Luke sighed. "That's just as plausible as anything else that's happened in the last twenty-four hours."

"Listen. Did you hear that?" She pointed to their left. "There it is again. That's Max barking. Come on!"

"Camry, wait!" Luke called out, chasing after her as she disappeared into the blinding snow. "You don't know what you might be running into!"

But when they reached the shelter of the dense evergreen trees, the visibility got considerably better. They stopped to listen again, then started running toward what sounded like both dogs barking.

They skidded to a stop when they saw Max and Tigger sitting under a huge spruce tree, in the sled made out of Podly's housing. Max immediately jumped out and ran up to them, and Tigger—wearing not only her pink sweater, but what looked like a tiny version of a wizard's hat— started yelping in protest.

"Oh, that's a good boy," Camry said, dropping to her knees to hug Max. "You helped us find you without abandoning your friend."

Luke walked over and scooped up Tigger, then reared back to avoid getting his face washed. "It's okay, Tig," he crooned. "Mommy and Daddy are here. We wouldn't have left this mountain without you."

"Mommy and Daddy?" Camry repeated with a laugh, walking up to them. She gave Tigger an affectionate scratch behind the ears, then straightened the dog's pointed little hat before looking down at the sled, which now had a small tarp fashioned like a tent over the top.

"Well, at least he made sure they were comfy. And judging by the snow on the tarp, they haven't been here more than an hour. Hey, there's something else in the sled," she said, reaching inside. She pulled out a small tin coffee can. "I don't think it's big enough to be the data bank."

Luke set Tigger back in the sled, on top of what appeared to be a straw-filled mattress, and took the tin from her—only to nearly drop it when whatever was inside suddenly chirped.

Camry snatched it from him and popped off the lid. "It's the transmitter!" she cried, pulling it out. "And it's been put back together!"

When she tried to hand it to him, Luke shoved his hands in his pockets. "That infernal thing is *possessed*," he growled, stepping away. He suddenly groaned. "Oh, God, now I'm *talking* like Roger."

Camry stuffed the transmitter in her pocket, then reached into the can again. "There's a note," she said, pulling out an envelope. She held it toward him. "And it's addressed to you."

Luke plopped down on the ground, tucking Max up next to him. "You read it. I've had my fill of Roger AuClair and all his hocus-pocus."

She dropped down beside him, pulled a colorful card out of the envelope, and held it for him to see the front. "It's just like the ones Fiona gave us."

Luke picked up the envelope. "But this isn't Fiona's writing." He looked back at her hand. "So, what's it say?"

"*Dear Lucian,*" she read. She stopped, eyeing him with amusement.

"What?"

She looked back at the card, cleared her throat, and continued. *"You may have had enough of my hocus-pocus, young man, but I'm afraid you're going to have to put up with a bit more of it, if you're hoping to hold on to that miracle sitting beside you."*

She smiled over at him. "In case you're wondering, he's referring to me."

When Luke merely arched a brow, she looked back at the card. *"You have less than two days to get Camry back into the loving arms of her mama and papa. Actually, it's one day, nine hours, and sixteen minutes from right now. You step foot in Gù Brath even one second after the winter solstice, and your marriage to the woman of your dreams will never have happened."*

"That bastard can't do that!"

"Tsk-tsk," she said. She held the card toward him. "That wasn't me. See, he actually wrote *tsk-tsk* right here." She held the card in front of her again. *"Tsk-tsk,"* she repeated, *"it's dangerous to call a drùidh names. And though you may not believe it right now, not only am I your greatest ally, I'm also your only means of accomplishing the seemingly impossible task ahead of you. Your science will only take you so far, Dr. Renoir, before you will have to concede that there's more to life than numbers, equations, and cold hard facts."*

She stopped reading and looked at him. "What impossible task is he talking about?" she asked, her eyes filling with worry.

"He's messing with us, Camry. It won't be the first time I've walked off this mountain in a blizzard. We're both strong and healthy, and it shouldn't take us even one day to get to Pine Creek." He gestured toward the tree next to the sled. "Especially with snowshoes."

She looked where he was pointing, then back at him. "But he left only one pair."

Luke stood up and walked over to the tree, giving Tigger a pat on his way by. He looked back at Camry and smiled. "Maybe my 'seemingly impossible task' is that I'm going to have to pull you all the way home in the sled."

She didn't return his smile. "I don't like this, Luke," she whispered, her eyes darkening with concern. "Why would he say that *you* had to get me home, when I am perfectly capable of getting myself home?"

"Because the old bastard is messing with us," he repeated, walking over and sitting down beside her. He hugged her to him. "He's just a bored old hermit, Camry, who loves drama." He snorted. "He even took it so far as to dress up like a wizard for added effect."

"Then where is he?"

"Gone in our snowcat. When we get back to Pine Creek, we'll probably find it parked on Main Street. Roger will be sitting in a bar, getting folks to pay for his drinks while he tells them about the two rocket scientists he duped into believing in magic."

She leaned away. "So you didn't believe anything that happened yesterday? When you said your vows to me, you were only . . . what . . . humoring me?" She looked down at the card in her hand. "So if you believe this has all been a charade, then you also believe that we're not really married."

He placed a finger under her chin and lifted her face to look at him. "As far as I'm concerned, we became husband and wife last night. And just as soon as we get back to civilization, we're going to make it legal."

"But the magic is *real*, Luke."

He kissed the tip of her nose, then smiled. "Yes, it is, because I just spent a very magical night with a very magical woman." He gave her another kiss, this time on her mouth, then stood up. "So, Mrs. Renoir, we better get going. I'd like to at least make it down to the lake before this storm gets too intense. We can wait it out at your sister's camp lot for the night, then start out fresh in the morning."

She looked back at the card in her hand. "But there's more."

"Don't bother reading it," Luke muttered, sitting down beside the sled and putting on the snowshoes. "I'm not interested in what else Roger AuClair has to say."

Chapter Eighteen

Cam sat in the sled, rubbing her cheek against Tigger, and stared at Luke's back as he trudged through the deepening snow. She'd insisted on walking, but by the time they'd made it back to their tent site and sorted through what gear they wanted to take, she'd realized not having snowshoes of her own only slowed down their progress as the storm intensified.

She sucked in a shuddering sob, her chest hurting so much she could almost feel her heart breaking in two. Not only did Luke *not* believe in the magic, he had felt it was necessary to pretend that he did. He'd stood there as serious as a groom on his wedding day and let Roger marry them, even though he thought it was all a charade.

Or maybe *farce* was a better word.

But why? If Luke loved her like he claimed, and thought she loved him equally as much, then why couldn't he have been honest with her?

Cam buried her face in Tigger's fur, wishing for her mama. She dearly needed her mother to explain to her why she'd fallen in love with a closed-minded, patronizing . . . know-it-all. She didn't care if Lucian Pascal Renoir was handsome and sexy and smart, or even strong and brave and loyal; if he couldn't wrap his mind around the magic, then he couldn't uncompromisingly, unpretentiously, and unconditionally love her.

The sled suddenly stopped, and Luke walked back to open the side of the tarp. When she wouldn't look at him, he slid his finger under her chin and lifted her face.

He sucked in his breath. "Are you crying?" he asked, wiping his thumb over her cheek. "Goddammit, you should have told me you were cold!" He reached down and started unlacing her boots. "Is it your feet? If they hurt, that's a good sign you haven't gotten frostbite yet. I'll find us a sheltered place to build a fire."

She covered his hands to stop him. "I'm not cold."

"Then why are you crying?" She saw him suddenly stiffen. "Camry, you've got to come back to reality. What I believe about magic doesn't matter, as long as you believe that *I love you*."

"I-I told you yesterday that loving me means accepting who I am."

"I do! You're Camry MacKeage—no, dammit, Camry *Renoir*—the physicist who's been driving me nuts for over a year." He cupped her face in his palms, his thumbs gently brushing her cheeks. "The woman I fell in love with within days of meeting in person." His grip tightened. "How can I make you understand that nothing else matters but our love for each other?"

She covered his hands with her own. "By *believing*, Luke," she whispered. "By honestly believing that miracles aren't something that happen only in books and movies, and that there's really more going on than our science can explain."

He visibly recoiled, sitting back on his heels. "So are you saying you can only love a man who thinks the way you do? And that I must not really love you because I can't understand how your five-month-old niece can also be sixteen, or how an old hermit can be your long-lost ancestor as well as a drùidh?" He hesitated. "Is that what you're saying, Camry?"

Unable to face him, she looked down at Tigger. "I don't know what I'm saying," she whispered. She suddenly looked back at him. "Would you believe my mother? If Dr. Grace Sutter explained the magic to you, would you believe *her*?"

He stood up and walked to the front of the sled. "We'll discuss this later," he said, the wind carrying his words away. He settled the rope over his shoulders, then glanced back. "You make sure you tell me if you get cold."

She nodded, unable to speak past the lump in her throat. Luke called Max to his side and started off, and the sled lurched forward. Cam buried her face in Tigger's neck, the image of Luke's wounded expression burning her eyes like hot sand.

It was well after dark when they reached Megan and Jack Stone's camp lot, and Luke was more than a little surprised that they actually found it, considering they had to battle both darkness and blizzard conditions. But with the last of his reserves fading from towing Camry, Tigger, and eventually Max, as well as their minimal gear, he'd given in to Camry's plea that he let her put on the snowshoes and tow him for the last few miles. He'd finally conceded when he'd realized they were mostly downhill miles, and that they'd both be better served if he conserved his strength for tomorrow's trek.

With an efficiency of effort and a few lumber scraps they found around the lot, they used the storm fly of the tent to construct a makeshift shelter, then crawled into the sleeping bag—with the dogs—to share their body heat. Luke sandwiched Camry between himself and Max and Tigger, then fell asleep almost before he'd even closed his eyes.

But when he woke up the next morning, he was alone. He bolted upright, shouting Camry's name as he scrambled to the entrance.

"I'm right here," she called back from the shoreline. She held her arms wide. "Look, Luke. Isn't it beautiful?"

He rubbed a hand over his face, shaking off the last vestige of terror, and took a calming breath as he stood up. He blinked in the sharp sunlight breaking over the east end of the frozen lake as he looked around, surprised by how utterly calm the air felt. It was a winter wonderland as far as he could see, everything blanketed in glittering, pristine snow.

"Yes, it's beautiful," he called to her, even as he thought about how difficult that beauty was going to make today's hike. But Roger's time constraint notwithstanding, their sitting still was not an option. Luke slipped into his boots and walked to her. "How much ice do you think is on the lake?" he asked, eyeing the snow-covered expanse.

"Anywhere from six inches to a foot. But some places could be only an inch." She shook her head. "And with the snow covering everything, there's no way of telling what's safe and what isn't."

Luke bent down, scooped up some snow and rubbed it over his face, giving a shiver as the last cobwebs of sleep fell away. "Then I guess we stick to the tote road. How long have you been up?"

"Half an hour. I started a small fire and melted some snow to make soup." She gestured toward the campfire burning a few yards away. "Max and Tigger and I have already eaten. The rest is yours."

"Why didn't you wake me?" he asked, going over and lifting the pot off the coals.

"I figured you'd wake yourself up, once you got the rest you needed." She knelt down beside him, picked up a stick, and pushed the embers into a pile. "I've thought about what you said yesterday," she continued softly, not looking at him. "And I agree that we should ignore Roger's ultimatum that we get back to Gù Brath before the solstice." She glanced at him, then back down at the fire. "The only people who have any say about our being married is us. We'll get home when we get there, and we'll be legally married when we want—by *who* we want."

She took hold of his sleeve, her sharp green eyes direct, her expression defiant. "We're a team, and together we can conquer the world if we want to, and trump Providence without even breaking a sweat." She reached down, lifted his hand, and fingered his ring. "Apparently *I'm* the one who forgot that the unconditional part of love works both ways," she whispered, smiling crookedly as she raised her eyes back to his. "I love you, Luke, for *exactly* who you are."

He slowly set the pot down in the snow before he dropped it, then just as slowly pulled her into his arms and held her against him with a sigh. "Thank you," he whispered into her hair. "For loving me just that much."

She melted into him, her own sigh barely audible over the sound of slurping.

"What the . . . ?" Luke glanced down to see Tigger's nose driven into the pot of soup. "Hey, that's mine!" he yelped, grabbing the dachshund and shoving her at Camry. "Your dog was eating my soup!"

"My dog? You were the one calling himself *Daddy* yesterday."

Luke picked up the pot and sat down, holding it protectively against his chest when Max came bounding up, his tongue licking his sniffing nose. "I think we should hook *them* up to the sled and make them pull *us* today."

"Come on, guys," she said with a giggle as she

scrambled to her feet. "Let's go pack up while *Daddy* eats his breakfast. We all have a long day ahead of us. But just think about the fabulous tales you'll have to tell Suki and Ruffles when you get back," she pointed out to them, her voice trailing off as she ducked into the shelter.

Luke frowned down at his soup, then used his finger to flick a whisker off the rim before he drank right out of the pot. Hell, if he was going to play the part of a sled dog today, what was a little hair in his soup?

Chapter Nineteen

$\mathcal{D}$espite the ineffectual sun hanging low in the southern sky, Luke was a ball of sweat not two hours into their trek. Breathing heavily from the incline that traveled along the ridge rising sharply to their left, he stopped in the middle of the tote road, shrugged off the rope, and flexed his shoulders. He pulled his GPS out of his pocket, punched some buttons, and realized they were only a couple of miles from the turnoff to Pine Creek, which still left another twenty-three miles after that.

"Okay, everyone walks for a while," he said, tucking the GPS back in his pocket, then putting his gloves back on. "Except Tigger, I suppose."

Camry had just set Tigger forward between her legs to stand up when a low rumbling whispered through the air. "What's that?" she asked, glancing around.

Luke looked up, adrenaline spiking through him when he saw the sheet of snow sliding down the exposed ridge above, heading straight toward them. "Avalanche!" he shouted, immediately snatching up the rope. "Stay in the sled! You won't be able to run in the deep snow!"

"Max! Come!" she cried, falling back when Luke jerked the sled and ran.

The rumble grew louder, echoing down the steep granite gorge, the snow pushing an icy wave of air ahead of it that sent chills racing up Luke's spine. He veered toward the stand of trees growing on the edge of the wash, but his snowshoes caught in the jumble of talus from previous rockslides, and he fell to his knees. He gave one last mighty heave on the rope to pull the sled past him, Camry's scream drowned out by the wall of snow slamming into them.

The rope jerked out of his hands, then tangled on one of his snowshoes as Luke helplessly tumbled in a sea of churning white, all the while fighting not to lose contact with the sled. The noise was deafening, the snow unbelievably heavy as it meted out its endless battering. The lacing on one of his boots snapped, the snowshoe attached to it pulling the boot off his foot. His hand scraped what felt like metal, but just then the rope gave a sharp tug before ripping the other snowshoe off his boot, releasing him to continue his turbulent free fall alone.

And just as suddenly as it had begun, it ended.

Luke slammed against an unmovable object, the air rushing from his lungs in a whoosh. An eerie silence settled around him, his body sheathed in what felt like concrete, every damn cell in his body screaming in agony. The snow had packed around him like a vise, squeezing his lungs and making it nearly impossible to breathe; when he opened his eyes, he literally couldn't see past his nose.

Camry! Unable even to hear his own scream, Luke frantically wiggled back and forth to free himself. His fingers brushed what felt like bark, and as he slowly increased the cavity around him, his knee connected with the tree that had stopped his fall.

Slowly, painstakingly, he was able to work his arms up beside his head, and he dug the snow out of his ears. He stilled, listening for any sound that might tell him Camry was okay, or at least that Max had made it to safety. But when he heard only the blood pounding through his veins, Luke focused on figuring out which way was up. His guess, based on the fact that the more he wiggled the farther he settled to his left, made him start digging past his right shoulder.

His fist suddenly punched through to open air! He gritted his teeth against the protest of his battered muscles and started jackknifing his body as he pushed at the snow above him. He suddenly heard barking. "Max!" he shouted through the small opening he was creating. "That's my boy! Come on, Max!"

The opening suddenly closed when a nose drove into it, and a warm tongue shot out and touched his wrist.

"Thatta boy, Max!" Luke said with a laugh. "Come find me, boy. Dig!"

With Max digging down from the top and Luke clawing his way up, he was finally able to break his upper torso free. "Good boy!" he chortled when Max lunged at his chest and started licking his face. He pushed the dog away, pointing beside him. "Keep digging. I've got to get free so we can find Camry."

With Max's help, Luke was finally able to lever himself up and crawl on top of the snow. He immediately got to his knees and looked around. "Okay, Max. Use that wonderful nose of yours and find Camry. Come on," he said, scrambling to his feet, again ignoring his screaming muscles and the fact that he had only one boot. He clapped his hands excitedly. "Find Camry, Max!"

The Lab immediately jumped into the hole from which Luke had just emerged, and started whining and sniffing around.

"She's not in there. Come on, let's play hide-and-seek. Find Camry!" he repeated, slapping his leg to urge the dog out. "And Tigger. Let's go find Tigger!"

Luke took several steps onto the uneven tangle of packed snow, his hopes rising when he realized it had been a relatively small slide, only about a hundred feet wide and two hundred yards long. He looked around for anything dark, like a hat or glove or . . . anything. He cupped his hands to his mouth. "Camry!"

He stilled, listening. "Goddammit, Camry, answer me!"

But all he heard was terrifying silence.

"Okay, AuClair," he growled, stumbling to the center of the small avalanche field. "If you're my greatest ally, then help me find my miracle!"

Luke was trembling so badly that he had to stop, plant his feet, and rest his hands on his knees in an attempt to calm his racing heart. "Help me," he whispered, closing his eyes against his burning tears. "Show me where to look."

He suddenly held his breath, not moving a muscle when he heard a faint chirping sound. Still not breathing, he cocked his head one way and then the other.

There—just to his left: that unmistakable chirp of Podly's transmitter! The last he remembered seeing it, Camry had tucked it in her jacket pocket in order to read the note Roger had left him.

Could it still be in her pocket?

"Max! Come!" he called, taking several steps to the left and dropping to his knees. He grabbed the excited dog and held him still. "Listen."

And there it was again, a slightly louder chirp.

"Hear that, boy? Get the toy. Come on, dig up the toy!" he urged, driving his hands into the snow. "Dig, Max!"

They dug a hole at least three feet deep before Max suddenly lifted his head, a tiny wizard's hat in his mouth.

"Yes, you found Tigger!" Luke cried, digging frantically. If Tigger was here, there was a good chance Camry was with her.

His hand suddenly struck metal. "Camry!" he shouted. "Answer me!"

"Luke," came a muffled sound, making him still again.

"Camry!"

"Lu—"

He dug harder, working his way along the metal sled in each direction, until he felt the tarp. He pulled off his glove to wiggle his fingers under the canvas, and touched her jacket.

"I've got you!" he shouted. He had to shove Max out of the way when the dog tried to drive his nose into the narrow opening. "Keep digging, Max. Right here," he said, patting the snow toward the front of the sled.

While Max dug, Luke carefully worked more snow away from the tarp until he was able to peel it back enough to see inside. But all he could see was the red of Camry's jacket. He climbed out of the hole, knelt down on the opposite side, grabbed the edge of the tarp, and pulled with all his strength.

It slowly peeled back, revealing Camry's folded body wedged into the sled so tightly, he was afraid she couldn't breathe.

"Max, no!" Luke grabbed Max by the collar when the dog started nosing Camry's hair, dragged the Lab up out of the hole, and pushed him away.

Luke then straddled the hole, bracing his feet on either side of the sled. "Camry, sweetheart," he whispered, slipping off his glove again and carefully threading his trembling fingers through her hair. He felt along her jaw to locate her neck, then held his finger against her weak pulse. "Easy now," he said when she stirred with a moan. "Don't move. We don't know what's broken."

"Tigger," she said weakly, her voice muffled because her face was pressed into her knees, facing down.

"To hell with Tigger," he growled. "I need to know where you're hurt. Can you feel your body, Camry? Your legs? Your arms?"

"T-take Tig . . ." she whispered. "C-can't breathe."

Luke felt along her body, carefully wedging his fingers between her arm and torso, and finally realized that she was wrapped around the dachshund so tightly, there was no room for her lungs to expand. He pressed deeper until he felt Tigger's sweater, then grasped the wool and slowly pulled. Camry moaned again as the limp body of the dog slowly emerged. As soon as he was able to get both hands around Tigger, Luke applied more pressure while carefully wiggling the dog back and forth, then finally pulled the dachshund free and set her on the snow above the hole.

He immediately looked down at Camry and saw her stir again, her torso expanding on a shuddering breath. "Okay, sweetheart, your turn." He clasped the shoulder of her jacket, at the same time wrapping his hand around her neck to keep her head still, and leaned close. "If you feel any sharp pain, you let me know, okay? I'm going to pull you out now. Don't try to help; just relax and let me do all the work."

He put just enough pressure into his pull to gauge how stuck she was, then stilled, watching for signs of distress. He pulled a bit harder, felt her sliding free, then lifted her just a bit more before he stopped again. He then slid his arm under her head for support and repositioned his hand on her jacket. Using his own body like a backboard, he slowly straightened as she unfolded out of the sled, until he was leaning back against the side of the hole with her in front of him.

"Can you feel your legs and arms?" he whispered into her ear, which was now even with his head.

"Right leg h-hurts."

Luke was so relieved he kissed her hair. "That's good. You'd have really scared me if you said you couldn't feel anything. Okay," he said, taking a steadying breath to calm his trembling. "I'll straighten my knees so that I'm standing, then reach under your legs and lift you into my arms. There's a chance your right leg is broken, but I've got to lift you up and lay you on the snow." He kissed her hair again. "Ready?"

She made a small sound, and her head, which

he was still supporting, nodded ever so slightly. He reached down and cupped her legs—gritting his teeth against her gasp of pain—and lifted her to his chest. "Easy, now. The worst is over," he said softly, brushing his lips against her cold, tear-dampened cheek.

Careful not to fall into the sled, he slowly turned around, raised her up, and gently set her beside the hole. He slid his arms out from under her, making sure her body was completely supported by the snow.

"Tigger," she whispered, sucking in deep breaths.

"You first," he hissed, having to shove Max away when the whining dog started licking her face.

"Not breathing," Camry said, weakly giving Luke a push. "Please . . . help Tig."

He glanced over his shoulder at the dachshund's limp body. Dammit! "I think . . . I'm sorry, I think she's dead," he said, turning back to carefully unzip Camry's ski pants leg.

"P-please, Luke," she sobbed.

He spun around with a muttered curse, stepped across the hole, and leaned down to put his ear against Tigger's side. He thought he heard a faint heartbeat, and moved his face to her snout, trying to find signs of breathing.

"Help her," Camry whispered.

Luke slid two fingers under Tigger's sweater, over her ribs, then used his other hand to lift the dachshund's nose so he could close his mouth over it. He gently blew, feeling the dog's chest rise, then blew several more times. Tigger suddenly stirred, giving a weak whimper, and Luke picked up the dog.

"Come on, baby," he whispered, turning to show Camry. "Thatta girl. Keep breathing." He set Tigger on the snow in the crook of her arm, then took her hand to stop her from trying to pull the dog onto her chest. "Don't try to pick her up. Just let her lie beside you. She's breathing. Just keep her tucked against you."

He brushed back Camry's hair and leaned closer. "Anything else hurt besides your right leg? Your ribs? Your back?" he asked, unzipping her jacket. He stopped and blew on his hands to warm his freezing fingers, then slowly pulled her sweater up and worked the hem of her turtleneck out of her pants so he could feel her belly. "Focus on *yourself,* Camry," he growled when he glanced up to find her straining to see Tigger. He touched her chin to make her look at him, then forced a smile to soften his demand. "I'm worried about internal bleeding. Do you remember anything jabbing you as you tumbled? Or did your head hit anything?" he asked, studying her pupils, which, thank God, appeared even.

"I-I'm okay. B-but my foot is throbbing."

He forced his smile wider, brushing his shaking hand over her forehead again. "You picked a hell of a way to get out of your turn to pull the sled."

Her gaze roamed his face, and she touched his cheek. "You're bleeding."

He also touched his cheek, then smiled at her again. "I've known you what . . . two weeks? And I've been beaten up twice. You should come with a warning label."

"I'm sorry."

He kissed her trembling lips. "I'm not," he whispered. He straightened, then turned toward her legs. "Okay. Time to assess the damage."

Max suddenly came bounding over, dragging one of the snowshoes. "Good boy, Max!" Luke said, quickly grabbing it when the dog nearly swung the three-foot-long snowshoe into Camry. "You found my boot! Go on," he said. "Find more stuff, Max."

Tigger whined and started squirming. Luke caught the dachshund just as she started slipping into the hole he was standing in. "Looks like you're recovering okay," he said, setting the dog on her feet and holding her steady. He let her go as soon as he saw her tail wag, then shot Camry a glare. "You tell anyone I gave mouth-to-mouth resuscitation to a dog, and I'm going to post the cell phone picture I took of you in your wench's costume on the Web."

Before she could answer him, he moved back to finish unzipping the right leg of her ski pants. "I don't see any bones sticking out," he said with false joy—because he sure as hell saw that her foot was twisted at an unnatural angle.

He pulled out his multitool and opened the blade, then bobbed his eyebrows at her. "I've always fantasized about playing doctor on a beautiful woman." He looked back down at her leg. "I need to slit your inner pants and long johns from the knee down, to see what's happening in there." He bobbed his eyebrows again. "Assuming I can see anything, since you haven't shaved your legs in what . . . days?"

"Just *do* it," she growled, stiffening. "And tell me if it's broken or just sprained."

Oh, he knew it was broken, all right; he just didn't know how badly. He pulled her wool pants and long johns away from her leg and slit them open with his knife, exposing angry red skin swelling up from under her wool sock.

"Yup, it's broken," he muttered, carefully cutting the sock down to her boot. He stilled when she sucked in a hiss, and looked at her. "I can't tell if it's your lower leg or your ankle. I have to take off your boot, Camry. I'll do it as gently as I can."

"Leave it on."

"No. Your foot's swelling, and it's only going to get worse."

She closed her eyes. "Then do it."

Luke carefully sliced her laces, then set down the knife in order to peel open her boot, wincing when she hissed again. "Easy now," he crooned, lifting back the tongue of her boot. He slid one hand under her ankle, then grabbed the heel of the boot and slowly pulled.

"No, stop!"

He stilled, turning to see her take several gulping breaths before she gritted her teeth. "Okay. Do it."

He held his own breath as he started pulling again, working as quickly as he could so he wouldn't prolong her agony while being careful he didn't do any more damage. The boot finally slipped free, taking her sock with it, and Luke closed his eyes. "I think your ankle is shattered," he whispered. He looked over at her. "No blood, though. So I'll just immobilize it as best I can. Then I'm digging out the sled, and we'll get you to a hospital lickety-split. Where's the closest house to here?"

She thought for a moment. "If we go down the

tote road about ten miles, then cut across the bay, I think there are some year-round homes out on the point."

Luke's gut tightened. "Do you think the bay is frozen solid?"

"I-it should be."

He glanced down at her ankle then back at her, and shook his head. "It's not a life-threatening injury, Camry, as long as you don't go into shock. So I'd rather not risk our drowning to save some miles. How far to your sister's house? Doesn't she live on this side of the bay?"

"Maybe eighteen or twenty miles from here."

Luke gently laid her foot on the open leg of her ski pants and turned in the hole he'd been standing in the whole time. "If I can find the other snowshoe, I can get us there by midnight." He got down on his knees and started rummaging around in the sled. He pulled out the sleeping bag and straw mattress, but didn't see the rest of their gear. "The gear must have broken free," he said, straightening with the sleeping bag, which he unrolled and laid over her. "I'll try to find it. I'd like to at least have the headlamp for when it gets dark, and the first-aid kit."

"How did you know where to dig for me?" she asked, helping him tuck the bag around her.

He grabbed the small mattress and tucked the

corner of it under her shoulders. But before he lowered her head, he kissed her gently on the lips with a soft chuckle. "That damn transmitter started beeping, and Max and I followed the sound."

She blinked up at him. "I don't have the transmitter," she whispered. "I-I threw it out onto the lake this morning, when I decided to . . . to see things your way," she said.

"You threw it away? But I heard it. Max heard it, too. It's how we found you!"

"That's impossible, Luke." She reached under the sleeping bag. "I don't have it anymore." She suddenly gasped, and her hand reappeared holding the transmitter. "Oh my God," she whispered, holding it toward him. "H-how is that possible?"

Luke damn near started laughing hysterically when the tiny instrument suddenly gave a lively chirp. He took the transmitter from her and studied it. "This thing keeps turning up like a bad penny." He looked at her. "It shouldn't even have its own power source, so what in hell keeps making that noise?"

She turned her head away. "I have no idea."

He gently turned her face to look at him. "Don't try to live by my beliefs, Camry, at the expense of your own," he softly told her. "I was wrong to pretend to go along with you and AuClair instead of telling you I thought it was all an act." He held the transmitter up for her to see. "But this *infernal thing*," he said with a crooked smile, "seems determined to make me believe." He shoved it in his pocket, kissed her again, then climbed out of the hole.

He freed his boot from the snowshoe Max had found, sat down and put it on, then crawled over and lifted the edge of the sleeping bag off her right foot. "It's still swelling," he said, carefully covering her foot again. "I'm going to hunt for our gear before I immobilize it. I'd like to find the first-aid kit, because I tossed what was left of our pain pills in it. Are you comfortable enough?"

"I'm okay. Where's Tigger?"

"She seems to be fully recovered, and is nosing the snow with Max. I'm giving myself twenty minutes to search, and then we're out of here, gear or no gear. Just close your eyes and rest. I'm afraid you might be in for a painful afternoon."

"I'm sorry. I wish I could help you."

He chuckled. "If you want to help, then picture our snowcat magically appearing while I go to work on my own miracle."

Chapter Twenty

*A*s "seemingly impossible tasks" went, Luke decided this one was a doozy. Getting back to civilization had appeared daunting enough when they'd both been hale and hearty, but getting Camry out of these woods with a broken ankle—without killing her in the process—might very well prove impossible.

Unless . . .

Luke shoved his hand in his pocket and touched the transmitter. How in hell did the damn thing keep turning up just when they needed it? He believed Camry when she said she'd thrown it away this morning—just as he had the other day, when he'd smashed it into that tree and watched it shatter into a hundred pieces. Yet here it was again, and they'd *both* heard it chirping just now.

Max had heard it, too. And dogs didn't know anything about miracles, did they?

Luke walked toward a dark spot in the snow and thought about Maxine's determination to rescue both Kate and him at the expense of his own life. If the fact was that Maxine had shown up at the pound just hours before they'd taken Kate over to pick out a dog, or that a five-year-old had seen something in the mangy old mutt that none of the adults had, was that the beginning of a miracle, or merely a string of sequential coincidences?

But then, did it matter *what* it was, as long as everything had turned out okay?

Well, except for Maxine.

Luke stopped suddenly and stared down at what looked like Roger AuClair's large pointed hat lying in the snow. Where in hell had that come from? Had it been in the sled all this time, and he just hadn't noticed? If Camry had found it, she certainly wouldn't have shown it to him, now, would she? Not after learning what he thought of AuClair's hocus-pocus.

Which she wholeheartedly embraced.

Maybe the question he should be asking was, If the magic really *did* rule science, could it be manipulated?

Even by a nonbeliever who was just desperate enough to try?

Luke looked around and saw Max and Tigger digging in the snow several yards away, apparently having discovered something worth salvaging. He looked at Camry and saw her lying quietly, her arm over her face to shield out the sun.

"How are you doing over there?" he called to her.

"I'm fine," she called back, not moving, "as long as I don't move."

Luke dropped his gaze to the hat, took a deep breath, and picked it up.

Something fell out of it. He bent over again, and picked up what appeared to be the card Roger had left for him. He opened it, scanned what Camry had already read to him, then continued from where she'd left off.

If you're harboring any dark thoughts that I had anything to do with the predicament you're in, Renoir, then think again. Free will dictates circumstances, not the magic. Life is a fragile gift, and if you can't embrace it all—the good, the bad, and the ugly—then you might as well stop breathing, since this is an all or nothing thing.

So the answer to your question is yes; just like your numbers, the magic can be manipulated. I was telling it straight the other day, when I told Camry that everyone has the power within them to create.

That is, assuming it's a creation of the heart.

The only brick walls people run into are of their own making. Take this particular brick wall, for instance, that you are right now trying to figure a way around. If I might be so bold as to suggest . . . why don't you take your own advice that you gave Camry, and simply go through it? You have the power to do that by merely turning off your analytical brain long enough to hear what your heart is telling you. I believe you'll find that when you do, what you consider obstacles might actually work to your advantage.

If you need more time, then stop the clock. And if you want to ease Camry's pain, then find a way. It's a simple matter of deciding what you need to happen, then acting as if it already has.

Miracles are really more about perception than actual fact. If all you see are obstacles, you'll be taking two steps back for every step forward; but if you can see the magic in them, you'll realize those obstacles might be blessings in disguise.

So the choice is yours, Renoir. Your logic can take you only so far, and if you want to get Camry home, you're going to have to rely on what your heart tells you to do. Just think back thirteen years, Luke, and ask yourself if you haven't already experienced what it is to create a miracle.

I'm afraid there's one other decision you're going to have to make before this is over, however, which will require a true leap of faith. But I'm hoping that by the time you have to make it, it will be a no-brainer—no pun intended, Doctor.

You see, Camry has an aunt who can heal her in a rather . . . well, let's call it an unconventional way, shall we? Libby MacBain will be at Gù Brath celebrating the solstice with everyone, so you might want to consider heading directly there, rather than wasting precious time trying to get Camry to a hospital and risk her never walking properly again.

"Goddammit, AuClair," Luke growled, glaring down at the card. "You almost had me up to this point, you old bastard. An aunt who can magically heal her ankle," he muttered, wiping a hand over his face.

"Did you find the first-aid kit, Luke?" Camry called to him. "One of those pills would be nice right about now."

Christ, what was he doing, reading some crazy old man's rantings! He crumpled the card and tossed it in the snow, along with Roger's stupid hat. "I think Max and Tigger have dug something up," he called out, running to the dogs. "What have you two found?" he asked, using his anger at himself to sound excited for them.

He edged Tigger out of the way, reached down into the shallow hole, and gave a tug on the material they'd unearthed. "Camry, they found our bag of gear!" He scrambled to his feet. "Okay, guys," he said, slapping his leg. "Come on. Now let's go find my other snowshoe!"

He walked over and knelt beside Camry, then picked up the snowshoe Max had found earlier and held it out to the dogs, letting them sniff it. "See this? Find the other snowshoe, and I'll make you each a whole pot of soup tonight."

They cocked their heads back and forth, listening to him, then both suddenly shot off in opposite directions. Luke smiled down at Camry. "If they come back with that snowshoe, I'm going to have to stop calling them simple beasts." He opened the bag and dug through their gear to find the first-aid kit. "Have you figured out yet if you're hurt anywhere else?" he asked, opening the kit and scanning the contents. He grew alarmed when she didn't answer. "What else hurts?"

"I think I may have cracked some ribs," she whispered, her eyes filled with pain. "I can breathe okay, so my lung isn't punctured or anything. But what if riding in the sled finishes breaking one of my ribs?"

Luke closed his eyes.

She touched his arm. "Maybe you should go for help alone. You can move me to the trees, build a fire, and the dogs can stay with me. You'll make better time if you don't have to tow me in the sled. Then Life Flight can fly me out."

"I'm not leaving you. If something were to happen to me, nobody knows you're out here."

"Daddy knows. We stole his groomer, remember?"

"But it might be days before he starts looking for us." He shook his head. "I'm not leaving you," he repeated. "We make it out together or we die trying—*together*."

He returned to scanning the kit, then pulled out the pills. "These should help," he said, opening the bottle. He pulled out one of the bottles of water they'd melted this morning, popped a pill in her mouth, then held her head for her to drink. "Okay, I'm going to dig out the sled while we give that pill time to kick in."

"Luke," she said, grabbing his sleeve when he started to stand up. "What were you doing a few minutes ago, when you were just standing up there? It looked as if you were reading something."

"I found AuClair's card, and was reading from where you'd left off."

"Anything interesting?" she asked, her eyes searching his.

He stood up. "Not really. Just more philosophical bunk about how I can make a miracle happen just by deciding I want one." He shrugged. "He even said I have the power to stop time, if I just put my mind to it. No, not my mind," he muttered, sliding into the hole beside her. He gave a forced smile. "He said I had to turn off my analytical brain, and think with my heart. Close your eyes, Camry," he said, not wanting to deal with the hopefulness he saw shining in them. "Relax and let that pill work."

With a muttered curse at the wounded look she gave him before she turned her head and closed her eyes, Luke also turned away and went to work on the sled. It took him about ten minutes to dig it out, and another ten minutes to straighten a bent ski and make it snow worthy again. He'd just finished tying their gear to the back when Tigger came trotting over, the GPS in her mouth. Luke felt in his pocket, realizing it must have fallen out during the avalanche.

"Good girl, Tig!" he said, roughing up the hair on her head. "I take back every bad thing I've thought about you. You and your buddy Max are a hell of a lot smarter than many people I know." He kissed the top of her head. "And I'm going to buy you a whole wardrobe of pretty sweaters."

Apparently not wanting to be outdone, Max came trotting over dragging the other snowshoe. Luke sat back on his heels. The dogs had actually found everything he needed? He shook his head in disbelief, wondering how they seemed to know how desperate the situation was.

"Okay, you pooches. You've definitely earned your soup—as well as a couple of hero medals, which I am personally going to see that you get."

They suddenly took off again in search of more treasure. Luke turned to show Camry what they'd found, but she was asleep. Lifting the edge of the sleeping bag, he actually winced when he saw how swollen her ankle was.

"Camry, honey," he said softly, gentling shaking her shoulder. "I need you to be awake while I immobilize your foot, so I know if I'm doing anything wrong."

Her eyes dark with drugged confusion and pain, she nodded.

Luke moved back down her leg. But just as he lifted the sleeping bag again, the dogs came bounding back, each carrying something. Only instead of bringing their newest finds to him, they brought them to Camry.

Max dropped the large pointed hat on her chest, and Tigger dropped the crumpled card. Then both dogs lay down, Max resting his chin on her belly and Tigger curling up beside her shoulder.

Luke sighed. Was he ever going to get rid of

Roger AuClair? "Here's an idea," he said, folding the sleeping bag back to expose her ankle. "You can finish reading Roger's letter to me while I play doctor on you." He shot her a smile. "And why don't you put on his hat, and try to sound just like him."

Her eyes filled with tears, and her chin quivered. "D-don't humor me, Luke."

"No! I'm not humoring you, I'm trying to distract you. And myself. Here," he said, uncrumpling the card and handing it to her. "Okay, let's hear what other sage advice good old Roger has for me." He arched an eyebrow. "Maybe at the end of the note, he tells us where he stashed the snowcat."

Probably as much from her own curiosity as wishing to humor *him,* Camry hesitantly started reading out loud from where she'd left off yesterday morning. Using the laces he'd stolen from her other boot, and a pair of pants he'd taken from their gear, Luke carefully started to wrap her ankle.

He paused when she stopped reading with a hiss of pain. "Sorry. I'm trying to be gentle. Go on, keep reading."

"But Roger said there's a chance I might never walk properly again," she whispered, her chin quivering again. "Luke, you have to do what he says, and take me straight to my aunt Libby. She's really a highly skilled trauma surgeon, but she also has a gift for healing people by only touching them."

"You won't just be walking properly, you'll be running a marathon by this summer," he said, giving her arm a squeeze. "Keep going. You've reached the part where I stopped reading."

Her eyes searched his, looking for . . . hell, for some sign he believed her, Luke figured. He went back to work on her foot, wrapping several layers of the heavy pant material around her leg, from her knee to down past her heel. He then gently tied it in place, careful not to make it too tight around the swelling.

He heard her take a shuddering breath; then she started reading again.

I warned you this was going to seem impossible, Renoir. But making a miracle is actually the easy part, whereas living with the realization that you really are in control of your own destiny is what's truly daunting.

So I wish you the best of luck, young man—not only on your immediate journey, but on your life's journey as well. Now don't you go feeling bad that I left before you got to thank me for all I've done for you; we'll be meeting again one day, so you'll get your chance. Godspeed, Renoir. Your faithful servant, Roger de Keage.

Luke snorted. "If we meet again, I'll likely wring his neck."

"My God," she whispered. "He's the father of the clan MacKeage."

"The father of practical jokes, you mean," he muttered.

"Um . . . there's a P.S."

Luke snorted again. "The old bastard does love to pontificate."

She dropped her worried gaze back to the card. "*P.S.*," she read. "*You're down to six hours and forty-four minutes, Renoir, so you might want to get cracking on making that miracle.*"

Chapter Twenty-one

Four hours later, Luke was worried that instead of saving Camry's life, he very well might be killing her. For the third time in half an hour, he dropped to his knees beside the sled, utterly exhausted from the grueling pace he'd set, and peeled back the tarp. Tigger blinked up at him from inside Camry's jacket with a mournful whine, then gently lapped her pale cheek before looking at Luke again.

"I know, Tig," he said between ragged breaths as he took off his gloves. He reached in and touched Camry's neck, feeling her faint pulse, which had grown steadily fainter in the last four hours. "I'm worried about her, too.

You're doing a good job of keeping her warm," he crooned, sliding his hand under the jacket to make sure the dog's weight was still on the mattress, and not putting pressure on Camry's ribs. He rubbed Tigger's ear. "Let's hope it's the extra pill I gave her that's making her sleep, and not shock."

He wrapped his arm around Max when the dog came over and nosed Camry, also whining worriedly. "Okay, gang, we need to come up with a new game plan," he whispered, his hand trembling as he patted Max. "Because this one isn't working."

Max drove his nose inside the sled beside Camry's body, then lifted his head with Roger's pointed hat in his mouth and dropped the hat on her face. When Luke quickly snatched it off, Max nosed Camry's hair with a whine.

"Okay, if it will make you feel better, I'll put it on her," Luke said, carefully replacing the wool hat she was wearing with the heavy velvet pointed one.

Camry stirred, and two faint flags of color appeared on her cheeks.

Luke touched his finger to her pulse again and found it much stronger. "Whoa," he whispered on an indrawn breath. "That certainly helped." He glanced at Max, then at Tigger. "Any other suggestions? Because at this point I'm open to anything, no matter how harebrained it might sound."

Max suddenly took off down the road, then just as suddenly veered into the woods. He stopped, looked back at Luke, and started barking.

Luke stood up, groaning when his muscles protested, and closed the tarp back over the sled. "Come on, Tig. Let's go see where Max thinks he's going," he muttered, hooking the rope back over his shoulders and starting off down the road.

But he suddenly picked up his pace with renewed hope. Maybe Max smelled a wood fire or something else that meant that help was close by.

When he reached the spot where the Lab had gone into the woods, Luke found what looked like a game trail. Max was standing about twenty yards in, facing him, his tail wagging. He barked again, then took off deeper into the woods.

Luke glanced down the road—the certain path to civilization—then back toward where Max had disappeared, trying to see through the trees. The sun had dropped below the horizon already, even though it wasn't even four o'clock. Today was the shortest day of the year, and Luke knew that he was facing the longest night of the year. But even in what little light that was left, he could see that the lake was about a hundred yards from where he was standing.

Out of sight now, Max started barking excitedly.

Luke looked back down the road. He didn't want to expend his energy on a wild-goose chase, but he didn't want to walk right past help, either.

Tigger suddenly jumped out of the sled and started lunging through the deep snow right past him, following Max's path.

"I guess that settles that," he muttered, stepping back to check on Camry. When he saw she was looking far less pale than she had been, he turned and started following the dogs. The trail emerged onto the shoreline, and Luke stopped beside Max and Tigger, who were looking out at the lake, their wagging tails brushing the snow.

Luke pulled his GPS out of his pocket, called up the screen that told him exactly where he was, and realized that he was still sixteen miles from Winter's house by way of the tote road. A chill ran down his spine as he recalled Roger's note; it appeared he *had* been taking two steps back for each step forward.

They had traveled only two miles in four hours.

Which meant that at the rate he was

walking—which was only going to get slower the more tired he grew—it was going to take him days to get them out of these woods. He zoomed out the map on the screen and saw that if he cut diagonally down the lake, Pine Creek was less than six miles away.

Of flat going.

With a full moon to light the way.

And possibly thin ice that he wouldn't be able to see.

Did he have the right to risk drowning Camry . . . to save her foot?

But it wasn't really her ankle that worried him; he was afraid she was going into shock. And though he didn't know much about medicine— emergency or otherwise—he was pretty sure shock was fatal if not treated in time.

He stepped to the sled and peeled back the tarp, plopped down in the snow and took off his glove, then reached in and wrapped his fingers around Camry's hand. He looked back out at the expanse of lake in front of him. Could he really shut down his brain long enough to follow his heart?

Just like he had thirteen years ago, when he'd found Kate and Maxine?

He hadn't stopped long enough to weigh the odds of his saving Kate versus their drowning.

Hell, he hadn't been thinking at all; he'd just acted on instinct. Nothing had mattered except getting her away from that river, and if they'd both drowned, well . . . he would have died knowing she hadn't died alone.

But by some miracle, neither of them had.

Was that what Roger had meant in his note, when he'd written that Luke had already experienced creating a miracle when he'd needed it?

Because honest to God, from when he'd found Kate's and Maxine's tracks under that tree to when he'd gone out onto the ice sheet after them, it had felt like time had actually stopped. He'd reached the river in what had seemed like only seconds, even though it had been over a mile away, then taken off his snowshoes, gone out to her, and flung her to safety with absolutely no sense of urgency. His actions hadn't been rushed or even in slow motion; time had truly ceased to exist.

So why in hell was he so determined to deny that miracles existed?

Because if they did exist, it would mean there really was some unknown factor ruling his beloved science, something that he couldn't quantify . . . or control.

And God knows he'd spent his entire pre-adult life feeling out of control—from his accidental conception and arrival into the world, to his being raised by three women determined to mother him, to his mother's marriage to a man who had been equally determined to father him. Even getting a baby sister he hadn't asked for.

So maybe the real miracle on that river had absolutely nothing to do with Kate, but rather with the fact that, for the first time in his life, he'd stopped being self-centered long enough to uncompromisingly, unpretentiously, and unconditionally love someone other than himself.

A condition that had lasted all of four weeks, until he'd returned to school and fallen right back into his old habit of putting himself first. And he'd tenaciously clung to his self-centeredness all through his career, not collaborating with anyone unless it served him more than it served the greater good, and even going so far as to steal someone else's work when he'd lost control of his own.

Christ, he deserved to die out here.

But Camry sure as hell didn't—because she loved him *exactly the way he was*.

And he sure as hell loved her more than he loved himself.

So maybe it *was* time he listened to his heart.

Luke looked at his watch and saw it was four o'clock. He lifted Camry's hand and kissed the stone ring on her finger, then tucked it back under the sleeping bag, got to his knees, and kissed her warm forehead.

"Okay, sleeping beauty," he whispered. "It's time for me to make some magic." He snuggled Roger's hat farther down on her head. "Too bad you're going to sleep right through the miracle I'm about to create."

He stood up, picked up Tigger, and tucked her back inside Camry's jacket. Then, after removing the bag of gear from the back of the sled and tossing it in the snow, he patted his leg. "Come on, Max. You're riding, too." He set the Lab in the sled, making sure the dog didn't crowd Camry and Tigger. "Santa Claus is arriving at Gù Brath on the solstice this year, and I'm the reindeer who's going to make this sled fly. So hang on tight, everyone," he finished with a laugh, closing the tarp and securing it to the side.

He stepped to the front of the sled, settled the rope over his shoulders, then reached into his pockets for his gloves. After putting them on, he pulled the GPS out of one pocket and the transmitter out of the other.

Luke tossed the GPS in the snow next to their gear, then held up the transmitter. "Okay, Rudolph, you guide my sleigh to Camry's house, because her mother's expecting her daughter to blow out thirty-two candles in a two hours and fifteen minutes."

The infernal thing gave a lively chirp.

Luke tucked it in his pocket with a laugh, then stepped out onto the lake. He took another step, and then another, keeping pace with the soft chirps coming from his pocket.

Chapter Twenty-two

So deep was Luke in the zone of putting one foot in front of the other that it took him a moment to realize that something was interfering with his hearing the steady chirp of the transmitter. He looked up from the moonlit snow in front of him and stopped dead in his tracks.

Max started yipping, and Luke shrugged off the rope and went back and opened the tarp. The Lab immediately jumped out and ran toward the bright lights of town, barking frantically. Luke peered in to see that Camry was still sleeping, her relaxed face rosy pink as Tigger's wagging tail made her jacket move. He petted the dachshund. "You did good, girl. You've kept her toasty warm. Hang on, we're almost there."

Luke closed the tarp and started after Max, soon walking up over the shoreline, past the shops, and directly onto Main Street. He then held up his hand to stop the pickup slowing down to let him cross.

But instead of crossing the road, he walked to the driver's window. "I need a ride to TarStone Mountain Ski Resort," he said when the driver rolled down his window. He gestured toward the sled. "My wife is injured. Could you please give us a lift?"

The man put the truck in park and got out, only nearly to trip over Luke's snowshoes. "Sure," he said, going to the sled and pushing Max out of the way to fold back the tarp. He suddenly reared upright. "Hell, that's Camry MacKeage," he said, spinning back toward Luke. "You say she's your *wife*?"

Luke tossed his snowshoes into the bed of the truck and walked over and pulled the tarp completely off. "You got a problem with that?" he asked, lifting Tigger out of her jacket and shoving the dog into the man's arms.

The man grinned. "No, sir. But I certainly do wish you luck." He nodded toward the sled. "Camry wrenched my brother's knee during a brawl at my bar about six months ago." After shifting Tigger to one arm, he held out his hand. "Pete Johnson."

Luke shook his hand. "Luke Renoir. So, Pete, does that mean you're not going to give us a lift?"

"Oh, jeez, no," he said with a laugh. "My brother deserved both the wrenched knee and the scathing lecture I gave him once he sobered up. Come on," he said, opening the back door of the crew cab to set Tigger inside. He motioned for Max to jump in, then walked back to the sled. "Jeez, she must be hurt bad if she's not waking up," he said, just as Luke straightened with Camry in his arms. "Hold your damn horses!" he shouted at the car behind them when the driver honked his horn. He rushed around to open the passenger's-side door. "What's the matter with her?"

"She has a broken ankle and maybe a couple of cracked ribs," Luke told him, gently setting Camry on the seat and sliding her to the middle. He crawled in beside her, then tucked her under his arm and laid her bundled right leg over his own. "Could you just pull the sled to the sidewalk? I'll come back and pick it up later."

Pete closed the door, ran to the sled, picked it up, and tossed it in the bed of his truck, then climbed in behind the wheel. "If she's got a broken ankle, I better drive you to the hospital in Greenville," he said, putting the truck in gear.

"No, I need to get her home before she goes into total shock. She has an aunt there who's a trauma specialist, who can help her while we call for an ambulance."

"Libby MacBain," Pete said. "I know her, and yeah, that's probably a good idea. Doc Libby's kept more than one person alive while waiting for an ambulance." He glanced over at Luke, then back at the road. "What happened? Was it a snowmobile accident or something? You look like you've been walking awhile."

"Avalanche," Luke said, setting his finger over Camry's pulse, sighing in relief when he felt it beating steady and strong.

"An avalanche? That's rare in these parts. Where'd it happen?"

"Just south of Springy Mountain."

Pete glanced over at him in surprise. "You hauled her all the way here in that makeshift sled? Down the *lake*?" He looked back at the road, shaking his head. "You either got more balls than brains, or one hell of a guardian angel." He glanced at Luke again. "The lake ain't frozen over in places, you know."

"Apparently the last six miles of it are."

Pete turned onto the TarStone Mountain Ski Resort road. "What's up with the funny hat?" he asked.

Luke settled it farther down on Camry's head. "It's a birthday gift from a relative."

"Oh yeah, that's right. Today's the MacKeage girls' birthday." He snorted. "Hell of a way for a woman to spend her birthday." He glanced at Luke again. "Talk in town when Camry was here last summer was that she didn't even have a boyfriend. How long you two been married?"

"A couple of days."

Pete chuckled humorlessly. "Hell of a way to spend a honeymoon, too. But I suppose honeymooning in the mountains in the middle of the winter, instead of on some warm beach in the Caribbean, ain't all that far-fetched for Camry." He turned off the road just as the resort came into sight, and pulled up into the driveway of Gù Brath. He stopped in front of the bridge leading to the front door, then shut off the truck with a sigh as he looked directly at Luke. "The MacKeages are pillars of the community, but they're . . . um . . . a bit on the strange side. They're a tight-knit clan, along with the MacBains." He opened his door, then shot Luke a grin. "I had a thing for Cam's older sister Heather when we were in high school, but her daddy scared the bejeezus out of me so bad, I never dared to ask her out. You need help getting Cam inside?" he asked, glancing at the well-lit house.

"No, I've got her," Luke said, opening his door. "If you can just bring the dogs."

"I'll let them out, and they can follow you in." He glanced at the house again, and Luke would have sworn the man shivered. "I got to get down to my bar. We open at five, and the staff is waiting for me."

Luke stilled just as he was getting ready to get out, and lifted his wrist.

Holy hell, his watch said four fifteen!

A vehicle pulled up behind them, doors opened and closed, and a man and woman walked up to Luke's side of the truck and peered in his open door.

"Oh my God, Camry!" gasped the woman holding the young toddler. "Robbie, take her. She's hurt."

"No, I've got her," Luke said, carefully sliding out of the truck with Camry in his arms, then shouldering past the tall man. "Thanks for your help, Pete," he called out as he strode onto the bridge. "I'll catch up with you later."

The man named Robbie rushed ahead and opened the door.

"Could you make sure the dogs come in?" Luke asked, stepping inside the foyer, the sounds of voices and playing children assaulting his senses. He stopped and looked around, blinking against the blast of hot air that made his eyes water, and even stepped back when several people rushed up to him.

"Camry!" someone cried. "Mom! Dad! Camry's here, and she's hurt!"

Another man stepped forward and reached out to take her, but Luke took another step back. "No, I've got her. Is her aunt Libby here?"

"Libby's my mother," Robbie said from behind him, placing a hand on Luke's back and guiding him toward the living room. "She should be here soon. Why don't you lay Cam down on the couch?"

Luke walked into the living room, but instead of laying her down, he sat with Camry in his arms, then carefully stretched her right leg out on the couch beside him.

"What's wrong with her?" asked one of the women.

"She has a broken ankle and maybe some cracked ribs." Luke unzipped her jacket, but quickly reached out when the woman tried to take off Camry's hat. "No, that stays on until Libby MacBain gets here."

The sea of people crowding around them suddenly parted. "Camry!" Grace cried, dropping to her knees in front of Luke. She touched Camry's cheek, then looked up and smiled at Luke, her eyes shining with tears. "You brought her home," she whispered, reaching up and touching his beard. "Th-thank you."

Greylen MacKeage edged past his wife and reached out as if he intended to take Camry into his arms. Luke pulled her against him. "No, I've got her."

"She's hurt," Greylen growled.

"Leave her, Grey," Grace said gently, caressing Camry's cheek again. "She's in very good hands, and she's going to be okay."

"What happened?" Grey asked, kneeling beside his wife and touching Camry's cheek himself. He glared at Luke. "Did ye crash the snowcat? Why won't she wake up? Does she have a concussion?" he asked, reaching to remove her hat.

Luke held it in place. "It stays on until her aunt gets here," he repeated. "And we got caught in a small avalanche, and her ankle is shattered. Libby MacBain will heal her," he said, somewhat defiantly.

Greylen snapped his gaze to Luke in surprise. "Ye know," he whispered.

"I know," Luke said with a nod. "And just so *you* know, she's my wife."

"I don't remember giving my permission, Renoir."

Luke grinned tightly. "A distant relative of yours gave it for you."

Greylen arched one brow. "And just who would that be?"

"Roger AuClair."

He frowned. "I don't know anyone named Roger AuClair."

"No? Then how about Roger de Keage?"

Greylen reared back, his sharp green eyes narrowing. "Ye met de Keage?"

Luke nodded toward Camry. "That's his hat." He grinned again. "And he thanks you for the snowcat he said you would want him to have."

"Aunt Libby's here," someone said.

The people who'd crowded around them again moved out of the way, and a slender woman in her sixties leaned over Grace's shoulder to touch Camry's forehead.

She stood silently for several seconds, then lifted her eyes to Luke and smiled. "You got her here just in time. Robbie," she said, motioning him over, "carry her up to her room for me, would you?"

"No, I've got her," Luke said, leaning forward to stand up.

"Let Robbie take her," Greylen ordered. "Ye look like you can barely walk."

"*I've got her,*" Luke growled, levering himself

off the couch to his feet. He fell into step behind Grace, who led the way through the sea of people to the stairs.

"Ye drop her, Renoir, and ye better hope you break your own neck in the fall," Greylen said, walking beside him.

"Oh, quit posturing, Grey," Grace said with a laugh, turning to loop her arm through her husband's and pulling him up beside her. "She's not your daughter anymore, she's Luke's wife."

"It wasn't a legal marriage," Grey muttered.

"No? Then would you care to lay odds that when we check at the courthouse tomorrow morning, we won't find their license duly registered?" she asked.

"Pendaär is supposed to marry our girls."

Grace laughed again. "I'm sure Daar will defer to Roger de Keage."

If Luke hadn't been seconds away from falling to his knees, he was sure he'd have found their conversation intriguing. But he was so exhausted, he just wanted to see Camry open her eyes and smile at him so he could fall into a coma for a week. They reached the balcony, and he followed Grace and Greylen down the hall as Libby MacBain walked beside him. She reached out and quietly took hold of his elbow, and in less than three steps his exhaustion vanished and he suddenly felt like he could run a marathon.

He stopped and looked down at her.

"You have amazing endurance, Luke," she said, smiling up at him. "And a powerfully strong and rather *loud* heart."

"Yeah," he said, feeling a bit drunk from the sudden surge of energy coursing through him. "And every so often, I can actually *hear* it."

Chapter Twenty-three

"Can you ever forgive me?" Cam whispered against her father's chest, snuggled up in his arms on her bed.

Her mother, lying with her arms around both of them, squeezed her tightly. "We forgave you one second after Luke told us."

Her father's arms also tightened, and his lips brushed her hair. "Actually, we forgave you before we even knew, daughter, because we love you." He ducked his head to see her face. "You are supposed to come to us when you're having a crisis."

Cam sighed, closing her eyes with a smile, and snuggled deeper into his embrace to prepare for the coming lecture.

"But even though you should have," her mother rushed to say, apparently hoping to way-lay her husband's scolding, "it soon became obvi-ous to your father and me that Luke would be able to help you better than we could."

"It did?" her papa muttered.

"Yes," Grace said. "That's why instead of going to Go Back Cove to get you himself, your father thought it would be better to send Luke."

"I did?" He sighed, smoothing down Cam's hair. "I am such a wise man."

"So, oh wise father," Cam said with a giggle, "did you know you were sending my future hus-band to fetch me, or were you just hoping that by waving him in front of my nose, I would fall madly in love because he's big and strong and handsome and smart . . . just like you?"

His arms around her tightened. "Your falling in love with him was your mother's idea. Whereas I was perfectly content for you to remain a spinster your whole life."

Cam snorted, then turned her head to look at her mom. "I . . . we couldn't find Podly's data bank. I'm afraid it might be gone for good."

Grace patted her arm and sat up. "Maybe. But you and Luke don't really need it, do you?" she asked, getting off the bed and turning back with a smile. "With your combined brainpower, I'm sure you'll duplicate my work in no time, once you lock yourselves in my lab."

Cam also tried to sit up, but she seemed to be stuck in her father's embrace. She patted his chest and grinned up at him. "I'm not going far," she whispered.

When he reluctantly opened his arms, she jumped off the bed, then turned back to him. "Except that I do have to take a quick trip to British Columbia, to meet Luke's parents and sister. But we'll be back right after Christmas."

"I'm afraid that if you're going to British Columbia, you're going to miss them," Grace said. "Because they're here."

"They're *here*? But how did you know to invite them?"

Grace walked to the bathroom door and waved her over. "Come on, you need a bath. The party starts in less than an hour. And to answer your question, it seems Luke's mom got a card in the mail, inviting them all to Gù Brath for Christmas." Her eyes shone with amusement. "When his mother called to question me about the invitation, she mentioned the card had a beautiful angel on the front, and was signed by a flourished *F.*"

"Oh my God," Cam said, covering her mouth with her hands. "She sent Luke's family a card, too?"

"Would ye happen to know who F is?" her father asked, getting off the bed.

Cam looked from one parent to the other. "Um . . . it's Fiona."

Grey arched a brow. "*Our* Fiona?"

Cam sighed. "It's a long story, Papa. I'll tell you about my rather interesting last couple of weeks tomorrow, okay? I'm just dying to sink into a tub of hot water." She looked at her mother. "Where's Luke's family now?"

Grace started filling the tub, pouring a liberal amount of lilac-scented bath beads into the cascading water. "I imagine Kate pounced on Luke the moment he stepped out of his own shower. That girl is positively enchanting." She pulled Camry into her arms and kissed her on the forehead. "Welcome home, daughter of mine. I've never missed you so much as I did when I realized you really were missing."

"But now I'm found," Cam whispered back, hugging her tightly. "Fiona and Luke and Roger AuClair helped me find myself." She leaned away. "And . . . and you, Mama. You were always right there in my heart, guiding me every step of the way."

Cam turned when her father walked into the bathroom, and threw herself at him. "And you, too, Papa," she cried. "I could almost hear you lecturing me, letting me know how much you love me."

He squeezed her so tight she squeaked. "Sorry. I'm afraid you'll get no more lectures from me. That's your husband's duty now."

Cam looked up. "But Luke's not very good at it, Papa. He actually tried once, and my ears didn't even come close to falling off. In fact, I fell asleep."

He hugged her to him with a laugh, then kissed the top of her head. "I will see what I can do to remedy that. Welcome home, my precious highlander."

Chapter Twenty-four

Luke sat in the huge dining room of Gù Brath, more than a little overwhelmed and utterly awed by the sheer magnitude of the festivities. The boisterous younger children—whom Luke had heard more than one person refer to as little heathens—had temporarily been relegated to the playroom downstairs, apparently to give the adults a few minutes of peace. But there still had to be forty people—sitting and standing around the table, which was thirty feet long if it was a foot, and crammed in among the balloons and streamers—and every damn one of them was wearing a birthday hat.

Except him.

And Tigger.

At Camry's somewhat threatening insistence, Luke was wearing *AuClair's* hat, and Tigger was wearing her own miniature version.

Kate's snickering wasn't at all helping his mood, nor were her repeated requests that he look at her; each time he complied she would then take his picture on her cell phone.

Luke figured several of them were already posted on the Internet.

While they waited for Winter, who seemed to be late for her own birthday party, Luke tried to concentrate on putting each sister's face to her name. He wasn't having much luck, though, considering he'd been introduced to all of them almost at once. As for their husbands and children . . . well, the only one he could place was Jack Stone.

But then, one usually does remember one's rescuer.

"Luke, let Max get up on your lap," Camry said, leaning close to be heard over the sounds of lively conversation. "His feelings are hurt because I'm holding Tigger."

Well, why the hell not? He already looked ridiculous in his hat, why not try to hold an overly excited fifty-pound dog on his lap, too?

He turned his chair slightly, bumped into

someone and apologized, then patted his chest. "Come on, Max. You sit quietly, and I'll share my piece of cake with you after they blow out the candles." Max jumped up, then immediately tried to crawl onto the table, apparently more interested in the gift sitting next to Camry's cake than he was in the cake. "No, boy. Sit," Luke commanded.

Max sat still for exactly six seconds, then made another lunge for the gift.

In his scramble to catch him, Luke's chair again bumped into the person behind him, and with a muttered curse, both Luke and Max fell to the floor—the gift clamped in Max's mouth.

Camry looked down, obviously trying not to laugh. "Are you having a bad day, Luke?" she asked, a snicker escaping.

"You don't know the half of it, since you slept through most of it," he said, standing up. He then tried to wrestle the gift out of Max's mouth, painfully aware that there was sudden silence, and that every eye in the room was on him. "Come on," he hissed under his breath, "give it up, Max."

The dog opened his jaws without any warning, releasing his treasure. Luke was so surprised that he bumped into his chair—which finally sent the long-suffering person behind him scrambling away—then fumbled to catch the gift that went soaring through the air toward the table.

It landed directly on top of Camry's birthday cake with a *splat,* sending tiny missiles of icing over anyone unlucky enough to be sitting nearby. Leaving the gift in the cake and Max on the floor, Luke straightened his pointy hat and sat down.

The gift suddenly gave a long, air-piercing, cake-shuddering *beep.*

Camry gasped so loud it had to have hurt.

Luke merely closed his eyes with a groan. Oh yeah, miracles notwithstanding, he was having a very bad day.

"Did you hear that?" Camry said, nudging him hard enough to leave a bruise.

"Half of Pine Creek heard it," he muttered, opening his eyes just in time to catch Tigger when she shoved the dog at him and stood up.

"Mama!" she shouted down the table—though he didn't know why, since the room was filled with absolute silence. "What's in my gift?"

Grace shrugged. "I have no idea." She gestured toward all the other gifts sitting beside each of her daughters' individual birthday cakes. "Your gift was delivered this afternoon by special messenger. There was a card, addressed to me, that said I could tuck my gift to you away for next year, because you would probably prefer this one instead."

"But who is it from?"

Grace shrugged again. "The card didn't say."

"And ye just brought it into the house without knowing what was inside?" Grey asked, standing up—as did Jack Stone, Robbie MacBain, and several other men, including Luke. Greylen walked down and snatched the gift out of the cake. "My God, woman, ye should know better than that."

"It's okay, Grey," Grace said, also standing up. "Because I have a pretty good idea what it is. The card also said that twenty years was a long time for a woman to wait for her dream to come true, but that he guessed patience was a motherhood thing." She gestured toward the gift. "And after what Camry told us earlier, I now also have a good idea who it's from. That's why I went and got it from the shed just five minutes ago, and set it on the table."

Camry gasped so hard again that she bumped into Luke—just before she snatched the gift out of her father's hand. "It's the data bank!" she cried, ripping open the dark green paper that was covered with what Luke just now realized were long strings of equations written in gold ink.

She tossed the paper on the table, popped open the box, and pulled out a black metal box the size of a six-pack of soda. She held it up for Luke to see, then turned and held it up to her mother. "It's Podly's data bank, isn't it, Mama?"

Grace collapsed down in her chair, her face as pale as a ghost, huge tears sliding down her cheeks as her smile outshone the three blazing chandeliers over the table. "Y-yes," she whispered.

Camry ran up to her, set the data bank in Grace's hands, and hugged her mother fiercely. "We have it, Mama. We have your key to ion propulsion."

"N-no," Grace said shakily, handing it back to her. "You have *your* key." She touched Camry's cheek. "You unlocked the secret to ion propulsion when you were twelve, one day when you were in the lab working on a school project. You came up and looked over my shoulder and suggested I transpose two integers in the equation I was working on. So that makes it your discovery, baby, not mine."

Camry reared back in surprise. "But why didn't you shout it to the world? Mom! We could be traveling to Mars by now!"

Grace looked at Luke, then at her husband, then down at the data bank in her daughter's hand. "I didn't want what came with shouting it to the world," she whispered. She looked up at Camry, her face flushing red. "I know it looks as if I've been unselfish to let you be the one to present our discovery, but it's actually the opposite. I didn't tell anyone because it would have meant leaving Gù Brath for days or maybe weeks at a time, to oversee its implementation." She looked over at Greylen, her eyes filling with fresh tears. "So I very selfishly kept silent, refusing to let the world intrude on my *true* dream, which was spending every day at home with a husband and family I love more than anything else in the universe."

She swiped the tears running down her cheeks with the backs of her hands, then cupped Camry's face. "But you, daughter . . . you have a husband who not only will travel with you, but who will also keep you grounded—as mine did," she finished strongly, looking at Greylen again, her smile tender.

Greylen strode back up the length of the table, edged Camry out of the way, and pulled Grace into his arms, lifting her off her feet to bury his face in her neck.

Camry walked to Luke, her own eyes spilling tears. He handed Tigger to whoever was standing next to him, and pulled her into his arms.

The front door suddenly slammed, shaking the chandeliers. "I'm here!" a woman shouted. "You better not have started without me! Fiona threw up all over my birthday dress just as we were leaving, and I had to go back in and change," she continued, rushing into the dining room. "I swear she did it on purp—" She came to a sliding stop. "What did I miss?"

Apparently no one thought to answer her.

"What's wrong? Mama, are you *crying*?" she asked, rushing around the table toward her parents. She suddenly skidded to a halt beside Luke. She looked at Camry still in his embrace, then up at him. "Who are you?" she asked.

"If you're Winter, then I guess I'm your newest brother-in-law, Luke Renoir."

"My what!" She shifted the infant in her arms to free up one hand, which she used to pull Camry around to face her. "My what?" she repeated. "You're *married*?" She touched Camry's wet cheek, then swung toward the head of the table. "Why is everyone crying? What did I miss!"

The infant she was holding suddenly gave a loud wail and burst into tears.

"Oh, give her to me," Camry said, shoving the data bank at Luke so she could take the baby. "Go see Mom and Dad. They'll tell you what's going on."

As Winter bolted for the head of the table, Camry nudged Luke with her hip. "Come on, let's go into the living room where it's quiet. I have someone very special I want you to meet."

Luke followed her through the crowd of

whispering people, smiling sinisterly at Kate as she held up her cell phone and snapped his picture again on his way by, then stopped to gently close his mother's gaping mouth. He gave her a kiss on the cheek, then stayed leaning close. "You think this is amazing," he whispered, "you wait until you meet some of her *distant* relatives."

With a nod to André, he followed Camry out to the foyer, where he found her smiling up at a tall, handsome, rather . . . intense-looking man.

No worry he would mix up this brother-in-law with the others.

"This is Winter's husband, Matt Gregor. Matt, this is my husband, Luke Renoir."

Matt extended his hand. "Welcome to the family, Luke." His piercing golden eyes, glinting with amusement, darted to Camry as she walked away with his now-sniffling daughter, then returned to Luke—specifically to his hat—before leveling directly on him. "How is good old Roger?" he asked.

"As outrageous as I assume he always is."

Matt's grin broadened. "Yes, but he means well. So what did he con you and Cam out of?"

"Greylen's best snowcat."

Matt arched a brow. "Really? In exchange for what?"

"Marrying us." Luke glanced toward the living

room, then back at Matt. "And your enchanting daughter signed as our witness, along with your grandson, Thomas Gregor Smythe."

Matt also glanced toward the living room, then heaved a heavy sigh. "That girl is going to be the death of me," he muttered. He looked back at Luke, shaking his head. "You and Cam decide to have children, pray they're boys." He gestured toward the once-again-boisterous dining room. "I swear I don't know how Greylen survived raising seven daughters." With a shudder, apparently to shrug off his fatherly terror, Matt slapped Luke on the shoulder and nudged him toward the living room. "You better go save your wife from Fiona, before the little imp gives Cam the idea that she needs a baby of her own.

"Oh, and Luke?" Matt said just as Luke was about to enter the living room. "Thanks for keeping a close eye on my daughter last week."

"Trust me, it was my pleasure," Luke said with a nod.

When Matt nodded back, then turned and walked into the dining room, Luke went over and sat down beside Camry on the couch.

She immediately plopped Fiona on his lap. "Where's the data bank?" she asked.

Luke peered down at the large blue eyes peering up at him, and smiled. "I left it on the table," he said absently, gently bouncing his knee. "Hello there, Miss Fiona. Been doing much traveling lately? And have you decided yet what you want to be when you grow up?"

Fiona's answer was to pat her hands together—though she missed more times than she connected—and blow bubbles as well as produce cute little belly laughs.

"She's going to be a rocket scientist like her auntie Cam," Camry murmured, leaning on Luke's arm as she smoothed down Fiona's soft blond hair. "Isn't she beautiful?" she whispered. She tilted her head back to look up at him. "Wouldn't you love to have a daughter just like her?"

Just as Matt had, Luke shuddered in terror.

Which made Fiona clap her hands together again with even louder belly laughs. But then the infant suddenly looked down at Luke's hand and touched the ring. Camry held her hand next to his, and the baby awkwardly went after her ring.

"They're really lovely, Fiona," Camry whispered. "And every time we look at them, we'll think of you."

"Five minutes to solstice!" someone shouted from the dining room. "Cam, get in here. Mom's lighting the candles!"

Still leaning heavily on Luke's arm, Camry tilted her head again to smile at him. "I guess that means you pulled off your miracle, Dr. Renoir, and we're legally married. Forever and ever."

He kissed the tip of her upturned nose. "Uncompromisingly, unpretentiously, and unconditionally, Dr. MacKeage-Renoir. Forever and ever."

She melted against him with a sigh. "Thanks to this little girl," she said, leaning forward to kiss Fiona's rosy plump cheek. She suddenly stood up. "Come on then," she said, heading out of the room. "I don't care if my birthday cake is ruined, I intend to eat every last crumb." She glanced at him from the door, her eyes sparkling. "I figure the sugar should kick in about an hour from now. Vroom-vroom, husband," she purred as she disappeared into the foyer.

Luke immediately covered Fiona's ears with his hands. "You didn't hear that!" He hugged her to him with a sigh. "Thank you," he whispered.

He finally stood up and held her facing him. "So, Miss Imp, when do you think I should tell Camry not to waste her time deciphering the data in Podly's data bank?"

The sweet little cherub closed one of her beautiful blue eyes in a wink.

"I thought so," he chortled, tucking her against him and heading after his wife. "So it *is* on the wrapping paper you gave Roger!"

Merry Christmas
and
Happy Winter Solstice!

Janet

Not sure what to read next?

Visit Pocket Books online at
www.simonsays.com

Reading suggestions for
you and your reading group
New release news
Author appearances
Online chats with your favorite writers
Special offers
Order books online
And much, much more!

POCKET BOOKS
A Division of Simon & Schuster
A CBS COMPANY

POCKET STAR BOOKS
A Division of Simon & Schuster
A CBS COMPANY

13456

"Boy, you listened to a word I said?"

the old man asked.

But all of Billy's attention was riveted to the TV screen, to that baby in the arms of Randi Wilding's sister. What *was* her name, anyway? A name of some upright and annoyingly admirable personality trait: Patience or something?

Whoever she was, she went on and on about her late sister, about how the birth of her son Jesse had changed her life.

Billy couldn't take any more. He grabbed the remote and shoved it toward the screen. It went blank.

"I'll be damned," his uncle said. "That was a Jones baby if ever I saw one. Yours, I take it?"

Billy stood, glaring at him.

The old man cackled in obvious delight. "A baby. I can't believe it. Bad Billy's got a baby boy."

* * *

"Ms. Rimmer has developed into a major, major talent."

—*Romantic Times* magazine

CHRISTINE RIMMER

THE

Taming

OF BILLY

JONES

Silhouette Books

Published by Silhouette Books

America's Publisher of Contemporary Romance

If you purchased this book without a cover you should be aware that this book is stolen property. It was reported as "unsold and destroyed" to the publisher, and neither the author nor the publisher has received any payment for this "stripped book."

SILHOUETTE BOOKS

THE TAMING OF BILLY JONES

Copyright © 1998 by Christine Rimmer

ISBN 0-373-48367-8

All rights reserved. Except for use in any review, the reproduction or utilization of this work in whole or in part in any form by any electronic, mechanical or other means, now known or hereafter invented, including xerography, photocopying and recording, or in any information storage or retrieval system, is forbidden without the written permission of the editorial office, Silhouette Books, 300 East 42nd Street, New York, NY 10017 U.S.A.

All characters in this book have no existence outside the imagination of the author and have no relation whatsoever to anyone bearing the same name or names. They are not even distantly inspired by any individual known or unknown to the author, and all incidents are pure invention.

This edition published by arrangement with Harlequin Books S.A.

® and TM are trademarks of Harlequin Books S.A., used under license. Trademarks indicated with ® are registered in the United States Patent and Trademark Office, the Canadian Trade Marks Office and in other countries.

Printed in U.S.A.

For Jesse...
...who asked me if I'd ever named any of the children in my books after him. I replied, "Come to think of it, I never have," and he said, "Well, is there a kid in the book you're writing now?" I answered, "Yes, but he's hardly more than a baby." And he told me, "All right, Mom. I'll take the baby. And about the dedication..."

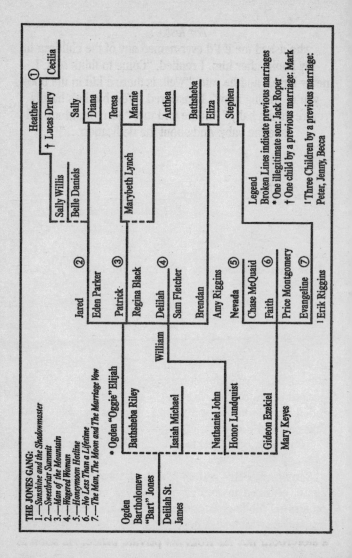

THE JONES GANG:
1.—Sunshine and the Shadowmaster
2.—Sweetbriar Summit
3.—Man of the Mountain
4.—Wagered Woman
5.—Honeymoon Hotline
6.—No Less Than a Lifetime
7.—The Man, The Moon and The Marriage Vow

Ogden
Bartholomew
"Bart" Jones

Delilah St.
James

* Ogden "Oggie" Elijah

William

Bathsheba Riley

Isaiah Michael

Nathaniel John

Honor Lundquist

Gideon Ezekiel

Mary Keyes

Jared ②

Eden Parker

Patrick ③

Regina Black

Delilah ④

Sam Fletcher

Brendan

Amy Riggins

Nevada ⑤

Chase McQuaid

Faith ⑥

Price Montgomery

Evangeline ⑦

¹ Erik Riggins

Sally Willis

Belle Daniels

Marybeth Lynch

Heather ①

† Lucas Drury   Cecilia

Diana

Sally

Teresa

Marnie

Anthea

Bathsheba

Eliza

Stephen

Legend
Broken Lines indicate previous marriages
* One illegitimate son: Jack Roper
† One child by a previous marriage: Mark
¹ Three Children by a previous marriage:
Peter, Jenny, Becca

Chapter 1

The ancient Eldorado, gold in color and as big as a boat, waited right by the front door of his club when Billy Jones pulled into the parking lot. Swearing under his breath, Billy slid his wraparound shades up onto his forehead.

The big, old car was clean for once. And it actually gave off a kind of glow, sitting there all by its lonesome. The late-afternoon Southern California sun poured down over it, bringing a deep luster back to the faded paint, making the hood ornament twinkle. Yeah, that car was a classic, all right.

Too bad it belonged to Billy's long-lost uncle, Oggie Jones.

Scowling, Billy settled his sunglasses over his eyes again, cranked up his stereo another notch and drove on around the back of the building to his personal parking space, which was next to a small door that led into a storeroom not far from his private office. As soon as he nosed the car into the space, he turned off the engine. The quiet, when the stereo cut out, seemed intense and oppressive. Billy Jones hated quiet. To him, quiet was something to be avoided at all costs—like marriage and church. Still, he sat there for a moment, in the dreariness of silence, staring out the windshield at the club he had owned for just about seven years now.

Bad Billy's was a two-story barnlike structure, sided in unfinished pine, with no windows to speak of. The lack of windows was a real bonus right then, because without a window to look through, the odds that the old man might have seen Billy drive up had to be just about nil.

Billy kept on staring at the building, considering. What if he just went ahead and turned his car around and drove back on out the way he had come? The place could do without him for a night. It had done without him before.

The silence got to be too much. Billy started tapping out a rhythm on the steering wheel, getting the music going in his head to complement the beat. He closed his eyes. Everything went away but that new song he'd been fooling around with the past few days. He let the music have him.

Then someone tapped on the window. He turned his head and saw a sweet little redhead with full, kissable lips and a come-and-get-it gleam in her eye. Billy was pretty sure she worked for him, but he couldn't for the life of him remember her name.

He looked at her through the window and smiled, slowly. She smiled back. Then she pantomimed a cranking motion: a signal for him to roll the window down. But to do that, he'd have to start up the car again. And there was no point in starting up the car when he'd decided to stick around, after all. Damned if he'd let Oggie Jones chase him away from his own club.

The redhead realized he didn't plan to do anything but smile at her. With a shrug and a tiny wave, she trotted off toward the storeroom door, her curvy rear end swaying an invitation at him as she went.

Billy waited for the door to close behind her before he reached over the seat for his straw Resistol. He slid the hat on his head, readjusted his shades and climbed out from behind the wheel, pausing only to beep on his burglar alarm before he entered the building.

He saw no one in the storage room. Good. He wasn't hiding from the old man, exactly. But the way he looked at it, the fewer people who saw him, the better. Maybe the old fool would give up and leave before he learned that Billy had arrived. Keeping his head down and his hat tipped low, Billy strode past the paper products and turned left at the bar nuts. A moment later, he was sticking his key in the lock of his office door. And then, at last, he was inside. And safe.

He flipped on the light and just stood there, his back against the door, surveying the cramped room as if it might have changed some since last evening. But no such luck. The big, scarred oak desk was still piled with food service magazines, brochures from different distributors and demo tapes from up-and-coming bands—things he should have read or listened to or thrown away a long time ago. The computer he never used crouched right in the center of the mess, gathering dust. The file cabinets had more papers stacked on top of them than inside. And it was damn dark, too.

He took off his sunglasses. There. He could see better. He tossed his hat, keys and the shades on the stand by the door and marched over to slide behind the desk. Once there, he took a big breath, looked around at all the papers—and decided it was just too damn quiet. He picked up a padded mailer and dumped out one of the demo tapes, along with a letter of introduction. The tape was of some group called the Prairie Wailers. Their songs had titles like "Rodeo Addiction" and "Love is Bull."

Billy shook his head and tossed the tape across the desk. He preferred to audition bands live anyway. He had no idea why the hell they all kept sending him tapes.

He fumbled around under a pile of receipts. "Hah!" he exclaimed, when he found the television remote. He pointed it at the Sony Trinitron, which sat across the room on a metal shelf, right above a long row of stereo components.

The news popped on. A perky blonde with incredible teeth babbled cheerfully about the weather. "Except for the leaves falling here and there, you'd never in your life believe it was October." Big smile, blinding in its whiteness. "But then, this is the Southland and it's *always* beautiful here."

Just then, the door flew open so fast and hard, it hit the wall with a bang like a pistol shot.

Billy jumped in his seat. "What the—?"

"Think you can hide, do you? You can't hide. Forget it."

Billy realized he was getting a headache. "Damn. Alexis. You *scared* me."

Alexis Sacadopolis, his head-waitress-turned-manager, had acres of platinum hair and a body like a Vegas showgirl. She also had a mind like a steel trap.

Nothing got by her—which made her a great manager and, on occasion, a pain in the ass.

Billy dropped the remote. "I'm trying to get some work done here, Alexis."

Alexis let out a snort. "Yeah. Right." She leaned against the door frame and studied a chipped fingernail. "He's out there again."

Billy considered pretending he didn't know who "he" was, but decided it would be futile. "I know. I saw his car."

"Well, Loretta saw *you*. She went straight in and told him."

"Loretta?"

Alexis folded her arms under her remarkable breasts. "Redhead. Gorgeous." He remembered the pretty girl in the parking lot. Alexis must have seen that he remembered, because she added, "That girl is barely twenty-one, which is too young for you."

"Yes, Mother," he muttered, not even really thinking about the girl, telling himself that he should have known. The old man had all of them, *all of them*, under his thumb.

Alexis reached into a back pocket of her skintight red jeans and came out with one of those little boards with sandpaper on it. She set to work on that chipped nail.

"Alexis, go somewhere else to fix your nails, okay?"

She shot him a sour glance and went right on filing away. "He just wants to talk to you, one final time."

"Get me some Excedrin, will you?"

She made a disgusted noise and disappeared from the doorway. Just when he thought maybe he'd actually gotten rid of her, she reappeared with a couple of tablets and a glass of water.

She marched straight to his side. "Here." He took the tablets and washed them down with the water, then looked around on his cluttered desk for somewhere to set the glass. "Give it to me," she said, rolling her eyes around in her head so he'd know just how much he was putting her out.

He gave her the glass. "Thanks. You can go now."

She just stared at him. He tried to appear abused. "Alexis, I've already talked to him one final time. Night before last, in this very cubicle. He blathered on for hours."

"He's an *old* man."

"Alexis...."

She leaned over, braced her hands on the desk and got right in his face. "Look, he swears this is the last time he'll bother you. He says if you don't want a thing to do with your own people, if you're that cold and unfeeling, that's your business. He's leaving, headed back up to that dinky town he's always talking about."

"North Magdalene," Billy provided grimly, sitting back in his chair to get some space from her.

She only leaned closer. "He just wants to say goodbye."

Billy swung his boots up onto the desk, causing a number of magazines to slide off. "Tell him to have a nice trip." He laced his hands behind his head.

Alexis rose to her full height again and braced her hands on her hips. "What am I, Western Union? Tell him yourself. And anyway, he says he won't leave, no matter what, until he speaks to you personally." Billy believed that. He'd never met a man so relentless as

Oggie Jones. "So, can I send him back?" Alexis demanded.

He shot her a sideways look. "Tiny Tim in yet?" Tiny Tim was Billy's head bouncer—all six foot six and three hundred heavily tattooed pounds of him.

"Yeah," Alexis muttered suspiciously. "So what?"

"So send *him* in to see me. Pronto."

Alexis sputtered and shook her huge head of hair. "Billy, that's an old man out there. An old man who is blood to you."

"I don't want to hear it."

"Billy, you can't sic Tiny Tim on your own flesh and blood."

"Watch me."

"Besides, Tim won't do it."

Unfortunately Billy had no comeback for that one. It was probably true. After all, Oggie Jones, with his threadbare dungarees, down-home palaver and smelly cigars, had managed to charm the sense out of every last waitress and busboy in Billy's employ. The odds had to be high he would have gotten to Tiny Tim, too.

Alexis batted her false eyelashes at him. "Billy, sugar. It's ten minutes of your time."

"Right. And if you believe that, I heard Graceland's for sale."

"Billy, come on. Just talk to him. One more time."

Billy swore some more. Then brought his boots thudding to the floor. "Is there any way I can get out of this?"

Alexis only shook her head.

Billy let out a long, weary breath. "One last time. And that's all."

Alexis beamed. "I'll go get him."

"No need," a grit-and-gravel voice announced. "I figured you'd see me, boy. So I'm already here."

Alexis blinked in mild surprise, then turned to the grizzled old coot who stood in the doorway. "Well, then." Her voice had gone as sweet as clover honey. "I'll just leave you two alone."

"Thanks." Oggie gave her a grin and a wink, edging into the room as she went out. "Nice girl," Oggie said, when she'd shut the door behind her.

No one ever called Alexis a "girl." She didn't like it and she made her opinions known. "I'm a woman, sugar," she'd say. "And don't you forget it." No one ever did. Except, apparently, Oggie Jones.

By the same token, Billy himself didn't particularly care to be called, "boy." More than once, he'd ordered the old fool not to do it again. The command had had about as much effect as a .22 cartridge in a twelve-gauge shotgun.

Oggie was glaring at the television. "You think you could shut off that idiot box, boy?"

Billy picked up the remote and turned the sound down a fraction.

Oggie looked from the television to Billy. He heaved a big sigh. "Guess that'll have to do." Leaning on his gnarled manzanita cane, he limped the few steps to one of the two extra chairs. Huffing and puffing, he lowered himself to a sitting position. He made a big production of laying his cane beside the chair. Then he sat back and folded his knotted hands over his paunch. "This is goodbye."

Promises, promises, Billy thought.

A sad look clouded the old man's rheumy little eyes. "At least you know now that you got a family."

"Yeah, I'd say you made that real clear."

"Spare me the sarcasm. Let an old man have his final say."

"You had your final say."

"I tried. But you didn't listen."

"I listened."

Oggie scowled. "You hear me out this last time. It's the least you can do."

Billy wondered at that moment if he would ever get rid of this old man. But what could he do now? He'd agreed to listen one more time. He shrugged and slumped back in his chair. "Say what you have to say. For the *last* time."

"Don't interrupt me, then."

"I won't. Just get it over with."

Oggie coughed and glared some more, shifting around in the chair, settling in all over again. Then, at last, he began, "On his deathbed, my brother Gideon told me of your father, my brother Nathaniel—and of you, his only child. Told me how your father was gone now, and his dear wife, too. How, of that branch of the family, you alone remained, down here in Los Angeles, runnin' this nightclub of yours and livin' wild...."

Billy stifled a yawn. As usual, Oggie was repeating himself. He'd already dispensed all this information more than once. If Billy thought it would do any good, he'd tell the old horse thief to get to the point. But that would be a futile endeavor if ever there was one. So he tuned Oggie out. His attention wandered to the events on the news.

Ten seconds later, Billy had forgotten the old man existed. He was too busy gaping at that TV screen, feeling as if someone had just sucked all the air right out of the room.

Meanwhile, Oggie droned on. "I been tryin' my damnedest to get through to you, hopin' with all my heart that you'd reach out to me. But you ain't reached out. I'm not a man who gives in easy. But I guess I know when it's time to fold my hand and head on home."

Billy tried blinking, several times in a row, hoping he would see something different when he looked again.

But nothing changed.

"Boy, you listened to a word I said?"

No matter how many times Billy blinked, he still saw Randi on that high resolution screen. Randi all dressed in white and smiling serenely—with a baby on her lap.

The newscaster announced, "Here you see the sex goddess, Randi Wilding, in another light, with her beloved baby boy, Jesse. This picture was taken just days before the fatal airplane flight that took her life. And now, just a month after the actress's death, representatives of her estate have announced the creation of the Jesse Wilding Needy Children's Fund."

"Boy? Yoo-hoo. I'm talkin' to you...."

Squinting, Billy leaned across the desk. But the baby in Randi's arms didn't change. It continued to look exactly like a picture Billy remembered of himself at just under a year, wearing ridiculous blue shorts and a silly little billed cap, chewing on a rubber frog. His mother used to keep that picture on her mantel. Billy had always hated the thing.

The studio photo of mother and child vanished, to be replaced by a shot of an ugly woman sitting in a wing chair: Randi's sister. The woman smiled tightly and introduced herself to the camera, but Billy didn't catch her name because Oggie sputtered out something just as she said it.

Billy frowned. What the hell *was* her name, anyway?

It was one of those names that could scare a man off all by itself. A name like his mother's name, which had been Honor. A name of some upright and annoyingly admirable personality trait: Patience or something?

Billy had met the woman once or twice, at Randi's Bel Air mansion, during those three months of burning lust he and Randi had shared. The times he'd seen her, she'd been sitting behind a desk in the office there, squinting at a computer screen. She managed all of Randi's money, Randi had told him. Randi said she did a bang-up job of it, too.

"Jesse really changed Randi's life," the sister was saying. "She settled down a lot, when she learned she was going to have him—and even more so after he was born. He awakened the natural mother within her. She became more contented. More relaxed. And more thoughtful."

Billy had to hold back a snort of disbelief. Randi Wilding, thoughtful? Right.

The sister hadn't finished. Unshed tears making her eyeballs seem to float behind her thick-lensed glasses, she continued, "Randi really *felt* for the homeless and disadvantaged children of the world. Every time she looked at Jesse, she would be reminded of all the children forced to grow up without the love and tender care she was able to lavish on her own little boy. She worked hard to establish this fund. And those of us who loved her are proud to see it become a reality, even after she is no longer with us. Randi was a wonderful, warm, giving—"

Billy couldn't take any more. He grabbed the remote and shoved it toward the TV. The screen went blank.

"I'll be damned," his uncle said.

Billy closed his eyes and muttered a few bad words.

Oggie slapped his knee. "That was a Jones baby if I ever saw one. Yours, I take it?"

Billy threw down the remote and stood. "Look. Let's cut to the chase here. I said all I had to say to you the other night."

Oggie's tiny raisin eyes twinkled in glee. "Cute as hell, that kid. Congratulations, son."

"You're leaving now. Aren't you." It was not a question.

The old man started cackling in obvious delight. "A baby. I can't believe it. Bad Billy's got a baby boy."

Billy said, "Out."

"All right, all right." The old man bent and collected his cane. He pulled himself upright, grunting. "I'll be at the same hotel, in case you need to get in touch with me."

"Why the hell would I need to get in touch with you?"

The old man shrugged—and chortled some more.

Billy scowled. "You said you were leaving town."

"That was before I found out about my little grand-nephew. Even if his father's a coldhearted S.O.B., that baby's got a right to know his people." Oggie hobbled to the door.

"I never said that baby was mine."

Oggie snorted. "You didn't have to. I know by the look of him—not to mention the look on your face when you saw him." Oggie pulled the door open and moved into the outer room.

Billy called after him, "You stay out of it, old man! Stay away from that baby! You go near that baby, I'll make you regret it!"

The only answer he got was that low, knowing laugh, which faded to nothing as the old man limped out of sight.

Chapter 2

For the next several days, Billy tried not to think about the baby named Jesse. What the hell good could it do to think about that kid? That kid would get along just fine with his aunt what's-her-name and all of his dead mama's money. That kid didn't need someone like bad Billy Jones in his life. Some men just weren't meant to be fathers. Billy knew that because he was one of them.

Oggie had been right about a few things, like when he'd said that Billy had no family feeling at all. Billy Jones was born to make loud music, make love to pretty women and just generally have a good time. He had always been that way, as far back as he could remember.

Twice, he'd gone and let himself get married. Both marriages had been disasters. On the positive side, they'd also been short. And childless.

No, he didn't need a kid. He didn't want a kid. And any kid with any sense wouldn't want him for a dad.

And yet damned if he could stop thinking about that beaming baby face.

He started having a recurring dream. The dream took him back to that clean, quiet house in Sweethaven, Kansas, where he had been born. In the dream, he slowly entered the parlor. He looked around, dreading what he'd see. His gaze would find the mantel. There, as always, stood that picture of him as a baby. And right next to it, in an identical frame, sat the picture of Randi and Jesse that he'd seen on the news.

In the dream, Billy would turn from the picture to find his mother and father sitting on the sofa nearby. They sat very straight, side by side, but not touching. They looked at him, looks that judged and condemned. And they spoke in unison, quoting from the Bible, he thought.

"If a son asks for bread from any father among you, will he give him a stone? Or if he asks for a fish, will he give him a serpent instead of a fish? Or if he asks for an egg, will he offer him a scorpion?"

Somewhere around the bit about the scorpion, Billy would wake up, running sweat. He'd look around, feeling kind of sick, wondering where he was—and then remembering: his own bedroom in Studio City.

For a few minutes, he'd wish that he'd brought someone pretty and soft home with him the night before. He would want gentle hands reaching for him. Someone to hold him close and make all the soothing sounds a lover will make for a man who wakes at her side from a nightmare. But then, as his sweat dried and his heart settled down to an easier rhythm, he'd be glad he was alone. This thing about the kid was nobody's business but his and the kid's. And Randi's, if she hadn't been dead. And maybe what's-her-name, the aunt's.

About a year ago, when he'd heard that Randi had added herself to the growing list of Hollywood single moms, Billy had experienced a moment or two of pure panic. He'd wondered if he might be the dad.

But then he'd dismissed the idea. After all, she'd never said a word about any baby to him. He figured it must have been some other guy, someone she'd hooked up with right after him. And Randi had known damn well how he felt about having kids. He'd been careful to tell her, to make the point very clearly right up front: no wedding bells and no rug rats. She'd said he didn't have to worry. She didn't want a kid, and he was hardly marriage material.

Still, if she'd found herself pregnant, she should have said something; she should have let him know.

And what about what's-her-name, the aunt? Did the aunt know who Jesse's father was? And if she did, what then? Did she plan to hide the truth forever, to raise the kid without ever telling him who he should be calling Daddy?

On a Monday at five a.m., a week and a half after seeing his son's picture on television, Billy woke in a sweat once again. He shot bolt upright in bed and let out a cry like a skinned cat. Then, as he gasped for breath and hoped his heart wasn't going to beat its way right out of his chest, he decided he'd had about enough of this crap.

Between the nightmares and the wondering, he just plain couldn't take it anymore. He had a few questions for what's-her-name.

He threw back the tangled, clammy sheet and swung

his legs over the side of the bed. Then, after switching on the lamp, he yanked open the drawer of the night-stand and fumbled through the junk in there until he came up with his well-worn black leather address book.

Randi's number came to him before he even flipped it open. There had been a time, after all, when he'd dialed that number a lot.

A funny ache went through him, as he started to dial it again. And for a moment, clear as day before him, he saw Randi, dressed in the kind of clothes she'd al-ways loved to wear: a skintight leather skirt and a lace-up formfitting leopard skin top. Black silk stockings. Spike-heeled shoes. She was grinning, her gold hair shining, her huge blue eyes full of fun and challenge. Ready for anything. Anytime. Anywhere.

He'd really tied one on when he'd heard she was dead. Just to think that she wasn't there anymore, in the same world he lived in, had depressed the hell out of him. It wasn't a torch-carrying situation. He'd known it was time to move on when she'd dumped him. But damn. He had *liked* her. And, in his own way, he mourned for her.

Now, sitting on the edge of his bed with the night-mare sweat cooling on his skin, the phone in his hand and her number half dialed, he found himself missing her all over again. She'd been a hell of a woman. The world was a little more boring without her in it.

And he wasn't going to call the mansion, after all.

Billy set down the phone. Then he rose from the bed. He spent a moment looking around for his jeans. But when they didn't present themselves, he forgot about clothes. The room wasn't cold, anyway. He got his Martin from where it waited for him in the corner and sat on the floor. The guitar felt good in his hands, as it always did. He strummed a few chords and fiddled with the pegs a little. Then he began to fool around with a new melody that had sneaked into his head.

Three hours later, he'd written a song: "Never To See You Again." He put the Martin back in its case and stood the case back in its place in the corner. Then he took a shower, found his jeans, a shirt and some boots and went out for breakfast at the IHOP a few blocks away.

Once he'd knocked back a plate of blueberry pancakes and four cups of coffee, he went to visit his agent, Waverly Sims. They discussed the songs Billy had written lately and he made arrangements to cut a few demos that Waverly would offer around.

Waverly wanted to take Billy to lunch, so Billy followed him into Hollywood. They ate at one of those chichi restaurants Waverly liked. It was on Melrose, in a tent. One of those places where they put lime slices in the ice water and the salad looked as if it was made out of weeds.

After the lunch, he said goodbye to Waverly and got back in his car. Without making any kind of conscious decision about it, he found himself headed west, for Bel Air.

Randi's mansion wasn't too far from the Bel Air Country Club. The huge house couldn't be seen from the street, which was lined with waxy-leafed magnolia trees and long stone walls. The stone walls appeared no more than decorative. Masses of bougainvillea, honeysuckle and jasmine tumbled down over the gray rock. But Randi had once explained to Billy that the top of the fence, beneath all the pretty greenery, was wired to an elaborate alarm system. To get in there, you had to ring at the big iron gates.

Billy drove up, rang and gave his name over an intercom, half expecting to be denied entry. But the gate opened. He drove up the twisting driveway, past expanses of emerald lawn dotted here and there with palms, jacarandas and lemon trees. The house came into view, an Italianate villa with a red tile roof, butter yellow walls, tall Palladian windows and white marble stonework. At intervals along the front, Doric columns loomed up, supporting balconies fenced in iron lace.

As he approached the imposing facade, Billy remembered the first time Randi had brought him here.

"I bought it because I could," she'd told him in that husky voice of hers. "Because when the palm trees rustle in the balmy breeze, they whisper to me. They say, 'You've come a long way, baby.'" She had laughed then, a laugh that was low and throaty and got him thinking about getting her prone. She tugged on his arm and grinned up at him. "You know what I mean—baby?"

In response, he'd let out a growl and started peeling off the little bitty tight piece of nothing she was wearing at the time.

Billy stopped before a long box hedge in the paved entrance court. A uniformed driver materialized, more or less out of nowhere.

"Just leave it right here," Billy told him. "I won't be staying long."

The man gave a brief nod and headed in the direction of the garages. As soon as he was out of sight, Billy turned and marched between two wide-spaced marble columns and up to the gracefully arched double front doors. He rang. The doors swung back.

A Tom Cruise look-alike in a tux greeted him. "This way, Mr. Jones."

Billy followed the butler out of the marble-tiled entrance hall and down a number of intersecting corridors. They passed a lot of large, sunny rooms stacked with packing boxes, where the furniture was covered in white drapes. Apparently the plain-Jane sister was ditching the villa for new digs.

After they'd walked about a mile, they finally came to the office room he remembered from before. The door was open. The sister—what the hell was her name: Verity? Constance?—was waiting for him behind her fancy inlaid mahogany desk, a stack of papers in front of her and one of those notebook computers at her elbow.

The studly butler coughed discreetly. "Mr. Jones is here."

The woman looked up, those ugly glasses of hers magnifying her eyes in a way that made them seem to bulge. Her brownish hair was skinned back, her face scrubbed so clean it gave off a shine like a newly waxed floor. She reminded him of some giant, solemn insect—an insect that had somehow got itself all dressed up in a tidy gray business suit.

She flicked a bug-eyed glance at the hunk to Billy's right. "Thank you, Lance."

Lance gave a brief nod, then turned and strode off, leaving Randi's sister and Billy to stare at each other for a minuscule period of time that somehow, to Billy, seemed as if it went on for about two hundred years.

Finally she spoke up. "I've been meaning to contact you. To be honest, as of yet, I hadn't quite gathered the courage."

Her words could mean only one thing: she knew Randi's kid was his.

Randi's kid was his. The reality hit him all over again, making his stomach churn and his knees turn to rubber.

He wondered bleakly what had come over him, to show up here, at the mansion Randi used to call home. Yes, he'd been putting up with a nightmare or two lately. And he was a little curious about the kid who looked so much like him.

But what the hell did he plan to do about it, now the sister had as good as admitted the truth? He knew nothing about fatherhood—he *wanted* to know nothing about fatherhood.

The sister was looking at him through those scary magnified eyes of hers. "Please," she said. "Don't just stand there in the doorway staring at me as if I've committed some unconscionable crime. I'm sure, somehow, that we can work this out." She gestured toward a chair opposite her desk. "Sit down."

It was so damn quiet. He hated quiet. He wanted to ask the insect woman to turn on a little music, but there was no stereo in sight.

She gestured at the chair again. "Please."

He stepped over the threshold. "I'll stand."

She gave a tiny have-it-your-way shrug, then took off her glasses and rubbed the bridge of her nose. He watched her, feeling a fraction easier for the brief moment that she didn't have those eyes pinned on him.

But the moment ended all too soon. She settled the glasses back in place and folded her hands on her desk pad, which was one hundred percent free of doodles and smudges. "Mr. Jones. I—" Her voice broke. She looked away, then seemed to force herself to look at him again, and to go on. "I loved my sister. She was generous and funny. And talented. And...good." He saw defiance in her giant eyeballs, as if she dared him to say a bad word about Randi.

Billy had made a lot of mistakes in his life, but he wasn't about to make one right then. He kept his mouth shut, though he couldn't help picturing that famous shot from a certain men's magazine, that shot of Randi spread out on a zebra skin rug, wearing nothing but a diamond watch, a butterfly tattoo and look of pure, unbridled lust.

Unaware of Billy's disrespectful thoughts, the sister continued, "Still, the fact is, she should have told you about the baby. I tried to convince her to tell you. But she felt you weren't cut out to be a father. That you had no *desire* to be a father. So when she found out she was pregnant, she—"

"Dumped me." He felt self-righteous, suddenly. It wasn't a bad feeling, especially not compared to scared spitless, which had been his basic emotional state since he entered that damn, silent room. He let his lip curl a little, giving the woman a good, solid sneer. "She dumped me flat."

The sister flinched. "Let's just say she ended your...liaison."

Billy decided to enjoy being the wounded one. He had a right, the way he figured it. He *had* been kept in the dark. "That's a fancy way of putting it." He made a low sound in his throat, one intended to indicate his total disgust with the way he'd been treated. "But dumped is dumped, no matter how you try to gussy it up."

The woman's mouth pursed into a tight little bud. "Please. Randi did what she thought was right. And now she's gone. Now *I'm* Jesse's guardian. And I will do what *I* think is right.''

Billy decided he felt a little too queasy to keep on standing, after all. He dropped into the chair opposite her, the one he'd refused a moment ago. He forced out his next words. ''And what exactly do you think is right?''

''Well....'' She patted the tight little bun at the back of her neck and fiddled with her glasses some more.

''Well, what?'' he demanded, pleased at how dangerous he sounded, since he felt about as menacing as limp spaghetti.

She gulped and blinked. ''Mr. Jones, I think your son should know you.''

''What the hell does that mean?''

''It means I think he should have a chance to build some kind of relationship with you. I think...'' The sentence kind of ran out of steam. She leaned toward him, frowning.

He threatened her by deepening his scowl. ''What?''

She seemed to have forgotten that he was scaring her. A strange, soft look came over her. The corners of her mouth turned up slowly in a tender smile. For a moment, even with those bug eyes, she was pretty.

Then she said, ''You're terrified.''

He realized that he hated her.

She rubbed it in. ''You're scared to death.''

He gave her the kind of dead, flat look he usually only granted an adversary in a poker game. ''The hell I am.''

She shook her head and let out a chuckle of amusement.

He felt the urge to leap across her desk, grab her by her scrawny neck and choke that knowing look right off her face. But he didn't move. Any show of emotion right then would only serve to prove her point.

"Would you like to meet him?"

What the hell was she babbling about now? "Meet who?"

She shook her head again, still wearing that smug little smile. God, he hated women like her. Women who thought they didn't need men. Women who thought they knew everything. Women who acted so damn upright and superior. Give him a good-time gal with a forgiving heart and a tolerant mind any day.

"Your son," she said. "Would you like to meet your son?"

No! a voice in his mind shouted. *I'm not ready for this. I'll never be ready for this!* "Yeah," he replied in his best nerves-of-steel tone. "Take me to him. Now."

She emerged from behind the desk. As she walked toward him, he realized that he'd never seen her— Charity? Faith?—except from the waist up before. Beneath that button-down gray business suit, she appeared to have a pretty good body: respectable breasts, a discernible waist and legs he'd look at more than once on any other kind of woman.

She moved right past him, stopping to turn at the door. "Please. Come. I'll take you to him."

His mind kept screaming no, but for some reason, his body got out of the chair and followed her. From behind, it became more clear that her body wasn't bad at all. And when she'd smiled, back there in the office, he'd seen that she could have been pretty, if she wanted to be. Still, she chose to hide her looks behind ugly glasses and skinned-back hair. It was just a mystery to him, what made a woman like that tick.

They turned left at the end of the hall, and then right at the end of *that* hall. Billy watched the gently swaying bottom of Randi's dowdy sister, concentrating on feeling superior to her—and trying his damnedest to keep his mind off where they were going and the child he would meet for the first time when they got there.

Finally, Hope or whatever-her-name-was stopped before a closed door. She rapped lightly.

After a moment, an older woman answered. "He's napping," the woman whispered, in a tone damn close to reverence.

Felicity or something turned to Billy. "We could just tiptoe in. See if he wakes up. How's that?"

He longed to say, *Let's forget it. I'll come back some other time—like in a couple of decades or so.* But instead he found that his head was bobbing up and down.

The older woman stepped back. Billy and Randi's sister entered a playroom, with murals of suns and rainbows bright on the walls and more toys than in FAO Schwartz. Dazed, Billy looked around him, wondering if maybe this was all just a bizarre extension of the nightmare that had brought him here in the first place. Any second now he expected his long-dead mother to pop out from behind one of the toy cabinets, ready to quote him a little more chapter and verse.

"I'll be in my rooms if you need me," the older woman whispered.

"Thank you, Alma," the sister said.

The older woman left them, going through a door a few feet away.

"This way," said Amity or Modesty. She started for a door opposite the one they had just come through.

She opened the door, slowly and quietly. He saw that it was shadowy in there, that the blinds were drawn.

She turned and discovered that he was still standing all the way across the room. She fanned the air in a come-on wave. He put one foot in front of the other, until he stood right beside her, before the open door to the shadowed room.

Smiling as if something wonderful was going on, Grace or Hope put a finger to her lips. "I'd better go in with you. In case he wakes up—since he doesn't know you. All right?"

Billy shrugged, elaborately, as if this whole thing was no big deal to him. "Fine."

She went into the darkened room. Seeing no other choice, Billy followed.

In there, in spite of the fact that it was pretty dark, he could make out more murals. There were airplanes in a blue sky and teddy bears dancing in a forest. And more toys. Damn, the kid had toys.

The crib stood in a corner, not far from a mural of flying toasters and dancing computer screens. What's-her-name approached the crib and Billy did, too. When she got there, she moved toward one end of it, leaving the other end for him. He stepped automatically into the space she'd left for him.

And then he had no choice. He was there. He had to look.

The kid lay on his stomach, his face turned toward Billy and one fat fist curled under his chin. He looked big and healthy—and *exactly* like the kid in the picture that used to stand on his mother's mantel back in Sweethaven. If there was ever any lingering shadow of doubt in Billy's mind, it was gone now. This was his kid.

His kid.

It was too weird.

Billy wanted music. *Loud* music. A drink. A *hundred* drinks.

The kid's fat little mouth made sucking motions. It was the cutest damn thing Billy had ever seen.

He could not breathe.

He had to get out of there.

He spun on his heel and made for the door, with Charity or Grace close behind.

"Are you all right?" she asked in a hushed, baby-in-the-other-room kind of voice, once they were back in the playroom again and she'd carefully shut the door behind them.

"I'm fine."

"You seem—shocked."

"Well, I'm not."

She started toward him. "Here. Sit down and—"

He put up both hands and backed away from her. "Look. I have to go."

At least she stopped coming at him. "But I thought—"

He waved her words away. "Later. Something important's come up and I—" He cut himself off when she started looking all soft again, those bulging eyes just brimming with sympathy and understanding. He knew that *she* knew the havoc inside him—and he was shamed to have her know it. He glared at her. "What the hell is your name, anyway?"

She fell back a little. "Excuse me?"

"Your name. What is your name?"

She swallowed, then said it: "Prudence."

"Prudence?"

She nodded.

He felt vindicated, cleansed. Under his breath, he muttered, "I knew it."

"What did you say?"

"Nothing. Look, *Prudence.*"

She seemed to realize she was cringing. She drew her shoulders back. "Yes?"

"I have to go now, but I'll be back. And when I do come back…"

Now she was wearing that knowing little smile again. "Yes?"

"…you'd better…" He fumbled for something to say.

"What?"

It came to him. "….get my kid out of that crib and into a damn bed."

That surprised her. She hitched in a tight little breath. "I beg your pardon?"

"I said, he's too big for a crib."

Her mouth pursed up tight. "Oh, and I suppose you're an expert on childrearing, *Mr.* Jones."

"Just do what I said. Don't make him into some wuss."

"Jesse is a very special little boy and—"

"*Boy,* Prudence. *Boy* is the operative word. He's old enough for a real bed."

"He's barely a year."

"Just…don't argue with me. Just do what I said. I'll be back, you hear?"

"Yes, I heard. Very clearly."

"Good. So do it."

"Mr. Jones—"

"I gotta go."

"But—"

He turned his back on her before she could say another word. The door to the hall was right there. He yanked it open, stepped through it and slammed it behind him.

Chapter 3

Prudence Wilding stared at the door Jesse's father had just slammed in her face. She was glad to be rid of him. At the same time, she wondered if she should follow him and see him to the front entrance—just to make sure he found it. After all, the house was huge. Guests were always getting lost in it.

But then Jesse began to cry. Prudence waited, listening. No doubt the raised voices and the slamming door had disturbed him. Maybe if she gave him a moment, he'd drift back to sleep.

But no such luck. The crying only got louder.

The nanny peeked her head out of her room. "Shall I—?"

"No, Alma. I'll get him."

Prudence turned and went through the door to her nephew's room. Jesse was standing up in his crib, his head thrown back, howling in frustration at the ceiling. The minute he saw Prudence, the crying stopped. He held out his chubby arms and hiccuped his own personal version of her name. "Woo, Woo!"

"Oh, honey. I'm here." She hurried over and scooped him into her arms. He cuddled up close and hiccuped a few more times, smearing his runny nose on the lapel of her jacket. She patted his back and rubbed her chin against the downy crown of his head. "There, now. All okay, right?"

He made a small, satisfied sound with a hiccup at the end of it. She eased him onto one arm and carried him with her as she went about opening the blinds to let in the afternoon sun. Then, when the room was full of light, she stood at the window, holding Jesse close, staring out at the pool and the cabana beyond—and trying not to stew about the hundred and one ways a difficult man like Billy Jones could complicate their lives.

"So, how'd you like that nephew of mine?" The rough voice came from behind her.

Prudence was already smiling as she turned to face the old man, her worries temporarily forgotten at the sound of his dear voice.

Oggie said, "He was swearin' up a storm, tryin' to find his way out of here. These old ears turned blue at the things he said when he went stompin' past my rooms."

She rubbed Jesse's back and kissed his round, sweet cheek. "Did you go out and help him find the door?"

Oggie cackled. "Hell, no. Unless there's a percentage in doin' otherwise, I stay out of trouble's way." His grizzled brows drew together. "You tell him I was here?"

"As a matter of fact, it never came up."

"Fine with me."

She rocked Jesse from side to side and went on smiling fondly at the old man. He'd come knocking on her door a week ago—to bring her the happy news of Jesse's huge family in North Magdalene. Of course, she'd been wary of him at first.

He'd suggested that she hire a detective to check out his story. "But make it quick," he'd commanded. "I want to meet my grandnephew. I'm an old man and gettin' older. I can't hang around down here in the palm trees forever, you know."

Oggie's story had been easily verified. Two days later, Prudence had called him at his hotel and asked him to come stay at the mansion for as long as he planned to be in L.A.

He'd come right over and he'd been there ever since. Prudence was just plain crazy about him. He was the father she'd never really had, the wise old granddad of which she'd always dreamed. He offered Jesse a family—and he automatically included Prudence in the offer, as well.

To have a family seemed very important to Prudence, especially since Randi's death. Prudence had shared a deep connection with her sister, a closeness and a feeling of belonging that she'd never known with anyone else, ever in her life. Their bond had been forged in a difficult childhood, and tempered over the years.

Without Randi, Prudence felt frighteningly unmoored. Like a tiny boat cast adrift in a wide, unfriendly sea. And she had worried so about Jesse, that she wouldn't do right by him.

But having Oggie around helped a lot. Since he'd appeared on the doorstep, Prudence had begun to believe that she and Jesse would manage after all, that everything would work out just fine in the end.

At least, she'd felt that way until this afternoon.

"I'm watchin' a smile turn to a frown," the old man said with gruff tenderness.

"Billy certainly is a volatile person." Prudence shivered a little, just thinking of Jesse's father.

Oggie grunted. "He's a man, that's all. A Jones. You'll get used to him. You got used to me already. And you hardly known me a week."

Jesse had had enough comforting. He pushed at Prudence's shoulder. "Dow, Woo. Dow."

Prudence set the child on the floor. He immediately ran off, falling forward from foot to foot, practicing his recently acquired skill of walking. "You're nothing like Billy Jones," she said to Oggie.

"Oh, yes, I am. That boy and me, we're more alike than you could imagine." Oggie knocked some toys off a chest with his cane, then lowered himself carefully onto the cleared surface.

"I see no similarity at all between the two of you."

Oggie rested with his arms out, both hands on his upright cane. "Truth is truth, whether you want to see it or not."

Prudence decided not to argue the point any further. With Oggie, arguing never did a lot of good anyway. She sank into a wicker rocker with a sigh, leaned her head back and began to rock. For a few pleasant minutes, both of them watched Jesse, who had found his favorite stuffed rabbit under his crib. He was cooing to it as he alternately chewed on one of its ears and petted its matted head.

"It's all gonna work out," Oggie said finally.

Prudence rolled her head to look at him. "Oh, Oggie. I hope you're right."

"I'm always right."

"I just…he makes me so uncomfortable. I understand that he's confused right now. Finding out all of a sudden that he's a father has upset him. Randi once told me that he was adamant about two things—never getting married again and not having children. Well, now, whether he likes it or not, he's a dad. He's furious and frightened. And I sympathize with that. But at the same time, he can be so intimidating. I can't help wishing I didn't have to deal with him."

Oggie only looked at her, a chiding sort of look.

She hastened to add, "I know, I know. It's the right thing. He is Jesse's father. He should be a part of Jesse's life. But I just…don't know how I'll be able to get along with him."

"You'll manage."

Prudence shrugged and rocked some more, watching Jesse, thinking gratefully again that Oggie's appearance in their lives, coming right when it had, was like some perfect gift from above. Randi had wanted Jesse to have a simpler, saner kind of life than he would ever have been likely to get as the son of a notorious sex symbol. And since her sister's death, Prudence had been determined to see Randi's wish fulfilled. Oggie had shown her how to do it.

"I didn't even get a chance to tell him about the move to North Magdalene," Prudence said.

"You'll make the chance." As usual, Oggie's tone left no room for disagreement.

Prudence went on rocking. "He said he'd be back."

"Good. You'll tell him then."

* * *

The next day, Oggie left for North Magdalene. Prudence and Jesse went, too. The town was just what she'd dreamed it might be. And she loved the wood-frame two-story house that Oggie had chosen for her. She paid cash for the house and arranged to have it painted inside and out. Then she and Jesse flew back to L.A.

Prudence put the last of her sister's affairs in order. By October 31, all the household staff had found new jobs. The mansion was in escrow. Very soon it would belong to a nice basket importer from Nepal. The Jesse Wilding Needy Children's Fund could run all on its own now; it occupied a building in downtown L.A. and employed a capable crew of five. Prudence was just about ready to take Jesse and go.

But before she could do that, she felt an obligation to inform Billy Jones of her plans. After all, he *was* Jesse's father. He had a right to know where to visit his son if he ever decided he wanted to see him.

But, in spite of his threat to return, he'd neither called nor come pounding on the door. Prudence knew she would have to take the initiative. Reluctantly she called the club Billy owned in Van Nuys. A nice man named Tim answered. Tim promised to tell Billy she'd called and to pass on her request that Billy call her back.

She waited forty-eight hours. Billy didn't call.

Prudence tried the club again. This time she spoke with the manager, a woman named Alexis. Prudence explained that it was very important that she talk to Billy right away. Alexis promised to pass on the message.

Another day went by. No word from Billy.

Prudence considered speaking with Alexis again.

Maybe the manager would work harder to get Billy to come to the phone if she knew it was his son's aunt calling.

But somehow, Prudence couldn't bring herself to do that to Jesse's father. She had no idea what Billy had told his manager about the son he'd recently learned he had. Probably nothing. Which made Prudence feel uncomfortable about broadcasting his private business. She kept thinking how Randi would have felt if Prudence had done something like that to her.

Randi's erotic exploits had been legend. Few people knew, though, that most of the stories had been started by Randi herself. Randi used to read them in the tabloids and laugh. "More shocks in the tabloids, more butts in the theater seats," she'd say.

But it always bothered Randi when the stories were true. Then she felt that her public was prying into her private life in a way they never could if she made up the stories herself.

Prudence sensed that Billy was a little like Randi. He seemed to live wild and free, but she didn't believe he'd want his private business known.

Why Prudence should even care what bad Billy Jones wanted known was a mystery to her. But at any rate, she didn't call Alexis at the club again. Instead she looked up Billy's home phone number in her computer files and called him at seven in the morning, an hour at which she felt almost certain she would find him in bed. She hoped that maybe the ringing phone would surprise him from sleep and he'd answer without thinking about it.

It didn't work. The phone rang four times and then a machine answered. "Leave a message," Billy's recorded voice growled.

Prudence stammered out something about the necessity that she speak with him immediately concerning Jesse, left her name and number and hung up feeling angry and foolish. When he didn't call her back, she tried again at three that afternoon. He didn't answer. She put the phone down and sat there, drumming frustrated fingers on her desk.

She had everything packed. Tomorrow, at ten in the morning, she would visit the title company and sign the final papers on the mansion. Meanwhile, the movers would be here, loading things up. By afternoon, she and Jesse would be on their way.

And if she intended to speak with Billy Jones before she left, she was going to have to think of some other way to reach him than by telephone.

At eleven that night, Billy sat at a table in the back room of his club. There was a nice pile of cash in front of him.

"That's it for me," said the man to his left.

One by one, the other men around the table threw down their cards. "Okay, you cleaned us out," one of them said. "You damn well better play us a tune."

Billy knocked back the rest of the drink he'd been nursing. "The band starts another set in ten minutes. I'll see if they'll let me sit in. I'm in a mood to wail."

"I'll bet," muttered another man, staring ruefully at the money he'd lost.

Agreeing to meet them all out front, Billy gathered up his winnings and took them back to the safe in his office. Then he went through the storage area and emerged near the long bar that took up nearly an entire wall of the lower floor of his club.

The place was jumping.

"Hey, Billy!"

"How's tricks?"

"Sing us a song, why don't you?"

Billy waved and smiled and signaled to the nearest bartender to pour him another shot of Jack Daniel's. A waitress—that cute little redheaded Loretta, as a matter of fact—scooped up the drink as soon as it hit the shot glass and carried it right to him.

"Here you go, Billy." Her full mouth bloomed in a smile full of gorgeous teeth. Southern California was an amazing place. Every face had fabulous teeth in it. Billy had lived in the L.A. area for nearly a decade and still, at times, he felt dumbfounded at all the dental perfection around him.

"Thanks, darlin'."

"Anytime." She drew in a deep breath and widened her eyes at him. "I mean that."

He knew she did. He also knew that he would never take her up on it. Even a man like Billy had to learn to draw the line somewhere. Beyond a little harmless flirting, he no longer fooled around with women who were likely to have attended a high school prom within the past four years. Really young women were just too damn romantic. They confused lust with love. If you told them you would never marry again, they would nod their pretty heads. But they never believed you meant it.

Both of his wives had been young. Young and determined. Just like sweet little Loretta, who was still sighing and smiling at him. He saluted her with his glass before he drank it down.

"Can I get you another one?" She licked her lips and widened those eyes even more.

"Sure." He set the glass on her tray and gestured at a table not far from the bandstand. "I'll be—"

"I know where you like to sit, Billy."

"Good enough. Thanks." He slid around her and worked his way through the crowd.

One of the guys from the poker game must have warned the band that he was on his way. The fiddle player handed him his guitar. He eased the strap around his neck and stepped up to the mike.

They swung into a couple of fast tunes first, to get the folks going. Billy fingered and strummed like a madman, tapping his foot in rhythm and singing lead full-out, giving it all he had. Down below him, on the big dance floor in the center of the club, couples whirled in each other's arms, separating to form lines when the pace quickened, then partnering up again when the rhythm slowed. At the tables on the raised platform that surrounded the dance floor, people laughed and drank and clapped along to the music. Upstairs, which was open in the center to the floor below, the last of the evening's dinner customers finished their coffee and watched the dancers below. Everywhere, waitresses in sequined Western shirts and red boots moved through the crowd, making sure that the liquor kept flowing.

It was a damn good night at Bad Billy's. And with the lights on him and his mind all wrapped up in the music, Billy could almost forget the kid he didn't know what the hell to do about—and that damn Prudence Wilding, who kept leaving him messages he knew he should return, but somehow never did.

Prudence came in just as Billy started singing a slow song. She stood in the back, not far from the door, listening. It was a song about a dying cowhand and the little boy who idolized him. A certain country-western star had made it famous, but Prudence knew it was Billy's song.

Once, during the time when he and Randi had been lovers, Prudence had heard him sing it. At the mansion, out by the pool. The music had drifted into the house through an open window. Prudence hadn't even realized that she was eavesdropping when she'd stopped to listen. The song was so sad and tender, so full of hopeless yearning and wounded, bewildered love. It reeled her in and wrapped itself all around her so that she couldn't help but try to get closer to it.

Outside, she saw Randi, sleek and gorgeous on a chaise longue, wearing nothing but a smile. Billy, bare-chested, but decent enough in old faded blue jeans, sat on a lawn chair right beside her, cradling a guitar, strumming and singing the beautiful song.

When the last note faded, Randi sighed. "You should have recorded that one yourself. That other guy didn't do it justice."

Billy laughed. "Come on. I just write 'em. You know that."

"You could be a star yourself, Billy."

"Naw. I'm too damn lazy to be a star." He put the guitar aside and leaned toward Randi. Slowly, still smiling, she'd turned her head so that their lips could meet.

Prudence had shaken herself then and turned away.

"You looking for a table?" a voice asked in her ear.

"No, not right now."

The waitress shrugged and moved on.

Up on the stage, Billy finished that magical song. There was silence, followed by an explosion of applause. Billy smiled shyly. Prudence found herself wondering how a man who could write a song like that could be such a complete jerk as a human being.

Right then, Billy turned to the band and gave a signal. They swung into a fast number that got everyone clapping and singing along.

Prudence stayed in the back, waiting, through three more songs. Then the band took a break. Prudence watched Billy, saw him sit down at a table not far from the stage, along with the drummer and the bass player and a big, noisy group that was already seated there.

Through the speakers mounted all around the club, recorded music began playing. Prudence started forward, weaving her way through the tables along the platform on the side of the huge room.

Billy had just received a shot glass full of whiskey and a look of blatant invitation from a waitress young enough to be his daughter when Prudence reached his side. She stepped right up to him before her nerve had a chance to desert her.

"Excuse me, Mr. Jones."

Billy set down his drink at the sound of that voice. He looked to his left and saw a white button-down-style shirt. He adjusted his gaze upward. Sure enough: Prudence.

He'd had a nice buzz on. But the sight of her sobered him up fast. Not knowing what else to do, he gave her a big smile. "Prudence. How the hell are you?"

She stared at him, those bug eyes hard with disapproval. "I'm just fine. And I'd like a few words with you, please. Alone."

Someone down the table chuckled. Billy hardly heard the sound. He was too busy feeling rotten and small and guilty. He knew he should have called her. He'd been *planning* to call her. Soon. Real soon.

"I assume you have an office, or some room where we can speak privately."

He decided he wouldn't let her railroad him. He stood. "Just a minute here."

"No, I really do want to—"

"Let me introduce you to a few of my best friends."

"Mr. Jones—"

"Prudence Wilding, meet Terry Sanduster." He ran right over her, gesturing around the table, reeling off names. "And Belle Evans, VanDyke Smith and, uh…"

The drummer's girlfriend grinned. "I'm Lucy. Billy always forgets my name."

Prudence forced a tight little smile. "Nice to meet you." She looked at Billy again. "Please. Let's go to your—"

"Wilding?" asked Loretta, still standing there holding her tray. "I love that name, Wilding. Randi Wilding—the movie star?—she was my idol." She turned all those shining teeth on Billy again, in a smile that said she knew about him and Randi.

Lucy, the drummer's girlfriend, had to toss her two cents in, then. "Randi Wilding was a woman who knew how to be a woman. But she was in-your-face, too. Someone nobody messed with. Remember *Firestorm?* I loved her in that."

"Yeah," said Loretta. "*Firestorm* was hot. And *Kerrigan's Honor.* She should have won the Oscar for that one."

Billy watched Prudence. She was looking way too polite. "Randi was my sister, actually." She surrendered the information reluctantly.

"Wow," said Lucy.

Loretta let out a little squeal. "No kidding?"

The fiddle player whistled low—probably in disbelief.

Billy muttered, "Damn hard to feature, isn't it?" before he let himself admit how nasty it would sound. Next to him, Prudence flinched. He told himself he didn't give a damn. He turned and looked right at her. "Were you the younger sister—or the older one?"

She glared back at him. "Are you going to talk to me or not?"

He gave her a slow smile. She backed up a step, betraying herself. She was scared. She didn't have a clue what he might do or say next. He found he liked her scared. Scared, she didn't seem so threatening to his peace of mind. Scared, he could handle her.

He pretended to study her. "You were the older sister, right?"

She said nothing, only went on glaring.

"What's the matter, Prue?"

"My name is Prudence."

"Am I all wrong about you?"

"I don't know what you're talking about. And I am not the issue here, anyway. You and I need to—"

"No. Really, Prue. If I've been a blind fool, I'll be the first to admit it."

"Mr. Jones. I am not here to—"

He moved then, swiftly and surely, closing the distance she'd created between them, reaching out as he stepped forward—and whipping off her glasses.

She gasped and blinked. Her eyes slid out of focus. "Mr. Jones!"

Before she could gather her wits, he stuck her glasses into his breast pocket, reached behind her and began pulling pins from her hair. Too stunned to protest, she let him do it, staring up at him through those unfocused eyes of hers the whole time.

He stared right back as her hair came loose. It fell over his hands as if it were a live thing, soft and thick and heavy. And it was so warm. And damned if it wasn't red. Dark red. Like cinnamon.

Like wine...

The bass player let out a whoop. "Hey, not half bad!"

"Yeah, not bad at all," another of the men agreed.

Everyone at the table started clapping. Billy kept on looking into those wounded, unseeing eyes. They were pretty eyes, really, without those hideous glasses over them, as blue as an innocent summer sky. And her heart-shaped face might not stop traffic or sink ships, but it could definitely lure a man who really bothered to look.

The truth, which he'd managed to ignore for the past several minutes, dawned like the morning after: inevitable and unpleasant. She was only trying to do the right thing, to talk to him about his son. She'd made a real effort, over the past several days, to get through to him. And for her pains, he had gone and made a spectacle of her in front of all of his yahoo buddies.

The applause slowly faded. Prudence went on staring at Billy, though she saw nothing beyond a blurry outline of his head. She wished her eyes could burn him; she wished she could sear him to a cinder right where he stood.

She commanded, with scalding civility, "Please return my glasses."

He handed them over without a word.

She put them on, carefully, taking her time about it. Then she smoothed her hair, squared her shoulders and faced him again. She felt a tiny flare of satisfaction to see that he looked just a little ashamed. "Now," she said briskly. "May I have a moment alone with you?"

One of his buddies let out a suggestive hoot. "Baby, if he won't go, you give me a try."

Billy actually shot the man a scowl.

The man put up both hands. "Hey. Sorry. No harm intended."

Suddenly everyone at the table became very interested in their drinks. Billy turned to Loretta. "A round on the house."

"Sure." She began taking orders.

Billy faced Prudence again. "We can talk in my office. This way."

Chapter 4

In his office, Billy shut the door and gestured at a chair. "Have a seat."

Prudence looked at him for a moment, not trusting him one bit, wondering what trick he might pull next.

"Aw, come on. I'm sorry about your glasses. And your hair. I shouldn't have done that."

"That's correct. You shouldn't have."

"I won't do anything else like that. I swear. We'll just talk."

She watched him apprehensively, wishing her hair was safely pinned in place again, instead of hanging down around her shoulders, feeling so loose and out of control.

His expression was truly contrite. He crossed his heart with an index finger. "Honest. I'll behave."

Warily she lowered herself into the chair.

Just as she was settling back, he picked up a remote and pointed it at the row of stereo components on the wall. Roy Orbison began singing "Only the Lonely." Loud.

She looked at the stereo components and then at him. "We have to *talk!*" she shouted.

"I hate quiet!"

"Would you please turn it down?"

He swore silently—she saw his lips move, forming the curses—but he did lower the volume enough that she wouldn't have to shout to be heard. Then he tossed the remote onto the chaos of his desk and dropped into the other guest chair, which was right beside hers. "Okay. What's up?"

"I have a few things to say to you. Concerning Jesse."

"Fine. Say 'em." He leaned an elbow on the metal arm of the chair and looked at her with an expression clearly meant to convey interest.

She decided a small amount of background was in order. "To understand what I have to say to you, it's important that you know something about Randi."

He shrugged. "Okay. Like what?"

"Randi really did change a lot, when Jesse came along."

"Yeah, you said that."

"I did?"

"On the six o'clock news, as a matter of fact."

She recalled the interview she'd given for the sake of the children's fund. "Yes. All right. Good. So you know she changed?"

"Okay, fine. She changed."

"She spent a lot of time reevaluating, thinking about what really matters in life."

"And?"

"She wanted Jesse to have those things."

"What things?"

"The things that money can't buy."

"Things like?"

"Well, like a normal kind of life."

He frowned. "A normal kind of life. What the hell does that mean?"

"It means that she wanted him to grow up... ordinary, I guess is the word. She wanted him to have a real family around him, to go to public school, to play Little League..."

Billy made a snorting noise. "A pretty tall order, considering his mother was the most notorious sex goddess since Marilyn Monroe." Prudence hated it when people called Randi a sex goddess, and it must have shown in her face, because Billy smirked, "What's the matter, Prue? Something I said?" Already, he seemed to have completely forgotten his promise to behave.

She shouldn't let him get to her, she knew it. He was just one of those people who refused to grow up. And he seemed to derive real pleasure from saying aggravating things. His opinion of her sister shouldn't matter in the least. Still, she couldn't help arguing, "Randi was a beautiful human being and a talented actress."

Insolence personified, he slouched low in the chair and stretched out his long legs in front of him. "Oh, come on. People didn't show up in droves to see her movies because of the beauty of her spirit."

Prudence sat taller, which allowed her to look down her nose at him. "She was a fine actress."

He grinned up at her. "I never said she wasn't. I only said—"

"This is pointless. We're getting off the subject."

"So?"

"I didn't come here to argue about Randi."

"I know." He had the nerve to let out a low laugh. "You look like you just sucked a lemon, Prue. And those glasses." He shook his head. "They've gotta go."

She sat even taller. "Do you want to hear what I have to tell you, or not?"

He hiked a boot up on his thigh and studied the leather tooling. "Fine. Sure. Get on with it."

"All right, then." She tried to think where she'd left off.

He glanced up from his boot and cocked an eyebrow at her. "Well?"

"Yes. All right." She remembered what she'd meant to tell him next. "As long as Randi was alive, Jesse would have been unlikely to ever have the kind of life she wanted for him. But now that she's gone, the situation has changed. As his guardian, I can be considerably more low-profile than Randi would have been. I can move anywhere I want and put down roots there. I don't have to take off for months at a time to go on location with a film."

Billy shifted impatiently in the chair. "So let me guess. You're getting married."

The idea seemed so preposterous, that she burst out with, "Me? *Married?*" Then she felt foolish. Struggling to regain her composure, she carefully folded her hands in her lap.

He watched her—still grinning, still insolent. "Okay. So you're not getting married."

"Correct. I am not."

"Then how do you plan to give Jesse a family and a chance to play shortstop?"

"Well, that's what I came to tell you."

"You mean you're about to get to the point here?"

Again, she let his rudeness pass. She imagined she'd never get anywhere in a conversation with him if she took him to task every time he said something she found objectionable. "I've made some plans recently."

"Yeah?"

She hesitated. From a few things Oggie had said, she was pretty sure Billy wouldn't be thrilled with her news—which was the real reason she was taking so long to break it to him.

"Spill it, Prue," Billy said.

So she did. "I've decided to move with Jesse to North Magdalene."

Billy sat absolutely still for a moment. Then he shot to his feet, grabbed the remote off the desk and aimed it at the stereo. Roy Orbison, who had just started wailing his heart out to someone named Leah, went silent.

In the deathly quiet, Billy turned and pointed the remote at *her*. "What did you say?"

He looked very angry. And the room seemed awfully small, all of a sudden. She tried for a combination of courage and calm reason. "Please do not point that thing at me."

His furious gaze shifted slightly. He looked at the remote. Then he swore and threw the device over his shoulder. It landed back on the desk, in almost the same spot it had been before he picked it up. He loomed over her, suddenly seeming bigger than before. She thought of that old television show "The Incredible Hulk," where a perfectly normal, handsome man kept turning into a huge green monster with muscles like boulders and hands like concrete slabs.

"North Magdalene," Billy said, very low and deliberately. "I could have sworn you just told me that you were taking my son and moving to North Magdalene."

Her anxiety made her speak with pained precision. "That is exactly what I told you."

"What the hell do you know about North Magdalene?"

"Jesse has a big family there."

"How do you know that?"

"Uncle Oggie told me."

His lip curled, so he looked like a mean dog about to bite. "*Uncle* Oggie?"

"He…he said for me to call him that. He thinks of me as part of his family, too."

"Oh, he does, does he?"

"Yes."

"And just how did you meet him?"

"He came to find us, at the mansion."

"When?"

"About two and a half weeks ago."

Billy just glowered. And then he turned, walked to the door and punched it hard with a fist. The door was made of metal, apparently, because Billy's bones made an unpleasant sound when they hit the door, although nothing happened to the door at all. For a moment after impact, Billy held his fist and moved his lips in a string of profanities that surely would have burned the air, had he uttered them aloud.

Prudence knew she shouldn't say anything, but she just couldn't help pointing out, "That can't be very good for your guitar playing, can it?"

He whirled and glowered at her some more, still cradling his hand. Then he muttered, "It's fine. It'll be fine."

"Well," she said. "That's good. I suppose."

He came closer to her once more. She really wished

he wouldn't. But there he was, standing over her. He said, "I told that old coot to stay out of it."

Prudence looked up at him, unwavering, determined that he wouldn't know how much he frightened her. "Well, Oggie didn't do what you said. And I'm so grateful he didn't." She felt better, stronger, just thinking of Oggie. "He's a wonderful old man, a man who knows how important a family is. Jesse is part of his family. And I'm honored that he considers me a part of it, too."

Billy glared at her for several more nerve-racking seconds before he said softly, "I will kill him. And then I'll stake his ancient carcass out in the desert to fry in the sun."

Prudence gasped in outrage. "You will do no such thing." She tried to look absolutely unyielding, though it wasn't easy, with him towering above her.

"Watch me." He started to turn.

She hastened to stop him by adding, "And besides, Oggie's not in L.A. now, anyway."

Billy snapped his attention back to her. "Where is he?"

"He's gone home, to North Magdalene. Which is where Jesse and I are going. Tomorrow, right after I attend the closing on the mansion."

Billy froze, he stood absolutely stock-still. And now he was gaping more than glaring. *"Tomorrow?"*

"Tomorrow." She could see it all on his face. He still hadn't decided what to do about being a father. But when he *did* decide, he didn't want the child in question at the other end of the state. He said, in pure disbelief, "You can't just take my kid and leave."

"I beg to differ. I can. And I will."

"I'm his father."

"And I'm his legal guardian."

"I still have rights."

"I know. That's why I'm here tonight, to tell you that you're welcome to come and stay with us. Anytime."

He turned, paced to the door and then paced back to stand above her. "What the hell are you talking about? I live *here* in the San Fernando Valley. You can't just take my kid and move four hundred miles away."

"Mr. Jones. Up to now, you have not shown a lot of interest in *your kid.*"

He swore some more under his breath. Then he spoke more directly to her. "Look, I didn't even know about him until a couple of weeks ago."

"I understand that."

"*You* didn't bother to tell me about him."

"I was remiss, I know."

"Remiss. That's a wimpy little word for careless, isn't it? Well, you weren't careless. You damn well didn't tell me. *Randi* didn't tell me. *Nobody* told me. I had to find out on the damn six o'clock news."

She did feel somewhat guilty about that. "I'm sorry."

"Sorry doesn't cut it. The point is, that in spite of the fact I told your sister I didn't want kids, she went ahead and had my kid anyway—and never said a word to me about it. Then she died. And you were in charge. You knew I was Jesse's father, but you didn't tell me, either."

"I planned to tell you. I *would* have told you."

"But you *didn't* tell me. I found out by accident."

"Well, yes. But—"

He didn't wait for her excuses. "It wasn't that long ago, either, that I found out."

"I understand."

"And since I found out, I've been...working up to dealing with it."

She looked at him coldly, then. "Working up to dealing with *what*, Mr. Jones?"

"You know what. The kid. Working up to dealing with the kid."

She thought about Billy's one visit to the mansion, during which he'd stormed out before anything important could be said. She thought about the time that had passed since then, all the calls she'd made to him that he had never returned. And she decided that if he'd been working up to dealing with Jesse, he hadn't been working very hard.

She told him, "Well, regardless of all that, I am Jesse's legal guardian. And I will decide—"

He threw up a hand. "Don't start that. *I'm* his father. I'll damn well take you to court. We'll see who ends up *deciding* about my kid."

She granted him a look of utter condescension. "Please. As if a judge would ever award custody of an innocent child to someone like you. I've heard the stories about you. It wouldn't take much to dig them up and present them in court."

That gave Billy pause. He thought about a few of his past exploits. Once he'd climbed a flagpole naked; that had been written up in *Guitar Pickers* magazine. And there had been that time several years ago when he'd let himself get hooked on downers. He'd gone in to rehab and stayed clean—well, except for the booze—ever since. But still, his past drug problem was common knowledge around the entertainment industry. And then there were all the stories concerning him and a large number of women. Some of them wouldn't sound so good in a custody hearing.

The woman was looking at him, all smug and prissy. He muttered defensively, "A man can change."

She stood. "Well, you'd better get started on it then, hadn't you? And in the meantime, if you want to visit, come on ahead." She took a small card from the breast pocket of that button-down shirt. "Here's the address of the house where we'll be living. The phone there is already hooked up and the number of my cell phone is on the card, too. And anyway, it's a very small town. If you want to find us, you'll have no problem." She shoved the card into his hand and turned for the door.

Billy wasn't about to let her get out that easy. He moved fast, sliding past her and blocking her path. "Just a minute, here, Prue."

She sucked in a hard breath. "Don't call me that. And step out of the way, please."

"Do not." He bit off each word. "Repeat, do *not* leave town with my kid."

She didn't give an inch. "I *am* leaving town with your kid. Tomorrow, as I said."

"If you do—"

She let out a mean little laugh and tossed her head so the red waves he'd set free from that bun of hers bounced audaciously. "You won't even know whether I go or not. Because as soon as I leave this building, you'll go out to the bar and get good and drunk. And you'll play in the band. And go to bed late. And tomorrow, you'll get up and start all over again. You don't have time for a son, Mr. Jones. You're too busy partying." The bug eyes were shooting sparks. "My sister was right not to tell you about Jesse."

"No," he said flatly. "No, she was not right. She

used me, to get a baby. And then she dumped me. I hit the ground like a safe.''

This time her laugh sounded a lot like a snarl. "Oh, come on. I *lived* in her house. And we were very close. She *cared* for you. A lot. *You* were the one who would never let it go anywhere. You set the parameters. You said you wouldn't get married again and you wouldn't have kids. She became pregnant accidentally.''

"Yeah, right.''

"She *was* careful. But sometimes, even when a woman's careful, things happen.''

"Sure they do.''

"Wipe that smirk off your face. You can't lie to me, Mr. Jones. I know the truth. I know how it was. When she told you she didn't want to see you anymore, you fell all over yourself agreeing with her. You walked away, and you never once looked back.''

"I did look back. I missed her. I—''

"Save it. I don't need to hear it. The point I'm making is, you don't deserve a son, especially not one as wonderful as Jesse, and I find that I honestly regret you ever found out you're his father.''

Billy had that urge again, that urge to reach out and wring the woman's neck.

She must have seen it in his eyes, because she stuck her nose right up to him. "Go on. Try it. You just try it.''

Billy had behaved badly with a lot of women, but he'd never actually hit a woman in his life—let alone tried to strangle one. He wasn't about to start now. So he just glared at her. And she glared back. Heat seemed to vibrate in the air between them. Billy chose to believe it was the heat of anger. She had him pegged, and he knew it. He resented the hell out of her for it.

And for some insane reason, he felt a growing determination to prove her wrong.

At last he spoke. "One way or another, I'll make you regret it, if you leave town."

"Is that a threat, Mr. Jones?"

"That's a *fact*, Prue."

They both glared and fumed some more. Then, with a mocking bow, Billy stepped out of her way.

Prudence reached for the door, pulled it open and swept out, not pausing and not looking back—and feeling wonderfully self-righteous.

After all, she had done her duty. Billy Jones knew where to find his son if he wanted to visit.

Which he wouldn't. The days would turn to weeks, then to months and eventually, to years. Somehow, he would just never find the time.

She had tried, she told herself. But it had simply done no good. Bad Billy Jones had neither the aptitude nor the inclination for fatherhood. He would never show up in North Magdalene. And that was just fine with her.

Chapter 5

At four in the morning, one week later, Billy packed up his Jeep Cherokee. He tossed his garment bag and suitcase in the back. Then he set his Martin, safe in its case, between the two pieces of luggage, where it wouldn't get knocked around.

He drove straight through to Fresno, where he filled up the Jeep and ate truck-stop waffles smothered in butter and maple syrup. He hit the road again around eight and made it to Sacramento before noon. There, he stopped again, for more gas and a burger. Then he headed for the foothills.

In Grass Valley and Nevada City, the sycamores and black oaks were aflame with the colors of fall. And the air had a bite to it. This wasn't L.A. Here, there would be snow on the ground when the winter closed in.

At a sign that said Downieville, Billy turned off the stretch of four-lane highway and drove on, deeper into the mountains. The two-lane road twisted and turned, leading him down into the South Yuba River canyon and then back up the other side. All around him, steep hills rose up, blanketed in tall firs and pine.

A half an hour after he left Nevada City, at one thirty-five in the afternoon, he was braking to enter North Magdalene.

The highway ran right through the center of town, so he found himself on Main Street. Billy drove slowly, looking the place over. If he'd had a woman with him, she would have been sighing and gushing, calling the place precious and quaint and charming. Women went nuts for covered wooden sidewalks and gift shops with country-looking stuff in the windows. A row of maples, their leaves turned bright red and gold, lined the street on one side.

In addition to the cute little gift and variety stores, Billy drove by a motel, a grocery store, a post office, a bar and restaurant and a coffee shop. He'd just passed some store called Fletcher Gold Sales when he realized he was headed out of town—and must have gone right by the street where Prue and Jesse lived. He swung into the parking lot of a new-looking town hall, turned around and went back the way he'd come.

This time he was paying more attention when he reached Prospect Street. He turned on his left blinker, since left was the only way to go. Then he had to wait for two old ladies carrying grocery bags to finish crossing the street in front of him.

They were a pair: one tall and scrawny, the other square and as solid as a bank vault. They caught sight of him through his windshield and both of them looked surprised for a moment. Then they frowned in unison, as if they already knew him and knew just the kind of trouble he was likely to bring to their peaceful little town. For a moment, he thought maybe his fame as a songwriter had preceded him. But that wasn't real likely. He was pretty well-known in some show business circles, but not by the public at large. And he doubted that many of his tunes would have much appeal for a pair of old biddies in North Magdalene, California.

Just for fun, he honked and waved. The thin one waved back, but disapprovingly, as if she only did it because she was too well-bred to do otherwise. Right then, he found himself thinking of Sweethaven, his hometown. Sweethaven had been a damn sight flatter than this place, windy as hell and not nearly so picturesque. But from California to Kansas, old ladies in small towns were pretty much the same. They moved around in pairs. And they recognized an undomesticated male on sight.

At last, the two ladies reached the other side of the street. Billy eased his foot off the brake and made his turn.

Not two minutes later, he pulled up in front of the address Prue had given him. He turned off the Jeep, silencing a great Randy Travis tune in midnote. Then, for a moment, he sat studying the two-story building where Prue had brought his son to live.

He estimated the place to be anywhere from forty to a hundred years old. It had been freshly painted white, with the trim and shutters a dark green. It had a nice, deep porch and a white picket fence around the yard. A big old rough-barked locust tree hung over the fence, looking a little scraggly now that it was losing its leaves for the winter. But the lawn was thick and green and the slate walk that led up to the porch steps seemed to just invite a man to come inside.

He had to admit it. The place seemed to be just what Prue had been looking for: the perfect setting for Jesse to get a good start on his "ordinary" life. It was also across and down from the white wood-frame community church. Leave it to Prue, he thought with some amusement, to find a house on the same street as the church.

Billy got out of the Jeep and went around back for his garment bag, suitcase and guitar. He slung the bag over his shoulder and took the suitcase and the Martin in either hand. Then he went through the front gate and up that pretty slate walk.

The look of stunned disbelief on Prue's face when she opened the door made the trip more than worthwhile. Now all he had to do was find that meddling uncle of his and knock his tonsils down his throat. Then Billy Jones would be a totally contented man.

"Billy." She said his name the way some might say, "measles," or "poison oak." Her glasses had a smudge on them. She wore jeans and an old shirt and her hair had a red bandanna over it.

"Getting a little cleaning done?"

"Billy," she said again, dazed. Disbelieving.

He savored her obvious stupefaction at the sight of him, here, where she had been so sure he would never come. "Your mouth's hanging open, Prue."

She snapped it shut.

"Can I come in?"

She fell back, still wearing an expression of pure bumfuzzlement. Feeling really good, really happy, really pleased with himself, Billy entered her house. It had no entry hall, so he stepped into her living room. It was just what he expected: hardwood floors and comfortable furniture, roses floating in a cut crystal bowl on the coffee table. The television was new, with a decent-size screen, but there was no stereo in sight. He'd have to do something about that.

He set the guitar and the suitcase down, though he kept the garment bag on his shoulder. "Where's Jesse?"

"Taking a nap."

He grinned. "In a bed, I hope."

She frowned. "He's too young for a bed."

He put on a reproachful expression. "He's still in a crib?"

"Uh, yes. Yes, he is."

"Well, I'll have to fix that." He grinned again. Ever since she'd left him in his office that night a week ago, he'd been making plans. For the things that he would fix.

Behind the smudged glasses, her eyes had lost that dazed look. They were starting to glitter dangerously. "Wait a minute. How dare you assume you can just march in here and—"

He cut in, sounding very reasonable, he thought. "He sure does sleep a lot. That worries me a little."

"He's hardly more than a baby. Babies do sleep a lot."

"Still, it could be a warning."

"A warning of what?"

He had no idea, but he wasn't going to tell her that. "Hell, lots of things."

She folded her arms under her breasts and tapped an impatient foot on the floor. "Oh, right. You're an expert on children now. After all, your experience with them is so *vast*."

She was starting to irritate him. "When it comes to my son, my experience is going to get *vaster*, Prue.

Just watch.'' He hoisted the Martin and the suitcase again. ''Now, where's my room?''

She blinked at him through those grotesque glasses that he knew damn well she wore as much to hide behind as to see through. ''Your room?''

He hefted the suitcase, just in case she hadn't noticed it. ''I'm staying a while. Contrary to your expectations, I'm taking you up on that offer of yours.''

''What offer?'' Boy, did she look bleak.

With relish, he reminded her, ''You know, to visit? To get to know my son. To learn how to be a father.''

''But, you can't—''

''Oh, yes, I can.'' He stepped a little closer to her. ''Unless…''

She moved back. ''What?''

''…you were lying to me.''

She gulped. ''Lying?''

''About how I was so welcome to come and stay. Anytime. Were you lying about that, Prue?''

Her eyes darted back and forth in their sockets, as she desperately tried to find herself some avenue of escape. But there was no escape, and Billy knew it. He'd done a lot of thinking about Prue. And he'd come to a few conclusions.

The woman was hopelessly honorable. And she possessed an ingrained determination to do the right thing. Honor and integrity. Such commendable qualities. They put her right where he wanted her.

''Prue,'' he prompted softly, ''were you lying?''

''No.'' She looked slightly pale. ''I wasn't lying. I meant what I said. You're Jesse's father. He should know you.''

''And he will know me. Now, where's my room?''

He watched the resignation come into her eyes. If

he'd been a better man, he probably wouldn't have enjoyed seeing it there so much.

"All right," she said. "This way."

She led him out of the living room, to a bedroom that branched right off the dining room. He tossed his suitcase onto the bed and hung up the garment bag in the closet. She stood in the doorway, watching him, looking all sad and haunted, as if she were some bespectacled Southern belle forced to bed down a damn Yankee in her plantation home.

She sighed. "The downstairs bath is off the kitchen."

"Fine." Carefully he stood the Martin in the corner, in a space between the bureau and the wall, where it wasn't likely to be disturbed. Then he felt in his pocket for his keys.

"You're going somewhere?" she asked faintly, as he strode past her.

"Yeah. Out."

"Out where?"

He was almost to the front door before he turned and gave her a grin. "To find my uncle."

That snapped some starch into her. "Why?"

"To knock his teeth down his throat."

She started moving then. Fast. Toward him. "Billy, you can't—"

"Watch me." In four steps he'd reached the door. He pulled it open and then paused to tell her, "I'll be back in time for dinner."

"Billy, you're not serious. You wouldn't really—"

He shut the door before she could finish. He was whistling as he strode down that charming slate walk.

* * *

In the house, Prudence stared at the door he'd closed in her face and debated whether to follow him.

She decided not to. She didn't really believe he'd hurt Oggie. Billy might be a hooligan by nature, but he didn't seem the type to brutalize a helpless old man. Besides, Oggie wasn't really all that helpless. He had four big, strong sons who lived in town. And if his sons couldn't save him, his quick tongue surely would. Billy would confront the old man, work off a little steam with shouting and swearing, and then he'd return—which was what she should be thinking about: Billy's return here. And how, exactly, she intended to handle it.

Because he clearly planned on staying a while. And she had no one to blame but herself for that. She *had* invited him, after all.

She started for the stairs. She still had some unpacking to do from the move, and she wanted to clean the bathroom up there. She would put away the last of her things and then get down on her hands and knees and scrub the bathroom tiles. She could decide how to proceed with Billy while she worked.

Billy was already back in the Jeep and heading for Main Street again before he realized he should have tried to get Oggie's address out of Prue. During those memorable evenings when the old man had followed him around Bad Billy's trying to convince him to join the family fold, Oggie had babbled a lot about his four sons and his daughter, their spouses and their children, about his niece named Evie and his granddaughter, Heather, who happened to be married to the world-famous horror writer, Lucas Drury. Thanks to the old man's incessant jabbering, Billy had learned more than he ever wanted to know about the Joneses of North Magdalene.

Unfortunately neither a phone number nor an address had been included in the torrent of information Oggie had unleashed on him. Since Billy had never intended to get near North Magdalene or its surplus of Joneses, not having an address hadn't mattered much at the time.

But now, he needed one.

So he went to the little coffee shop on Main Street: Lily's Café. Usually, in a small town, all the gossips hung out at the café. He could ask there about his dear old uncle, Oggie Jones. Some talkative soul would be more than happy to fill him in. He slid on his Resistol and settled his shades over his eyes before he went in.

Everybody turned and looked when he pushed open the café door. For a moment, he knew how Garth Brooks must feel. He spotted the two pillars of society he'd watched crossing the street earlier. They sat in a back booth, sipping tea and giving him the evil eye. He felt sure they would know where he might find his uncle, but he doubted they'd tell him if he asked.

A man at the counter let out a hoot right then. "Well, I'll be hornswoggled. Another damn Jones. Even with them sunglasses on, there's no missin' that look."

The waitress, a big, motherly type, leaned across the counter and told the man, "Rocky, why don't you just toddle back on over to the Hole in the Wall."

"Can't," Rocky muttered in bleary regret. "Eden's over there now. She says get sober." He held out his coffee cup. "Fill 'er up." The waitress looked at him with equal parts affection and disapproval. He sighed, "Please?"

Eden, Billy was thinking. That would be one of Oggie's daughters-in-law. More of the old codger's ramblings came back to him. The family owned a bar and restaurant: the Hole in the Wall and the Mercantile Grill. Billy realized he'd driven by them more than once now. They were across the street and down a few doors, past the post office.

Billy slid onto the stool next to the drunk. "Hey, Rocky."

"Hey, yourself," Rocky said. "You *are* a Jones, ain't you?"

"I sure am."

"Which one?"

"Billy Jones. I'm a nephew of Oggie's."

The waitress poured Rocky's coffee, then held the pot toward Billy.

He turned his cup up and she filled it. "Thanks." He pulled a five from his pocket and slid it across the counter. "That'll do it." Ignoring the continued hush in the place, Billy picked up the cup and took a sip.

Rocky sipped, too, with some effort, since his hand was a mite shaky. "You Evie's brother or what?"

"No, my father was Nathaniel. I think Evie's father might have been Gideon."

"Right," said Rocky. "Gideon." He shook his head. "Died in prison, did you know?"

"I think Oggie mentioned that." Hell, Oggie *might* have mentioned that. He'd mentioned just about everything else, for God's sakes.

Rocky lifted his cup again, then set it down and lowered his mouth to the rim. He slurped in a sip.

The waitress, who had taken Billy's money to the cash register, marched over and slapped Billy's change on the counter. "Here you go."

"Keep it," Billy said.

"Thanks." She slid the change into her palm and dropped it into an apron pocket.

"Yeah," Rocky was saying. "Crazy old Gideon. Died in the slammer. But Oggie gave him a real purty funeral right here, at the church, back just a few months ago. Buried him right here, too, in the North Magdalene cemetery."

Billy decided it was time to cut to the big question. "Speaking of Oggie. I wonder, do you know where I can find him?"

Rocky's seamed face split in a gap-toothed grin. "Sure. The Hole in the Wall. The back room."

"He's there right now?"

"Ten minutes ago, he was."

Billy took one more sip, then set down the cup and slid off his stool. "Thanks, Rocky."

Rocky went on grinning. "Hey. You betcha. You take care a yourself now, Billy."

"I'll do that." Billy tipped his hat to the waitress. "Great coffee, ma'am." The waitress folded her arms across her middle, leaned back on the service counter behind her and granted him an itty-bitty nod.

He headed for the door, feeling about ten pairs of eyes burning holes in the back of his shirt. At the last minute, he turned, took off the sunglasses and hung them on his breast pocket. The two biddies in the back were looking right at him—as he had known they would be.

He gave them a slow grin. "You ladies have a real nice afternoon."

The skinny one stared and the big one blinked. He kept up the grin as he pulled the door open and went out.

Two minutes later, he was pushing back the swinging doors and entering the Hole in the Wall. It was dim inside, as a bar should be. Billy stood for a moment, letting his eyes adjust. As they did, he saw dark wood walls and small round tables with bentwood chairs grouped around them. Three men sat at the bar to his left, sipping drinks, saying nothing. Beyond the bar lay a narrow hall—to a back exit, it looked like. To the right of the hall, about midway along the wall, hung a heavy green curtain. The way to the back room, Billy had no doubt.

"What can I do for you?"

Billy looked toward the voice, which had come from behind the long bar. A tall, rangy character stood there. A familiar character, who resembled the guy Billy saw in the mirror whenever he bothered to look.

"You Jared?" Billy asked.

"You Billy?"

They both said, "Yeah," at the same time.

"The old man's been expecting you," Jared said.

Billy wondered what that meant. He had an urge to ask, but thought that might put him at a disadvantage, so he said nothing.

Jared offered, "Beer?"

Billy shrugged. He might be here to grind the old man's bones to dust, but he could take a minute for a cold one first. "Yeah."

"Bud?"

"Fine." Billy slid on up to the bar.

Jared filled a mug and set it down. Billy moved to pull out some bills.

"On the house," Jared said.

"Thanks." Billy drank, not stopping until he'd drained the mug. When he was done, he set it down.

"Refill?"

"That'll do it. For now."

A woman came through a door behind the bar. She had short strawberry-colored hair and carried a cash drawer, which she put in the ornate old-style National cash register. She stopped at one point and shared an intimate look with Jared. Billy decided that she must be Jared's wife, Eden, the one who had sent Rocky across the street to sober up.

"I'm going on home now," she said to Jared.

He nodded and she disappeared through the door again. Two of the men at the bar got up and went over to the pool table, which stood about five feet in front of the green curtain. They began racking up balls. The third man remained on his stool, staring morosely into his beer. He was a giant of a man, broad-shouldered and deep-chested, with red-gold hair clubbed into a ponytail down his back.

"My brother-in-law, Sam Fletcher," Jared said of the long-haired giant. Billy and Sam Fletcher nodded at each other, then Jared added, "Listen, if you're looking for the old man, he's not here."

Billy asked, "Where'd he go?"

"Back to the house, I think," said Sam.

Billy turned to the big man. "The house?"

"Our house. Delilah's and mine."

Delilah, Billy thought. Sam and Delilah. Real cute. Then he realized what the giant had just told him. "Wait a minute," he said in disbelief. "You *live* with that old snake oil salesman?"

Sam's expression remained carefully blank. "*He* lives with *us*."

Billy shook his head. "My condolences."

Sam nodded, looking weary.

Billy asked, "You think you could tell me how to get to that house of yours?"

Sam and Jared exchanged a look. Then Sam shrugged. "You go down to Bullfinch Lane. Hang right. Cross Sweet Spring Way. Our house is in the middle of the next block." He named an address.

"Thanks," Billy said.

"No problem."

Billy decided he liked both of these men and owed them the respect of honesty. "I guess you should know that I'm not feelin' real friendly. That old geezer has pushed me too far."

Jared shook his head, his expression regretful. "He's my father. I know how he gets." Sam didn't say anything. His eyes said it all.

Right then, the phone behind the bar rang.

Jared picked it up. "The Hole in the Wall." He listened. "Hold on." He held out the phone to Sam. "It's that new clerk of yours."

Sam took the phone. "Hi, Sharlee. Yeah. All right. I'm on my way." He gave the phone back to Jared and stood.

Jared said, "What's with her, anyway? She can't handle that store alone for ten minutes?"

"She's new. She needs the benefit of my expertise."

"She's got a thing for you," Jared said quietly. "People have noticed. They're starting to talk."

"People can go to hell." Sam headed for the door.

Billy and Jared watched him go out. Then Jared dumped out the rest of Sam's beer, wiped the counter and washed the mug.

Billy said, "I'm gonna check the back room, just in case."

Jared shrugged. "Suit yourself."

Billy strode over and looked behind the curtain. He saw a felt-topped table with a hooded light above it, ashtrays, a few cigar stubs, but no Oggie. Satisfied, he turned for the door.

At the house on Bullfinch Lane, he knocked and got no answer. He'd turned for his Jeep again when a black-haired woman pulled up in a hatchback car. He waited on the step while she got out and came toward him.

"I'm Delilah. May I help you?" She was small and curvy. Her dark eyes told a man he'd better not mess. Billy found himself pondering the call from Sam's clerk and the cryptic remarks Jared had made. He had a feeling that if Sam didn't watch it, little Delilah would be clipping his hair but good.

Not that it meant a damn thing to Billy personally. "I'm Billy Jones—your cousin?"

She smiled then. "Oh, yes. Father said you just might be coming to town."

I'll bet he did, Billy thought. "Yeah. Well. Here I am. Got any idea where I might find your father?"

Delilah said he could try Evie's—either the shop she owned on Main Street or her and Erik's house, over on Pine. Or then again, Oggie might have gone to Patrick and Regina's, which was right next door to Evie and Erik's. Or possibly to Jared and Eden's, way out on River Road. Or Brendan and Amy's. Or even Jack and Olivia's.

Using the directions Delilah had given him, Billy went to each house. He struck out every time. But he did end up meeting a passel of relatives. He found it a sobering experience, all those cousins and their wives and kids, and all within about a three-mile radius.

By the time he finally gave up and wandered back

to the Hole in the Wall, it was after five in the evening. And he was ready for another Bud.

Jared poured one without having to be told. Billy murmured thanks. Then Jared said, "By the way, the old man's been here the whole damn time." He slid the beer to Billy. "Just stepped out to take a whizz, that was all."

Billy swore low, with feeling, then drained the mug. Down the bar, he saw the drunk from the café, Rocky. He nodded. Woozily, Rocky lifted his glass in a salute.

Billy asked Jared, "He in back?"

Jared nodded.

Billy turned for the green curtain.

Chapter 6

"Hey, boy, good to see ya," the old man chortled. He sat at the felt-clothed table, a shot of whiskey at his elbow, a cigar clamped between his teeth and five cards in his hand. He waved his cigar at the other three men around the table and reeled off their names.

"I want to talk to you," Billy said. "Alone."

Oggie chortled some more and flicked his ash. "All right, all right. Just let me finish this hand."

Billy stood waiting as the bets went around the table. Oggie pulled in the pile after the rest of them laid down. Then, one by one, the other men got up and left.

A long silence followed. In the middle of it, Jared came through the curtain. He set a bottle on the table and a clean shot glass beside it. Then he went back out to the main room again.

Oggie filled the glass Jared had brought and then refilled his own. "Sit," he said. "Drink."

Billy stayed on his feet. But he did pick up the glass

and knock its contents down his throat. It was smooth and hot going down. Good stuff.

Oggie said, "So. I suppose you got a longing to rearrange my face."

Billy did. But he wouldn't act on it. He had never intended to act on it. It had been fun, though, telling himself—and Prue—that he would.

Oggie shrugged and puffed some more on his cigar. The smoke trailed and curled in the light of the hooded lamp over the table. "I could call the boys back in. We could play a few hands. Have a few drinks. A few laughs."

Billy said, "I told you to stay away from my kid."

"So. Now you admit he's your kid."

"Yeah. He's my kid and he's none of your damn business."

"He's a Jones. That makes him my business. The way I look at it, I only did what needed to be done." Clamping the cigar firmly between his teeth, Oggie began gathering up the cards from around the table. "And I don't mind tellin' you, I'm glad to be home. I was gettin' real tired of followin' you around that club of yours." He picked up the last card, then began to shuffle the deck. "I got bored with waltzin' the help all the time, puttin' on the charm. It was gettin' old, you know? I was longin' to be back here where people have to put up with me just 'cause I'm me. And I sure as hell wasn't getting through to you. But then, I saw that kid. I saw my chance. And I took it. Talk to anyone in this town. They'll tell you. Oggie Jones ain't a man to miss his chance. So. You want in the card game, or not?"

Just then, someone put a quarter in the jukebox. "Up Against the Wall, Redneck Mothers" came on. A true classic by Ray Wiley Hubbard, sung by Jerry Jeff Walker himself.

Oggie slapped the deck on the table. "Cut."

Billy cut. Then he went over to the curtain and looked out into the main room. The men who had just left the card game were lined up at the bar. Billy caught the eye of one of them and signaled with a jerk of his head. One by one, they got up, walked around the pool table and came back through the curtain. They took the same seats they'd had before.

Oggie began to deal. "The game is five-card draw."

Billy slid into the vacant chair.

A nice dinner, Prudence decided. She would fix Billy a nice dinner, and afterward, they would talk. They would talk reasonably, calmly. About what his expectations were. About what he wanted from this visit and how long he intended to stay.

Jesse sat in his high chair, gurgling and gumming crackers, while Prudence bustled around the kitchen. She prepared her favorite chicken casserole, one made with lemons and rice. It was very low fat and healthy, but also quite tasty, too. She cut up broccoli and put it in the steamer, all ready to go. She made a nice salad.

While the casserole was cooking, she bathed Jesse and read him a Dr. Seuss story, using lots of facial and vocal expression. Even at his age, he seemed to listen and understand. She firmly believed that you couldn't start too young when it came to reading to a child.

The casserole was finished at six-thirty. But Billy had not returned. Prudence left the food in the oven to stay warm and took Jesse up to her room. There, he played with blocks on the floor while she sat at her computer, redesigning her résumé for about the fifth time.

Prudence was a C.P.A. Even while working for her sister, she'd kept up her continuing ed and renewed her license every year. She had thought, when she moved to North Magdalene, that she might find a job with a local firm. But North Magdalene had a population under 250. Even in the larger towns of Grass Valley and Nevada City, C.P.A.s weren't in great demand. Fiddling with her résumé had become a sort of game to her, really. A way to start thinking of how she might make some kind of job for herself here. Eventually, when Jesse got a little older, she'd probably start a small bookkeeping service, just to keep her hand in.

Not that she'd ever need money. She'd made plenty and invested well while she worked for Randi. Then Randi had left her a small fortune when she died. And then there was Jesse's huge inheritance, which was always available if they needed it.

Prudence glanced at her program clock: almost seven-thirty. She was starting to wonder if something might have happened to Billy. Maybe he had gone too far with Oggie, after all. Perhaps Oggie's four big sons had been forced to step in. Billy could be over at the town clinic right now, getting patched up by Will Bacon, the practical nurse who handled all the local medical emergencies.

Over by the bed, Jesse was chewing on the bed linens.

"No, no," Prudence chided. "That is not food."

He looked up at her, puzzled, then turned to frown at the soggy corner of bed ruffle he held clenched in his plump fist. "Not?"

She got up and went to him. He dropped the bed

ruffle and reached out his arms, his face blooming into one of those smiles that always turned her heart to mush. She bent and scooped him up. "Bedtime for you, mister."

He made what she thought of as a stinky face, wrinkling his nose and scrunching his eyes shut. "Nawp," he said, as if it were a real word.

"Yawp," she replied, and carried him downstairs.

It took about an hour to get him to bed. Jesse liked to have her sing to him and tell him stories before he'd go to sleep. Lots of songs and lots of stories. If she dared to stop before he'd heard enough, he'd start crying. All the books she read said she was just supposed to let him cry, and she knew that Alma always used to get him to go down with a minimum of fuss. But somehow, since Prudence had taken sole charge of his care, bedtimes had become protracted affairs.

The truth was, she couldn't bear to hear him cry. So she indulged him. So what if the books said she shouldn't? She had the time. And an excess of attention could hardly hurt him.

Finally, at eight-thirty, Jesse fell asleep.

A little tired from all the singing and storytelling, Prudence wandered back downstairs and took the casserole out of the oven. It looked a bit dry by then. But she was starved. She ladled a serving onto a plate, dished up some salad and ate.

Then she put the broccoli, still unsteamed, back in the crisper and cleaned up after the meal. If Billy Jones wanted dinner, he could get it himself.

But then again, maybe something really had happened to him. She decided to call Delilah's house, where Oggie lived. Maybe somebody there could tell her what had happened to her supposed houseguest.

Delilah answered on the first ring. She said that Billy had been there briefly that afternoon, searching for Oggie. "Try the Hole in the Wall," Delilah suggested, with the authority of a woman who had grown up with Jones men.

Prudence did try the bar. The night bartender, Nick Santino, answered.

"He's in the back room with Oggie and the boys," Nick said. "Been there for hours now."

"Doing what, may I ask?"

"Playin' poker, ma'am."

Billy sipped his whiskey as he studied his hand. He shot a glance at the old man.

The old man was looking back. He pulled out a card and sloughed it. "So. How long you stayin' in town for?"

Billy sloughed two cards. "Depends." He picked up the two the dealer had laid in front of him.

Oggie picked up his single card and added it to his hand. "Where you stayin'?"

"At my son's house."

"In point of fact, that house belongs to Prudence."

Billy shrugged.

"That's a fine house," Oggie declared. "Used to be the Conley house, for years and years. It went to my granddaughter Heather when her first husband, Jason Lee Conley, passed on. A sad story, that was. Barely in his twenties, with his whole life ahead of him. Killed in a landslide, working on a county road. Left poor Heather alone. But not for long. Lucas Drury came for her. You heard of him, ain't you?"

"Yeah. Writes scary books."

"Horror novels, son. Horror novels. And now,

Heather don't need that fine house anymore. Lucas has
built her and their children a big fancy place up on
Piety Hill." Oggie puffed on his cigar, making the tip
glow read. "So Prudence has bought the Conley place,
and brought your son to live there." He took the cigar
from his mouth and looked at the end of it. "A nice
woman, that Prudence. A woman of heart and grit."
He stuck the cigar back between his yellowed teeth.
"And she is fine-lookin', too, behind those disagree-
able glasses and that scraped-back hair."

The dealer said, "Dealer takes two," and dealt himself two more cards.

Oggie arched a grizzled brow and looked straight at
Billy. "Don't you think our Prudence is fine?"

Billy reached for the bottle next to the pile of money
on the table. "You in this game or not?"

Oggie grunted, scowled at his cards and then, finally,
placed his bet.

"You want me to get him on the phone for you?"
asked Nick the bartender.

Prudence said, "No, thank you," and hung up.

She couldn't believe her own foolishness. She'd actually been worried about Billy Jones. Concerned that
he'd been injured. That he might be in pain. But no.
Bad Billy Jones was feeling no pain. He was playing
poker at the Hole in the Wall. With Uncle Oggie. Who
ought to know better, at his age.

I'll make you regret it, if you leave town, he had
threatened when she told him she and Jesse were moving here.

Already, he was proving his point.

The poker game broke up around midnight. Feeling
pleasantly plotzed, Billy gathered up his winnings and

bought everyone in the house a couple of rounds. He and Oggie stood together at the bar. The old man told a joke or two, then asked Billy if he happened to know that great show tune, "Have Some Madeira, M'dear."

There was a battered upright piano in the corner. Billy banged out the tune and Oggie playacted the old rake intent on seducing a sweet young thing. Even Rocky, who could barely sit up by then, laughed long and loud. Oggie knew a few other great tunes as well. Billy played some more and the old man performed. The guy was pretty amazing, really. In his eighties at least, and still up for partying hearty till all hours of the night.

The only sour note in the evening came around twelve-thirty, when one of the old bats Billy had seen crossing Main Street when he first hit town came in looking for her husband. The husband's name was Owen. He was one of the men Billy and Oggie had been playing poker with. The old bat's name, as it turned out, was Linda Lou. Linda Lou demanded that Owen come home right now. When the poor man hesitated, she grabbed him by the arm and hauled him toward the door.

Billy, totally by accident, ended up in her path as she dragged her husband out. He moved right back, but still, she shot him a look that would have curdled sweet cream.

Oggie slapped him on the back. "You should know better than to get in *her* way."

"One too many whiskeys," Billy explained. "My reflexes have slowed."

"Have another," Oggie suggested. "It'll settle your nerves."

"I believe I will do that," Billy replied.

Two o'clock came the way it always did: too soon.

Billy helped Oggie and Nick close up. Nick drove Oggie home and Billy pretty much carried Rocky to his apartment above the grocery store. And then, since he still felt way too good to be getting behind the wheel of a car, Billy strolled back to Prudence's, which was just around the corner and down the street anyway.

But then, somehow, he must have ended up on the wrong block. He went in Prue's front gate—he thought. And he went up the walk, which he should have noticed was made of concrete and not slate. The porch looked a little different, too. But by then, he was starting to think about hitting the sack, and not feeling real picky about details. He opened the door and went in.

He'd turned on a light in the living room and was looking around, trying to figure out where he was, when he heard the screaming. He blinked and turned toward the sound. A tall, skinny woman stood in the hallway that branched off from the far side of the room. She was clutching a blue quilted robe at her neck and wearing a blue hair net on her head.

"Oh my Lord! Help! Somebody, help me, please!" she screamed. About then, he realized where he'd seen her before: crossing Main Street the previous afternoon, along with that other battle-ax, Owen's wife.

"Help, oh, help me! A murderer! An intruder!"

Even as drunk as he was, Billy managed to deduce that she wanted help because she was terrified of *him*.

"Uh, look." He backed toward the door. "Sorry. So sorry. Big mistake. Leaving now."

She started running toward him, still screaming for help, as he got the door open and put it between himself and her. Something crashed against it and shattered; she must have picked up the vase on the side table and thrown it at him. He sprinted off down the walk, kicked the fence open and headed back toward Main.

A few minutes later, when he went through a second gate, he was more careful to check for familiar objects: the locust tree by the fence, the slate walk, the Adirondack-style porch furniture. Yeah, this was Prue's house. No doubt about it this time.

The problem came when he tried to open the front door. It was locked. Billy stepped back, puzzled. Then he smiled to himself. Probably she'd left a key under the mat. He bent over, braced himself on the door frame and lifted the thing. Nothing. He took a minute to straighten up again, and then he noticed that the house was really dark. She hadn't left the porch light on.

Billy started to understand. He'd stayed out later than he should enough nights in his life to know what it meant when a woman didn't even leave the porch light on. It meant a man would have to make a hell of a lot of racket, pounding on the door and shouting— and then maybe, if he got lucky, the woman would have a little pity and let him in. But then again, maybe even a lot of noise and shouting wouldn't work. A man got no guarantees when it came to a woman who didn't leave the porch light on. No guarantees at all.

But that was all right with Billy. He'd handled situations like this before. He went back down the porch steps and around the side of the house to the window of the room Prue had assigned to him. He had to crush a few bushes to do it, but he got up close enough that he could study the screen, which was hinged at the top and had a hook at the bottom. As luck would have it, the hook wasn't engaged. He lifted the screen and eased it up. Then he slid it sideways and it came right off the hinge. He tossed it behind him, onto the side lawn. Now, for the window. The lock was the old-fashioned kind, a slide latch that anchored the top pane to the bottom one.

He grinned woozily to himself when he started to shimmy the bottom pane. The house was newly painted, but those windows were old. A few good nudges with the heel of his hand and the latch started to give. He hit the frame again, sharply, and then pushed. The latch slipped completely free and the window slid up.

"Hah!" he said, but quietly. After all, he knew it was late. He didn't want to wake anyone up. He just wanted a bed to sleep in. He swung his boot over the sill.

He saw her standing there, a shadow in the doorway, as he slid into the room. She flicked on the light. He groaned as the sudden burst of brightness attacked his eyeballs. Where in holy hell had his sunglasses gone? He'd had them with him earlier—and his hat, too. But he must have left them at one of the Joneses while he was looking for Oggie, because he didn't think he'd been wearing either while he played that poker game.

After a moment, his poor abused eyes adjusted to the glare. He looked at her, from the bottom up. Her feet were bare. She had long, pale toes. Very nice toes. She wore white pajamas—at least, what he could see of them was white. They disappeared under her white robe, which was belted good and tight around her waist. Her face was pink from sleep. Altogether, she looked better than usual. Her hair helped. She wore it in a braid down her back. Little crinkly red strands of it had gotten loose and stood up around her face. Unfortunately, even in the middle of the night, she had those ugly glasses on—and a snapping-turtle look in her eyes.

He tried a sheepish grin. "You forgot to give me a key."

Her mouth was a flat line. "What I forgot to do is to call the sheriff's office and have you arrested."

He let out a tired breath. "Come on. Lighten up."

"Breaking and entering. That is what you just did."

As usual, she was irritating him into sobriety. "What? Is there some curfew around this joint that I should know about?"

"No, Billy. No curfew. Just common courtesy, that's all."

He tried to look pitiful. "I was being courteous. I didn't pound the door or shout, did I?"

"Oh, certainly. You break into my house. But you're quiet when you do it, so it's all right." She had her arms wrapped hard around her middle, as if she was holding her anger in there, good and tight.

He decided looking pitiful wasn't cutting it. He dropped to the edge of the bed. "There's nothing I hate more than a tight-assed woman, you know that, Prue?"

"I assume you're referring to me."

"If the shoe fits—"

"Oh, stop it. I'm not the issue here, and we both know it. You've been out gambling and drinking till the middle of the night."

"I surely have."

"Why?"

"Because I wanted to."

"You could have gambled and drank at your club in L.A."

"I make myself at home wherever I go. I like a good time. And I *have* a good time."

She gave him another of those long, mean looks. Then she sighed and shook her head. "I just don't understand."

"What's to understand?"

"You said you came here to get to know Jesse." She didn't look mad anymore. She just looked tired. And a little bit sad.

And all of a sudden, he found he felt about as low as he had that other night, at Bad Billy's, when he'd stolen her glasses and taken down her hair in front of his friends.

She was leaning against the door frame now. "Billy, there is no point in your being here, if you're just going to run wild in the bar all night long."

He rubbed his tired eyes and fell back on the bed.

"Billy…"

The light fixture overhead had two cut-glass shades shaped like flowers. In the center of the flowers, lightbulbs bloomed. He shouldn't be staring at them, but he was, anyway. The brightness made weird afterimages that floated in a circle around the central blossoms of light. He closed one eye and then the other, causing the afterimages to pop back and forth like the ball at a tennis match.

"Billy, have you gone to sleep on me?"

"No. I'm awake. And I did come here to get to know Jesse."

"Well, then." Her voice had softened. It was almost kind. "When are you going to start doing that?"

He was still a little drunk, he supposed. The flowers of light kept becoming four, then fading back to just two again.

"Billy, when are you going to start getting to know your son?"

"Tomorrow," he said on a heavy exhalation of breath. The flowers of light were fading, moving away.

She said something else, something quiet and low. But he didn't hear it. The wave of unconsciousness rose up over him. It was taking him under.

He went with it, murmuring, "Tomorrow, Prue. Hones'. Tomorrow. I will get t' know him. Tomorrow. I will...."

Chapter 7

When Billy woke, he felt as if someone had freeze-
dried his brain. He rolled over and squinted at the little
clock radio by the bed: after nine. With a groan, he sat
up and pushed back the blanket.

He hung his head and studied his socks. He was still
fully dressed, except for those socks. Even though it
hurt to do it, he smiled. Prue had a good heart. She'd
pulled off his boots and thrown a blanket over him.
Lots of women wouldn't have bothered.

His stomach felt dangerous. And his head…

Better get moving. Get some Alka-Seltzer. Pronto.

He launched himself at the door and stumbled out
into the dining room. He saw his kid beyond a low
gatelike contraption, sitting on the kitchen floor, chewing on something yellow—a rubber duck or a toy
chicken, he supposed. The kid stared at him. He stared
back.

"Oh, Billy." It was Prue, standing beside the kid, sounding very discouraged.

"Bathroom," he muttered at her shoes, since he couldn't bear to face the disappointment in her magnified eyes.

She moved forward, unhooked the low gate and pulled it back. "That way." She pointed. He went through, barreling past her, headed for the door she'd indicated. He made it just in time to lose the contents of his stomach in the toilet bowl.

Even after he rinsed his mouth and splashed cold water on his face, he continued to feel like twenty miles of bad road. He looked in the medicine cabinet: no Alka-Seltzer.

She knocked on the door. He marched over and yanked it open. "What?"

She held up a glass filled with water. As he watched, she dropped two white tablets into the glass.

He took it from her. "Thanks." He shut the door. As he started to drink it down, he heard the phone in the kitchen ringing.

A few minutes later, he left the bathroom and headed back to bed. Prue was talking on the phone. The kid still sat on the kitchen floor. Now he was gnawing on a piece of biscuit. The kid looked up at him and made a gurgly, friendly, questioning sort of noise. "Awanna?" He held out the gooed-up biscuit.

Billy shook his head and kept on walking, almost tripping on the gate, which she'd put back across the door to the dining room. Somehow, though, he readjusted his stride for it just in time and managed to get over it. Then he staggered on, through the dining room and back to the bedroom, where he fell across the bed and shut his eyes with a grateful moan.

But not for long.

"Billy?" Prue was standing over him shaking him.

"Uh. Yeah." He opened one eye and looked at her. "Wha'?"

"That was Jack Roper on the phone."

The name sounded familiar. But Billy's mind wasn't operating at optimum efficiency. "Jack? Rope?"

"Jack Roper. He's Oggie's son by a woman he knew before he met his late wife, Bathsheba."

"Why are you telling me this? Why are you talking? Why are you here?"

"Jack Roper is also a deputy, over at the sheriff's station."

"Whatever it is, I didn't do it."

"Nellie Anderson filed a complaint last night."

"Never heard of her."

"She said a man broke into her house. She described the man. Her description sounded exactly like you."

Billy had a vague recollection of a blue hair net and a lot of shrieking. "Wait a minute. Tall, skinny broad? Hangs out with Owen's wife, Linda Lou?"

Prue just looked down at him and sighed.

He lifted a hand and waved it in front of his face. "It was an accident. I thought I was here."

"Oh, Billy..."

He dropped his hand and shut his eyes again. The world, blessedly, went away.

The next time he woke, it was two hours later. And he felt better. Not good exactly, but better. He swung his legs over the edge of the bed and sat there for a while, gathering his energy, thinking of pulling on his boots. But pulling on his boots would take more effort than he was willing to expend right then.

He wanted coffee and a shower. He knew his own constitution. By the time he got a good shot of caffeine in his system and cleaned himself up, he'd be feeling just fine.

There was no one in the dining room. He started for the kitchen, but then he heard women's voices and children's laughter coming from out front. He looked that way and saw that the door was partway open. He started toward it. The sun was out and shining brightly. It looked like a warm afternoon, for November in the mountains.

Billy moved quietly through the dining room to the living room and the open door, drawn by the sunshine outside, by the soft drone of feminine voices.

When he got closer, he edged to the left, so he could see out. He spotted his son, playing on the lawn. The kid wore long pants and a red jacket and he was pushing a small plastic cart filled with stuffed animals. A little girl with shiny strawberry-colored hair sat on a blanket nearby, grooming the mane of a stuffed blue horse. The girl was Jared and Eden's. Billy had seen her yesterday, when he'd stopped in at Eden's house to ask after the old man. The comb she used must have been studded with rhinestones; it caught the sunlight and glittered as she worked. As Billy watched, his son grabbed a teddy bear from the cart and toddled over to the girl.

Jesse held out the bear.

The girl said, "You want me to comb it?" Jesse nodded. The girl set her blue horse aside. She went to work on the bear. Jesse dropped down beside her in a monkey crouch and watched the process with great interest.

Right then, Billy noticed a creaking sound. He

turned his head a little and saw a baby, moving in and out of his view, swinging in a windup chair that had been set up on the porch. The baby had the same red-blond hair as the little girl. It was Eden's, too. Eden had been holding the child in her arms when she answered his knock the day before.

"Oh, Eden. What am I going to do?" That was Prue's voice, from farther down the porch, pitched low and confidential. Billy had been just about to pull the door open all the way and step through it, but instead he froze where he stood.

Prue went on. "Jack Roper called this morning. Evidently Billy walked into Nellie Anderson's house late last night by mistake. He was really drunk and he thought he was here."

"Oh, no..."

"Oh, yes. I guess Jack managed to convince Nellie not to press charges, but the poor woman was frightened half out of her wits. And that's not the end of it. You should have seen him when he finally did get here. He climbed in the guest room window around three a.m., so plastered he couldn't see straight. When I tried to tell him what I thought of him, he told me to lighten up. Then he passed out. This morning, he got up just long enough to vomit. He's been out cold ever since."

Eden said something about how difficult it must be for a confirmed bachelor like Billy to deal with the reality of having a son. Billy thought he could get to like Eden.

But Prue wasn't finished. "Eden, he's an alcoholic, I'm sure of it. I never should have invited him here. It was foolish and wrong. Even at Jesse's age, it can't be good for him to see his dad like that. They say little boys need a father, in order to learn how to be a man. But I shudder to think what kind of lessons Jesse will learn from Billy. I just…I hope he gets bored with hanging around here. I hope he goes back to L.A. where he belongs and never bothers to return. And I hope he does it soon.''

Eden started talking then, reassuring and advising. But Billy was already backing away from the open door, from the two children playing in the November sunlight, from the anxiety and frustration in Prue's voice.

He went to the kitchen, where he should have gone in the first place. He found she'd left the coffeemaker all ready to go. He pushed the button and the brew cycle started.

Then he returned to his bedroom, got some clean clothes and headed for the bathroom. When he came out, freshly showered and shaved, Jesse was sitting in his high chair by the table and Prue was feeding him what had to be mashed bananas, from the look and smell of it. There was no sign of Eden, the little girl or the baby.

Billy stood for a few moments, watching Prue stick spoon after spoon of banana into the kid's mouth. She didn't even look at him. He cleared his throat. ''Good morning.''

Prue shot him an injured, long-suffering look. ''Coffee's ready. Help yourself.''

''I will.'' He was carrying his dirty clothes. ''I'll just…put these away first.''

She shrugged and went back to feeding the kid. Billy knew he should just go toss his stuff in his room and get himself some damn coffee. But he couldn't stop thinking about what she'd said to Eden out there on the porch.

He shuffled from foot to foot. "Look. Maybe I didn't get off to such a great start here."

She shot him a glance.

He raised his voice—just a little. "I am trying to say I know that I went too far."

She glanced at him again, a mean little eye-flick of a look. "You're right. You went too far." She dipped another spoonful of banana.

He gritted his teeth. "I apologize, is what I'm saying."

"Fine." She gave the kid another bite and dipped more from the bowl, carefully scraping the excess off the rim as she did it.

"I'll do better."

She paused, looked at him—and didn't say a word.

The kid pounded his fists on the chair tray. "Nana," he demanded.

Prue offered the bite of banana she'd already scooped onto the spoon. The kid gulped it down.

Since she looked so unconvinced, Billy said it again. "I will do better, honestly."

Another frigid glance. "That would be…nice."

Nice, Billy thought darkly. She called him an alcoholic behind his back, and when he promised to improve, she said that would be *nice.*

And he didn't care what she said, he was no alcoholic. He'd always been able to handle his liquor just fine. Pretty much. Maybe lately, since he'd learned about the kid, he'd been hitting the bottle a little harder than usual. But damn it, he would deal with it. He would show her he could play this thing straight.

If it killed him.

She was looking right back at him, her eyebrows raised, waiting to see if he had anything more to say.

"Na-na, na-na!" the kid demanded.

She turned from Billy to dip another spoonful.

"Wait," Billy said.

She froze with the spoon still empty. The kid continued to pound his fists and chant, "Na-na, na-na."

"Give him the spoon."

She looked worried then. "Why?"

Billy said it again. "Give the spoon to him."

"Na-na! Na-na!" The kid was starting to get worked up.

Prue suddenly looked frantic. "Billy, he wants another bite."

"Now, Woo. Na-na now!"

"Give him the spoon."

"But…"

"Na-na! Na-na!"

Billy dropped his dirty clothes. "Give it to him. Now."

She didn't move. So he reached out and took the spoon from her.

"Na-na, na-na, na-na, now!"

Billy dipped up a spoonful of banana, grabbed the kid's pudgy hand and wrapped it around the handle. "There. Eat. And shut up."

Prue gasped. "There's no reason to be harsh with him. He doesn't know how to feed himself yet and when he's hungry he—"

Billy put a finger to his lips, in a signal for silence. By some miracle, she obeyed.

Eyes wide, the kid looked at his own hand and the spoon clutched there. Then he looked up at Billy. His little face started to crumple.

"Uh-uh," warned Billy softly. "None of that damn wussy crying. You eat now. Just eat."

The kid stared at Billy.

"Eat. Feed yourself. You can do it. You can."

Slowly, Jesse raised the spoon to his mouth. He poked in the bite of banana—most of it, anyway. He swallowed. And then, slowly, he smiled.

"Good goin'," Billy said, and smiled back.

Jesse hit the spoon on the tray and threw back his head. "Na-na!" he crowed in triumph. "Na-na, now!"

Billy turned to Prue. "See, he can feed himself."

The blob of banana hit him on the side of the neck before Prue managed to warn him it was coming.

About forty-five minutes later, Prudence put Jesse down for a nap. Billy was kind enough not to help her with that.

When she came downstairs from half an hour of singing Jesse to sleep, she found that Billy had left.

"Oh, no," she said in despair to the empty kitchen. No doubt he'd gone on over to the bar again. He'd be home after closing time, just like last night.

She sank to a chair, thinking that she had to find some way to get through to him, some way to convince him that he should return to L.A. and leave her and Jesse in peace. As she was shaking her head and sighing, she noticed the note stuck between the salt and pepper shakers: Gone shopping. Back by six. She blew out a breath in disgust. "I'll believe it when I see it."

She crumpled the note into a ball and tossed it into the trash under the sink.

Billy returned at five forty-three. He came strolling into the kitchen, carrying a bulging shopping bag, a huge bouquet of flowers and a toy truck.

He dropped the truck on the floor for Jesse, who immediately started pushing it around and making *vroom-vroom* sounds. Then he held out the flowers. "Put these in water. And whatever it is you're cooking, save it."

He held up the shopping bag. "CDs. About fifty of 'em. And I mean it, put that food away. We're going over to the Mercantile Grill for dinner. We have a few things to talk about it, you and me."

She dropped the carrot she was scraping, grabbed a towel and wiped her hands, irritation at him rising. He simply had no concept of what it meant to be responsible for a child. "Billy. Jesse's too young to take to a nice restaurant. He just won't sit still that long and I—"

"Jesse's not going." He shoved the flowers at her.

She took them, grudgingly, and then glared at him over the top of them. "And just what do you suggest we do with him while we're away?"

Someone knocked at the front door. Billy gestured at the bouquet. "Come on, chop, chop. Deal with those, will you?"

"There's someone at the—"

"It's Marnie. Patrick's second daughter. They say she's a hell of a soccer player, and she'd rather hang out with the guys than other girls. They also say she's pretty good with little kids."

"You found a *baby-sitter?*" Her irritation abated a bit. The flowers, mostly yellow roses, smelled lovely. And Billy actually appeared to be sober.

"I've had a busy afternoon." He was already half-

way to the door. "Go on up and fix your nose, or
whatever you have to do to get yourself ready."

She trailed after him, feeling uncertain about everything all of a sudden. "My nose is fine."

"Good. Then you're ready to go." He pulled open
the door and ushered Marnie Jones inside.

The food at the Grill was excellent. And they had a
candle on their table. It was very civilized and adult
and Prudence felt a little guilty at how much she enjoyed taking a night off from baths and bedtime stories.

"We do need to talk about this…situation we're in
here," she said when their salads arrived.

"We will. Later."

"But I thought you said—"

"Prue. I promise. We'll talk. Now relax. Enjoy the
food." He smiled at her so sweetly, making her understand what Randi had seen in him.

"You're just trying to get on my good side," she
accused, only half teasing.

"You bet I am."

It was so strange. It was almost like a date.

He ordered wine, which made the meal seem more
festive, but also got her worrying that he'd end up
drinking too much. And then he surprised her again,
by only having one glass, which he raised in a toast to
her.

"For loving my son," he said. Then he laughed low.
"Maybe too much sometimes."

She laughed, too, though she didn't really believe it
was possible to love Jesse too much.

For dessert, they had chocolate cheesecake and coffee. And then they started back toward the house, walking, since they'd walked over in the first place. It felt

good to be out in the chilly night air. Overhead, the stars seemed brighter than in the city. Shadowy clouds scudded across the face of the full moon.

Prudence heard herself suggesting a stroll along Main.

"Let's go," Billy said.

But then she remembered Jesse. He hadn't fussed much when they left, but Billy had pretty much pushed her out the door before the poor child had a chance to understand what was happening. "On second thought, maybe we should just go on back to the house. It's Jesse's bedtime now."

"So?"

"He's very demanding at bedtime. I wouldn't want poor Marnie to have to put up with too much fussing."

"Marnie will do fine."

"But—"

"Prue."

"What?"

"Look up the street. Now look down. You can see all the way to the end both ways. It's an extra ten minutes, max. That's all we're talking about here."

She knew he was right, though she still felt uneasy about it.

He took her arm. "Come on."

They started up the street, toward the post office and the town hall. Just before they reached the post office, they passed a man and a woman Prudence had never seen before. Still, they waved and exchanged greetings. Since coming to North Magdalene, Prudence had learned to say hello to everyone she met. She considered it one of the real benefits of small-town life, that she felt safe exchanging pleasantries with strangers.

They met up with Nellie Anderson and Linda Lou

Beardsly at the town hall. The pair emerged from the double doors in the center of the wide front veranda.

"Ladies," Billy said, with elaborate politeness. "What a pleasure to see you again."

The two women looked at him, then pointedly looked away. Each forced a smile for Prudence's sake as they hurried past.

After they were out of earshot, Prudence suggested, "I'd say you owe poor Nellie an apology."

"I did apologize. I think." He looked confused. "I seem to remember backing toward the door with my hands up, insisting the whole way how sorry I was. But the memory is pretty hazy. The way I recall it, she threw a vase at me for my trouble."

"I'm sure she was terrified."

"Yeah, well. She sure screamed like she was terrified. That woman has a set of lungs on her."

"She's actually very nice, once you get to know her. And so is Linda Lou Beardsly—that's her friend."

"Right. I've run into her before, too."

"When?"

"She came into the Hole in the Wall last night, to pick up her husband."

"Linda Lou is very highly respected here in town. She just retired, after thirty years of teaching primary grades at the North Magdalene School. And Nellie Anderson is a pillar of the community church."

"A pillar, eh?"

She slid him a glance. "I'm picking up some serious sarcasm."

He faked a look of pure innocence. "From me?"

"Yes, from you."

"I know their type, that's all. They were born to hate guys like me."

"Oh, come on. You're exaggerating."

He wrapped her hand more snugly around his arm. She was surprised at how natural it felt to have him do that. "Let's forget about them, all right?"

She decided there wasn't much point in saying more anyway. They crossed the street and proceeded down the other side, past Sam's gold-sales store and Santino's Barber, Beauty and Variety, on by Lily's, and then past Evie's gift and clothing shop, which was called Wishbook.

It was five after eight when they got back to the house. They found Marnie in the living room watching television.

"Where's Jesse?" Prudence asked.

Marnie switched off the set. "In bed."

"Already?" Prudence couldn't believe it.

"You said to put him down at seven-thirty."

"I know. But he always gets a story or two."

"I read him a story. And then he went right to sleep."

"I think I'll just check on him."

Ignoring the look that passed between Marnie and Billy, Prudence headed up the stairs. She heard nothing from his room as she approached it, which surprised her. She'd expected a few hopeless sobs, at least. She tiptoed in and found him as Marnie had said she would: sound asleep. She adjusted the covers, resting a hand on his back for a moment, seeking the reassurance that only touch could bring her. His little body felt so good and warm and she loved to feel the movement of his small chest as it expanded and contracted with each breath.

He was fine. And if she didn't leave him alone, she would probably wake him. She tiptoed back out.

* * *

The yellow roses Billy had brought her sat in a crystal vase on the dining-room table. Prudence paused at the foot of the stairs to admire them. They seemed to glow in the spill of light from the living room. Yellow was such a warm, alive color.

She shouldn't be so pleased with them, really. Roses were a little inappropriate, coming from Billy. Roses meant love. And romance. Prudence wasn't looking for either—and especially not with bad Billy Jones.

"You like them." He was standing just beyond the arch to the living room, watching her.

"Yes. Very much. But you shouldn't have."

"Why not?" She knew his eyes were green. But with the light behind him, she couldn't see their color. They only looked dark. And very soft. "Why shouldn't I buy you roses, if I want to…and if you like them?"

She didn't know why they were talking about this. "Never mind. It doesn't matter."

He went on watching her. It seemed way too personal, the way he was looking at her.

She thought of Randi, who could handle any man. Randi hadn't done so well with Billy.

"I think it matters," he said.

Her chest felt tight. And she wished her heart would just settle down and quit bouncing around so energetically inside her chest. "Thank you for the roses. Now, let's talk about something else."

But he didn't talk. He just looked at her. And she looked back. After a minute or two, it became ridiculous. She began to wonder if he planned to just stand there, staring at her all night long.

She made herself walk toward him and she assumed a no-nonsense tone of voice. "We have to talk now,

Billy. About what you plan to accomplish here and how long you intend to stay.''

He said nothing, only watched her approach.

She stopped a few feet from him and demanded, ''Billy. I mean it. I want you to talk to me. Now.''

He spoke, then. But not about anything they needed to discuss. ''You hide behind those ugly glasses, don't you, Prue? What are you hiding? What are you hiding *from?*''

She gaped at him for a moment. Then she shook her head. ''I do believe you are the rudest man I've ever met.''

He actually smiled, a charming, rueful kind of smile. *''Ever?''*

And suddenly, she was thinking of her mother. Betsy Wilding had gone through a lot of men in her endless search for true love and a good provider. Some of those men had been considerably ruder than bad Billy Jones.

She sighed. ''All right. I've met ruder men. But not many.''

He was still smiling. ''Now, about those glasses...''

''What about them?'' She tried to sound confident, unfazed by him and his impertinent questions. ''I need them. To see.''

''You could get contacts.''

''I don't know why I'm discussing this with you. We need to—''

''Contacts, Prue? Why don't you get contacts?''

''They....don't work for me. They make my eyes water.''

''Soft contacts, what about them?'' His voice was like velvet, the way he could make it when he sang those beautiful songs he wrote.

''Really. No. Not for me.''

"And they're doing incredible things with laser surgery lately. I read about it in *Newsweek,* I think. Have you heard about that?"

"I don't want surgery."

"Well, fine. But even if you stick with glasses, they make thinner lenses nowadays, even for really powerful glasses, and I know they can blend them so you won't have that old-lady line in the middle."

"It's a bifocal line, I'll have you know."

"Right, and you can have it fixed so that line doesn't show."

"It's none of your business, Billy. Just leave it alone."

He lifted a hand in a gesture that indicated her glasses as it dismissed them. "How long have you had those things?"

"A long time. And I like them. And we really have to get down to—"

He shrugged. "I know." He turned without another word and went into the living room.

They sat at either end of the sofa.

He said, "I told you this morning I'd do better, and I meant it."

She didn't really believe him, but for Jesse's sake, she felt an obligation to give him another chance. "Say I take your word for it."

"All right. Say you do."

"How long, exactly, are you planning to stay?"

"A couple of weeks. How's that?"

Two weeks, she thought. How would she get through it? She wasn't used to the kind of tension being around him caused her. Whether he was climbing in the window drunk or showing up with roses and a baby-sitter, he had a talent for keeping her nerves on a razor's edge.

She cast about for reasons he shouldn't stay. "What about your club?"

"What about it?"

"Well, can you afford to be away from it for two weeks?"

"My manager, Alexis, runs the place just fine without me. The only thing she doesn't do better than me is book talent. But I took care of that before I left. So unless she calls me, she doesn't need me. Any other objections?"

She decided to just lay it right out there. "Your drinking."

"What about it?"

"I don't approve of it."

"I gathered."

"I don't want any more nights like last night. And I don't want to see you staggering to the bathroom in the morning, with Jesse looking on."

He glanced away, toward the far wall.

"I am serious, Billy."

He met her eyes. "All right. I won't get drunk again while I'm staying here."

"And if you do?"

"Then the visit ends. I'll take my guitar and go."

What else could she say to that but "All right"? She slipped off her shoes and gathered her knees up to the side. "Two weeks, then. And what's supposed to happen in that time?"

"We'll learn a few things."

"Like?"

"Like if I'm capable of being a decent father."

"And if you aren't?"

He looked around the room. "It's too quiet here. I hate quiet. I can hear the damn leaves falling off that locust tree out by the fence."

"Answer my question."

"You don't give a guy an inch, do you, Prue?"

"I want to know. I think I have a right to know. If you're not capable of being a decent father, what then? Will you just…go away?"

He actually looked thoughtful, then he grunted. "No. I don't think I could do that. It's crazy. I never asked for a kid, but now I've got one.…" He let a shrug finish the thought. "I'll want to visit sometimes. I'll want to help out, with the money, you know?"

"Jesse doesn't need money. He's a very rich little boy."

"Look. I'll do what I can, all right? I'll help out some way. We can figure out how when the time comes. And I'll come to see him, now and then."

"You'd have to call ahead when you plan to visit. I don't want you just dropping by anytime the mood strikes."

"I could learn to call first, if that's how you want it."

"It is."

"All right, then. I would check with you ahead of time."

She gathered her legs up closer to her body—and made herself ask the next question, though she didn't really want to hear his answer. "What about if it turns out the other way?"

"What other way?"

"If you're…good with Jesse. If he's good with you."

He let out a short laugh then. "You think that's likely?"

"We're just talking. Covering the bases, considering all the possibilities. Aren't we?"

"Yeah. Okay. Right."

"So, what if it turns out you're good with Jesse?"

He lifted a hand, ran it back through his thick, dark brown hair. "I can't believe you're even considering that."

She told him honestly, "I don't want to consider it. And I certainly don't believe it will happen. But anything's possible. And I'd like to know what you'd want to do—if it turned out that being a father suited you, after all."

He tipped his head and studied her. "Prue, you're all right." It was a compliment, delivered with a musing smile.

His praise pleased her. And that made her feel vulnerable. She spoke briskly. "You haven't answered the question."

"Okay, let me put it this way. You're not exactly an easygoing gal. But you're fair."

"I try to be."

"Well, then. Whether I'm good with Jesse or not, I'll expect you to try to be fair in two weeks, when we talk about how much time Jesse should spend with me."

For some reason, Prudence thought of Randi then. Of the two of them, as teenagers, stretched out on the ugly shag carpet in their mother's house trailer, watching *Some Like it Hot* on television.

"Damn, she was good," Randi had said of Marilyn Monroe. "She was the best. But they used her. They won't use me, Pruey, you wait and see...."

And they hadn't. They hadn't used Randi Wilding. Randi Wilding had beat them all at their own game.

And still, she was gone. Lost to Prudence, forever.

How would she bear it if she lost Jesse, as well?

"Prue? Are you all right?" Billy's dark brows had drawn together.

That wasn't going to happen. No way in the world would Billy Jones prove himself capable of raising a child. Still, she felt the tears rising, pushing at the back of her throat. She tried to swallow them. "You are his father. I want to do the right thing."

One tear escaped and slid down her cheek. Billy watched that tear, remembering how he had raised his glass to her earlier, in a teasing toast about loving Jesse too much.

He saw then that her love was nothing to joke about. She loved Jesse enough to do what she thought was right for him, no matter the cost to herself. He didn't know if he'd ever seen love that pure before.

And for the first time he consciously admitted to himself that his son was not the only one he'd come to North Magdalene to get to know.

Chapter 8

The delivery van showed up in front of the house at nine the next morning. Prudence answered the door to find two men standing there. They wore matching shirts with the words Stereo Express embroidered on the breast pocket. "Delivery for Mr. Jones."

Billy came up behind her then. "Oh, yeah. Great," he said when Prudence cast a questioning glance over her shoulder at him. "Bring the stuff right on in."

"You got it." The men headed back for their van.

Prudence turned to face Billy. "What *stuff*?"

"Stereos, Prue. Two of 'em. One for my bedroom and one for the rest of the house."

"Stereos?" she repeated, as his meaning slowly sank in.

"I told you I was busy yesterday. I drove into Grass Valley. And I went shopping. You saw all those CDs I bought."

"Yes. I saw them. So what?"

"Well, where did you think I planned to play them?"

"How about your car stereo?" she suggested hopefully.

He smiled and shook his head. "I got extra speakers, too. To put in the kitchen and dining room."

"Billy, I think you're unsure of the concept here. This is my house. And I don't need *one* stereo system. Let alone two."

"But I do."

"Billy, you can't just—"

He pulled her away from the door, so the men could get through with the boxes of equipment. "Please, Prue. I can do without the booze. But don't ask me to give up my music jones. I won't be able to do that, no way."

"Oh, stop it. There is no such thing as an addiction to music."

"Yes, there is. And I've got one."

"Billy—"

"I got headphones. Remote headphones. If it drives you too crazy, you won't have to listen. But then again, there is Jesse to consider."

"Jesse?"

"A music jones is an inherited condition, didn't you know? Think of it. The kid's probably sustained neural damage already, from poor management of his disease."

"Oh, you just stop."

"I mean it, Prue. Headphones. This won't be a problem for you, I swear."

One of the delivery men stepped up with a clipboard. "Mr. Jones?"

"That's my name."

"Sign here."

Billy was still setting up his stereos when the bed arrived two hours later. Prudence, who'd somehow ended up hovering nearby and handing Billy things when he asked for them, looked out the picture window over the sofa and saw the furniture van pull up.

She had a sinking feeling. "What is that?"

Jesse, who was sitting in one of the stereo boxes, wearing a currently nonfunctioning pair of headphones and chewing on a teething ring, let out a happy little chortle and a few nonsense syllables.

Billy took his head out of the back of the stereo rack and looked through the window, too. "Oh, that. It's the bed."

"Pardon me. I don't need a bed."

"I know. But Jesse does."

Billy stopped fooling with the stereo long enough to show the men the way to Jesse's room. Prudence scooped up the child and trailed along after them.

"The crib has to go," Billy said, and started shoving it to the other side of the room. Prudence stood in the doorway, holding Jesse, wondering how to stop this madness before it went any further.

Grunting and breathing hard, the deliverymen set the frame down. It was a bunk bed, bright red, made of some kind of metal tubing, with the springs built right into the frame.

"C'mon, Leroy," one of the men said to the other. "Let's get the mattresses. And the ladder." The two men went out, edging around Prudence muttering, "'Scuse me, ma'am."

She was left holding Jesse, staring at Billy, who was looking at Jesse's crib as if he'd like to burn it.

She tried to remain reasonable. "Billy, he won't stay in a bed. I can barely get him to go to sleep in his crib."

"You got an attic, right? Or a basement? Someplace we can store this thing, until you can get rid of it?"

"Billy, you're not listening to me."

"Sure I am. And we still need a place to put this crib until you can have it hauled away."

"I'm trying to tell you that I'm not ready to have it hauled away."

He looked at her levelly then. "Jesse's ready for a bed."

"No, Billy. He's not."

"Dow, Woo. Dow." Jesse was pushing at her. She bent and let him go. He headed right for the big red metal thing that sat where his crib had been. He wrapped both hands around the lower part of the frame and braced himself there, then he babbled out, "Abee me?"

"Yeah," said Billy, as if Jesse's chatter made perfect sense. "That is your bed. You'll be sleeping in it from now on."

Jesse bent and put his mouth against the frame. After gumming it happily for a moment, he looked up at Billy again and pronounced, "Awa baba."

"Yeah, you're gonna love it."

"Billy, I don't think this is a good idea."

"Prue, you have to let go a little. Let him grow up."

"He's barely a year old, for heaven's sake."

"Let me handle this."

She spoke with careful precision. "All right, I will. I'll let you handle it one hundred percent. I'll let you be completely responsible for putting him to bed. And making sure he stays there, for as long as you're visiting here. But I am not getting rid of that crib. I just might need it again, when you go."

"'Scuse us again, ma'am." The deliverymen were back with one of the mattresses. Prudence edged out of their way. "Uh, would somebody move that kid?"

Billy went over and grabbed up Jesse. The men set the mattress on the bottom bunk, then went out again.

Billy eased Jesse to the floor once more. "I bought sheets and blankets, too. Yesterday. They're out in my Jeep."

"Billy, you never said a word about this bed to me."

"Sure I did. I've said lots about this bed. You just haven't been listening."

"You know what I mean. You never said you actually went out and bought one."

"Look. Lighten up, will you."

"I hate when you say that."

"This is gonna work out just fine."

"I mean it, Billy. Until you give up this idiocy and let him go back to a crib, bedtimes and naps will be your responsibility."

"Don't you worry. I can deal with it."

She looked at the top bunk. "Wait a minute. You're not thinking of putting him up there, are you?"

Billy looked injured. "Hell, no. What kind of father do you think I am?" He caught the look she gave him and frowned. "Never mind, don't answer that. The top bunk's for later. You know, when he wants to have friends over."

"Oh, right. You're just looking ahead."

"You bet I am."

"You have never looked ahead in your life."

Jesse babbled out something incomprehensible.

"See," Billy said, "this kid is ready. Aren't you?"

"Me yeah," Jesse replied.

Billy had to suspend his stereo assembly that afternoon, so he could stand guard over Jesse's nap time. Once she saw that Billy really intended to deal with the problem he'd created, Prudence resolutely stayed out of it. Soon enough, she knew, Billy would grow tired of spending half the afternoon and a good portion of his evenings making sure Jesse stayed in his bed. Jesse would go back to his crib. And Prudence would be proved right.

Billy spent that night in the top bunk in Jesse's room. The next morning, while Prudence was feeding Jesse his breakfast, he carried the crib down to the basement.

"You'll have to bring it up again yourself," Prudence said to him when he came into the kitchen, heading straight for the coffeepot.

"I'll bring it up. When whoever you give it to comes to collect it." He poured himself coffee, then turned around and leaned on the counter, sipping. "Let him feed himself."

Prudence mentally counted to ten. "Billy, you can't take over everything."

"Come on. Give him the spoon."

Actually she had read somewhere that most babies could feed themselves by the end of the first year. Maybe she had been a little slow to encourage Jesse to move on. On this particular point, anyway. She handed Jesse the spoon.

Twenty minutes later, there was baby cereal and canned fruit everywhere. But Jesse had fed himself an entire meal for the first time.

Prudence was changing his diaper, getting him cleaned up for church, when Billy leaned over her shoulder and suggested, "Have you thought about teaching him to use the toilet? I thought maybe I'd get him one of those little kid's potties, you know? And maybe we could switch him to training pants and—"

"Stop. We can talk about this later. Right now, I'm going to church."

"Fine. You can leave Jesse here. You only take him to some nursery anyway, right?"

"That's true." Prudence reached for a pair of toddler-size red corduroy overalls and started snapping Jesse into them. "Maybe you'd like to go to church with us?"

"Sure. And maybe your friend Nellie Anderson would like a double Scotch on the rocks."

Prudence shot him a long-suffering look. "I don't believe that Nellie indulges in alcoholic beverages."

"Fine. Nellie Anderson doesn't drink. And I don't go to church. We all enjoy different forms of entertainment."

"Oh, Billy," Prudence said, smiling because she couldn't help herself, though she knew it only encouraged him. "Are you sure you can handle Jesse alone?"

"I'm sure."

"Have you ever changed a diaper in your life?"

"Don't worry. I'll figure it out. I've watched you a few times."

"All right, then." She picked up Jesse and handed him to Billy.

Billy adjusted the suspenders on Jesse's overalls. "You get to stay here with me today. How's that?"

"Yah," Jesse said, grinning and drooling.

"We'll have a little discussion about toilets and how to use 'em."

Jesse nodded, his expression suddenly grave.

"And then we'll talk about how independent you're gonna feel once you learn to dress yourself."

Prudence left them, crossing the upstairs hall to her own room, where she showered and got ready for church. As she pulled her hair back and put on a gray skirt and white sweater, she realized she didn't have a single qualm about leaving Jesse alone with his father.

Three days ago, when Billy had first appeared on her doorstep, she wouldn't have trusted him to take out the garbage. Now, she found she was willing to leave Jesse in his care. Was that progress—or delusion?

"Oh, my dear. Are you out of your mind?" Nellie Anderson asked.

They were standing on the steps of the church right after the service. Nellie had just inquired where that sweet little Jesse was. Prudence had made the mistake of answering honestly.

Nellie huffed in outrage. "Did anyone tell you what that man did the other night?"

"Yes, Nellie. I heard about it."

"It took ten years off my life, I was so terrified."

"I am sorry. And so is Billy."

"I don't believe that for a minute. Men like him are never sorry."

Prudence had sense enough not to belabor the issue of Billy's remorsefulness. She said, "Well, it was kind of you not to press charges."

Nellie sniffed. "I must be honest. It was an option I did consider. But this is a small town. And it's full of Joneses. My grandchildren's stepmother is a Jones—

you know Evie Riggins? And I do love her. And then there's Delilah, born a Jones just like Evie. Delilah is one of my dearest friends. But then, Evie and Delilah are women. The women of the Jones family tend to be quite decent human beings. The men, however, are possessed of the devil.''

"Well now, Nellie, I don't think they're *that* bad."

"Oh, but they are. Why, just look at Ogden Elijah himself. He married Bathsheba Riley, bless her sweet soul, over forty years ago now. And even I am willing to admit that he has probably remained true to his vows. I can almost admire him for his fidelity, especially taking into account the fact that, for the past twenty-eight years, his devotion has been to a memory.

"But faithfulness aside, Oggie Jones is still trouble. Capital *T*. He drinks whiskey and smokes cigars and gambles at the drop of a hat. He is loud and uncouth and when he wants something, he will go to just about any lengths to get it.''

Right then, Prudence somehow managed to interject, "I love Uncle Oggie."

Nellie waved that remark away. "Yes, I'm sure. Ogden can be charming when it suits his aims. But for the most part, he's like his sons and that nephew of his—a trial, pure and simple. Trouble waiting to happen. A walking slap in the face to good Christian folk. Don't try to convince me otherwise. I do my best to get along with them, because I have to live in the same town with them.'' She paused, but only to gulp in a breath. "And that one, that Billy. He's the worst of a bad lot. Which is why it was extremely unwise of you to leave that child with him.''

Prudence felt she had to say something in Billy's defense. "Honestly, Nellie. Billy is trying hard to learn to be a father. *I* believe he deserves support and encouragement. And a little trust, as well.''

Nellie's small eyes seemed to get smaller. And then, out of nowhere, she gasped. ''Oh, my dear!''

Prudence jumped back. ''What? What's the matter?''

''Now I see what's happening here.''

''What are you talking about?''

Nellie leaned in closer. ''Don't let him...take advantage of you. That's all I'm going to say. Be careful. Keep your head.''

''Excuse me?''

''The Jones men are...notorious with women. I could tell you stories. And I'd bet my mother's second-best china that *that* one, that Billy, is no different from the rest. He may even be worse, from a few things I've heard.''

Prudence could hardly argue with Nellie on that point; bad Billy Jones had a real reputation when it came to women. But Billy was no danger to Prudence personally. And she told Nellie so. ''There's nothing like that between Billy and me.''

''He's staying alone in that house with you, isn't he?''

''With me and Jesse, yes he is.''

''Well, you just be careful, dear. That's all I'm saying. He's a Jones and you're a woman. A very nice woman. There's something about those Jones men and nice women....''

''What do you mean?''

''Those Jones men can't resist nice women. Haven't you noticed? To a man, they've all taken absolutely lovely wives.''

Prudence was becoming a little confused. "Is that bad?"

Nellie looked down her rather beaky nose. "Well. What do you think?"

Prudence thought it was time to end the conversation.

Nellie said, "Never mind. Don't answer. Just be careful around that man. I warn you. He will toy with you, if you let him."

"Honestly," Prudence said again. "There is nothing like that going on between Jesse's father and me."

"Let's talk," Billy said.

Prudence looked up from her copy of *Forbes*. Billy was standing in the arch to the dining room, a set of headphones dangling from his hand. She glanced at the mantel clock. "It's only ten after eight."

He braced a hand against the frame of the arch and leaned there, managing to look both cheerful and insolent at the same time. "Impressed?"

"What did you do, tie him to the bed?"

He cast a glance toward the ceiling, as if seeking heavenly intervention. "Oh, ye of little faith..." Then he pulled himself away from the arch and sauntered toward her. She watched him coming, feeling uneasy all of a sudden—even more uneasy than she usually felt around him.

When he was just a few feet from where she sat on the sofa, he stopped and dropped the headphones on the coffee table between them. "So. What do you say?"

"About what?"

"Put that magazine away."

She frowned. "I don't understand what you're up to."

"I told you. I want to talk."

"About what?"

He hooked his thumbs in his belt loops and looked at her in a way she couldn't quite define. "About you."

"What about me?"

He let out a long breath. "It's too quiet."

"What?"

He turned for the stereo rack, which he'd set up on the far wall, between a pair of bookcases. He punched a few buttons and a moment later, music filled the room. Soft, seductive music. And a throaty, sexy woman's voice.

"Sarah Vaughan," he said.

She listened for a moment, charmed. "I thought you were strictly a country and rock 'n' roll kind of guy."

He came toward her again. "Don't try to pigeonhole me."

She put up both hands. "Sorry."

He dropped to the sofa beside her. She scooted down to the other end, putting a little bit of distance between them. In the process, her magazine fell off her lap.

He picked it up and tossed it on the table beside his headphones. "You scared of me, Prue?"

As if that was news. "You make me nervous."

"Why?"

"I never know what you're going to do next."

He laid his arm along the sofa back and his fingers brushed her shoulder. A shiver skittered across her collarbone. She couldn't decide if the touch had been intentional or purely by accident.

"So. How was church today?"

She couldn't help scoffing at that one. "As if you care."

"I care."

She frowned at him. "What *are* you up to?"

"Getting to know you."

"You know me. As much as you need to know me."

"Tell me about church."

She shrugged. "The sermon concerned abundance. *My Cup Runneth Over,* it was called. Somebody mentioned that the Reverend Johnson has a thing for the twenty-third psalm."

"I'm with the reverend."

"Sure, you are."

"I mean it. At least concerning abundance. I'm a big believer in abundance. It means plenty for me, and that's good."

"Only you could make abundance sound reprehensible."

"Tell me more—about your morning."

"After church, I spoke with Nellie."

"How sad for you."

"She warned me about you."

"I'll bet."

"She said all the Jones men are possessed of the devil and that you're even worse than the rest of them."

He leaned a little closer to her. "Well, enough about Nellie. I want to hear about you."

She craned backward to get some distance. "What about me?"

"How did you start working for your sister?"

"Could you move down just a little? You've got more than half the sofa."

"You bet." He actually backed off an inch or two. "Now, tell me."

"What?"

He repeated, with great patience, "How you started working for your sister."

"She asked me."

"When?"

"About eight years ago. I was fresh out of college, slaving away at my first job."

"Doing what?"

"Working for a big accounting firm. Randi was still on 'Eden Beach' then." "Eden Beach" was the television series that had made Randi a star. "She was bringing in a huge amount of money. And throwing it all away. She asked me to manage her finances. I agreed."

"She said you did a great job with her money."

Prudence smiled a little, remembering. "It worked out fine for both of us."

"You went to college?"

"UCLA, yes."

"Randi told me she never went to college."

"Randi always knew what she wanted to do with her life. And for what she wanted, she didn't need college. I did."

"Randi told me you two grew up poor."

"That's right."

"So how did you afford UCLA?"

"I earned a few scholarships. And I worked."

"Prue. You are so admirable. What was your mother like?"

She said the first word that popped into her head. "Hungry."

"For what?"

"Love. Attention. Someone to take care of her. She had a lot of lovers." Now, why had she told him that?

"And what about your father?"

"What about him? He left shortly after Randi was born. He just went to work one day—and never came back. I was three then, so I hardly remember him at all."

"And after that, for your mother, the men came and went, is that it?"

"Is this information going to be useful to you in some way?"

"You bet. So the deal is, you and your sister reacted in opposite ways to the same situation. Randi became a sex goddess. And you became—"

"Look, Billy. I really hate it when people call Randi a sex goddess."

"I know you do." His tone was gentle. "But that doesn't change the truth. Randi *was* a sex goddess."

Prudence stood. "I don't know what you're up to tonight."

"Don't go." He looked at her hopefully, his expression open and boyish. And vulnerable.

Which she shouldn't buy for a moment. After all, a man who had seduced as many women as Billy had would need a whole repertoire of appealing expressions.

"Come on. Stay." He tipped his head at the empty space beside him on the sofa.

She remained standing. "I'm going to bed now. If you're bored, why don't you go on over to the Hole in the Wall and have yourself a drink."

His face went blank. And then his eyes grew hard.

She realized how rotten that must have sounded. Shame flooded through her, making her palms sweat and her face feel too warm. "Look. I didn't mean that."

"The hell you didn't. You want me to blow it."

"No, of course I don't."

"You want me to go get blasted, so you can tell me to get the hell out."

"No. No, I don't want that."

"You're lying. But get this. I'm not going to blow it. You're not going to get rid of me. We have an agreement. And I'm sticking by it—no matter how many times you point me toward the bar."

"I did not point you toward the bar." It was an outright lie. Her shame increased as it passed her lips.

He made a low, disgusted sound. Then he picked up the remote and pointed it at the stereo. The nostalgic, seductive music stopped. He punched another button and ominous drums began playing. A man started to sing in a low, rough voice.

Billy smiled, but it wasn't a friendly smile. "This is the soundtrack from *Natural Born Killers*. Stick around. You'll love it."

She longed to leave him there, to simply turn and walk away. But she knew she had been in the wrong, and she wouldn't be able to live with herself until she had truly apologized. "Billy. Please."

"What?"

"I won't do that again."

"You won't do what?"

"Try to get rid of you by sending you over to the bar."

He gave her a long, assessing look before muttering, "Okay." Then he picked up his headphones and settled them over his ears. He pointed the remote at the stereo and the speakers went quiet. He leaned back and closed his eyes.

Prudence watched him for a few seconds, feeling edgy, wanting to shake him, make him look at her so that she could tell him—what?

She had nothing to tell him.

She turned and left him there.

Chapter 9

The next morning, Prudence felt apprehensive about facing Billy at breakfast.

However, when he joined her and Jesse in the kitchen, he seemed friendly enough. He greeted her in a pleasant tone and then immediately took over the supervision of Jesse's meal, followed by a visit, just the two of them, to the bathroom, where Billy showed his son how to use a toilet.

As soon as that was over, Billy went to his room and shut the door, which was just fine with Prudence. She and Jesse had a very pleasant and uneventful morning. Jesse played with his toys and Prudence put in some work on her stock portfolio. Now and then, she heard guitar music coming from behind Billy's closed door. She guessed he might be writing a song in there. It rather pleased her to imagine him writing a song in her guest room that famous singers would perform for years to come.

Billy emerged at a little before noon. They ate lunch. Jesse covered himself, his high chair and a good section of the kitchen floor with his meal. Next, while Prudence cleaned up the mess, Billy took Jesse into the bathroom and put him on the toilet again. Prudence tried not to think about the possibility of Jesse falling in. Instead, she reminded herself that Billy was in there with him, and would surely either hold him in place or catch him if a dunking looked imminent. She told herself to look on the bright side: at least Billy hadn't demanded his son stop wearing diapers.

Not so far, anyway.

Not long after the bathroom ritual was completed, it was time for Jesse's nap. Billy, of course, went with him—to stand guard. The two of them came downstairs at a little after two, looking rumpled and still sleepy, but otherwise content.

Prudence felt a certain tightness in her chest at the sight of them. They really did look a lot alike. And then, occasionally in Jesse, she could see Randi—in the tilt of his head or the flash of his smile.

At a little before three, Billy decided to take Jesse out for a walk. It was a gray day, and windy. Prudence started to advise against subjecting the toddler to the cold and damp. But one look at the set of Billy's jaw and she knew any protest would be futile.

She settled for insisting that Billy dress Jesse warmly. She even got the stroller out for them. Billy looked at it with disdain.

"This is a walk, Prue. A *walk*."

Prudence experienced a distinct and quite powerful urge to pick up the lamp from the side table nearby and bop him over the head with it. "Billy, be reasonable. He's hardly more than a baby."

"He can walk."

"You'll just end up carrying him."

"That's my problem, isn't it?"

They went out the door a few minutes later. Prudence stood in the living room, watching through the picture window as they set off side by side, with Billy holding Jesse's mittened hand. By the time they made it through the gate, Jesse was already starting to balk a little.

Resolutely Prudence turned from the window. By the end of the block, Billy would be forced to carry Jesse. They would be home much sooner than they would have been had Billy agreed to use the stroller.

"Which is good," Prudence muttered out loud. It was cold out there and the clouds threatened rain any minute now. The sooner they came back the better.

Jesse sat down at the intersection of Prospect and Rambling Lane.

"Get up, Jess," Billy said sternly, tugging on the small hand.

"Nawp," Jesse said.

Billy tugged harder. He ended up lifting the kid clear off the sidewalk, but Jesse only hung there, refusing to put his weight on his legs.

The wind was up pretty good, reddening Jesse's button of a nose and making Billy shiver a little, even in his warm leather jacket. He wanted to turn around right then and head back for the house.

But at the house there'd be Prue to deal with. He'd get one of her smug little I-told-you-so looks when he walked back in the door not five minutes after having walked out of it. He could do without that.

And he was a little bugged at Prue anyway. She'd

cut him off cold last night. Getting so upright and injured just because he'd called Randi exactly what Randi had been. And then as good as inviting him to go get drunk and blow what he was trying to accomplish here.

"Da?" Jesse said, using the name he'd started calling Billy just yesterday. He hugged his arms around himself. *"Brrrrrr."*

"I know," Billy said. "It's colder than a tax collector's smile out here. Come on." He knelt. Jesse reached out his arms.

Billy stood and walked on toward Main Street, carrying his son against his chest. Jesse was a pretty goodsize kid, but he wasn't that much of a burden. And his little arms felt good, holding on tight.

"We're just going to walk on over to Lily's Café, what do you say?"

"Yeah, me."

"We'll have ourselves some fruit juice or something."

"Foojoo."

"Yeah, something healthy, so when Prue asks later, we can tell her we looked out for your nutritional needs just fine."

"Woo?"

"Yeah, Woo. She's a pain in the ass, but we won't hold it against her, okay?"

"Tay."

Billy turned onto Main Street, headed north, toward the café. Jesse laid his head against his shoulder and sighed, "Da."

Billy felt something absolutely terrific right then. A kind of swelling sweetness in his chest, a pressure at the back of the eyes. A father's job wasn't easy. But it did have its rewards.

He was feeling so good that he passed up the chance to say something provoking to his two favorite battle-axes, Nellie and Linda Lou, who gave him a wide berth as he and Jesse met up with them just beyond the North Magdalene Garage.

Jesse huddled closer. The wind did have a bite to it. Billy started walking faster, hoping Jesse wouldn't end up with the sniffles—and give Prue more to criticize.

They were just approaching the shop called Wish-book that Evie Riggins owned when they heard the scream. Startled, Jesse pulled back. "Da?"

Right then, a chair came flying through the window of the Hole in the Wall across the street.

Jesse whipped his head toward the sound. "Wha'?"

"Hell if I know," Billy replied.

Now there were shouts coming from the bar and the sounds of things crashing, of wood splintering. Another chair came through the window, followed by a second scream.

And then Jared Jones flew headfirst through the dou-ble doors. He fell across the sidewalk, faceup. After that, he didn't move. Eden shoved through the doors after her husband. At the sight of him lying there, out cold, she gave a cry of dismay and dropped to her knees at his side.

From beyond the shattered window of the bar, the crashing and splintering continued.

Right then, Evie Riggins stuck her head out of her shop. "What's going on? Should I call Jack?" Billy must have frowned, because she started to explain, "Jack Roper, he's Olivia's husband and he works as a—"

"Never mind. I know who Jack is."

"Should I call him?"

"You better—and an ambulance, too. And will you hold my kid? I think they need some help over there." Evie held out her arms. Billy passed Jesse over. "Thanks," he said over his shoulder as he took off across the street.

When he reached the opposite sidewalk, he paused to ask Eden, "How is he?"

Just then Jared groaned. "He's coming to, I think," Eden said. With great care, she lifted his head and cradled it in her lap.

"Evie's calling the ambulance."

"Good."

More furniture went flying beyond the double doors. Something hit them. Hard. Shaking his head, Billy started forward.

"Be careful," Eden warned.

Billy pushed through the doors. Inside, he saw a lot of broken furniture—and Sam Fletcher, backing Oggie toward the corner where the upright piano stood.

Oggie had both hands up, and for once he looked worried. "Now, Sam. Now, listen—"

"I'll kill you," Sam growled. "I'll wring your neck like a chicken. I'll—"

"Hey, Sam!" Billy called.

Sam didn't so much as pause. He seized the old man by his grimy red suspenders and lifted him right off the ground. Then he started to shake him. Oggie's head wobbled back and forth like the head of one of those silly little dogs people put on their dashboards. Pitiful bleating sounds came out of his mouth.

With a sigh, Billy grabbed a chair. He move swiftly

up behind Sam and brought the chair down hard across Sam's shoulders. The chair broke apart.

Sam grunted—and let go of Oggie. He turned on Billy.

Billy put up both hands. "Look. Let me explain. I was just trying to get your attent—" That was as far as he got. Sam delivered a swift right cross, followed by a doozy of a left hook to Billy's jaw. Then he picked Billy up and threw him across the room.

Billy landed against the bar, hard. A jolting numbness went out from his lower back, the actual point of impact. His jaw had no feeling in it and the room spun in circles.

Meanwhile, across the room, Oggie had managed to get out of the corner. Now, he backed and dodged, alternately pleading and arguing with Sam, who advanced on him, silent and determined as the grim reaper himself, picking up chairs and tables and tossing them aside just as fast as Oggie could push them in his way.

Billy knew he had to do something, and fast. With a grunt at the effort, he reeled to his feet—and headed for the storeroom in back.

He found what he needed right away, thank God. A nice big jar of maraschino cherries. He staggered back into the main part of the bar, where luck was with him. Sam was facing the other way. He was busy dangling Oggie against the wall by the suspenders again.

Billy rushed up on Sam, hefted the cherries high— and brought them down squarely on top of Sam's head. The jar shattered. Red syrup and cherries splattered and flew.

Sam froze, releasing Oggie, who slid down the wall. Sam started to turn. Billy knew he was a dead man.

Sam got around, his blue eyes twin points of blue ice. "You…"

And that was as far as he got, because he went down. He just dropped, hitting the floor with a sound like a thunderclap.

Oggie and Billy looked at each other. And then they heard the siren coming.

Prudence heard the siren, too. It sounded to her as if it came from Main Street. She almost walked over to investigate. But then the siren stopped and she told herself it was nothing, after all.

By five, Billy and Jesse had yet to return and it was pouring rain. Prudence had done the laundry, mopped the kitchen floor and fiddled with her résumé for a while. And she was worried. They'd been gone for two hours. What in the world could they be doing?

Lots of things, her wiser self answered. In a small town so thick with Joneses, Billy could have found any number of places to get in out of the rain.

But then again, he hadn't even taken an extra diaper. Jesse would certainly have needed changing by now. The little sweetheart had a mild diaper rash already. Having to sit around in a wet diaper would be bound to aggravate the condition. And if Billy had put him on a toilet in a public rest room, Prudence thought she might just buy a pistol and shoot the man.

And Jesse usually had a snack of fruit or graham crackers and juice sometime around four. Four was long past. Had Billy given him anything? And if he had, was it good, healthful food? She could just see Billy now, offering candy and soda pop in place of something with nutritional value.

She was staring out the front window again, trying

to decide whether or not to make a few phone calls, when a light-colored van pulled up in front of the gate. Prudence recognized the vehicle immediately; it belonged to Evie Riggins.

Evie got out, went around to the back and took Jesse from the car seat there. Prudence had the door open for them as Evie ran up the steps, in a hurry to get out of the driving rain.

"He needs changing," Evie said as she handed Jesse over. "I keep some spares over at the store, but they're smalls, for Stephen." Stephen was her baby. He'd been born about a month and a half before.

"Where's Billy?"

Evie let out a big sigh. "Long story."

"Tell me."

"Tange, Tange!" Jesse demanded.

Prudence kissed his rain-damp cheek. "I will, sweetie. Right away." She started for the stairs.

"I have to get back to the shop and close up," Evie said. "I left Tawny there with Stephen." Tawny was her sister-in-law. "And it isn't fair to ask her to watch the baby *and* the store."

"Don't you dare leave until you tell me something about what is going on," Prudence commanded over her shoulder as she reached the foot of the stairs.

"Billy should be here soon. He'll explain everything. I really have to—"

Though Jesse was squirming, Prudence turned and faced Evie once more. "Just tell me what it's all about."

Evie shook her head. But then she said in a rush, "All right. Sam got so mad at Oggie, he came after him at the Hole in the Wall. Jared stepped in. Sam knocked Jared out cold with a bottle of Glenlivet and then threw him in the street.''

Prudence thought of the siren she'd heard over an hour before. It must have been the ambulance, coming for Jared. ''Is Jared all right?''

''He'll be fine, after the swelling goes down and the headache passes.''

''But why did Sam get so angry at Oggie?''

''It's a long story. And I do have to go now.''

''But what does Billy have to do with this?''

''He and Jesse were walking up Main Street when the problem started, so he ended up getting mixed up in it, too.''

''Is he—?''

''He's fine.''

Prudence realized that poor Evie was looking at her pleadingly. ''All right, I know. You have to go. Thanks for looking out for Jesse.''

''I was glad to do it. And Billy knows the whole story. As soon as he gets out of jail, he'll tell you all about it.''

''He's in *jail?*''

''Relax. It's nothing serious. Jack just put him and Sam in there until he can check with Eden and make sure she doesn't want to press charges.''

''Press charges? For what?''

''Prudence....''

''I know, I know. You have to go.''

Before Jack Roper locked Billy and Sam in the small holding cell at the North Magdalene Sheriff's Substation, he allowed them to clean up a little.

'''Preciate this,'' Billy said to Jack as he washed the cherry syrup off his face and neck.

"No problem," said Jack.

Sam said nothing. He rinsed himself off and went into the cell.

There were two skinny cots in there, one against each of the cinder block side walls. Sam dropped to one, on the far end, so he was facing the back wall with its one tiny barred window way up high. He closed his eyes and didn't say another word. Billy stood in the middle of the room for a minute, then wandered over and took the other cot, stretching out on it, groaning a little at the pain in his poor, abused back.

Fifteen minutes crawled past, and then the door to the main room of the station swung open. Billy sat up, hoping it would be Jack to tell them that Eden had said they could go.

But instead of Jack, it was Oggie.

Slowly, his expression bleak, Oggie hobbled toward the cell. When he got there, he stood huffing for a moment, as if the walk from the door had completely tuckered him out. He peered through the bars at Sam, waiting for the big man to turn. But Sam didn't move.

"Sam?" For once in his life, Oggie sounded subdued. "Sam, would you talk to me, please?"

Sam still refused to turn. He didn't so much as move.

Oggie cleared his throat. "Well. I'm here to say goodbye, is all. I'm here to say, I only done and said what I thought was right. For you and for Delilah. Because she is my blood and *you* are as good as blood to me." He waited. Even Billy thought he was damn pitiful. But Sam remained facing the wall, as still as a stone.

Oggie continued, "Yes, I know I have been wrong. I have spoken out of line. And for that I sincerely apologize.'' He waited some more. Still no response from Sam. ''So I have come to tell you I am leaving town, taking off for God-knows-where. I can't say when I'll be back—or *if* I'll be back, to tell you true.''

With a heavy sigh, Oggie looked at Billy. ''Goodbye,'' he said, all the sadness the world could hold in his tiny black eyes. ''You look after our Prudence and that little boy.''

Though Billy seriously doubted Prue would welcome being looked after by him, he nodded anyway. He'd learned his lesson about arguing with Oggie. It never turned out to be worth it in the end.

With slumped shoulders and halting steps, the old man departed.

Once the door had closed behind him, Sam moved around to face the center of the cell. He leaned his head back on the cinder block wall and let out a long, sad groan.

Billy said, ''You all right?''

Sam shrugged. ''Doesn't matter. Nothin' matters. Nothin' matters a damn. Not anymore.''

Billy had the feeling that Sam wanted to talk. And why the hell not, thought Billy. He had the time. ''Tell me about it.''

Sam lifted his head and looked hard at Billy. ''You really want to know?''

Billy nodded. That was all it took. Sam launched into his tale of woe.

Chapter 10

At ten past seven, Billy sauntered into the upstairs bathroom, where Prudence was giving Jesse his bath. Prudence let out a shriek when she happened to glance over her shoulder and there he was, leaning in the door to the hall, wearing sunglasses and a straw cowboy hat. His shirt and jeans were streaked with some kind of pinkish stain.

"Billy! You scared me."

Billy was grinning his best killer grin. He had a big bruise on his chin and a cut on his lip. "Found my hat." He tapped the brim. "And my shades."

"Well. Good. I guess." Actually she hadn't even realized he'd lost them.

In the tub, Jesse bounced up and down, clapping his hands and chortling in glee. "Da! Da!"

Billy pushed away from the door frame and entered the bathroom. He took off the hat and the sunglasses and set them on the sink counter. In addition to the bruise on his chin and the cut on his lip, he had a bandage on his forehead and a purple bump high on his cheekbone. With the sunglasses off, she could see that both of his eyes were clear and bright.

He hadn't been drinking.

Prudence realized then that she'd been worrying, subconsciously, all afternoon. She'd feared that maybe he'd show up drunk again—and she'd have to make the bleak choice between giving him another chance and asking him to leave. But here he was, after all. Still on the straight and narrow. Still sticking to their agreement.

He blew out a breath. "Yeah, all right, I'm a mess. But Jared's worse, from what I've heard."

"What about Oggie?"

"Not a scratch on him."

"Evie told me a little of what happened, when she brought Jesse home. Was anyone seriously hurt?"

"Aside from Sam's broken heart, I'd say no."

"Sam's broken heart?"

Billy nodded. "Delilah left him."

Prudence let out a small sound of dismay. "But why?" She didn't know either Delilah or her husband that well yet, but Oggie was always insisting that each of his kids had married well and forever.

Billy just shook his head. "The poor sucker."

He knelt beside Prudence and splashed Jesse playfully. Jesse giggled in delight. Prudence watched them. Billy smelled like sweat and dirt and something sweet, almost syrupy. She couldn't quite put her finger on what.

Jesse's giggles faded. He leaned toward his father. "Boo-boos," he said, his little face gone solemn. He reached out to touch Billy's chin.

Billy chuckled. "You bet, lotsa boo-boos." He pulled back then, and rolled up his sleeves. "But your dad is tough." He fished around in the water until he came up with the soap. "Let's finish this bath."

Prudence watched him for a moment, as he soaped up the washcloth. He looked so battered—and so pleased with himself. Jesse splashed water at him and giggled. Prudence canted back on her toes and then pushed herself to her feet.

Father and child stopped soaping and splashing to gaze up at her.

"Woo?"

"Where you goin'?"

"I think you two can handle this job alone."

He came to find her in the living room after he put Jesse to bed.

"Seven fifty-nine," she said. "I think it's some kind of record."

He stood just beyond the coffee table, in the center of the room. He almost looked nervous. "I smell like a hard-ridden horse. I could really use a shower."

She felt her face coloring a little, as if he'd said something terribly intimate. "Oh. Well, I…"

"If I cleaned up quick, would you still be here…you know, to talk?"

"Certainly. Of course. Go right ahead."

He was back in ten minutes, his hair still shiny with water, wearing a clean pair of jeans and a soft-looking shirt with the sleeves rolled to just below his elbows. The bandage on his forehead was gone.

"That's a nasty gash," she said.

"It's nothing." He went over to the stereo and put a CD in the cartridge. It was something classical and soothing, with piano and strings. He adjusted the volume, then came and sat on the sofa with her, not so close as he had last night, but close enough that she could smell his clean, just-showered scent.

He really was an attractive man. Attractive in the way of someone totally comfortable in his physical body. Maybe that was what Randi—and all those other women—had seen in him. His naturalness. His ability to live right in the moment. He did what he wanted to do, and he enjoyed every second of it.

He was smiling at her strangely. "Have I got soap on my nose?"

She realized she was staring and laughed, a nervous laugh. "No, of course not. I'm just…anxious to hear what happened."

The strange smile was still there. "You could have called Eden and got the story from her."

"Well, I know. But I didn't want to bother her. With Jared injured and all the uproar, I figured she wouldn't need me calling up to ask what was going on. And besides, I knew I could ask you. As soon as you got home. So what happened?"

"Well, like I said, Delilah left Sam. I guess things have been pretty rough between the two of them lately."

"Because?"

"They want a kid."

"But they can't have one?"

"I don't know if they *can't*. It just ain't happening. Sam says they've been to two different fertility clinics. He says he wouldn't even explain to another man the things he went through there—or what he and Delilah have been through at home. Making love by thermometer, Sam calls it."

"Sam was the one who told you all this?"

"Yeah, while we were waiting in the jail. The deal is, the doctors haven't found anything wrong with either Sam or Delilah, but Delilah's never managed to get pregnant and both of them are in their forties now. It's put a big strain on their marriage. Especially in a small town like this one, where too many people pay too much attention to other people's business. Sam told me that in the last year or so, it's gotten pretty damn close to unbearable. Delilah can't walk down Main Street without someone stopping her to ask if she and Sam are ever going to produce a little bundle of joy."

"I can see how that would be hard to take."

"Yeah. And have you noticed that all the rest of the Jones women have at least one kid each? And most have two or more. Sam says even Jack's wife is pregnant now."

"Yes. Eden says Olivia is four months along."

Billy nodded. "According to Sam, that's another link in the chain of frustration for Delilah. Until Jack's wife got pregnant, at least there was one other childless couple in the family. But as soon as Olivia has her baby, Sam and Delilah will be the only ones."

"I imagine that *would* be hard."

"Sam told me they feel like a pair of freaks."

"Oh, no…"

"Yeah." He leaned in a little closer. "You know, if you think about it, the number of babies in the Jones family right now is pretty damn eerie."

"Well, I don't know if I'd call it eerie. I mean, people get married and they have babies. It's the natural thing to do."

"Fine. It's natural. But not for Sam and Delilah, evidently. And that was making them both miserable.

Added to that, Oggie lives with them. And Oggie wants grandchildren.''

"He *has* grandchildren.''

"You know the old man. He's never satisfied with plenty when he might be able to get more. Evidently he's made one too many remarks to Delilah lately, about how she's not fulfilling his expectations.''

"I do love him, but he can be thoughtless.''

Billy grunted. "Thoughtless. Right. Put it mildly, why don't you?''

"He means well.''

"He means to get what he wants. Anyway, he's been making remarks to Delilah. And then there's that new clerk Sam hired. She's young and pretty. And she's been playing up to Sam.''

"But Sam wouldn't—''

"No, he says he wouldn't. He swears he didn't. But Delilah's been feeling pretty damn insecure lately.''

Prudence filled in the rest. "And seeing a young, attractive woman chasing after her husband has just added to her misery.''

"Right.''

"So she left him.''

"Yeah. Evidently she dropped in at Sam's store this afternoon, and found him making way too friendly with the help.''

"Making friendly? What does that mean?''

"Sam says it really wasn't anything. That he and Sharlee—that's the clerk, Sharlee—were just looking over some equipment catalogs together, laughing and talking. That Delilah got the wrong idea. But she stormed out. Sam followed her home and found her packing a bag. He tried to reason with her, but she wouldn't listen. She told Sam that Oggie had warned her about that clerk, that Oggie had said she would lose Sam if she didn't watch it, and now she knew that Oggie was right. She accused Sam of betraying his marriage vows. Then she left.''

''Where to?''

''She took a room at the motel. And Sam just snapped. He went after Oggie—which doesn't surprise me a bit. Do you know that old man has been living with them for almost their whole married life? I figure if I lived with him for much longer than a half an hour, I'd end up trying to kill him, too.''

''But did Sam actually hurt Oggie?''

''Hell, no. That old geezer has more lives than a black cat. First Jared stepped between them—and got his head bashed in for his trouble. And then I showed up. In the meantime, Oggie just backed and dodged— and somehow managed to come out untouched. When I got there, Sam hit me in the face a couple of times and threw me against the bar. That was when I knew serious action would have to be taken.'' He told her of the big jar of cherries and what he'd done with it.

''Poor Sam,'' she said when he was through. ''Did he have to visit the clinic, too?''

''Naw. He refused medical help. By then depression had set in. He said if he ended up in a coma or something, maybe at least Delilah would come and sit by his bedside till he wasted away and died. Jack let us wash up a little, over there at the jailhouse. Then he locked us in. A few minutes later, Oggie showed up to say goodbye.''

Prudence hoped she hadn't heard right. ''Goodbye?''

''Yep. It was kind of sad, really. Sam wouldn't look at him, but the old man apologized for meddling, anyway. Then he said goodbye, said he was leaving for a while, maybe never to return.''

"Oh, no. Do you really believe he would leave here for good?"

Billy waved the question away. "Hell, no. He'll be back. He's Oggie Jones and this is his town—I'm telling you, Prue. This is a hell of a family I've gotten myself in to." He was shaking his head—but his eyes were shining. He added, "Oh, and then, last of all, Rocky came by while I was in the cell to return my hat and my shades."

"The ones you lost, you mean."

"Right."

"And who, exactly, is Rocky?"

"Rocky Collins is more or less a fixture over at the Hole in the Wall. And as it turned out, I happened to leave my hat and shades at his place that first night I was in town. You remember that night?"

As if she could ever forget it. "So that's the whole story?"

"Yeah."

"Where's Sam now?"

"Home. Alone."

"And Oggie's really left town?"

Billy nodded. "He took off in his Eldorado. Probably for Tahoe or Reno. He likes to go both places and gamble, from what I heard."

"And Delilah?"

"She's still over at the motel."

It sounded so sad. Delilah at the motel and Sam at home, each of them all alone. "They'll probably work it out in the end, don't you think?"

He shrugged. "Who can say?"

The mood seemed so heavy suddenly. She tried to

lighten it by teasing, "And you were quite the hero."
She reached across and put her hand on his arm, right
below his rolled-up sleeve. "You and your nice, big
jar of maraschino cherries."

Before she finished the sentence, she recognized her
mistake.

His eyes changed. She saw heat in them. At the same
time, she felt as if all the breath had fled right out of
her body. The rain on the roof sounded louder, more
insistent, suddenly. And Billy's eyes looked way too
soft.

Very carefully, Prudence withdrew her hand. They
sat for a moment, listening to the rain and the beautiful,
haunting music on the stereo.

At last, Billy said, "You do hide behind those
glasses, don't you Prue?"

How many times had he asked her that, now? Several times, surely. And each time, she'd felt invaded.
Offended. Insulted.

Because it was true.

"Tell me why."

Why. She thought of her mother, in the bathroom,
putting on her makeup, spending hours on her hair.
And of all her mother's boyfriends, who had started
eyeing Randi when Randi was barely in her teens. And
of herself—hiding, yes—behind her glasses, her hair
pulled back so tight it hurt sometimes. Safe from men
and their hungry eyes.

"Come on," Billy coaxed. "You can do it."

Prudence stared at Billy, wondering when the moment had come that she had started to like him, trying
to remember that he was bad Billy Jones, a rouser and
carouser, a seducer of women, born wild and not meant
to be tamed.

"Come on," he coaxed.

And she found herself confessing hesitantly, "There's…a game that women play."

"A game?"

"For men."

"Women play a game for men."

"Well, I mean they play it to attract men. They…dress provocatively and they make themselves up just so. When women play the game, they aim all their energy at men, at pleasing them. At making men want them. My mother played that game. It ate up her whole life. And Randi…she was a master at it. But in the end, I think the game controlled her. In the end, when people looked at her, they didn't see what a beautiful person she was. They only saw the game."

"Maybe she wanted it that way."

"I don't believe that. I really think she wanted more. But she didn't know how to get it. She was trapped by the game, like most women are."

"And what about you, Prue?"

"I told you. I'm just someone who doesn't want to play the game at all. I want to live my life with dignity. I want fulfilling work and good friends. And to do the right thing by my sister's little boy. Is that too much to ask?"

"Naw," he said, his voice low and tender. "Not too much. Not too much at all." He leaned closer. "If anything, I'd say it wasn't enough."

"It's enough."

"But what if you could have more? Wouldn't you like more?"

"No."

"Prue. More is always better than enough. And everyone wants more, no matter what they say."

"Not me."

"I don't believe that." He had her backed against the arm of the sofa again, just like last night.

She hardened her expression, stiffened her spine. "You're pushing me, Billy."

Slowly that devil's smile appeared on his lips. "I am. It's a fact. I'm in your face and in your space."

"Back off." She bit off each word sharply and clearly.

And he did. He withdrew to his half of the sofa, though when he got there, he went on watching her in a way that made her want to get up and leave.

Prudence folded her hands in her lap and looked down at them. In her mind's eye, she saw Nellie Anderson's pinched face, heard her dire warnings: *"Just be careful around that man. I warn you. He will toy with you if you let him…"*

She asked, very carefully, "What are you trying to do here, Billy?"

"What do you think I'm trying to do?"

She smoothed her hair, straightened her blouse. "If I told you, you would only laugh."

"Tell me anyway."

She shot him a challenging glance. "If you keep after me, I will. I really will."

"Good. Go on. Hit me with it."

She made herself look at him full-on, right into his glittering green eyes. "It appears to me that you are trying to seduce me."

That shut him up. For a minute, anyway. He gaped at her.

And then he threw back his head and laughed. It was a deep, rolling laugh and it lasted a long time. Prudence waited it out. Eventually the laugh wore down.

PLAY

RUN
FOR THE
ROSES

and get

THREE FREE GIFTS!

HOW TO PLAY:

1. With a coin, carefully scratch off the silver box at the right. Then check the claim chart to see what we have for you — **FREE BOOKS** and a **FREE GIFT**—**ALL YOURS FREE!**

2. Send back the card and you'll receive two brand-new Silhouette Desire® novels. These books have a cover price of $4.25 each, but they are yours to keep absolutely free!

3. There's no catch. You're under no obligation to buy anything. We charge nothing — ZERO — for your first shipment. And you don't have to make any minimum number of purchases — not even one!

4. The fact is, thousands of readers enjoy receiving books by mail from the Silhouette Reader Service™. They like the convenience of home delivery...they like getting the best new novels months before they're available in stores...and they love our discount prices!

5. We hope that after receiving your free books you'll want to remain a subscriber. But the choice is yours — to continue or cancel, any time at all! So why not take us up on our invitation, with no risk of any kind. You'll be glad you did!

© 1998 HARLEQUIN ENTERPRISES LTD.
® and TM are trademarks owned by Harlequin Books S.A., used under license.

This surprise mystery gift
Will be yours **FREE –**
When you play
RUN for the ROSES

DETACH AND MAIL CARD TODAY!

PLAY
RUN FOR THE ROSES

Scratch
Here
See Claim Chart

YES! I have scratched off the silver box. Please send me all the gifts for which I qualify. I understand that I am under no obligation to purchase any books, as explained on the back and opposite page.

RUN for the ROSES			Claim Chart
♛	♛	♛	**2 FREE BOOKS AND A MYSTERY GIFT!**
♛	♛		**1 FREE BOOK!**
♛			**TRY AGAIN!**

Name
(PLEASE PRINT CLEARLY)

Address   Apt.#

City   Prov.   Postal Code

(C-SIL-PT-10/98)   **326 SDL CJAY**

Offer limited to one per household and not valid to current
Silhouette Desire® subscribers. All orders subject to approval.

PRINTED IN U.S.A.

The Silhouette Reader Service™ — Here's how it works:

Accepting free books places you under no obligation to buy anything. You may keep the books and gift and return the shipping statement marked "cancel." If you do not cancel, about a month later we'll send you 6 additional novels, and bill you just $3.49 each, plus 25¢ delivery per book and GST.* That's the complete price — and compared to cover prices of $4.25 each — quite a bargain! You may cancel at any time, but if you choose to continue, every month we'll send you 6 more books, which you may either purchase at the discount price...or return to us and cancel your subscription.

*Terms and prices subject to change without notice.
Canadian residents will be charged applicable provincial taxes and GST.

If offer card is missing, write to: Silhouette Reader Service, P.O. Box 609, Fort Erie, Ontario L2A 5X3

CDMA
Member

0195619199-L2A5X3-BR01

SILHOUETTE READER SERVICE
PO BOX 609
FORT ERIE ONT
L2A 9Z9

MAIL▶POSTE
Canada Post Corporation/Société canadienne des postes

Postage paid   Port payé
If mailed in Canada   si posté au Canada

Business   Réponse
Reply   d'affaires

0195619199   01

He gave her one of those long, insolent looks of his, a look that started at the crown of her head, went down to her shoes and then back up again. "Seduce you, huh?"

"Yes." She refused to be cowed by his ridicule. "Yes, I believe that you are trying to seduce me. Am I wrong?"

He pretended to consider, making a big show of furrowing his brow and scratching his chin—carefully, because of the bruise there. She wanted to demand again, *Am I wrong?* But somehow she made herself sit there and wait. Finally, when her patience felt stretched right to the breaking point, he answered her.

"No, Prue. I'd say you pretty much hit the old nail right square on the head."

Chapter 11

Once the words were out of his mouth, Billy felt pretty damn stunned that he'd said them. After all, he'd only put it together himself just a minute before. She'd asked if he was trying to seduce her. And it had been like one of those light bulbs going on over the head of a character in a cartoon.

He wanted to get it on with Prue.

He wanted to take off her glasses and let down that red hair. He wanted to get naked with her. And he wanted to do it ASAP, because ASAP was always how he wanted the things he wanted.

All those sappy strings were irritating him. "Where's the damn remote?"

"Right here." Prudence picked it up from the coffee table and handed it to him. He pointed it at the stereo and the music stopped. Now only the rain filled the silence between them.

He tossed the remote down. "So, what do you say?"

He felt impatient with her, suddenly. She didn't look as if she was going to be throwing herself into his arms anytime soon. "You don't want to be seduced?"

She blew out a weary breath. "Oh, Billy."

Damn, she was an irritating woman. "Oh, Billy what?"

"I thought I just explained it to you. I don't want to play any of those games."

The damn rain bugged him, the way it drummed away. No change in rhythm, just a steady, nerve-flaying, never-ending roll.

"Billy, are you listening to me?"

"Who turned off the music?"

"*You* did."

He grabbed the remote and pointed it. Something livelier this time, he thought. A little zydeco. Seconds later, a bouncy accordion riff drowned out the rain.

She was watching him, looking grim. He suggested, "It could just be fun, you know?"

She hitched in a gaspy little breath. *"Fun?"*

"Yeah. Fun. You're a woman. I'm a man. I'm single, so are you. We're both one hundred percent free of entanglements and that means no one gets hurt."

"But I just told you—"

He put up both hands, determined to get through to her. "No. Wait. Listen."

"This is insane."

"No. It's not insane. It's natural. It's good. You don't want to play any games. And I don't, either. You can be…just you. I don't want you to dress any other way, or to paint your face. It's true I wouldn't mind if you would let down your hair and get a new pair of glasses. But even if you won't make those two tiny concessions, I gotta admit it. I still got a thing for you.

You get to me. You…irritate me. But in a way that makes me want to get down. So what do you say we go with it? Right now would be fine with me.''

She just went on staring at him.

He said, ''Your mouth's hanging open, Prue.''

She snapped it shut, then instructed, ''Find someone else.''

He tried to stay patient, though patience was not an activity at which he excelled. ''That's not the point. It's not just…anyone. I've been there and done that. It gets old, I'm telling you. No. It's strange, it's impossible. But it's you. You get to me. I thought it was because I hated you. But now I see it was only attraction. That I was fighting it. And that's pretty stupid. I mean, why fight it? Why not just go with it and see what happens?''

''Billy, I do not want to have an affair with you.''

He decided maybe the zydeco was a little *too* lively. He pointed the remote again. Got Elvis. ''Love Me Tender.''

''Billy, do you hear me?''

''I hear you, Prue.'' He dragged in a breath. ''So I guess you're saying, not tonight, huh?''

''I'm saying not ever.'' Her eyes looked wide and scared and her face was flushed. A few strands of hair had escaped their scraped-back imprisonment and curled along her forehead and at her temples.

He said, ''I really do want to kiss you. Maybe we could start with that. With one kiss.''

''No.''

He pointed the remote once more. For quiet. Into the silence and the endless drumming of the rain, he said, ''You're really telling me no.''

''That's exactly what I'm telling you.''

"Not just for tonight. For good. Period. Zippo."

"Exactly."

"This could create tension."

She jumped to her feet and threw up her hands. "Tension? There's already tension. Do you think it's a picnic for me, having you here?"

He sat back and considered. "Well, I never really thought about how it's been for you."

"Oh, I'm sure you haven't." She windmilled her hands. "You never think. You just...act on your appetites. You get an urge and follow it. Feel an itch and you scratch. You never think of consequences. The morning after does not exist for you. For you it's always the night before!"

He grabbed one of her flying hands. "Prue."

"Don't!" She tried to jerk away.

He held on. He liked holding her hand. It felt good. Right. "Prue. Come on. If you're not interested, you're not interested. It's okay." It wasn't, not really. But she didn't have to know that. Her face was all screwed up tight. "Are you going to start crying on me?"

Her sweet, wide mouth quivered and her eyeballs had that swimmy look behind the lenses of her glasses. "No, I am not."

"Sit down." He tugged on her hand.

She just stood there. He thought of Jesse, that afternoon, hunkered down on the sidewalk, refusing to budge.

"Come on." He tugged again.

And she just sort of crumpled back down beside him. Once she was seated, she jerked her hand away, then scooted over against the armrest and held onto it as if it might save her from his evil self.

"Prue, look—"

She cut him off. "You know my sister loved you! She *told* you she loved you."

"Huh?"

"Randi told you she loved you. Admit it. She did."

He wondered what it was about women. When they were upset, they felt no obligation to stick to the subject.

"Billy. She told you. She told me she told you."

"So?"

"You made such an issue out of how she dumped you. But we both know why she dumped you. Because she told you how she felt about you, and you didn't care. So she said that she wanted to stop seeing you."

He wished he hadn't turned off the stereo. He picked up the remote again—and she shot him one of those just-you-try-it looks of hers.

He tossed it down. "Why the hell are we talking about Randi?"

"You know why. You can't just…tell me you want to sleep with me, and then not face up to what you did to Randi."

"I can't? Watch me. And, by the way, *sleeping* with you wasn't really what I had in mind."

"Oh, right. Fine. Play word games with me now."

He'd had about enough. He stood. "Look. This was a bad idea. Just forget I even brought it up, will you?"

She stuck that nose of hers high in the air. "I'd be glad to."

He said, "We'll get through the rest of my two weeks, somehow. And then we'll make some decisions concerning Jesse. And that will be that."

"Fine. Good night."

He started for the guest room.

"Wait."

He should have known. She just couldn't leave bad enough alone. Slowly he turned to face her again.

"Admit it. Randi told you she loved you."

He would have slapped his own forehead in frustration, if he wasn't afraid he'd open the gash there again.

"Admit it, Billy. I just want to hear you admit it."

"All right. Fine. She told me she loved me."

"If she dumped you, if she didn't tell you about Jesse, it was because you didn't care. Admit it. You didn't care."

He wasn't admitting that. No way. "I did care."

"You didn't."

He looked at her straight-on and he said it out flat. "I cared. Just not the way she wanted me to. And she gave me no choice about Jesse, no choice at all. You know that as well as I do."

That reached her. She had to look away.

He laid a final point on her. "Randi was a hell of a woman. But she was no candidate for sainthood. Maybe you just ought to face that, and move on."

He thought she sighed. But she wouldn't look at him. He turned and left her there.

Prudence waited until he closed the door to his room. Then she climbed the stairs. She looked in on Jesse. He slept like an angel, in the bottom bunk of the bed his father had bought for him.

She went to the bathroom, filled the tub and took a long, hot bath to try to relax. But it didn't do much good. She ended up lying awake half the night, putting on her glasses now and then to see how late it was getting, thinking about the things Billy had said and telling herself she'd put him firmly in his place.

He certainly wouldn't be making any more passes at

her. If nothing else, in confronting him about Randi, she'd completely turned him off. And that was good. That was fine.

She had better things to do with herself than provide some transitory sexual amusement for bad Billy Jones.

In the morning, she woke late. She looked at the clock and saw it was after ten. Downstairs, she discovered the note waiting on the table, stuck between the salt and pepper shakers: "We went to Grass Valley. Don't worry, took diapers. Back by five. Will feed no junk food."

By eleven, minus Jesse to care for and Billy to argue with, Prudence began to feel pretty much at loose ends. She started to call Delilah and Sam's house, wanting to talk to Oggie, who always cheered her up. But then she remembered that Oggie had left town. She hung up before she even dialed.

She called Eden, who assured her that Jared was fine. "He's even gone into work today. He's not a man to let a knot on his head get him down. And how's the family hero?"

It took Prudence a second or two to realize that Eden referred to Billy. "Oh, he's fine, too. A little beat-up, but fine."

"I have to tell you, he showed up just in time yesterday."

"Yes. So I heard." She could see him, in her mind's eye, lounging on the sofa last night, telling her the whole story of how he'd knocked poor Sam out cold.

Eden asked, "How's he been, the past few days?"

"Pardon me?"

"You were worried, about his drinking."

"Oh, that. He's been…good. He's stayed sober and he's put in some real effort with Jesse."

Eden laughed. "So there's hope then? For him as a father."

"Yes. Yes, I suppose there is."

They talked for a few minutes about Sam and Delilah. Eden said Delilah had stopped in to see that Jared was all right. Jared had told her to go back to her husband, and Delilah had walked out in a huff. Eden added that Delilah had never been one to sit still for advice from her hell-raising brothers.

After the call to Eden, Prudence decided to walk over to Main Street. The rain had stopped sometime in the night. Outside, it was clear and cold.

She went to Lily's Café and had a sandwich. All the talk there centered on Sam and Delilah. Prudence learned that, in spite of everything, Delilah had gone to work that morning—she taught fourth and fifth grade at the North Magdalene School. Also, Sam had opened up his store right on time. The clerk, Sharlee, was still on the job.

"Business as usual," Linda Lou Beardsly was heard to whisper. "Except for the distinct possibility of *d-i-v-o-r-c-e* in the future."

After lunch, Prudence wandered into the shop next door, Santino's Barber, Beauty and Variety. A small dark-haired woman smiled at her from behind the register counter when Prudence entered the store. "Hi, how you doing? I'm Maria. Santino, like the front window says."

Prudence murmured hello and glanced toward the back of the shop. She could see two barber's chairs there, a sink and a hair dryer.

"You need a cut?" asked Maria.

"Oh, no. I didn't…"

Maria emerged from behind the counter. "I tell you true, I'm bored to death. You do me a favor, let me cut your hair. I give you a break on the price."

"Um, well, I…"

"Come into the light. Let me see." She took Prudence by the arm and led her back to the barber's chairs, where a big window let in the afternoon sun and the overhead lights were much brighter than in the rest of the shop. "Sit. Sit here." Prudence allowed herself to be pushed into one of the chairs. Maria stood behind her and began removing the pins that held back her hair. Absurdly Prudence found herself thinking of that night in Billy's club, when he had stolen her glasses and let down her hair.

"Not bad," Maria declared.

Prudence smiled to herself. That night in the club, one of Billy's friends had said the same thing.

"What's so funny?" Maria wanted to know.

"Oh, nothing. Really. Nothing at all."

"We shorten it," Maria murmured. "Four or five inches. Take it up some in back. What do you say?"

"Well, I…"

"A nice shampoo first, a little head massage. So relaxing. You'll see." Maria was already guiding her out of the chair, leading her to the shampoo sink.

Half an hour later, Maria hooked her blow dryer back in its rack on the wall by the mirror. "So. What do you think?"

Prudence's hair barely touched her shoulders now. It fell, smooth and sleek, from a center part. "It's just so…red."

"A beautiful red." Maria handed Prudence a hand

mirror. "Like dark fire. And this cut is good for the shape of your face."

Prudence used the hand mirror to check the back. "You think so?"

"I know so. I'm the expert, right? But let me give you a little bit of advice."

Prudence lowered the mirror and looked at Maria.

"Those glasses, they gotta go. You pay a visit to my cousin, Benny, in Grass Valley. He's an optometrist. He'll fix you up good. Wait right here. I'll get you his card."

Prudence left Santino's at a little past one. She went home and sat down in the kitchen for a moment and thought about brewing a pot of tea. Instead she called the number on the card Maria had given her. Benny Anselmo's assistant said he had a three o'clock slot on his appointment schedule.

Prudence said, "Well, maybe we should just forget this."

"Miss Wilding, that's certainly up to you."

Prudence closed her eyes, slid her thumb and forefinger under the nosepiece of her glasses and massaged the bridge of her nose.

"Miss Wilding, are you there?"

Billy was wrong about a lot of things, she thought. But probably not about her glasses. They were plain ugly. And it was time she stopped using them to hide from the world.

"Miss Wilding, will we see you at three today, or not?"

She sucked in a deep breath and forced out "Yes."

Chapter 12

Billy knew the minute he saw Prue's new haircut that he was making headway, after all. Over dinner, he told her it looked good.

She said, "Thank you," as if the words caused her pain coming out.

He asked, "What made you decide to let it down?" as if he didn't know.

She said, "I thought it was probably about time. Pass the squash."

Jesse fell asleep two minutes after Billy put him in his bed. Now *that* was a record. But the kid was beat. Billy had kept him hopping all day. They'd visited two playgrounds and gone to McDonald's for lunch. Jesse had climbed around on the play-sets and dug in the sandboxes until he was plain wiped out. Yeah, Billy decided, standing over his sleeping son, holding the Martin on which he'd been playing variations on the theme of "Puff, the Magic Dragon," he just might turn out to be an okay dad, after all.

At 7:37 he tiptoed from his son's room and went down the stairs to find Prue sitting on the sofa, reading.

"Good book?"

She looked up. For half a second, he dared to hope she might crack a smile. Her newly liberated hair shone so pretty in the light from the lamp beside her. He wanted to run his hand down it, from the crown of her head to where it brushed her shoulders.

Then her face pruned up. "You know, the music you're always playing for Jesse is great. Children love and need the sound of music. But you have to make a point to read to him, too. Most studies show that a child who is read to consistently learns to read and write much earlier and with much less effort. And the state of a child's reading and writing skills are a direct measure of his success in his future working life."

"Thank you, Dr. Wilding."

She sighed. "Will you just try to read to him more?"

"Sure. I can do that."

"Good." She looked down at her book again.

He stood there, staring at her bent head, feeling dismissed. Then he turned on his heel and went to his room. He got his keys, put on his hat, his shades and a jacket. After that, he returned to the arch that led to the living room and leaned there, just as before. "Look. I think I'll go out for a while."

That got her attention. Her head snapped up. "Go out? Where?" He knew just what she was imagining: booze, naked women and broken furniture.

He shrugged. "Hell if I know. Maybe I'll go over and see how Sam's holding up. Can you watch Jesse?"

"I am his guardian." She spoke each word distinctly, as if making some major point. "Of course I'll watch him."

"Terrific. Do you think I'm old enough now to have my own key?" She'd been off somewhere that afternoon when he and Jesse got home. They'd waited on the porch, playing peekaboo and patty-cake, for twenty minutes until she showed up.

"Of course." Her face remained pursed tight. If she didn't watch it, it would probably get stuck that way. She set her book aside and stood. "I'll get you one." She had to walk past him to reach the stairs. He made a point of watching her go by because he knew it bugged her.

But then, once she disappeared from the upper landing, he felt edgy and discouraged. He didn't really understand what she did to him. She got to him. In ways he'd never been gotten to before. Last night, they'd had fun together, during that too-short time while he was telling her about Sam and Delilah and the fight at the saloon. Or at least, he'd thought they were having fun. But then, as soon as he admitted that he wanted to get naked with her, she'd turned on him. She'd given him nothing but grief from there on in.

What in hell did he see in her? She had way too much honor and integrity for someone like him. Most of the time she just plain annoyed him. She made him want to annoy her right back.

However, in the past couple of days, he'd discovered he wanted to do a lot more than irritate her. He wanted to reach out and touch her. To smooth a hand down her silky hair, to pull her pretty body close. To unbutton all her buttons and see what exactly she looked like under there. To take away her glasses and have her stare up at him through those half-blind sky blue eyes.

In short, he wanted to get started on the love affair they were going to have. And if she'd only stop aggravating him, he would make another move on her.

He heard her footsteps on the stairs. He turned and watched her descend. At the bottom, she held out a key. "Here."

He took the key and headed for the front door, pausing at the threshold to advise, "Don't wait up."

She gave him a tight, mean little smile. "Don't you worry. I won't."

Once he was out in the cold night air, he wondered what to do next. He considered a visit to the Hole in the Wall, and then rejected the idea almost before he thought of it. He was feeling too uneasy. And when he felt uneasy, he got an urge to howl. When he howled, he tended to drink too much.

And if he drank too much, Prue would throw him out. That, he couldn't afford. For Jesse's sake, mostly. And beyond that, for the sake of the father he was learning to be.

So howling was a no go. He shivered a little and flipped up the collar of his jacket. And then he thought of Sam, probably sitting all alone in that house out there on Bullfinch Lane. That first day Billy came to town, when he'd been hot on the trail of the old man, it hadn't taken him more than ten minutes or so to get out there from the bar.

Yeah, all right. Maybe he *would* go see Sam.

Sam took so long to come to the door that Billy almost turned around and left. But at last, the long-haired giant appeared.

"Yeah," he said, staring blankly at Billy as if he'd never seen him before. "What do you want?"

Billy shrugged. "A beer, maybe. How 'bout that?"

"A beer," Sam repeated. He looked completely dazed—the walking wounded in the aftermath of a major natural disaster.

Billy decided he shouldn't stay. "Look. Bad timing, huh? I'll come back some other—"

Sam cut in. "No. Don't go." And then he just stood there.

Billy really felt sorry for the poor guy. "What you do is you step back and ask me in."

Sam stepped back. "Come on in."

Sam led him into a living area, with a switchback stairway leading to the second floor, high, angled ceilings, and lots of full bookcases. Billy liked the place immediately. It was one of those houses that invited a man to sit down and relax. The furniture looked comfortable and there were lots of carvings around. Sam's work, he was pretty sure. Oggie had told him once that Sam was a real artist with a whittling knife.

Sam stared at the room as if he didn't recognize it. "Maybe we ought to just go in the kitchen, all right?"

"Hey. Fine with me."

They went to the kitchen and sat at a big wood table. Sam got a couple of bottled Buds from the fridge and popped off the caps. "You need a glass?"

Billy shook his head.

Sam pulled out the chair across from Billy, dropped into it and slid Billy's beer over to him. Billy took a long pull, then removed his shades and his hat and set them on the table. He gestured with the bottle. "How's your head?"

Sam frowned, not picking up the reference through the fog of his misery. Billy felt another surge of pity for the man. Delilah better come back to him soon, or he'd end up forgetting his own damn name. Finally Sam caught on. "Right." He felt in his hair, for the spot Billy had popped him. "Tender. But no big deal."

"Glad to hear it." Billy drank again. When he set the bottle down, he wondered what the hell to say next. At this rate a twenty-minute visit would come out feeling like a year.

Right then, the doorbell rang. Sam jumped up. "That might be Lilah." He flew out of the kitchen, headed for the front door.

Billy sat sipping his beer, grateful toward whoever it was. He could use a little help here, in keeping the old conversational ball on the move. And if it *was* Sam's runaway wife, he'd have a fine excuse to take his leave.

A moment later, Sam reappeared, followed by a small, early-twentyish blonde, a pretty little thing with a round, dimpled Kewpie-doll face. She carried a large rectangular casserole dish covered in foil. She was talking a mile a minute, as she trotted along in the giant's wake. "Sam, I'm only *worried* about you, that's all. I was sitting at home, thinking how you most likely weren't eating right, and it occurred to me that maybe I should just do something about that and so I—" Right then she caught sight of Billy. "Oh. You didn't say you had company."

Billy looked at Sam. No help there. The big man had stopped over by the sink and was staring blindly into the middle distance. Billy stood. "Hi. I'm Billy."

"Oh. Yes. I think I've heard about you. Billy Jones, right?"

"Yeah." He offered to shake.

The blonde held out her casserole and giggled. "Sorry. I do have my hands full. I'm Sharlee." The husband-stealing clerk. He should have known. "Pleased to meet you," she simpered. "I hope you're going to be all right."

He wondered what the hell she meant by that.

She giggled some more. "Your face, all those bruises."

He touched the bump under his eye, which was already going down. "Oh, right." He dropped into his chair again. "I'll be fine."

"Well, good then." Little Sharlee bustled over to the stove. "I'm just going to heat this up a tad, and then—Sam, you haven't eaten yet, have you?" She set the casserole down and began fiddling with the oven knobs. "Sam?"

The big man blinked. "Huh?"

"I asked, have you eaten?"

"Eaten?" Sam's brows furrowed. "No, not lately, I don't think."

"Oh, I just knew it. You must keep your strength up, Sam. Good nutrition is the key to getting through a difficult time." She whipped the foil off the casserole.

Just then, they all heard the sound of a door shutting.

"Now, what was that?" Sharlee asked brightly as she put the dish into the oven.

Billy said, "Sounded like the front door," just as Sam breathed, "Lilah," in equal parts agony and longing.

They heard footsteps, coming through the hall and dining room. And then, there she was: Delilah Fletcher, standing in the doorway, wearing some gypsy-looking swirly red skirt and a red jacket, her thick, caterpillar-curly black hair sticking out loose and wild around her face. "Sam, I—"

Right then, the oven door slammed shut. Sharlee squeaked, "Oh!"

Delilah's head whipped around. She saw her rival, standing at her own stove. Her creamy skin went pink. All at once she looked fit to chew nails. What a woman, Billy thought. He felt a swift welling of pride, to know that he could call her his cousin.

"Lilah," Sam said again, on a whisper of pure yearning.

Delilah looked toward Sam once more. Her face seemed to crumple. "I thought we could talk, Sam. I thought maybe..."

"Lilah, listen." Sam took a step in her direction.

She put up both hands. "No, Sam. No." She gathered herself. "You just tell me. What is that woman doing in my house?"

"Well," Sharlee started to say, rubbing her hands together. "It's a difficult time for Sam and I just came over to see that—"

Delilah cut her off with a chopping motion of her arm. "No." She pointed at her rival. "*You*, I don't listen to. *You*, I don't hear. I want my husband to tell me, I want *him* to explain."

Billy stood. "Actually we were just leaving."

Delilah's hot gaze swung on Billy. "What?"

"I said, Sharlee and I are going to go now." He went over and took Sharlee by the elbow.

She tried to jerk away. "I'm heating a casserole here!"

"Leave it. We are out of here. Now." He half pushed, half dragged her toward the door to the dining room. Delilah had the sense to step aside when they got to her. "Thanks for the beer, Sam," Billy said over his shoulder.

Sam muttered something indistinguishable in reply.

"Wait." Delilah's voice stopped Billy in midstride.

He turned, keeping a good grip on the uncooperative Sharlee. "Yeah?"

"Did *you* bring her here?" Delilah's black eyes burned with accusation.

Billy shook his head. "She came by herself. And Sam didn't invite her. When the doorbell rang, he thought it might be you."

The fire and rage seemed to flow out of Delilah, then. She slumped against the door frame. Behind her, Sam said her name once more. She turned to him. "Oh, Sam…"

Sharlee was still squirming, making little, yippy complaining sounds. Billy headed for the door again. She dragged her feet all the way, but somehow he managed to hustle her out of there.

She started crying before he could get her into her little compact car that waited on the street behind his Cherokee. "Oh, I only wanted to help. I only wanted to do something nice for Sam. I…care for Sam. He's been so good to me, so patient with me on the job. And *she* doesn't appreciate him. She's a cold woman. She's forty, at least. And she never gave him any children. It's all over town, everyone's talking about it. She doesn't deserve him. She doesn't even begin to understand the needs of a man like Sam. She—"

There was more in the same vein. Billy tuned it out as he tried to decide what the hell to do with her. If he put her in her car, she'd only sit there behind the wheel, blubbering away. She might even decide to wander back into the house. Or Delilah might come out again, or glance out the front window. Anyway he looked at it, he only saw more hell to pay.

"Oh, Sam, Sam," Sharlee chanted between hiccups and sobs. "Sam, why won't you let me help you? Sam, why won't you see me as the woman I am?"

Billy led her back to the Cherokee and boosted her into the passenger seat. She went on wailing and jabbering as he buckled her in. "I am no one, I *have* no one. I came to this town hoping to make a new start. But there's no new start for me. Oh, Sam, Sam, you were my new start!"

"Where do you live?" Billy asked, after he'd climbed into the driver's seat and started the engine.

"Live, live. Where do I live? *How* will I live? Who am I? Who will ever care?"

He flipped open the glove box, shoved a few CDs out of the way and found the little package of Kleenex he'd stuck in there a while back. He handed it to her.

"Thank you. Oh, thank you." She managed to get a tissue out and blow her nose resoundingly. "You're nice. A nice man."

It was the first time in his conscious memory that anyone had called him *nice*. He couldn't decide whether he liked it or not. He asked again, "Sharlee, where do you live?"

She muttered an address on Pine. He put the Cherokee in gear and steered it out onto the main part of the street.

As he drove through the darkness, Sharlee alternately sobbed and blew her nose and bemoaned the emptiness of her life. When he pulled to a stop in front of the small, rather run-down cottage at the address she'd given him, she turned to him. "Thank you. I heard so many terrible things about you. Now I know never to trust what other people say." She paused, to sob and sniffle. "Tell Sam goodbye for me, please. I won't be bothering him anymore. After tonight, I'll never bother anyone again.'' She popped herself out of her seat belt and leaned on her door.

Billy watched her as she started up the concrete walk, thinking that her chatter could drive a man bonkers, but she really did seem like someone who needed a friend.

And he hadn't liked the sound of her final remark. It sat on his mind, heavy and ugly with meanings he hated to let himself understand: *After tonight, I'll never bother anyone again....*

He pushed open his door. "Sharlee. Wait up."

She stopped in the middle of the walk, a small, forlorn figure, shivering in the light of the waning moon. He jumped down from the Cherokee and ran to her side. "Look. I don't think you should be alone tonight."

She stared at him, her eyes wide and wet, her mouth working in misery. And then she let out a loud wail and threw herself against his chest. "Oh, I can't ask you! It isn't right! I'm not your problem, not at all!"

He gave her an awkward pat on the back. "Hey. You come on, now. I'll take you home with me." Prue probably wouldn't be thrilled about this. But she'd no more be able to turn away poor, pitiful Sharlee than he could right then.

The porch light of the house next door to Sharlee's popped on just as Billy was leading her toward the Jeep again. He paused, caught by something familiar about that house.

And then he got it: it looked a lot like Prue's house.

Right then, a tall, skinny woman in a blue robe with a blue hair net on her head came out the front door.

"What is going on out here?" Nellie Anderson demanded.

He should have known. He herded Sharlee toward the Jeep, calling over his shoulder as he went, "Nothing, Mrs. Anderson. Everything's under control."

"Is that you, Billy Jones?"

"Yes, Mrs. Anderson, it's me."

"What are you doing to that girl?"

Sharlee piped up. "It's all right, Mrs. Anderson." She paused to try to control a sob. "He's...helping me."

"Oh, my dear. Help from *him* is the last thing you need."

Billy hustled Sharlee to the passenger side and pushed her in. Then he hurried to get in on his side.

"Billy Jones, do you hear me? I will call the sheriff's office!"

He jumped in. "Good night, Mrs. Anderson!" He pulled the door shut and drove off.

Prue must have heard them coming up the walk. She pulled open the front door before they even got there. And then she didn't say a word. She just looked very slowly from Billy to Sharlee and back again.

Sharlee, still clinging and crying for all she was worth, gave an extra loud sob. "I...I needed help. And Billy was there...."

Prue moved back. "I suppose you'd better come in."

Billy pushed Sharlee inside and kicked the door shut. "This is Sharlee. Sharlee—?"

"St...St...Stubblehill," the girl said, stuttering to try to control her sobs.

Billy added, "Sharlee is Sam's clerk."

"Oh," Prue said, as understanding dawned. "I see."

Billy explained, "There was some trouble, at Sam's house. Sharlee came by after I showed up. And then Delilah arrived next." This description of recent events sent Sharlee into a fresh fit of weeping. She grabbed Billy's jacket front and pinned herself against him again.

"Sharlee is…real upset," Billy said.

"Yes. I can see that."

"I thought we could put her in my room."

Prue started to get pinched-faced. "*Your* room?"

He gave her a look of high-principled disdain. "And I can take Jesse's upper bunk."

She blushed—in embarrassment over how she'd misjudged him, he knew. "Oh. Yes. All right, that makes sense."

He peeled Sharlee off the front of him and gave her a gentle push. She fell into Prue's arms. "Oh, oh. Thank you, thank you," the girl whimpered, clinging as hard to Prue as she had to Billy.

Prue immediately did what women do. She rubbed and patted and made soothing sounds. "There now, come on now. It's all right. It's going to be all right…."

"You settle her down a little. I'll go ahead and change the sheets on that bed for her."

"There, there…" Prue paused to give him a nod. "Yes. Change the sheets." And then she began leading Sharlee toward the sofa. "Come on, sit down. Here are some fresh tissues. You cry it out. And then, if you'd like, we can talk a while."

The phone started ringing.

"I'll get it," Billy said. Prue didn't even hear him.

She was too busy hugging Sharlee and urging her to let it all hang out.

It was Jack Roper on the phone. "What the hell's going on, Billy? I just got a call from Mrs. Anderson. She said—"

"Let me guess. That I kidnapped her neighbor."

"Something along those lines."

Billy briefly explained the events of the evening.

When he was finished, Jack suggested wryly, "As an officer of the law, I'd advise you to avoid all contact with Mrs. Anderson."

"I'm trying, Jack," Billy said. "I truly am."

Sharlee took an hour to stop sobbing. And then, intermittently breaking down again, she told Prudence her life story. Her father had died when she was very young. She'd been raised in Southern California by an indifferent mother and a stepfather who favored his own natural children over her. She'd completed two years at business college. She'd come to North Magdalene to make a new start.

"But I can see now, I'm never going to fit in here. Sam never did fall in love with me at all. He was just trying to be nice to me, to help me out, since I worked for him and I was new in town. I understand that now, after seeing the way he looked at that awful wife of his tonight. And I can see the writing on the wall. I'm not a complete fool. Even though Sam didn't touch me, I've ended up the bad woman anyway. Everyone thinks I'm some kind of husband-stealer. And that wife of Sam's, she's a Jones. Everyone will take her side. No one goes against a Jones in this town. Oh, it's just not going to work for me here. Like always, I've failed."

Prudence sat on Billy's freshly made bed with the girl, hugging her and passing her tissues and listening.

"I have to leave this town. I have to get out of here."

"Sharlee, listen. Don't try to make any decisions tonight. You'll get some sleep. Things will come clearer in the morning."

"Yes, you're right. I know you're right...."

It was a little past one in the morning when Prudence finally left the guest room. Alone in the dim dining room, she paused to take off her glasses and massage the bridge of her nose. When she put them back on again, her gaze fell on the roses Billy had given her. They sat in a cut crystal vase on the dining-room table. They were halfway open now. Prudence smiled, looking at them.

She went to the living room and turned off the light. Then she climbed the stairs, ready for the comfort of her bed.

Outside the door to Jesse's room, she paused. And then, as quietly as she had closed the door on the sleeping Sharlee, she turned the knob.

The light from the hall spilled in. If she wasn't careful, she would wake the two in the bunk bed across the room.

Quickly and quietly, she slipped inside and closed the door all but a crack. Then she tiptoed over to where father and son slept. Jesse lay sideways, his head against the wall and his little toes hanging off the side of the bed. She gently straightened him up and then covered him with the blankets he'd kicked down. She indulged herself and kissed him, very lightly, on his warm, soft cheek. And then she rose and turned for the door.

"You gonna tuck me in, too, Prue?" The whisper came out of the darkness of the upper bunk.

She smiled in spite of herself and whispered back, "Not a chance."

"Sharlee said I was *nice,* Prue. What do you think of that?"

"She was right. You *were* nice to her."

"Could this be a trend?"

The question sounded rhetorical, so she didn't attempt to answer it. She went on toward the door.

Just before she slipped out, he murmured, "G'night, Prue."

"Good night, Billy." She slid around the door and out into the hall.

The next morning, Sharlee called Sam and told him she thought it would be best if she didn't work for him anymore.

"Well," Sharlee said, after she'd told Sam goodbye and hung up. "That's that, I suppose. He was very nice. He said he...understood. And that he'd make up a final paycheck for me. It'll be ready for me to pick up anytime after eleven at the store." Her lower lip quivered a little. "He left my casserole in the oven too long. It burned to a crisp and then he ran cold water on it and the dish cracked."

Billy, sitting at the kitchen table nearby, could see that the tears were on their way. To forestall a whole new shower of them, he suggested, "Come on, I'll take you over to pick up your car, how's that?"

"And then I have to go to my house, don't I?" She

sank forlornly into a chair, her lower lip quivering away.

Prue jumped in. "Well, if you'd like to come back here—"

Sharlee didn't even let her finish making the offer. "Oh, yes. I would. Please."

Billy shot Prue a sideways why'd-you-do-that? glance. Her gaze slid away so fast, he knew she understood.

"Uh, yes." Prue forged on with it. "We can discuss your options. And you can come to a decision about where you'd like to go next."

Billy ended up going over to the store to pick up Sharlee's check for her. She felt it would be too difficult to face Sam again, after all that had happened.

At the store, Sam handed him the check—and the hat and shades he'd left at Sam's house—and thanked him for stepping in and taking Sharlee out of the picture the night before.

"Did you work things out with Delilah?" Billy asked.

Sam, who had seemed reasonably alert when Billy entered the store, got that faraway look in his eyes again. "We talked. But nothing's solved." He looked down at the register counter, then off toward a barrel of shovels that stood in a far corner. "She went back to her room at the motel." He shot a glance around the store, though they were the only two people there right then. When he spoke again, he leaned across the counter and pitched his voice low. "She says she feels like she's not woman enough anymore."

Billy remembered his cousin, dressed in red, standing in the kitchen doorway, her hair all wild around her face. "If she's not woman enough, I don't know who is."

Sam grunted. "Yeah. But all the same, she's killin' me with her damn doubts. She says those doubts are all about herself. But that isn't true. Those doubts of hers have spread wide enough to include me. She doubts me, too. She thinks I'm just gonna find another woman, one to have kids with. She doesn't trust me—and how's a man supposed to live with that?"

These were not questions to which someone like Billy was likely to have answers. But he didn't much mind standing there, listening and nodding and shaking his head. Somehow, he'd become the guy that Sam could talk to. And he supposed that was okay with him.

Sam said, "And who says *she* couldn't have a kid, if she found someone else? All those damn tests we took came out showing there wasn't a thing wrong with either of us. But do *I* accuse *her* of lookin' elsewhere?"

Billy shook his head.

"Hell no, I do not," Sam answered his own question. "Maybe I got a few doubts of my own, you know? Maybe I wonder, am I *man* enough? But she's the woman here. And she thinks that makes her the only one with feelings. You know what I'm sayin'?"

Billy nodded.

Right then, the shop bell rang. Two men came in. Sam sucked in a breath and drew his huge shoulders back. "Thanks for listenin'."

"Anytime."

Sam dredged up a smile for his customers. "Can I help you folks?"

Three days later, Sharlee was still sleeping in Billy's bed.

And Billy had had enough. Exactly one week remained of his visit. And then decisions would be made, changes would come.

Before his time was up, he wanted his damn bed back. And he wanted a chance to have that love affair with Prue. It was a chance he couldn't see himself getting with Sharlee underfoot all the time, looking forlorn and pondering her "options."

In one of their rare moments alone, he gave Prue clear instructions. "Get rid of her. Now."

She cast him a long-suffering glance—and Sharlee walked into the room.

Finally, on Friday, after he got Jesse into bed, he marched downstairs, where he found Sharlee on the sofa and Prue in the armchair. Sharlee, as usual, was babbling away.

"And I just, well, I know I should get myself motivated. I know I need to pack up my things and move on. And I intend to, Prudence. You know I do. Really soon."

Billy strode over and grabbed Prue's hand. "Come with me." He looked at Sharlee. "We need a little time. Alone." He tugged on Prue's hand and she actually got up.

Sharlee said, "Well, of course. I don't want to *interrupt* anything, I honestly don't. You just go ahead. You just—"

"Fine. We will." He pulled on Prue's hand again and she followed along behind him, up the stairs. When they got to the top, he asked, "Your room okay?"

Her eyes narrowed. Clearly, she didn't trust him anywhere near a bed.

"Oh, come *on*," he said.

"Well, all right."

He pulled her in there, shut the door and leaned against it, so she couldn't get away until he'd said what he had to say. He glanced around. The room reminded him of the inside of a cloud, all soft grays and different shades of white. She had a nice, wide four-poster bed, with a white lace canopy and a fluffy white quilt and lots of big, soft white pillows. The windows had white trim and almost-white lace curtains. On the walls she had pictures of flowers and botanical prints, all matted and framed, along with several photos of Randi and Jesse.

"This is nice," he told her.

"You got me in here to admire my room?"

He cast her a look of great patience. "Prue. She really has to go."

"Well, I know that, Billy. And actually, I have been thinking..."

Relief washed over him. "You have?"

"Maybe if we helped her to find a job...."

"That occurred to me, too. So I've already called Alexis—the manager at my club? She'll take her on as a waitress."

Prue shook her head. "No, I think she'd be happier doing something else."

"Such as?"

"Well, she has a bookkeeping background. And she's told me she has a hunger to contribute something meaningful to the world." If Sharlee had a hunger, Billy doubted it was for meaningful work, but he had sense enough not to say that. Prue smiled, "Maybe the foundation."

"The foundation?"

"The Jesse Wilding Needy Children's Fund."

"Whatever you say."

"You disagree?"

"Hell, no."

"Billy, you just snorted."

"Look. If Sharlee wants meaningful work, let her have meaningful work. Especially meaningful work four hundred miles away from North Magdalene."

"I really think the foundation is the place for her."

"Fine."

"I'm sure, if I call, they can find a job for her."

"All right, then. The Needy Children's Fund it is. And tomorrow, we will all—you, me, her and Jesse— go over to her house and see that she gets packed up."

"Yes. That would be helpful to her, I'm sure."

Billy smiled. Prue looked good standing there, with the bed behind her. She'd look even better *in* the bed. But all in good time. "Prue, you're getting so agreeable all of a sudden."

"Well, it *is* time that Sharlee moved on."

"Amen," he said on a breath. "Let's go tell her what we have planned for her."

"I'd rather work at Bad Billy's, I think," Sharlee said.

Prue looked a little hurt. "Why is that?"

"Well, no offense, Prudence, but the foundation thing seems pretty dry."

"Dry?"

"Yes. It sounds like serious work. *Meaningful* work, you know?"

"But you told me you felt you needed to find meaning in your life."

"Yeah, but later. Right now, after all I've been through, I need a little fun. I've been to Bad Billy's once or twice a couple of years ago, when I first turned twenty-one. It was hot. The waitresses wear sequins, right? And cowboy boots.''

"You bet," Billy replied.

"Oh, yeah," Sharlee declared. "A job at Bad Billy's is just what I need right now."

Billy glanced at Prue. She shrugged. He smiled at Sharlee. "Alexis—that's the manager—said you could start Tuesday, so we'll have to get you packed up and on your way."

"Fine, fine. Good bands play there, too. I might meet a drummer or a bass player who needs a special lady to make his life complete. It's a whole new start. Thank you, thank you. You've given me hope and the will to go on...."

Chapter 13

Sharlee left for Van Nuys two days later, pulling a rented trailer behind her car. "Thank you, thank you. I'll never forget you," she called out the window as she drove away.

"And Alexis will probably never *forgive* me," Prudence heard Billy mutter under his breath as they stood waving goodbye on the sidewalk in front of the little house Sharlee had rented.

"Bye, bye, bye!" Jesse called and began toddling off down the street after the retreating car.

Laughing, Prudence went to catch him. "Come back here. *Sharlee's* the one who's leaving, not us." She captured Jesse's hand and turned him in the right direction. As she did, she glanced toward Nellie's house. Sure enough, Nellie stood in the front window, peering through a gap in the curtains.

Billy chuckled. "Wave to her." He lifted his hand.

Jesse cheerfully imitated his father, flapping his hand at the woman in the window. "Bye, bye, bye!"

Nellie jumped back and the curtain dropped shut. By then, the car and trailer had disappeared beyond the intersection of Rambling Lane. Billy took Jesse's hand. "Come on. Let's go home."

Jesse went along willingly, chanting, "Home, home, home."

Soon after they returned to the house, Prudence walked across the street to church. Nellie caught her on the steps right after the service.

"Oh, my dear. How are you holding up? I heard Billy brought that troubled young woman to stay in your house. I was there, you know, when he abducted her."

"Excuse me?"

"I was there, the night he forced her into his car and—"

"Billy did not force anything on Sharlee. She was very upset and he didn't want her to be alone. So he brought her to my house."

"I'm sure he told you that."

"Nellie, that was how it happened."

"Whatever you want to believe, my dear. I heard she was leaving town, though."

"I thought you *saw* her leaving, Nellie."

"Yes, well. I like to know what's going on with my neighbors."

"I noticed."

"And I must say, it's good that girl is gone. Nothing but a home-wrecker, that one." Nellie shook her head, then put on a sugary smile. "And where is the little one?"

"Home. With his father."

Nellie's head went back and forth some more. "Oh, my dear. No. No. You really must not leave that child alone with that man."

"Jesse is just fine with Billy."

"How do you know that?"

"He adores his father."

"The child has told you this?"

"Nellie, I *know* Jesse. I would see if there was something wrong."

Nellie leaned closer. "How can you be sure what goes on when you're not there? You might think that little boy is fine now. But the emotional scars of childhood run deep. If you're leaving him alone with that man too much, he could be damaged for life."

"I happen to disagree with you, Nellie."

"I'm sorry you're so sadly misled."

That did it. "Nellie, I have had enough."

"I beg your pardon?"

"I happen to think Billy Jones is a fine father. And if you don't think so, then you can just…keep it to yourself." Prudence realized she must have raised her voice a notch. The people nearby had stopped talking to glance her way.

"Oh, my dear." Nellie's thin, veined hand flew to her throat. "It's happening. It's happening to you."

"*What* is happening?"

"He's after you. I'm so sorry. You'll end up just like all the other Jones women."

Prudence had the urge to argue, *No, I won't. The other Jones women are* married. *And Billy Jones is never going to marry anyone.* But that would only serve to move the conversation along from bad to worse. So all she said was, "He's not after me," which felt like a flat lie, considering the things he had said to her the night before he brought Sharlee home.

Nellie kept on shaking her head. "Oh, my dear, my dear..."

Right then Evie Riggins emerged through the open church door behind them. "Nellie, there you are. Reverend Johnson wants to speak with you—something about the Christmas Carnival, I believe."

"Oh, yes. Yes, of course. Isn't it just impossible, that the holidays are nearly upon us again already? I'm coming. Right now." She patted Prudence's arm. "At least think about what I've said." She turned and hurried back inside before Prudence could muster a suitably scathing reply.

Once the older woman was gone, Evie leaned close to Prudence. "Don't mind Nellie. She can be nosy and narrow-minded—but she's got a good heart, underneath."

Prudence shook her head. "She just won't let up on me."

"Because she likes you."

"Well, that makes a lot of sense."

"It's true. She likes you very much. And she doesn't like Billy."

"There is nothing between me and Billy," Prudence insisted, too strongly by half.

Evie's smile was gentle. "I'll talk to her."

"Will it do any good?"

"Who can say? But I'm willing to give it a try."

A moment later, Evie's husband came to find her. Prudence headed home. As she let herself in, the phone was ringing.

Billy called from the kitchen, "That you, Prue?"

"It's me."

"You want me to get the phone?"

"No, I've got it." She picked up the cordless extension from the side table near the television.

It was Sam Fletcher. He greeted Prudence with a glum, "How you doin'?" and then asked if Billy was there.

Prudence started through the dining room. "He's feeding Jesse, I think. Just a minute."

"It's all right. I guess I can talk to you."

She paused in the doorway to the kitchen. Sure enough, Billy had Jesse in the high chair and was pouring Cheerios on the tray for him. Billy flashed her a smile.

Sam went on, "It's about Thanksgiving. Remember? Lilah invited you to our place?"

"Yes, it was so nice of her." The first day Prudence and Jesse had arrived in town, Delilah had paid them a visit. She said she'd come to welcome them to North Magdalene—and to invite them to the big Thanksgiving dinner party she was planning. "The whole family's coming," Delilah had announced. "Every Jones—husbands, wives and kids—for miles around. I hope you can make it."

Prudence had promised that she would.

Now, Sam was muttering, "Well, I'm still having it." He sounded defiant. Prudence didn't quite dare to ask if Delilah would be there, too. "Will you still come?"

The event sounded potentially disastrous. "I, well…"

"Look. Please come."

He sounded so weary—and yet so determined. She didn't have the heart to turn him down. "Sure. All right."

"Great. Billy, too."

"Just a minute. I'll ask him." She tucked the phone beneath her chin. "It's Sam. He wants you and me and Jesse to come to his place for Thanksgiving."

Billy lifted an eyebrow at her. She gave him a shrug. He nodded then. "Count me in."

She spoke into the phone again. "We'll all be there."

"Thanks."

"What time?"

"Say around two."

"Good enough. What can we bring?"

"What's the matter? Don't you think I can cook?" His voice was teasing—but with an edge.

"Sam. If you want to do it all, that's just great with me."

"Good. Just come. That's all I ask."

"We will." Discussion of the celebration brought Oggie to mind. Prudence hadn't heard a word about him since he'd supposedly left town after the incident at the Hole in the Wall six days before. She asked Sam, "Have you heard anything from Oggie?"

A silence, then Sam admitted grudgingly. "I heard he was in Phoenix. With Nevada—that's one of Evie's sisters. He stayed there a few days, I think. And then he took off again."

"Do you know where he went next?"

"Haven't a clue."

"I hope he's all right." Prudence recalled Oggie's lined face, the way he leaned on that cane of his and sometimes winced when he walked. Once, in the nursery at the mansion, he had been sitting in the rocker, holding Jesse on his knee. Prudence had stood over him and looked down at the bald, age-spotted crown of his head. He'd seemed, at that moment, so frail to her. Someone infinitely vulnerable, though he'd never for the life of him have let anyone else know.

She told Sam, "I don't like this. He's not young, you know."

Sam let out a low laugh. "No, but he's tough as old boots. Don't you worry about Oggie Jones. He's fine. He's always fine."

"Maybe he'll be back for your Thanksgiving party."

"Right. Maybe. Listen, I gotta go. Lots of calls to make, to get the word out."

After Prudence hung up, she turned to find Billy watching her. "So Sam's giving a party," he said. "You think Delilah will come?"

"I guess we'll find out on Thanksgiving."

He frowned. "Some problem with the old man?"

"Pawbem?" Jesse stuffed a handful of cereal into his mouth and looked at her with the same curious, concerned expression his father wore.

Prudence stared at the two of them, thinking that the life she led with them now felt very much like the kind of life a family might share. But it wasn't, of course. It was only a temporary situation. She really must keep remembering that.

"Prue? Did you hear me?"

"Yes. Yes, I heard." She picked up the cereal box, closed the waxed paper liner and secured the cardboard flap on top. "And no, nothing's wrong with Oggie that I know of. He went to visit Nevada—that's Evie's sister, in Phoenix. He left there a few days ago. Sam hadn't heard where he went after that." She took the box back to the cereal cabinet and put it away.

Billy came up behind her before she had a chance to turn around again. He put his hands on her shoulders and spoke softly, close to her ear. "Hey, Prue, feelin' blue?"

She should have jerked away, she knew it. Jerked away and told him in no uncertain terms to keep his hands off. But she didn't. His silly little rhyme of "Prue" and "blue" charmed her. And those hands of his felt good. He was standing very close behind her. She could feel his body's warmth, a warmth that seemed to communicate comfort and understanding and someone to lean against when things got rough.

Prudence did not consider herself a person who leaned. And bad Billy Jones was hardly a man suitable for leaning *on*. But still, there he was. Rubbing her shoulders gently, easing the tension away, making her feel better just by being there—coaxing her, without saying a word, to go ahead and lean.

Prudence leaned. With a sigh.

Billy murmured in her ear, "Come on, what's wrong?"

"I guess I'm just worried about him."

"About Oggie?"

"Mmm-hmm. I just…I hope he's okay." *And Nellie Anderson thinks you're a terrible man who is up to no good. And, for the most part, I used to agree with her. But I just don't anymore....*

Billy chuckled, a warm, low, pleasingly rough sound that vibrated all through her, since he was so close. "The old man is fine. He's Oggie Jones."

She sighed again. "That's pretty much what Sam said."

"Listen to Sam." He slid his hands down, eased them under her arms and clasped them around her waist.

It felt good to have his arms around her. It felt right.

Just as it must have felt good and right to Randi. And the legion of other women bad Billy Jones had known.

Prudence put her hands on Billy's hands and gently broke his hold. Without a murmur of protest, he stepped back and dropped his arms away.

She turned to face him, thinking she should say something to acknowledge and perhaps clarify the nature of the moment that had just occurred. The problem was, she couldn't decide *what* to say about it.

And then she discovered that no words were required. Billy had already turned away himself. "How 'bout some milk?" he was asking Jesse.

Jesse pounded his little fists on the tray. "Yeah, yeah. Meeook, meeook!" Cheerios flew.

"Next up," Billy announced as he opened the refrigerator, "a few lessons in table manners."

"Man-ners. Man-ners. Meeook. Meeook."

Prudence leaned against the counter and watched Billy get the milk, fill Jesse's safety cup and hand it to the child. Finally he turned to her again.

"You're staring, Prue."

"Yes. Perhaps so."

"Something you want to say?"

She considered, then shook her head. With a shrug, he returned his attention to his son.

That night, once Jesse had been tucked in his bed, Billy sought her out again. He came down the stairs and he lounged there in the arch to the living room, the way he had done a number of nights before.

"Sixty Minutes" was just ending. Prudence picked up the remote and turned the television off.

They regarded each other across the width of the

room. She knew what he would say before he said it: "Too quiet."

He went over to the stereo and put several CDs into the cartridge. She sat there on the sofa, feeling content, watching him choose the discs he wanted and shake his head over others that didn't quite make the cut. Finally he put the cartridge in place. Then he turned the music on.

He chose the easy chair nearest her end of the sofa. She watched him approach, watched him lower his lean body to the cushions and stretch out his legs, wondering the whole time where her instinct for self-preservation had gone. She wanted to drum up a little fire and fight, say something quelling that would send him on his way.

But then again, she had a problem: she didn't want him to go.

Perhaps, during the days Sharlee had stayed with them, she'd become too complaisant. After all, with Sharlee around, they were never really alone. The girl could pop in on them at any moment, eager to discuss her poor, battered heart and what she should do with her life.

Tonight however, Sharlee wouldn't be popping in.

"You look sort of friendly tonight, Prue." Billy spoke low and teasingly.

She tried to summon a crisp response, but couldn't come up with a thing beyond a shrug and a smile.

"You're gonna talk to me, right? You're gonna tell me things."

She leaned on the arm of the sofa, toward him. "What things?"

"About you."

She felt a sort of shimmer all through her body, a

ripple of sensation that might have been unease—or anticipation.

Oh, this was bad. And delicious. And lovely. For a moment, she had to look away, toward the fireplace, where a fire danced behind the glass of the fireplace insert.

Billy said her name, softly.

She met his eyes again and challenged, "I have an idea. Why don't we talk about you instead?"

He let out a low laugh. "Me? I know about me."

"But I don't."

"You know enough."

"Come on, Billy. You had your turn quizzing me about my life. Fair is fair."

He shifted around, sat up straighter for a moment, then slumped into the cushions again, stretching his booted feet out once more, crossing them at the ankle, and then proceeding to stare at them. "All right. What do you want to know?"

She wasn't prepared for him to give in quite yet, so she had to think for a moment before she asked, "Well, how about your marriages—there were two of them, right?"

He stopped communing with his boots long enough to shoot her a look from under his eyebrows. "Two. Right."

"Is this difficult for you?"

"I can take it. What else?"

"Well, tell me about them."

"About my marriages?"

She gave him a patient look. "Yes."

He sank farther down into the chair, and studied his boots even more intently than before. "Not much to tell. I married the first one, Serena, one night after a big party. Somehow, we ended up in Reno and I woke up wearing a wedding band. That lasted a year. My second wife, Lisbeth, said she was going to marry me the day that she met me. I said I wasn't a man any woman should marry. But she was relentless. She got to me one night.'' He shot her a grin. "You guessed it. After a big party. It was a party that started in Malibu.''

"And the next morning—?"

"I woke up in Vegas. Married again. That only lasted six months.''

Prudence really wanted to understand how he could have done such foolish things. "You probably had a terrible childhood, didn't you?''

He shook his head. "There was nothing wrong with my childhood. I was never abused. Unless you consider being bored to death abuse. My folks were too quiet and too religious. That was all that was wrong with them. All the dumb mistakes I made in life, I did all by my lonesome.''

She watched him, thinking how handsome he was—in a totally unconscious sort of way. She'd lived in L.A. most of her life and she knew very well that men could be every bit as vain about their looks as women were supposed to be. But Billy wasn't vain. Maybe that was part of his attraction. He didn't care in the least how he looked.

An up-tempo country song came on. Billy put his boots flat on the floor and began tapping rhythm on the sides of his knees. For a moment, he seemed lost in the beat of the song. Then he caught her eye. "You know the two-step, Prue?''

She refused to be lured off the subject. "Billy, we were talking about *you*.''

He went on tapping out the beat. "So what else you want to know?"

"Well…early love affairs?"

"Lots."

"Did you go to college?"

"Nope."

"You did finish high school, though, right?"

"You bet. Barely. GPA: 1.9."

"Impressive."

"Hold the irony, please."

"What did you do after high school?"

"I got out of Sweethaven, Kansas."

"Where did you go?"

"Nashville, where I worked odd jobs during the day and played country-western clubs for peanuts at night. I sold my first song in my early twenties. For fifty dollars, outright. To tell you true, I sold a lot of songs way too cheap. But then I hooked up with Waverly Sims, my agent, eleven years ago. Since then, I've been making good money on what I write. What else?"

"When did you move to L.A.?"

"When I was twenty-eight. I opened Bad Billy's when I was thirty. And talking about all this is almost as boring as being raised by two aging Bible-thumpers in Sweethaven, Kansas, you know?"

"I'll bet Sweethaven is a very nice town."

"Aw, Prue. You would say that." He stood. "This song is almost over, Prue."

"So?"

In two strides, he was standing over her. "So come on. Let's dance."

"I don't know the two-step."

"I'll teach you." He held down his hand.

She didn't think she was ready to do that, to go

willingly into his arms—even for something as seemingly innocent as a dance. "No. I don't think so."

"Aw, Prue. You've shamed me into staying out of the Hole in the Wall. I haven't had a wild night in over a week. The least you can do is try a little two-step with me."

"No, Billy."

He dropped his hand. "Well, listen to that. The song's over, anyway." He picked up the remote from the coffee table and turned the sound down. Then he tossed the remote over his shoulder. It landed neatly back on the seat of the chair he'd just vacated. He looked down at her, open appeal in his eyes. "Prue, what are we gonna do about this?"

"About what?"

"This. You and me."

She wondered how everything had managed to get away from her so fast. "Billy, didn't we discuss this before?"

"Yeah. And that time it didn't work out so well."

"You mean because I told you no."

He winced. "I really hate that word." He reached for her hand. For some crazy reason, she let him take it. He gave a tug—and she was on her feet. He put his right hand at her back and led her out into the middle of the room. They swayed to the music for a few lovely moments, Billy leading without effort, Prudence surprised at how easy it was to just follow along.

Still, her wiser self could not be entirely silenced. "I shouldn't be doing this," she whispered against his shoulder.

He pulled her marginally closer. "Don't talk, dance."

She danced, for a minute or two more. And then she

pulled back a little. "When I said no, didn't I say never?"

"I don't remember. My mind's a complete blank."

"Liar."

"Hey, I've got my own agenda here. You oughta know that by now."

"I am actually flirting with you."

"Nice, isn't it?"

"It would just be so…foolish of me."

He snuggled her closer. It felt good. So very good. "How many times in your life have you been foolish, Prue?"

She tried to remember at least one.

"I thought so," he said, though she hadn't given him an answer. He pulled back, looked down at her. "You need to be foolish, Prue. You need to be reckless."

"Says you."

"Yep. I'm sort of an expert on recklessness."

"So I noticed."

"And Prue?"

"What?"

"You not only need to be reckless—you need to be reckless with me."

"Why with you?"

"Two reasons. Because I'm so experienced at it. And because *I* want to be reckless with *you*."

"This is insane."

"Naw. This is *fun*."

"But what about later, what about Jesse?"

"What about him? I'm his father. You're his aunt. What the two of us do in private will never change that."

"You mean he'll never even have to know."

"Now you're thinkin'."

"Well, but..." Her mind seemed suddenly about as sharp as molasses.

"Reckless, Prue. That's the word. The whole idea, when you're reckless, is you don't give a damn about later."

She stared up at him, thinking that all of a sudden, she could fully understand what the serpent must have done, back there in the Garden of Eden. "You really are trying to tempt me."

"I never *try,* Prue."

The song ended. They stood a foot or two from the coffee table. Prudence started to pull away.

Billy said, "Wait." He put his hands on her shoulders.

"What, Billy?"

He said nothing, only raised his hands to her temples and began sliding her glasses off.

It wasn't like that other time, at his club, when he'd moved so fast she couldn't have stopped him if she'd wanted to. This time, she could have stopped him easily. This time he did it slowly, giving her a wide-open window of opportunity to reach up and still his hand.

But she didn't.

And soon enough, her glasses were gone. The room, Billy—everything—went blurry, distorted and soft, all shimmery. Unreal.

He moved away, but only enough to set her glasses aside. And then he was standing tall, pulling her close once more.

"Billy?"

"Yeah."

"Every possible error of refraction there is, I've got."

"What does that mean?"

"It means my cornea is shaped all wrong and so are my eyes themselves. I'm severely astigmatic, as well as hypermetropic. In both eyes."

"So?"

"So I can't see a thing, Billy."

"Well, I know that. That's good."

She started to speak again. But before she could find words, he pulled her even closer. She stared, seeing the vague shape of him, feeling the heat of him, closer, hotter.

"Billy...."

"Shh." He touched her hair, his palm sliding down, from the crown of her head to where the strands curled under just above her shoulders. "Silky. Warm," he whispered.

He clasped her shoulders again, so gently. She knew he must be looking at her, and she smiled, a wobbly smile. She felt breathless, a woman frozen on the brink of something dangerous and splendid. Her heart sounded loud in her chest, but steady and deep. She was not frightened. She was...exhilarated.

And then his face came closer. She dragged in a breath. Her heart beat a fraction faster.

His mouth touched hers, very lightly. It felt... perfect. So right. He said that name he always called her, which she had told him not to call her—which he called her anyway. "Prue."

She felt the sweet caress of his breath across her skin and remembered to exhale. He breathed in the air she let out, his lips moving against hers in what she knew was a smile.

He said it again, "Prue." His mouth settled more firmly on hers and his arms slid around her, pulling her even closer than before, surrounding her—but not in a bad way, not at all. She heard a moan and it took her a split second to realize that she had made that sound herself.

He started kissing along her cheek, nuzzling her hair aside. Then he whispered in her ear. "Put your arms around me, Prue." She lifted her arms, slipped them up and around his neck. He made a low sound of satisfaction and approval. Then his mouth found hers again. "Kiss me back."

It sounded like a very good suggestion. So she did.

Chapter 14

The longer the kiss went on, the better it got. But then Billy put his hand at the small of her back and tucked her up against him so close that there was no mistaking the hard ridge of his arousal pressing against her. It felt shockingly good. But it also reminded her that if she intended to stop this, she had better do it soon.

She slid her hands from around his neck to his chest. By applying steady pressure, she somehow managed to pull her mouth loose from his. "Billy…"

"I'm not done yet, Prue." He slanted his mouth the other way and captured hers once more.

"Billy…"

"Shh."

"Billy!"

That got his attention. He lifted his head. She knew he was looking down at her, though all she could see of his eyes were a pair of slightly darker spots halfway up in the fuzzy shape of his face.

"What's the problem now?"

"I just would really like some time to think about this."

He grunted. "Bad idea. You'll only change your mind." His blurred face came toward her again.

She pressed against his chest and craned her head away. "Billy."

He muttered a rude expletive—but at least he did let go of her. Then he turned away. When he faced her again, he took her hand. "Here." She felt the reassuring shape of her glasses in her palm.

She put them on. The world swam back into focus. In the center of her visual field stood Billy. He didn't look happy.

"Billy, I just..."

He put up a hand. "Let's not beat this thing to death. You know what I want. If you make up your mind you want it, too, you let me know."

Later, since sleep wouldn't come, Prudence lay in bed and worried about Oggie. She hoped he was all right. She reminded herself that no one else seemed the least concerned about him, and that everyone said he often took off like this, without telling anyone where he would go or when he'd be back.

Her thoughts turned to Randi.

Randi in a red crop top and striped leggings, sitting in the breakfast room of the mansion, her gold hair a glorious tangle around her incredible face, her untouched morning cocktail of blenderized vegetables and herbs waiting on the table in front of her.

Prudence had set aside the *Wall Street Journal* and watched her sister. Randi hadn't even seemed to notice she was being observed. Finally Prudence prompted, "Something's up. What?"

Randi shrugged. "A man." She picked up her drink, looked into it and then set it down untouched.

"What man?"

Randi sighed. Then, delicately, like a cat licking up the last bit of cream, she traced her upper lip with her tongue. "Billy Jones is his name."

"You like him."

Randi rested her chin on her hand and wiggled her perfect eyebrows. "I like him. I want him. I'm gonna have him. And then I'm gonna end up paying the price."

"What price?"

"He's a no-strings kind of guy. He's gonna hurt me."

Prudence couldn't understand. "Then why even start with him?"

And Randi smiled the saddest, sweetest smile. "There are some men a woman shouldn't pass up if she can help it, whether it lasts or not, whether she gets her heart broken or not."

"I don't get it."

Randi reached across the table and chucked her sister under the chin. "Phooey, Pruey." They looked at each other for a moment, and then they laughed together.

Then Randi said, "I want you to meet a man like him someday. I want you to have what I'm gonna have with him."

"No, thanks."

"There is nothing sadder than a life only half lived."

"I said, no thanks."

Randi shook her head. "Oh, Pruey, the way you

limit yourself…'' She let the thought trail off and reached for her vegetable drink.

In her bed in North Magdalene, alone, Prudence stared into the darkness and couldn't help wondering if her sister had been right.

The next morning, Billy seemed cool. Civil enough, but cool.

He spent most of the day with his son. While Jesse napped, he went into his bedroom and played his guitar. That night, he went over to Sam's house. He came home around eleven, after Prudence had gone to bed. Since she hadn't managed to fall asleep yet, she heard him come in.

She wanted to throw on a robe and go downstairs, to ask him how Sam was doing. And also, to ask him if he would please just go ahead and do all those things to her that she shouldn't let him do.

But she didn't. She stayed in her bed and she tossed and she turned.

The next day, Billy and Jesse left the house at a little after nine in the morning. ''I think I'll take him down to Grass Valley again. He's got a thing for that big play-set at McDonald's—you know, the one with the balls and the tubes?''

''Yes. He does like that.'' She knew she sounded wistful, like someone hoping to be invited along.

But Billy didn't invite her. He said, ''I've got the list you keep tacked on the refrigerator. I'll pick up the groceries.''

''Thanks.''

''Anything else you need?''

An endless kiss. Incredible sex. ''No. That's all.''

After they left, she felt so terribly lonely. She stood

looking at the yellow roses on the dining-room table for a long time. They were way past their prime by then, many of their petals gone, the blossoms that remained drooping and brown-edged. She had been silly, to keep them so long.

She threw them away and washed out the vase. Then she called Eden. They talked about the weather—and poor Sam and Delilah, who remained apart. Eden said no one had heard anything from Oggie since he'd left Nevada's house five days before.

"Is anyone starting to get worried yet?" Prudence suggested, with maybe just a hint of an edge in her voice.

"Hmm," said Eden. "Feeling a little tense, are we?"

"Even if no one else is, *I'm* worried about him."

"I gathered. And yes, we all get a little concerned when we don't hear from him for several days. But it's happened before. And he always comes back safe and sound—and what else is on your mind?"

"What do you mean?"

"It's in your voice. Something's got you good and bothered. It's Billy, am I right?"

Prudence tried to think of what to say.

"I'm right," Eden answered the question herself. "Want to talk about it?"

"No. Better not."

"I'm here, if you change your mind. Off the record. For my ears alone."

"Thanks."

"And can I say just one thing?"

"Well…"

"I'm saying it, before you tell me no."

"Saying what?"

"Here goes...if you don't send your ship out, chances are, it ain't gonna come in."

"What?"

"Take a chance, maybe, huh?"

"Could we talk about something else?"

"Sure." Eden good-naturedly shifted the subject to something innocuous. They chatted for another twenty minutes or so, and then baby Diana started crying and Eden had to go.

It was nine-thirty. To Prudence, the day seemed to stretch out in front of her, empty and vast. She trudged upstairs and worked on her résumé. She fiddled with different fonts, trying to make her name look better; she reworded the descriptions of all the responsibilities she'd assumed as Randi's business manager.

And more than once, she found herself just sitting there, staring at the computer screen, remembering the feel of Billy's lips on hers, picturing ships sitting in dry dock, or wherever ships that weren't sent out sat, hearing her sister's voice: "There are some men a woman shouldn't pass up if she can help it, whether it lasts or not, whether she gets her heart broken or not...."

Finally Prudence shut down the program, admitting with a bleak sigh that she hadn't made any changes that amounted to anything—which was nothing new. She *never* made changes that amounted to anything. Because there was nothing really wrong with her résumé. It was ready, if and when she needed it.

Which just might end up being sooner than she had originally thought. In three days, on the day after Thanksgiving, Billy's two-week testing period would come to an end. She was going to have to make a hard decision, to try to make the *best* decision for Jesse. It wasn't a task she relished.

The doorbell rang. Prudence's sagging spirits lifted a little at the prospect of company. She ran down the stairs and pulled open the door.

Nellie stood beyond the threshold, clutching a clipboard. "Hello, my dear. I'm here to help you decide on your contribution to the Christmas Carnival."

Prudence seriously considered muttering, "Forget it," and shutting the door on Nellie's narrow face. But good manners won out. She led Nellie to the kitchen where she poured them each some coffee.

"Now," Nellie said, "as far as the carnival goes, let me tell you what I had in mind for you."

The Christmas Carnival was slated for Saturday, December 6. There would be game booths and Christmas crafts for sale, raffles and a bakery goods auction. In the evening, at the town hall, the kids from North Magdalene Elementary would put on a Christmas show. Prudence found herself agreeing to run a craft booth for a few hours and to bake a rather daunting number of brownies.

At last, Nellie tucked her clipboard under her arm and stood. "Thank you for the coffee, Prudence. And for your commitment of time and effort to the carnival. Now, I must be on my way."

Prudence herded Nellie toward the door, feeling gratified that they'd gotten through an entire conversation without one reference to bad Billy Jones.

But then, just as Prudence slid around Nellie and pulled the door wide, Nellie said, "I can see the child's not here. I suppose he's off with that man."

So much for feeling gratified. Prudence leveled a hard look on Nellie. "Do not start."

Both of Nellie's thin eyebrows rose toward her hair. "Pardon me?"

"I said, do not start."

"Someone must speak truly to you."

"You have, already, lots of times."

"Watch yourself, dear. Protect your character. Not to mention, your poor heart."

"Nellie, this is just none of your business."

"You could end up like poor, dear Delilah. Crushed and humiliated, living in a rented room."

"Delilah has not 'ended up' in a rented room. She's living at the Foothill Inn temporarily, until she and Sam work things out."

"In the divorce courts."

"You don't know that."

"You'd be surprised the things I know."

"And anyway, Delilah's situation and mine aren't the least bit similar."

"They are perfectly similar."

"How?"

"The men, Prudence," Nellie intoned. "Sam Fletcher and Billy Jones. They're cut from the same cloth, those two. Everyone knows Sam Fletcher is as much a Jones as any real Jones. Ogden has always thought of him as another one of his sons. And he's certainly *behaved* enough like one of them over the years. Why, I could tell you stories—"

"Please don't." Prudence took Nellie by the arm and guided her over the threshold. Nellie was still spouting dire warnings as Prudence murmured goodbye and gently closed the door on her. About fifteen seconds later, Prudence heard Nellie's footsteps retreating across the porch. She peeked out the picture window and saw the older woman, shoulders back and head high, marching down the slate walk toward the front gate.

With a sigh, Prudence sank to the sofa. A moment later, it occurred to her that she would go stark, raving out of her mind if she hung around the house all day, missing Billy and Jesse, pointlessly revising her résumé, at the mercy of the opinions of anyone who knocked on the door.

She jumped up, went to get her purse and coat and then headed out into the chilly November morning.

Once beyond the gate, she lingered on the sidewalk for a moment, trying to decide if she should head over to Lily's. It was almost noon, time for lunch.

But then she turned for her car. She would go in to Nevada City and have lunch there. The steep, tree-lined streets and authentic gold rush Victorian houses always pleased her. She would shop for nothing in particular and forget her troubles for the afternoon.

At each and every sharp bend in the twisting road to Nevada City, Prudence found herself half expecting to pass Billy's Jeep headed back for North Magdalene. But it never happened. Which was all to the good. If she saw the Jeep going the other way, she'd only end up wondering how Billy and Jesse were doing at home, wishing she were there with them instead of enjoying the solitary pleasures of a free afternoon.

She had lunch at the Country Rose Café on Commercial Street, then she wandered up Pine Street to Broad. At Broad Street Books, she went in—to browse and to treat herself to a sweet, creamy cup of cappuccino. And then she wandered back down Broad, looking in the shop windows, thinking what a beautiful town Nevada City was—and wishing she could stop thinking about Billy.

It was just before two when she got back into her car. She meant to go on home. But somehow, she found herself headed the wrong way on the freeway that ran between Nevada City and Grass Valley. For no reason she could fathom, she got off at Brunswick Road, turned left at the end of the exit ramp, and drove back over the freeway to Sutton Way. A few moments later, she was parking in front of Longs Drugs.

Inside, she wandered the aisles for a while, pausing to look over the magazine racks and check out the stationery supplies. She'd progressed to the pharmacy section and found herself pausing in front of several shelves filled with contraceptives before she finally admitted to herself why she was there.

Jesse had been cranky all day. As far as Billy was concerned, the trip to Grass Valley had been pretty much of a bust. Jesse fussed in every store they visited, and squirmed and cried when Billy took him to the park. Probably Billy should have given it up early and gone home.

But Prue was home. And he was mad at her. They had three days left on the agreement they'd made. Not much time for a hot and heavy affair. Hell. He had to face it. There probably wasn't going to be a hot and heavy affair. He'd had his best shot at it the other night—and he hadn't made the grade. She'd said she wanted to *think* about it. Billy had known enough women in his life to realize that when they said they wanted to *think* about it, a guy didn't have a chance.

So he was mad at her. And he was punishing her by avoiding her. Which was pretty damn ridiculous, considering she probably felt nothing but grateful to see less of him.

Hell, this whole mess was driving him nuts. He wanted her. Now. It made no sense. She wasn't his type at all. But he was willing to just go ahead and take a chance if she would.

But she had to *think* about it.

So he spent the day in Grass Valley with a cranky kid.

Finally, at about two-thirty, he gave up and headed home. By right around three, he was walking up to the door carrying a crying child on one arm and a bag of groceries in the other. He was looking forward to handing Jesse to Prue, tossing the groceries onto the kitchen counter and retreating to his room. There, he would put on his headphones and lie down on the bed and forget for an hour or two that cranky kids and *thinking* women even existed.

But then he found the damn door locked. He almost dropped the groceries while he fumbled with the key. When he got the door open, he yelled, "Prue!" good and loud, which startled Jesse and made him wail all the harder.

Prue didn't come. He was forced to admit that she must have taken off somewhere. He set the groceries on the coffee table and sat down with Jesse. A few moments of soft talk and cuddling, and the kid seemed a little better. He hugged up close and sniffled and sighed.

Billy felt the kid's forehead, as he'd done more than once that day. But he didn't seem hot. He didn't even seem sick, not really. More like unhappy or maybe uncomfortable.

Billy carried him upstairs and checked the diaper he was going to damn well make sure the kid stopped needing pretty soon here. It was wet. Billy changed him.

"There. Feel better?"

"Nawp." Jesse cried some more.

Where the hell was that woman when a man needed her? "Come on, Jess. Tell your dad what's wrong."

Jesse puckered his lips and rubbed at his face and said something that sounded like. "Awut, awut."

"Something hurts?"

Jesse squirmed and pushed, so Billy put him down. He lumbered over to the bed and started chewing on the bed frame. Billy let him chew for a few minutes because it seemed to soothe him, and then he went and pulled him away. Billy didn't approve of kids sticking things in their mouths all the time and he was trying to break Jesse of what he considered a bad habit.

But the kid started crying again the minute his mouth lost contact with the red metal frame. Billy tried to soothe him. Jesse cried louder. Billy tried singing—a little Shel Silverstein, because his stuff was funny and could be acted out.

Jesse was not amused. He shoved his little fist into his mouth and went on sobbing.

Billy felt like screaming.

Maybe there was something really wrong. Where was Prue? She should be here at a time like this. He hoisted Jesse up and headed downstairs.

"Maybe a little snack, huh?" He got Jesse into the high chair and poured out some Cheerios.

Jesse looked down at them and then up at his father—and started calling, "Woo, Woo, Woo!"

Billy wanted to shout, *Woo is not here, and when she gets here, she won't be any good to you anyway, because I'm going to kill her!* However, all he said was, "How about some juice?"

His fingers fumbling in haste, Billy filled one of Jesse's safety cups with apple juice, then handed it over. Jesse took one sip, tried to bite the top off the cup and then threw it across the room. It landed on the sink counter, the top popped off and apple juice exploded onto the splashboard, across the counter and finally dribbled down the side of the cabinet toward the floor.

"Cute," Billy said.

Jesse went on crying, wailing Prue's name.

"That does it, I'm calling the clinic." The number was posted in a list of important numbers, right beside the wall phone. He dialed.

Just as a woman's voice answered, "North Magdalene Medical Clinic," he heard the front door open.

"Never mind," he told the voice, and hung up.

"Woo, Woo, Woo!" Jesse sobbed.

Billy heard her footsteps and then, there she was, standing in the door from the dining room, still wearing her coat, carrying a small brown paper bag and her purse. She set the purse and the bag on the table. "What's going on?"

Billy was furious at her—and he'd never felt so relieved to see anyone in his entire life. "I don't know. He's been fussy all day. Now he won't stop crying."

"Woo, Woo!" Jesse waved his arms and sobbed in a sort of urgent despair.

Billy backed out of the way as she went right to Jesse, pulled him from the chair and carried him to the refrigerator. She took an object from the freezer, removed the plastic wrapping and handed it to him. With an audible sigh, he stuck it into his mouth and started gnawing on it.

Billy backed up enough that he could lean against the sink rim. "What is that?"

"Half a frozen bagel. He's teething. He needs something to chew on. And the cold helps."

Jesse gnawed away, still hiccuping a little, but noticeably calmer. Gently Prue set him on the floor.

Billy stared at his son. He couldn't believe it. A damn frozen bagel and the kid was just fine. "He's been crying all day."

"Why didn't you take one of his teething rings with you?"

He didn't like her tone, so prissy and judgmental, but he answered her reasonably enough. "I don't like to see him gnawing on things all the time."

She started unbuttoning her coat. "Well, teeth hurt, coming in." She scooped up her purse and the brown bag. "Unless you want him in pain, you'll have to make an exception, I think." She turned around and left the room.

He stared at the place she had been, anger churning inside him, making his gut burn and his skin feel too tight.

A few moments later, she reappeared, minus the coat, the brown bag and her purse, but carrying the groceries he'd left on the coffee table. Pausing only to hook the child gate in place, she marched to the counter right beside where he stood—and set down the bag in the middle of the puddle of apple juice.

She pulled a head of lettuce from the bag and went to the refrigerator, where she knelt and put the lettuce in the crisper. About halfway back to the counter, she noticed the spilled juice. With a long-suffering sigh,

she lifted the bag and looked at the bottom of it.
"Great." She looked at him, a look that clearly said,
The least you can do is get out of my way. He stayed
right where he was. Sighing again, she walked around
him and set the bag on the other side of the sink. She
sighed a third time as she was reaching for the sponge.
He'd had about enough of those sighs by then. So he
stuck out a hand and snared her wrist.

She gasped and stiffened—which he found quite satisfying.

He said, very precisely, "I do not *want* my son to
be in pain."

"Let go of my wrist."

"Do you believe that I want my son to be in pain?"
She tried to jerk away.

He held on. "Do you?"

She gave him one of those haughty, high-chinned
looks she was such an expert at. "No. Of course not."

He released her. "Good."

She started for the sponge again.

"Don't."

She stopped in midreach and looked at him with one
eyebrow raised above her glasses' rim. "Why ever
not?"

"I'll clean it up."

"Don't be silly."

"I said, I will clean it up."

"Fine." She stepped back, folded her arms and
waited.

He put the safety cup and lid into the sink and picked
up the sponge. With great care, he blotted up the puddle of juice on the counter. Then he rinsed the sponge
and wiped down the splashboard and the woodwork.
That accomplished, he rinsed the sponge a final time

and squeezed it out. Through the whole process, she stood there, waiting.

When he set the sponge back on the sink rim, she asked, so politely, he wanted to shout obscenities at her, "Are you finished?"

"Yeah."

"Then *I'll* finish putting the groceries away."

It was like that the rest of the day. They spoke to each other only when they had to, and then in short, precise sentences.

Billy wanted to yell at her. He wanted to grab her and kiss her. He wanted to walk out the door and never come back. He wanted to break something. He wanted release from the tension that gnawed at him from the inside and didn't seem likely to go away until he either got his hands on Prue—or got clear of her for good.

Dinner was pure hell. Billy chewed and swallowed and scowled.

Prudence pushed her food around on her plate and wondered how things had gotten so awful all of a sudden. He'd seemed to blame her for everything since she got home this afternoon. He was downright nasty.

She thought of the small brown bag she'd left on the bureau in her room and wondered what could possibly have possessed her, to imagine she might need contraceptives this evening. She shot a glance at Billy. He glowered back at her.

Never, she thought grimly. Never in a hundred thousand years. Not if he was the last man and I was the last woman and the future of the human race depended on it.

No way.

He growled, "You gonna eat that, or just shove it around on your plate?"

She inquired sweetly, "Why? Do you want it?"

"Hell, no. But you shouldn't play with your food. It sets a bad example for Jesse."

She granted him a cold smile. "Thank you, Dr. Spock."

In his high chair, Jesse mimicked, "Spaw, Spaw, Spaw." When both adults turned unsmiling faces his way, he put his nice, cold half bagel into his mouth and said nothing more.

It took Billy until after eight to get Jesse down. Not a record night, but the poor kid had sore teeth and deserved an extra bedtime story.

When he left Jesse's room, he told himself he was going straight to his own room and shutting the door. If it turned out he couldn't stand it alone in there, he'd go visit Sam. He and Sam could commiserate on the evilness of women.

But then, when he got downstairs, there was Prue, sitting on the sofa in the living room. She had her nose buried in a book, though he didn't believe for a second that she was actually reading. No, she was just pretending. Her real purpose was far more sinister. She'd been lying in wait for him to come down the stairs. She didn't want to miss an opportunity to cut him down to size with that acid-dipped razor blade she called a tongue.

Well, he wouldn't disappoint her.

He lounged in his usual spot in the archway. She didn't look up. He coughed. She turned the page.

He straightened from the archway and approached her, not stopping until he stood right over her, looking down at the open book, which he saw was titled, *Income Property Appraisal*. She was on chapter six: "Compound Interest and Discount Factors."

"Now I know what your problem is."

"Go away, Billy."

He reached down and grabbed the book.

Her head shot up. She glared at him, furious, her lips pressed together, her bug eyes full of fire.

He shook the book at her. "No woman should be reading something like this in her spare time. A book like this is *bad* for you."

"Give it back."

"It's too dry, Prue. You don't need dry. You need juicy. Adventure. Romance. Something to heat you up a little. Something to get your imagination in gear."

"Give me my book."

He held it high and grinned at her, at the same time wondering what the hell was wrong with him, snatching her book up, waving it over her head, *bullying* her.

She stood. "Good night, Billy." Red head high, she walked around the other end of the sofa and headed toward the dining room.

"Prue."

She just kept walking.

"Damn it, Prue!"

She turned at the stairs and disappeared.

Billy stood there, more angry at himself by then than he'd ever been at her. He listened as her footsteps attained the landing, then faded away overhead. And then, very carefully, he set her book on the coffee table. He looked down at it, shaking his head, knowing that he'd gone too far—and not sure what the hell he ought to do next.

* * *

By the time Prudence reached her own room, she was trembling in rage.

She dropped to the edge of her bed, shaking, remembering...

Her mother and those awful boyfriends she was always bringing home. Men who usually started out nice, but turned mean soon enough, when they drank, or when Betsy did something that they didn't like. If Prudence closed her eyes, she could see their ugly, sneering faces, yelling at Betsy. And Betsy crying and yelling right back at them.

And Prudence and Randi huddled in a corner, trying to be small, trying not to be noticed—while furniture got broken and terrible things were said. A couple of times, Betsy got beat up bad. She'd wander around their double-wide house trailer for days after that, looking like something from a horror movie, crying and smoking cigarettes and swearing that men weren't worth it at all.

But then, within a month or two, she'd come home with a new one.

Never, Prudence had sworn to herself, would she let a man talk to her that way, let a man *invade* her world that way. Never would she give one the chance.

She had planned her whole life around self-sufficiency, around total independence from the male of the species. And her plans had worked out just fine.

Until bad Billy Jones came along.

Prudence sprawled backward on the bed, closed her eyes and ordered her body to relax. But she couldn't relax. She was just too full of frustrated wrath.

Right then, she heard a tap at the door.

She could not believe his nerve. "Go away, Billy,"

she whispered at the canopy overhead.

He only knocked again.

''Go away.'' She said it loud enough that she knew he would hear, and then she waited, listening hard, for the sound of his footsteps retreating down the hall.

It was a sound that never came. He tapped again and said something that might have been, ''Please.''

She sat up.

Another tap. ''Please, Prue.''

He sounded so pitiful. Her rage faded a little. She waited. He didn't knock again, he didn't speak. But she knew he was still standing there. She could see his shadow beneath the door.

Let him stand there all night if he wants to, a hard voice inside her head seemed to whisper.

But she knew she couldn't do that. Slowly she stood. And then she went to let him in.

Chapter 15

He didn't know what to say when she opened the door. So he just looked at her. Even with those glasses on, she looked good to him now. He wondered what the hell was happening to him.

She said, "What?"

He said, "I'm sorry."

He thought she was going to shut the door on him. But she didn't. Her eyes looked stranger than usual. Maybe she was going to start crying on him. But she didn't do that, either. Not her. Not Prue. She pressed her lips together and stood a little taller.

He said, "I guess I'm just used to getting what I want."

She only went on looking at him, not quite crying, not quite mad.

He couldn't take it. He glanced away, down the hall.

"Billy?"

He made himself look back at her. "Yeah?"

"What is it you want?"

"You know." She waited. And he said it: "You."

She lifted a hand and brushed a few strands of that fiery hair away from her cheek. He wished with all his heart that she would have let him do that.

Something happened in her face. Another change. Now, instead of trapped between anger and tears, she looked purposeful. She moved back, clearing the doorway.

He stared, not understanding.

"Come in," she finally instructed in a small voice.

He stepped over the threshold warily, expecting at any moment to be told to leave. She gestured at the bed.

The bed.

He wondered if this was a dream. An incredible, impossible dream that had somehow begun to come true at last.

But then again, it didn't have to mean anything that she'd let him in, that she'd signaled him toward the bed. He was probably just getting carried away with wishful thinking.

And damn, it was quiet in here. He sent a swift glance around the room. No stereo. It occurred to him that he might go nuts in this room, wishing and hoping in a silence so vast, it seemed to echo off the pale gray walls.

She was watching him, waiting for him to make the next move. He did what she'd told him to do, crossing to the four-poster bed, and sitting carefully on the edge of the fluffy white quilt.

He waited for her next command. What the hell else could he do? Whatever was going on here, he wasn't running it.

She flicked off the wall switch. The corners of the room turned shadowy. The only light left was the small lamp on the bed stand, making a golden pool of light across the whiteness of the pillows and quilt.

A tall bureau stood not far from her. She went to it. He saw that bag then, the brown paper one she'd brought in with her this afternoon. It was sitting on top of the bureau.

She picked up the bag and turned. "I went to Nevada City today. I had lunch. Then I went to Grass Valley. I stopped at Longs Drugs. I didn't admit to myself what I was doing there, at first."

Was he supposed to say something in response to that? He couldn't think of a damn thing. So he kept his mouth shut.

She came toward him. She was wearing a pair of gray chino-type pants and a white blouse, with flat-heeled black shoes and a black belt. She looked like some lady executive on her day off. A direct, no-nonsense, cut-the-crap sort of woman.

He wanted to grab her, mess up that silky cap of hair, slide off that belt, take down those chino-type pants. But all he did was watch her, hardly daring to breathe, hearing his own heartbeat, loud and hungry in his ears.

She stopped right in front of him, so close that one of her legs brushed his knee. The bag was rolled shut. Carefully she unrolled it, pulled the sides open and turned it upside down.

Two boxes of condoms, a dozen each, fell into his lap. One stayed there. The other bounced off and landed on the nubby gray throw rug beneath his feet.

His heart froze. Everything went absolutely still. And then he remembered that breathing was necessary.

He sucked air into his lungs and let it out, still staring down at the one box of condoms that hadn't bounced to the floor. Altogether, twenty-four of the suckers. Wow. She really had faith in him.

She said, "I thought, if we were going to do this, we should be...responsible about it. You know?"

He gulped. "Uh. Yeah. Good thinking."

"I mean, especially in our case. After what happened, with you and Randi. After Jesse..."

He reached out, still not daring to actually look up at her, and caught her hand. It felt so good, so soft and warm. Best of all, she didn't pull back. For a moment, she was still. And then she wrapped her fingers with his. He took the box of condoms from his lap and set it on the nightstand. Then he tugged on her hand. She stepped forward, so she stood between his thighs. He looked up, smiled. She smiled back, with some effort.

He said, "Jesse's turning out to be the best thing that ever happened to me."

She nodded, her eyes thoughtful. "Still..."

"What?"

"We don't need another accident. Having a baby should be a conscious decision."

He squeezed her hand. "Prue. Always on the high road."

She pressed her lips together, looked away. "You don't agree?"

He tugged on her hand once more, to make her look at him again. "I agree. One hundred percent."

She closed her eyes. "I guess it's not your fault— that Randi loved you and you didn't love her back."

"That's really bothered you, huh?"

"Yes."

"Prue."

"Um?"

"You keep looking at the wall."

With visible effort, she met his eyes. "I feel... disloyal."

"To Randi?"

She nodded. "At the same time, I feel as if Randi's up there in heaven, cheering me on."

He couldn't resist. "So you really think Randi made it to heaven?"

She let out a small sound of irritation. "Billy, stop."

"Come on." He bent to scoop up the other box of condoms and set it beside the first. That accomplished, he patted his knee.

She made another sound—this one disbelieving. "You want me to sit on your lap?"

"Yeah."

"I am not the kind of woman who sits on a man's lap."

He laughed, realizing that his heart had settled down to a slow, deep rhythm. That he was anticipating, but no longer scared stiff that one wrong move would blow this whole deal. "Make an exception."

She sighed. He tugged again. She dropped onto his knee.

He put his arms around her and pulled her closer. She went, if somewhat reluctantly. He rested his head against her shoulder, breathing in the scent of her, which was a little bit like roses and also something else—baby powder, maybe. He couldn't be sure, he only knew he liked it and could recognize her anywhere by sense of smell alone.

He also liked the feel of her, soft, but sort of resilient. She seemed smaller in his arms than she looked most of the time.

She coughed.

He chuckled. "What?"

"Well, what do we do next?"

"Wing it."

"Easy for you to say."

"Come on." He fell backward onto the bed, pulling her with him. She went, but slid off him in the process, so they ended up lying next to each other, his arm beneath her neck. They stared up at the lace canopy.

"Billy?"

"Yeah?"

"I have a feeling I'm going to be very bad at this."

He rose up on an elbow and leaned over her. "This your first time, Prue?"

She gave him the tiniest of nods.

He studied her plug-ugly glasses, her cheekbones, the really fine, slim shape of her nose, thinking that he was about to break one of the cardinal rules of being Billy Jones: no virgins. Billy had always considered a virgin as someone a man like him shouldn't mess with. Call it respect. Call it fear. Call it self-preservation. He didn't make love to women who had never made love before. He left the rites of sexual initiation to braver men than he'd ever be.

She was watching him. "Are you changing your mind?"

"What makes you say that?"

"I don't know. Just something in your expression."

He gave her a slow smile. "No, I'm not changing my mind. So don't get your hopes up. You're not getting out of this."

She lifted her hand and her fingers brushed the side of his face. "I don't want to get out of this." Her voice was all whispery. The sound of it, the little quiver in it, did him in. His pulse went crazy and his heart felt too big, thudding away in there, hard and insistent. Behind the buttons of his 501's, there was suddenly a shortage of space.

He kissed the tip of her nose. "You have a very fine nose, did you know that?" He kissed her lips, one soft, quick kiss. "And a good mouth."

She was smiling, relaxing a little. "Oh, Billy. A fine nose and a good mouth?"

"I like your eyebrows, too. What I can see of 'em, behind your glasses."

"They're too pale."

"Pale is good. Pale is fine." He lifted his hand.

She knew what he was going to do, and turned her head slightly away. "I won't be able to see."

"Please."

She looked at him forever. At last, she murmured, "All right."

He took her glasses away, set them behind him on the nightstand, between the condoms and the alarm clock. When he turned back to her, she looked at him in that soft, unfocused way he remembered from the night at his club—and the other night, when they had danced and he had kissed her for the first time, and then she had turned him down.

She said, "I can't see, but I am not defenseless."

He touched her pale, golden red brows, one and then the other, tracing the shape of them, following the curves.

"Did you hear me, Billy?"

"I heard." He put his mouth against her temple, felt the pulse beat there, dared to put out his tongue, taste the rhythm of her heart.

"I think that's my deepest fear, Billy. To be defenseless in front of a man."

"You're not, Prue," he whispered into the sweet, dark central hollow of her ear. "You know you're not." He pulled back, looked down into her blind, yearning eyes. She looked back. What she saw, he would never know. But the way she looked at him made him hunger. Made him burn.

First, he wanted to watch her lose herself.

And then he wanted to get lost in her.

He laid his hand on that black belt she wore. Those pale brows drew together. But she didn't say a word, didn't try to move away. He pulled the tip from the keeper, the prong from the buckle. He undid the button of her gray pants and slid the zipper down. Underneath, he found silk panties. Silver gray silk. It didn't look as if they had any lace on them. Nothing fancy. Just fine, plain silk.

He slid his hand beneath those panties, felt satiny skin, a warm tangle of hair.

She was already wet. He had known by the look in those eyes that she would be. She moved her legs farther apart, giving him access. He stroked that sweetness, bending to take her mouth when she could no longer hold back the moans.

He swallowed her cries. They tasted so good. She moved against his hand, and he drank in what happened to her, all of her turning liquid, baby powder, roses, all around him as she came.

He broke the kiss at the last minute, to watch her toss her head, watch the way that dark red hair rubbed the white quilt, to see the sweat of loving on her pale skin.

When she went limp, he bent close again. He took

her lips, biting them a little, tugging at her clothes, getting them off her as he kissed her. Her body felt easy, warm and ready under his hands. She helped him, in a slow, lazy sort of way, pulling her arms from the sleeves of her shirt, toeing off her shoes, lifting her hips so he could pull down the gray pants and the silk panties.

He had her down to her gray silk bra and a pair of ankle socks when she started shoving at him. He thought for a moment that she was going to want to stop. He swore and then scowled at her. "What?"

But then she whispered, "You, too..."

And he understood that all she wanted was for him to get his clothes off, too. So he did. He could do that pretty damn quick, as a matter of fact.

Within seconds, they both were naked. She looked just like he'd thought she would: slim and pale and a hell of a lot prettier than she did with her clothes on.

She was smiling at him, blindly. "I can't believe it."

He reached out, touched her shoulder, felt the silky smoothness of her skin. "What?"

"This is...just fine. Natural. Okay."

He grinned back at her. "I told you so." He pulled her close, got that first incredible shock of her naked body against his own. "Kiss me, Prue."

She obliged, with enthusiasm.

A moment later, she was sighing. And then she was moaning.

When he pushed her back on the white cloud of the bed and put himself inside her, she cried out. He stilled and waited.

She was looking at him. "That hurt."

"Sorry."

"But it's starting to...not hurt."

"That's good." He waited some more, sincerely hoping that he would not explode.

"Billy?"

He tried to say, *Yeah?* but it came out as more of a groan.

"Billy..." And then she moved against him, pushing her hips up to him, offering him more.

And more was fine with Billy Jones. He pressed deeper. She took him. And from about that point, there was only her body and his body and the white cloud of the bed, the golden pool of the bedside lamp. It all swam together, became an endless pulse, a glow, a sensation of expansion and glorious heat. Billy held on, he drowned in baby powder and roses, in silky skin and fiery hair and the soft, urgent cries that Prue made as she moved beneath him.

At the end, he was probably too rough for her. He pushed himself in hard and deep. She took him, but with a startled gasp. His climax rolled through him, yanking him under, then tossing him up, turning him inside out, so his body and his mind were one endless, exploding sensation. White heat. Expansion.

Then contraction. A feeling of falling. And the blessed sweetness of landing lax, satisfied—and still naked, still with Prue.

"Did I hurt you too bad?" Billy whispered in her ear.

Prudence smiled. He was squashing her, especially her hipbones and her breasts.

"Did I?" He sounded worried.

She rubbed her cheek against his. "No, you didn't hurt me too bad."

He let out a big, relieved-sounding breath. "Good."

She pushed at him, a light push.

"Don't make me move." But then, as soon as he got the words out, he was rolling, holding onto her as he did it, so that she ended up on top.

She looked down at his blur of a face.

He said, softly. "Please don't go away. We have twenty-four condoms to use, remember?"

She kissed his nose. "Twenty-three."

He let out another long breath. "Right. Twenty-three." She slithered backward, toward the night table. His arms tightened around her. "I said, you can't go."

"I'm just getting my glasses."

"Why?"

"So I can see."

"You don't need to see."

"Billy, I *want* to see. And I'm not going anywhere."

"Swear it."

"Billy, come on."

"Hell. All right. Get 'em."

She sat among the pillows and felt on the nightstand until she found them. When she put them on and saw Billy, stretched across her bed, naked and grinning, she went ahead and grinned right back. Then she noticed the red stains on the quilt. He saw where she was looking. He frowned, then he looked at her once more— and they were grinning all over again.

He said, "I'm starved."

Her stomach actually growled right then. "Me, too."

"Let's raid the refrigerator." He grabbed her hand and pulled her off the bed toward the door.

She hung back. "But, Billy, we're naked."

He looked down at himself, then he looked at her. And then he shrugged. "We sure as hell are."

"Billy, I don't think I'm quite ready yet to go wandering around my house in the buff."

He laughed. "In the *buff?*"

"That is what I said."

"Well. Get a robe, then."

She did as he suggested, collecting her white robe from the closet.

"Ready?" he asked, as she belted the robe at her waist. She nodded. He pulled the door open and led her into the upstairs hall.

They stopped briefly in the upstairs bathroom, where he got rid of the condom. Then they went on down the stairs.

He took her to the living room first, led her to the sofa and said, "Sit down. Let me put on some music."

She dropped obediently to the cushions, tucking one foot up under herself and waited as he went through the CDs. Once he'd made his choices about what he wanted to hear, he went on to load up a cartridge, tapping his bare toes and humming to himself the whole time. Prudence watched him, thinking that there wasn't an ounce of fat on him. His muscles were all long and sharply defined. She marveled at how fine and hard his body was, as she knew how he liked to drink and she'd never seen him exercise on purpose in the time he'd been staying with her. But he had that easy grace of very lean men, that look of economy, of nerve endings right up close to the surface of the skin. When he turned to give her a smile, she noted that the bruises from the fight with Sam had faded to almost nothing, to green shadows against his skin.

"You'll wake Jesse," she chided, when the first tune came on, too loud.

He shook his head, but he did turn it down. Then he

came for her, reaching out his hand, tugging her off the couch and into his arms.

They danced through the dining room and into the kitchen, where they made peanut butter and jelly sandwiches. They ate the sandwiches standing at the counter.

"Milk," Billy said, after the first bite. And she thought of Jesse, pounding his fists on his high chair tray, demanding, "Meeook, meeook, meeook!"

She went and got the milk and poured them each a big glass. He toasted her, then drank down the whole thing in one long gulp.

They started kissing again as they were rinsing their dishes and putting them into the dishwasher. Billy untied the sash of her robe and pushed it to the floor. The counter tiles felt icy against her bare bottom when he hoisted her up there. But soon enough, Prudence forgot the discomfort. She looked down at Billy's head, which was buried between her open thighs. She could see very clearly what he was doing, as he'd let her keep her glasses on this time.

She wondered, could this really be her, Prudence Wilding, doing these naughty things with bad Billy Jones?

But then Billy did something impossible with his tongue. Prudence held onto his head, closed her eyes—and forgot everything but his endless, incredible, forbidden kiss.

At the end, after he pushed her right over the edge, she looked down at him. And he looked up at her, his green eyes gleaming with a devilish light and his lips all swollen and wet from what he'd been doing to her.

"You even taste like roses," he said.

And her heart just lifted up inside her chest. She

cupped his face and bent over and kissed her own wetness right off his lips. He whispered her name. And then he stuck out his tongue and licked the corner of her mouth.

"Peanut butter," he said.

She wiped the spot. He caught her hand, rising up, so they were face-to-face. He set her hand on his shoulder, felt for the other one and put it there, too. Then he laid his own hands on her thighs. Gently, in long, feathery strokes, he caressed the tops of her thighs, from her knees to the place where her hips joined her torso. He leaned in, fitted his mouth to hers and kissed her until she forgot where she was and let her head fall back to bump against the cabinet behind her.

He made a noise of concern and pulled away enough to meet her eyes. "Hurt?" She thought of Jesse, asking, "Boo-boo?"

She rubbed her head. "I saw stars."

He laughed, and then the laughter faded. He looked at her, and went on looking, at the same time slowly caressing the tops of her thighs.

She stared back at him, a half smile on her lips to match the one he wore. And something happened. Something shifted deep inside her. Awareness dawned.

Twin creases formed between his dark brows. "What?"

She scanned his face, her gaze moving from his slightly crooked nose to his finely shaped mouth to the beard-shadow on his cheeks and chin. Her skin burned a little, on her face and in more private places. Beard burn. Randi used to say that, *Beard burn*. And then Randi would rub her tender, reddened cheek and smile, a satisfied smile. A smile that said it had all been worth the minor pain.

Billy was still frowning at her. "What, Prue?"

Prudence thought, *But this is a lot worse than beard burn....*

She heard Randi's words in her head: "I like him. I want him. I'm gonna have him. And then I'm gonna end up paying the price... He's a no-strings kind of guy. He's gonna hurt me...."

This is bad, Prudence thought. *This is trouble. This is a man even Randi couldn't handle....*

Billy lifted his hands to cradle her face. "What's wrong?"

I've gone and let myself fall in love with you, Billy. "Nothing. Kiss me."

For once, he simply did what she asked.

Chapter 16

They went back to Prudence's bed soon after that. They used two more of the condoms that night. Just before they dropped off to sleep, Billy murmured, "Twenty-one to go."

She woke to gray daylight, Billy's caresses and the sound of rain drumming steadily on the roof.

She suggested on a sigh, "We should check on Jesse."

"I just did. He's still asleep."

"But not for long."

"Let's not waste time, then." He pulled her closer and immediately began doing things that made her sigh some more.

They didn't leave the house that whole day. Of course, with Jesse around, they weren't able to spend all of it making love. But they had their own kind of nap time when he took his—and they ended up in bed again within a half an hour of the moment that Jesse's little head hit his pillow that night.

By the time they went down for breakfast the next morning, the rain had let up a little. While Billy put Jesse in his high chair and mixed up his oatmeal, Prudence poured herself a cup of coffee and wandered over to the window that looked out on the backyard. Beyond the big walnut tree in the middle of the lawn, the sky was like a sheet of gray steel. Everything looked misty and cold.

Billy came up behind her and wrapped her in his arms. "Happy Thanksgiving." He lifted her hair and breathed a kiss onto the side of her neck.

"Same to you." She leaned against him, enjoying the feel of him at her back, thinking that tomorrow would be the last day of his two-week trial period. It would be time for the big talk.

That was how she had started to think of it: *the big talk.* Something grim and enormous that would ruin the fantasy she had foolishly allowed herself to start living.

Perhaps, now they were lovers, they could just go on as they were for a while, let the big talk wait.

But for how long? A few days? A week? Not much longer than that, surely. Billy had his life in Southern California, after all. And decisions would have to be made.

Billy asked, his voice a pleasant rumble in her ear, "What time do we have to be at Sam's?"

"Around two."

"Hmm. There'll be time for a little nap before we go." He lifted his hands and cupped her breasts. Inside her, everything turned molten, a delicious, hungry, burning ache. He must have picked up her body's response to him, because he let out a teasing growl.

Behind them, Jesse pounded his chair tray and crowed, "Meeook, meeook!"

"Hell," Billy muttered, dropping those wonderful hands away.

She turned to watch him fill the safety cup, her love a deep, warm, sad little secret down in a place she doubted she would ever let him see.

Perhaps because she was Delilah's friend, or maybe because Evie's stepchildren were her grandchildren, Nellie turned up at Sam's Thanksgiving party.

"Look," Billy whispered to Prudence at the sight of the older woman. "It's the president of my fan club. Should I introduce you?"

She gave him a poke in the ribs and a long-suffering sigh, which only made him laugh. Eden came over and led them to the downstairs bedroom, where they piled their coats on the bed with everyone else's. Billy set his guitar, which Prudence had urged him to bring, in the closet, where it wouldn't be disturbed.

When they returned to the living room again, Sam appeared from the kitchen, his long hair tied back and a white apron around his waist. "Welcome. I hope you're making yourselves comfortable." He gestured at a table near the wall, where several Jones children lurked around a big bowl of something pink and a variety of chips and dips. "Punch and stuff's over there. If you want anything stronger, I set it all out on the kitchen counter. And there's hot spiced cider on the stove." He looked around, his eyes going vague. "Lilah's not here yet. But she'll come. I know she'll come." Without another word, he turned and headed back for the kitchen.

Billy, who stood close to Prudence, muttered in her

ear, "You get the feeling that means she told him she *wouldn't* come?"

Prudence whispered back, "Unfortunately, yes."

They shared a fond, knowing smile, after which Billy planted a quick kiss on her nose. Beyond his shoulder, she could see Nellie, watching, her thin lips screwed up tight in disapproval.

"Dow, Da. Dow." Jesse had started to squirm in Billy's arms. Billy set him down.

Prudence suggested, "I'll follow him around for a while. You go see if Sam needs any help in the kitchen."

"The kind of help Sam needs, only Delilah can provide."

"Still…"

"I know, I know. I'm going." He headed for the kitchen.

Across the room, Nellie started on the move—in Prudence's direction. At the same time, Jesse took off the opposite way. Grateful for small favors, Prudence turned her back on Nellie to follow the child.

For the next hour, Prudence managed to avoid conversation with the older woman. She chatted with Eden and drank punch with Evie. Billy appeared and took charge of Jesse again. Relieved of her responsibility for child care, Prudence sat on one of Sam's big, leather sofas and enjoyed a nice talk with Heather Drury, who was Jared's daughter by an earlier marriage and who had sold Prudence the house on Prospect Street.

But Nellie Anderson wasn't someone who could be avoided indefinitely. She was lurking on the stair landing, sipping a cup of hot cider, when Prudence emerged from the upstairs bathroom at a little after three. At the sight of her, Prudence considered heading for one of the bedrooms. She could lock herself in, and not come out until she felt certain Nellie had given up and gone away.

However, knowing Nellie, that might never happen. So Prudence pulled her shoulders back and marched for the stairs.

Nellie spoke up just as Prudence reached her—and before she could move on past. "Evie has told me I must learn to accept that your private life is none of my business."

Well, Prudence thought philosophically, it was a better opening than some. She put on a smile. "Evie is right. And I believe I've told you the same thing myself, more than once."

"I'm entitled to my opinion—my opinion, which is right."

Prudence shook her head. "Oh, Nellie."

Nellie gestured with her cider cup. "However, I know it's too late now. I can see by the way that man looks at you that the worst has happened."

Prudence said nothing.

"My warnings just never do any good." Nellie looked sincerely distressed. "I mean to be helpful and honest. A true friend."

Prudence thought of Billy, of the love affair they were having that they probably shouldn't be having. Her wiser self agreed with Nellie. Bad Billy Jones hardly represented a wise choice in a man. "Nellie, it's good to be honest. But once you've made your point, you have to let people lead their own lives."

Nellie hung her head. "I suppose." She straightened a little, sipped from her cup. "I was watching him, just now, with the child...."

Prudence braced herself for the worst.

Nellie surprised her. "I must admit, he actually seems quite good with the boy."

Prudence relaxed a little. It just might be possible, over time, that she could learn to like Nellie. "Yes," she agreed, "Billy's turning out to be a real father, after all."

By four-thirty, when they sat down to eat, neither Delilah nor Oggie had appeared.

To make it possible for all the Joneses to sit down at once, Sam had put four tables together, down the center of his large living room. He had borrowed china and silver from his sisters-in-law, but he'd cooked the huge meal himself, including the turkey and the ham and the mountains of potatoes and stuffing and vegetables. He had everything carved and piled high on platters, ready to pass. And when he sat down at the head of the table, with that empty chair opposite him way down at the other end, Prudence thought she had never seen a man look so sad.

As soon as all the chairs but two were filled, Sam tapped his spoon against his water glass. Everyone fell silent, even Jesse and two other small Joneses, Diana and Eliza, in their high chairs.

"I want to thank you all for coming," Sam said in his deep, rumbling voice. "I guess..." He hesitated, breathed in deeply and let the air out slowly. Then he made himself go on. "Well, I guess I thought some things would get worked out by now, for me. And for Lilah. That I would have what I most want. But as you can all see, that hasn't happened. Yet." A melancholy smile played at the corners of his mouth. "But still, sitting here, looking down this table, I figure I am grateful, after all. I might not be a Jones by birth, but when I look at all of you, and see you all came here for your Thanksgiving just 'cause I asked you to, well, I know I got a true family, no matter what. And I say, thank the good Lord for that.''

"Amen," said Jared. And down the table, the word was picked up and repeated, "Amen, amen, amen..."

After the "amens" faded, there was silence. Outside, the rain had started coming down again. It drummed against the windows, as steady as a long, drawn-out sigh. Beside her, Prudence felt Billy shift a little in his chair. His hand found hers.

There are moments a woman never forgets. Prudence knew she was living one right then. A moment that had everything in it. Sam's sad and beautiful little speech. The rain on the roof. The Thanksgiving feast. A roomful of Joneses—and Billy's hand in hers.

Brendan, the youngest of the Jones brothers, announced, "I'm starved. Let's eat."

Sam picked up the platter piled with turkey, speared himself a big slice, and passed it on. Within seconds, the room was filled with talk and children's laughter and the clink of silver against china plates. The doorbell rang about ten minutes later, after everyone had been served and they'd all settled down to some serious eating.

At the sound, Sam's head shot up and his eyes went blank. The whole table fell silent, so the drumming of the rain outside seemed louder, more insistent again.

Eden pushed back her chair. "I'll get it."

Even the little ones stared as she walked the length of the four pushed-together tables and disappeared into the foyer. A moment later, she returned—with Delilah at her side.

Eden returned to her own chair. And Delilah went and stood behind the empty chair opposite Sam.

"You're all wet," Sam said, his pale blue eyes taking in all of her, from the drops of water that gleamed in her wild black hair, to the high color and sheen on her cheeks, and the dark waterspots on her clothes. Prudence, in the seat directly to Delilah's right, could smell the rain on her, wet and fresh and cool, a smell of the forest, green, secret and dark.

"I went for a walk," Delilah said. "Then...I couldn't stay away." She looked around the table, her black eyes soft and shining in what seemed to Prudence to be equal parts joy and pain. "This is beautiful, Sam."

He said, "Sit down. Eat."

She looked at him, and in those black eyes, Prudence saw that the pain had overshadowed the joy.

Sam said, "It's all right, Lilah. It doesn't have to mean anything, if you stay. If you eat with your family, on Thanksgiving day."

For a moment more, she hovered there, tottering on the edge between leaving and staying. At last, she pulled back the chair and sat down.

One by one, they passed the bowls and platters to her. She piled her plate high. By then, everyone was talking and eating again.

After dinner, they cleared the plates and all but the youngest ones helped to scrape and stack. Then Sam brought out the coffee and three kinds of pies. They sat down again, for dessert.

It was past seven by the time all the eating was done. Billy brought out his guitar. And Regina, Patrick's wife, sat down to the piano that Delilah said had once belonged to her mother, Bathsheba. They played together, and everybody sang, mostly children's songs, to keep the kids entertained. By nine, a few of the youngest ones had started to droop. Jesse sat in Prudence's lap, his little head nodding, more than ready for bedtime, but unwilling to let go of all the fun he'd been having. She kissed his warm, fuzzy head and looked up to meet Billy's eyes.

He set his guitar aside. "Time for us to be heading on home."

Jenny and Becca, Evie's stepdaughters, protested. "Just one more song," they begged. But the adults were already up and moving toward the downstairs bedroom, where all their coats lay in a high, rain-damp tangle on the bed.

Prudence sat, rocking Jesse gently, and waited for Billy to come back with their things. By the time he was standing over them, wearing his own jacket, holding out her coat, Jesse had slipped off into dreams. Carefully she traded the child for the coat, slipping her arms into the sleeves and buttoning up.

The doorbell rang just as they were standing in the foyer, saying their goodbyes to Sam and Delilah. Prudence's heart leapt a little at the sound. Who else could it be but Oggie? The sight of him, safe and well and ready to meddle in everyone's lives again, would make the magical evening complete.

Delilah, closest to the door, reached out and pulled it open.

A big, gray-haired man in a khaki uniform stood there. The nameplate on his breastfront read Pangborn. And the patch on his jacket sleeve said he was the sheriff.

"Mind if I come in, folks?"

Delilah stepped back. Sheriff Pangborn entered the foyer. Delilah shut the door behind him, closing out the driving rain.

From just beyond the foyer, Jack Roper caught sight of his colleague, "What's up, Carl?"

The sheriff looked from one expectant face to the next. He shook his head. "I just got a call, folks. From the boys over in Tahoe."

An ominous silence descended. Someone in the living room murmured, "Oggie…"

Pangborn nodded. "I'm afraid so."

"Where is he?" Delilah's face had gone chalk white.

"Tahoe Forest Hospital."

"What's happened to him?"

"He blew a tire. It happened out on Highway 80, up near the summit early this afternoon."

Delilah demanded, "A flat tire? He's in the hospital because of a flat tire?"

Pangborn put up both hands. "Easy, Delilah. Give me a minute." He looked around at all the Joneses, then met Delilah's eyes once more. "Maybe we should talk alone."

Jared spoke up from the arch to the living room. "Is this something the kids shouldn't hear?"

Pangborn thought about that. "Well, no. I suppose they'll be finding it out, anyway."

"Then you better just tell us. We're all family here, and we'll all want to know."

A chorus of agreement went up.

"Yes."

"Tell us."

"Tell us, please…"

Pangborn eyed the group warily "You're sure?

"Positive," said Jared.

"Just tell us what you know," Delilah insisted.

Jared spoke more calmly. "You said he blew a tire?"

Pangborn nodded.

"So just start with that. Where did it happen?"

"Past Truckee. Not far from Donner Summit. It was a steep, twisting section of road. Really treacherous, a canyon on one side and a mountain on the other, with almost no shoulder. And it was raining hard—sleeting, really. It's almost cold enough for snow up there now. When the highway patrol got there, they found the car up against the mountain, good and snug. Oggie had pulled in as tight as he could. But it just wasn't tight enough. It was the left rear that blew, the side out toward the highway."

"But what *happened?*" pleaded Delilah.

Pangborn cast her a pained look as Jared commanded, "Let the man talk."

Pangborn continued, "The point is, Oggie ended up pretty close to the oncoming traffic while he knelt there to change the tire. A semitruck went by. At the same time, some idiot in a camper tried to pass on the trucker's left. The trucker had to swerve to give the camper room."

Delilah interrupted again, her voice tight as a hard-coiled spring. "You're saying my father's been hit by a semitruck?"

Sounds of distress went up from the group.

Pangborn hastened to reassure them. "No, he wasn't hit by the truck. He evidently scrambled off his knees just in time to avoid getting clipped. But in the process, he knocked the jack loose."

Delilah put her hands over her mouth and let out a little moan of distress.

"That Cadillac dropped like a rock," Pangborn said. "It more or less ejected the jack, which bopped Oggie a good one up the side of the head."

Someone murmured, "Oh, God."

"Luckily the trucker was one of the good guys. He called for help, then pulled over as soon as he could and ran back with flares, to wait with Oggie until the ambulance came." Pangborn glanced around at all the shocked, worried faces. "Look. It could be worse. There's no skull fracture, and no hemorrhaging that they've been able to find so far. And that's good."

Delilah had a wild light in her eyes. "What are you saying, Sheriff? What are you telling us? Are you saying he's all right? Are you saying he's just fine?"

Sam stepped up close and wrapped an arm around her, pulling her against his side. "Lilah, go easy...."

At first she stiffened, and then she acquiesced to lean on her husband. She sighed. "Sam, it's my fault. I drove him away...."

He pulled her closer. "If anyone drove him off, it was me."

She reached up, touched his face. "Oh, Sam..."

Eden chided, "Don't you two go blaming yourselves. You know how Oggie is, always taking off for somewhere. This could have happened on any one of those trips of his."

Jack stepped forward. "Carl, tell us. Is he going to be all right?"

Pangborn let out a long breath. "He should be."

"*Should* be?"

The sheriff cleared his throat. "There is one little problem."

Everyone waited—silent, fearing.

The sheriff said, "The old man seems to have forgotten who he is."

Chapter 17

Delilah, Sam, Jared and Eden all went to the hospital right away. Eden told Prudence later that Oggie was sleeping when they got there. They took turns in his room through the night. The next morning, when Oggie woke, he didn't seem to know any of them. Wearing a blank, pleasant smile, he looked from one face to the other.

"Well, hi. It's so nice to have visitors. Who are you folks, anyway?"

Shaken, they turned to the doctors, who counseled patience. They still found no physical signs of brain damage. More than likely, very soon, Oggie's memory would return.

Through the entire day, Friday, Sam and Delilah both refused to leave Oggie's side. The two of them slept in his room that night, sitting up in chairs, holding hands.

And a miracle happened. When he woke the next

morning, Oggie greeted his daughter and her husband by name. In a gentle, patient voice, he said he was sorry for all the pain and frustration he'd caused them over the years. From that day forward, he vowed, they would find him a changed man, a man who minded his own business and let others mind theirs. Since Oggie had always been prone to grandiose declarations, they didn't take him too seriously at the time.

Twenty-four hours later, Oggie was released into the care of his family. They brought him back to his room at Sam and Delilah's house. Once she saw Oggie settled in, Delilah returned to the motel—but only to pay her bill and collect her things. Then she went home to her husband and her father.

Sunday afternoon, while Jesse napped, Billy paid a visit to the old man. When he returned, Prudence was waiting at the door for him.

"How is he?"

Billy shook his head. "I don't know. He's fine, I guess."

"You're frowning. Something's wrong."

"He's just so...different."

"Different, how?"

"I can't explain it. He's so...nice. So soft-spoken. So polite. It's not like him at all. And do you know, he never once called me 'boy'? That really bothered me, for some crazy reason."

"But did he know who you were?"

"Yeah. He knew me. He asked how you and Jesse were doing."

"So he is okay?"

"Hell. I don't know. What's okay? I talked to Delilah afterward. She said he really has changed, that he claims getting hit on the head has helped him to see the world in a new light. He says he'll do no more interfering. No more telling people what they should be doing with their lives. He swears he's never going to meddle again. That should be good, right?''

''Yes. I suppose.''

''You don't *sound* like you think it's good.''

''Quite frankly, I don't know what to think.''

The next day, Prudence went to see the change in Oggie for herself. Delilah showed her to Oggie's room, where she found him sitting in a reclining chair, staring out the window at a leafless tree in the backyard.

''Father. Prudence is here.''

He turned his head and smiled amiably. ''Ah. Prudence. Real nice of you to drop by.''

Prudence took a straight chair near his recliner. They visited for a half an hour, during which time he never once called her ''gal,'' which bothered her just as much as not being called ''boy'' had bothered Billy. In fact, at more than one point in the conversation, she had the eeriest feeling she was talking to a very sweet, very well-behaved stranger who just happened to look like Oggie Jones.

Finally she couldn't stand it anymore. She leaned across and put her hand on his. ''Uncle Oggie. Are you *really* all right?''

He laid his other hand on hers. ''I am just fine. I have learned my lesson is all. Turned over a whole new leaf, yessirree. It's live and let live for this old fool from now on.''

She spoke to Delilah before she left. ''I can't get over it. He really does seem different.''

Delilah nodded. ''You'd think I would like it, after the way he's driven me crazy for just about all of my life. But I'm not sure....'' She let the thought trail off.

Prudence dared to ask, "And how are *you* doing?"

Delilah's face looked softer, suddenly. "It's funny. Sometimes you can be so hungry for that one important thing, that you lose sight of all you do have. And then, something happens to wake you up. You look around and you realize you have a lot already. And you're so busy suffering over not having that one other thing, you're throwing away all the rest. Does that make any sense at all?"

Prudence nodded. "It makes complete sense. I'm glad for you." She started for the door, but Delilah stopped her with a hand on her arm.

"How did things turn out for Sharlee Stubblehill?"

"As far as we know, she's fine."

"She went back to Southern California, didn't she?"

"Yes. Billy got her a job at his club in Van Nuys. She was glad to go, glad for a new start."

"I have to admit, I'm glad she moved on."

"It was the best thing."

"But I do believe she was a sweet kid at heart— even if she was after my husband."

"Sam never looked twice. You know that, don't you?"

Delilah's smile went all the way to her eyes. "Sharlee was never really the problem. I understand that now."

The day was cool and breezy, but sunny. Prudence pulled her sweater a little closer to block out the bite of the wind as she walked down Rambling Lane, headed home. She pondered the change in Oggie, and remembered the softness in Delilah's face when Prudence had asked her how things were going.

Sam and Delilah had a good marriage, Prudence

could see that. A marriage strong enough to withstand
the worst disappointments life can dish out. Until she'd
moved to North Magdalene, Prudence hadn't seen
many good marriages. Now, though, observing what
was possible, Prudence couldn't help but feel just a
little bit envious.

Billy was lounging in the open front door when she
got home, with the stereo going behind him. Prudence
shook her head at him as she went up the walk. "You
know, it costs money to heat the whole outdoors."

"You give me the heating bill when it comes. I'll
take care of it."

"That's not the point. It's wasteful."

"Don't nag, Prue." He had a certain look in his eye.
A look she knew very well now, a look to which her
body responded automatically.

She mounted the steps, her gaze locked with his.
When she got about a foot and a half away, he reached
out, grabbed her hand and yanked her over the threshold into his arms. "I've been waiting for you." He
kicked the door closed behind them and leaned against
it, pressing a hand at the small of her back so that her
body fitted right to his.

That delicious, warm ache was spreading down inside her. She tipped her head up to him. "Glad to see
me, are you?"

He pressed her closer. "Feel how glad."

She remembered Jesse. "What about—?"

"Nap time." He kissed her. When his nose bumped
her glasses, he took them off. Then he grabbed her
hand and pulled her toward his room.

As he pressed her down onto his bed, she thought,
we really can't go on like this forever. The big talk
had to happen. It was supposed to have happened two

days ago, on Friday. But neither of them had breathed a word about it. They'd waited near the phone for news of Oggie and taken care of Jesse and continued on, playing house as if it was never going to end.

Billy pushed her sweater out of the way and kissed her breast right through her shirt and bra. It felt good. Wonderful. She pushed herself up toward him. His hands went roaming. Incredible, what he could do with those hands of his.

Prudence let those hands have her. The big talk could wait.

That night, as soon as Jesse went to sleep, Billy went to find Prudence. She was waiting for him, where he'd hoped she'd be, in her bedroom.

It surprised the hell out of Billy, how good Prue had turned out to be in bed. She was better than booze or any drug he'd ever tried. She gave endless pleasure. And he never had a hangover after.

She dropped off around midnight. He lay there beside her, watching her in the pale wash of starlight that came in through the window several feet away.

Her hair looked almost black in the darkness, her skin so pale and fine. Billy liked to look at her. She had so many different ways she could look. From butt-ugly, to downright beautiful. Sometimes, in the morning, when she woke up, before she groped for her glasses and settled them on her nose, she would blink and then open her blind eyes so wide. She would look just like Mr. Magoo. And then other times, like now, as she lay sleeping, he would think that he'd never seen anyone so damn beautiful in his life.

She turned her head, sighing, showing him the side

of her neck. He lowered his head, put his mouth there. She lifted her arms, pulling him closer. "Billy..."

"One more time," he whispered, trailing his hand down over her belly, kissing his way up the smooth line of her neck.

"Billy..."

He covered her mouth with his own.

The next morning after breakfast, Billy had some calls to make—to Alexis and to his agent in Los Angeles. Prudence took Jesse and went over to Eden's, where she drank more coffee than she should have and she and Eden discussed the change in Oggie and the touching reconciliation of Sam and Delilah.

Around ten, Jared came into the kitchen. "Heading over to the Hole in the Wall," he said, and dropped a kiss on Eden's forehead.

She grabbed his arm before he could escape her. "Check the produce over good when it comes in, will you? Some of the lettuce has been coming in looking pretty ragged lately."

"Yes, ma'am."

They looked at each other for a moment, then Jared bent briefly and brushed his wife's lips with his own. Eden promised, "I'll be in by two."

"Good enough."

Watching them, Prudence had the sudden, embarrassing urge to burst into tears. She got up, went into the living room and checked on Jesse, who was playing happily by himself under the conscientious supervision of Sally Louise, Eden's four-year-old.

"He's doing fine," Sally Louise announced in her most grown-up voice. "He tried to eat the chair leg, but I said, 'no, no, no.' So he stopped."

"Very good. Thank you." Prudence glanced at Sally's baby sister, Diana, who lay on a blanket nearby, sucking on her toes, in clear view of Eden in the kitchen. "And I see Diana looks happy, too."

"Everybody is haiving."

It took Prudence a moment to realize that "haiving" stood for behaving. "Yes," she said, "you are quite a good baby-sitter."

"I certly am."

Prudence praised the little girl some more and then wandered back into the kitchen. Jared had left and Eden was waiting for her. Prudence tried a bright smile.

Eden wasn't buying. "Okay. What's the deal?"

Prudence considered denial and rejected it. In the past weeks, Eden had become a true friend. Someone Prudence could trust. Someone she could really talk to. Prudence sank to the chair she had left a few moments before.

"What?" Eden prodded. "Tell me."

Prudence folded her hands on the table, her coffee cup between them. "You and Jared look so great together. So solid, you know? So permanent."

Eden let out a groan and raked both hands back through her short cap of red-blond hair. "It's Billy."

Prudence stared down into her empty cup. When she looked up, Eden was nodding grimly. "It's Billy," she said again.

Prudence leaned her chin on her hand. "At first, I thought there was no chance of anything, you know, happening between us."

"Okay."

"And then, when he first…expressed interest, I told him no way. Ever. Forget it. Get lost."

"And now, you're in love with him."

Prudence picked up her cup, went to the coffeemaker and got a refill. "More?"

Eden shook her head. "Have you told him?"

Prudence leaned against the counter and sipped. "No."

"You should tell him."

"No. It's never going to be anything but temporary with him. I know that. That's...the way he is."

"Prudence, that's the way he *was*. Maybe, with you—"

"Oh, stop it. Have you heard the stories about him? Every woman he's ever been with has thought that."

"Still, I think you should tell him. Tell him how you feel and what you want. You do know what you want?"

"Yes."

"What?"

She dared to say it. "What you and Jared have."

"Marriage?"

Prudence turned, set her coffee cup on the counter and spoke without turning back to her friend. "Oh, it's crazy. I never wanted that. Never in my whole life. I wanted...to take care of myself. To lead a productive life. And then, lately, to bring Jesse up right."

"But now?"

"Now Jesse has a father. A *real* father. You know what I mean?"

"You mean Billy is fully capable of bringing up Jesse himself."

"Yes."

"You would let him do that?"

"Yes. Yes, I would. Selfishly I wouldn't want to. But for Jesse, I really believe it's the right thing."

Eden asked softly, "And what about you and Billy?"

She turned then, and faced Eden. "You said it a minute ago. I'm in love with Billy."

"And where does that lead you?"

"It leads me to…want it all. And if I can't have it all, I want to know. So I can move on."

"So tell him."

"Oh, God."

"You have to tell him."

"I know."

"Talent problems," Billy said the minute Prudence and Jesse walked in the front door.

Prudence knelt to help Jesse out of his jacket, then, still wearing her own, she went to sit by Billy on the sofa. "What kind of talent problems?"

"I had Buddy Bobiles and the Hawaiian Rockers starting Friday and scheduled through the end of next week. But the band broke up. I called around a little, trying to come up with something from here. But it doesn't look like that'll work. Everybody I can think of already has a gig. That means I've got to go down there and listen to a few new groups. I figure, if we leave tomorrow morning, I'll have tomorrow night, Thursday and all day Friday to come up with another group. It shouldn't be that big a deal." He leaned toward her, brushed her shoulder lightly with the tips of his fingers. "But then I got to thinking, maybe we could just stay on for a while. I could line up a few more acts, get together with Alexis, go over the books and all that stuff, so things will be under control until at least after the holidays."

Prudence stared at Jesse, who sat on the floor a few

feet away. He'd found a rubber hammer under the coffee table and was gently tapping his knee with it.

"Prue?" Billy touched her shoulder again. "You in there?"

She blinked and looked down at Jesse's jacket, which she still held wrapped over her arm. "Yes. I heard what you said."

"So can you handle this? A few days, maybe longer, in L.A.? The weather should be nice. You can shop. Visit old friends."

She made herself look at him. "Billy." He knew immediately. She saw the veil of wariness come down in his eyes. "That two weeks we agreed on when you first came here has been and gone."

He pulled away, back to his own side of the sofa. "Yeah, so?"

"So, before we go running off to Van Nuys together, we really have to...discuss a few things."

"No, we don't."

She stood and cast a significant glance at the child on the floor. "We can talk all about it at nap time, how's that?"

Billy made a low sound in his throat. "Do I have a choice?"

Now she found herself beginning to feel angry. In some ways he was just like a child. He wanted what he wanted when he wanted it, and he didn't want anything interfering with his fun. She spoke carefully. "A few decisions do have to be made."

"Why? Things are going just fine, as far as I'm concerned."

She had the distinct urge to shout at him. She cast a glance at Jesse, who'd picked up the tension between the grown-ups and stopped hammering his knee to stare at them. "Let's just talk about it later."

He looked at Jesse, too. "Fine. Later." He stood and went to kneel before his son. "Hey, mister. How 'bout lunch?"

Jesse stuck the rubber hammer into his mouth and drooled out something that might have been yes.

Two hours later, Billy stood over Jesse's bed. The kid looked so sweet and peaceful when he slept. Watching him made Billy want to climb into the top bunk and catch a few z's himself.

Sleeping would sure be preferable to what waited for him downstairs: Prue, in a mood for a serious talk.

It was enough to ruin a guy's whole day.

Sure, he'd known it had to come sooner or later. But later would have been a hell of a lot better, if you asked Billy.

Which nobody had.

With a rueful shrug, he turned from the sleeping child and headed for the door.

She was sitting in one of the easy chairs when he got down to her.

He dropped to the sofa. "Okay, what?" As if he damn well didn't know.

She rubbed the chair arms with her hands, looking toward the fireplace, the front window, and then finally at him. "This is so difficult."

He sat forward, braced his elbows on his knees. "So don't do it."

She blinked. "Excuse me?"

"Look. Things are going along fine. Just let it be. Let what happens happen."

She stared at him, the way people stare when they're

spoken to in a language they don't understand. "Billy, maybe that works for you. But it doesn't work for me. I want to know *where* we're going together. I want to know what we really are to each other."

He decided he might as well go ahead and make his offer. "You want me to marry you, Prue, is that it?"

She hadn't been prepared for that one, he could see it in her look of round-eyed surprise. "You would actually marry me?"

"Yeah."

"But…"

"But what?"

"Billy. You've always sworn you would never get married again."

He shrugged. "I changed my mind."

"But why?"

He sat back, let out a long breath. "You want me to say I love you, right?"

He knew her next words before she said them: "*Do you love me?*"

He looked at her, thinking that with women, it always had to come to this. To negotiations. Definitions. To tying everything up in a neat little bow. To tying *him* up, if they could manage it.

Generally, once it got to this point, he was ready to move along anyway. No woman had tied him up yet—excepting the two who'd had the sense to get him good and drunk before they whipped out the rope.

Prue, however, was another situation altogether. He wasn't even close to being through with her yet. Even now, irritated as he was with her for springing this crap on him so early on, he wanted her.

And besides, there was Jesse to consider. The three of them—him and her and Jesse—got along just fine together. Why bust up a good thing when all he had to do to keep it was to trot out a few love words and slide a wedding ring on Prue's finger? True, love words and wedding rings went against his principles. But now, with Jesse in his life, some things would have to change.

"Time's up," she said dryly.

"I was going to answer." He sounded defensive, even to his own ears.

But she only smiled sadly and shook her head. "Look. Let's put aside this marriage thing, okay? Let's settle the question of Jesse's custody. That's the real issue anyway, isn't it?" He supposed that it was, though he didn't reply. She demanded, looking pinched, "*Isn't* it?"

He shifted uneasily, dreading what she'd hit him with on this front. "Fine. All right. It is. So get it over with. What are you going to do?"

"I'm going to sign over full custody to you."

Chapter 18

If she hadn't been so hurt and angry, Prudence would have laughed out loud at the blank shock on Billy's face.

He asked, very quietly, "Would you repeat that?"

She kept her tone strictly businesslike. "I'm going to sign over custody of Jesse to you. You're going to be responsible for raising him. I'm sure you'll do a fine job."

She could see he still couldn't quite get his mind around what she was telling him. "You're going to let me have him?"

She nodded. "I'm not certain yet just how we'll go about it, since Randi didn't put your name on Jesse's birth certificate. I imagine blood tests might be necessary, and certainly there'll be a hearing. But eventually, guardianship will be yours."

The stereo remote sat on the coffee table. Billy reached for it.

"Don't," she said, thinking she would scream if he turned on his music right then. "Let's finish this."

He sat back without touching the device. "All right. Finish."

She watched him, wondering how in the world, if she just *had* to love a man, she'd managed to choose this one. "I have a few suggestions—conditions, really."

He was looking at her sideways, not at all sure what was going on here. "Fine. Let's hear 'em."

"I think any single parent raising a child should have…community around them, people who can and will help out sometimes."

"Wait a minute."

She didn't want to wait. She just wanted to get this over with. "Listen to me, Billy. If you want custody of Jesse, I really will insist that you make arrangements to live here permanently."

He put up both hands. "Whoa. Hold it. Single parent? What about you?"

"I said I'm giving you custody. Full custody. I won't be staying here."

He stood. "What the hell? I said I'd marry you."

"No, thanks."

He dropped to the couch again, rubbed a hand down his face and then slumped against the cushions. "Come on, Prue. Don't go there."

"I don't know what you mean."

"You do. Don't go there. Don't play this game."

"It's no game."

"The hell it's not."

"I'm not going to marry you, Billy," she told him again, since he seemed to have such difficulty believing her. "It wouldn't work. I can see now that it's better to just cut it clean."

"Cut it clean." He gave her words back to her in a voice that lacked inflection.

"Yes."

"When did you decide that?"

"Just a minute ago. Now, can we get on to what matters here?"

He looked at her for a long time before he said, "Sure. Get on with it."

She realized she was clutching the chair arms as if they could save her—from what, she couldn't have said. She ordered her grip to relax. "Randi wanted Jesse raised in a place like North Magdalene. And I think she was right. I think this is just the right place for him to grow up, in this particular small town, with his family all around him. Will you raise him here?"

He was staring at her. Just staring.

She prodded, "Billy. Will you raise Jesse here?"

"You're done with me. Finished. All at once. Just like that."

She knew if she said the word, *yes,* it would come out a hoarse croak, without power. Without dignity. She settled for one fast nod—and got back to what had to be dealt with. "Will you raise Jesse here?"

He seemed to shake himself. "Yeah. All right."

"Maybe while you're down in L.A., you could come to some agreement with the manager of your club. Maybe she could handle things most of the time and you could—"

He waved a hand. "I'll deal with it. It's my damn club."

"Well. All right. Of course." Her voice caught. She had to swallow before she could go on. "Actually I think you do like it here, for yourself. You like your family. I think you *want* to stay."

"You're just jam-packed with opinions, aren't you, Prue?"

She flinched at his sarcasm, then told herself to ignore it, to stick to the issue here, to get things settled. "Do you want this house?"

He lifted an eyebrow. "Oh, that's right. You're leaving. You won't need it."

"Yes."

"And where are you going?"

"I thought...Sacramento." She hadn't really thought about where she would go, not seriously. Not until this very moment.

"Why Sacramento?"

She cast about for reasons—and found them easily. "It's less than two hours away. There are several major public accounting firms there. I would even be able to cultivate a client base if I wanted to open up some kind of bookkeeping or financial planning service on my own. And I'll be close enough to visit Jesse often."

"Yeah. We'll really be looking forward to visits from you, Prue."

His ridicule was getting old fast. "Billy. Come on."

He surged to his feet again and came around the coffee table toward her. "Come on, what?"

She realized she should have escaped the chair before he stood. Now, he had her cornered in it. "Let's just...not do this."

He looked down at her, his lip curling in a nasty snarl. "Not do this? What does that mean?"

"Let's not get angry. Let's not say ugly things. Please."

"But I *am* angry, Prue." His tone was a mean caress. "Out of the blue, you're telling me it's over. And I am thinking a lot of very ugly things."

"Well, keep them to yourself."

"The hell I will."

She managed to slide to the side and get free of the chair, which she immediately put between them. "I mean it, Billy. Let it go."

"I'm not ready to let it go."

Something inside of her snapped then. "Right. That's it. That's it exactly."

"What are you babbling about?"

"You're not ready to let it go."

He glared at her, refusing to understand.

So she explained it to him. "You want things—and people—when you want them. For as long as you want them. That's all that's bothering you. That I'm leaving before you're through with me."

"Bull." But his eyes shifted away.

She kept her gaze dead on. "It is not bull. It's the truth. I know the way you operate. I saw you with my sister. And it worked out just fine with her, didn't it?"

"Why is it you always end up talking about Randi?"

"Because she matters. Because you hurt her. Because by the time she started making those scary commitment noises, you were ready to walk out the door anyway. But with me, it's not working out so well. I'm making the scary noises, and you're not done with me yet. So you pull out the big guns. You break your own rules about women. You agree that you'll marry me."

He let out a derisive snort. "And you fix me up good on that score. You turn me down flat. Because your damn pride's hurt."

"No, that's not it."

"Your pride's hurt, Prue. I didn't come up with the

I-love-you's fast enough. I didn't drop to my knees and beg you to hook a ball and chain to my leg.''

"This is not about pride."

He grunted. "Right."

"It is not."

"Then what? Lay it on me. What is this about?"

"This is about...my own foolishness, to have ever let myself become involved with you in the first place, after what I know from my own sister's experience."

"Randi, damn it. Randi again."

"This is about my own foolishness," she repeated, low and tautly controlled. "It is also about your disgusting willingness to do whatever you have to do in order to get what you want."

"My *disgusting* willingness?"

She refused to waver. "You want me around now, so you'll say anything to keep me around. You'll agree to marry me. You even would have said that you love me. Eventually. If I'd stood here waiting long enough. You have no...respect, Billy. You take no care with people. You don't think about what's right. You don't think about the future. About the consequences to both of us—not to mention, Jesse—if we get ourselves into a marriage that isn't going to work."

"Stop. Stop right there. I think about Jesse. I think about him all the time."

She sighed—and knew she couldn't deny that. "Yes, all right. I know you do."

"Really kills you to admit that, doesn't it?"

"No, it doesn't. Not at all. I think you are a wonderful father. And I believe that you will do a fine job of raising your son. However, in your relationships with women, you have a lot to learn. I hope you do learn. But you will not be learning with me. Is that clear?''

An ugly laugh escaped him. "Yeah. As glass. We're finished. Fine with me." He turned from her, and dropped to the couch again. "Anything else?"

Weakness washed over her. Pity. For him. For herself. For a brief time of beauty that was suddenly ending in such small meanness. She wanted to reach out, to cry, *Wait. I don't know how we got here. We have done this so badly. Let's try one more time....*

He picked up the remote, weighed it in his hands. "Finish it up, Prue."

So she did. "I expect you to take Jesse with you to Van Nuys tomorrow. I suppose it will take a while to work out all the legalities, but as far as I'm concerned, you're his father and he lives with you. However, this afternoon and this evening, I would like to spend as much time with him as possible." She paused, to give him a chance to say something if he wanted to. He didn't speak, just continued to balance the remote on his palm, waiting for her to be done. She went on, "As soon as you are gone, I will pack up and be on my way. Of course, I will keep you informed of my whereabouts at all times, should you need me for anything concerning Jesse's care." She remembered the issue of the house. "You still haven't told me, do you want this house?"

He shrugged. "Yeah, I want it."

"All right. I'll talk to Heather and get the number of the agent who handled the sale when she sold it to me. I'll have the agent call you, in a week or two. Good enough?"

He muttered, "Sure."

''As far as my furniture goes, once I get settled, I'll want my bedroom set and my desk. The rest of it—''

He waved the remote at her. ''Look. Do we have to go into every little detail right now?''

He was right, she knew it. ''No. Of course not.'' She hovered for a moment, behind the chair, feeling as if there was something else she ought to say. But then he looked away.

She knew then that the talking was done.

The music started as she mounted the stairs. And then, abruptly, it stopped. She hesitated on the third step, thinking maybe he would be coming after her, to tell her he wanted another chance, too. To say, *Let's start over. Let's give it one more try.*

But he didn't come. She realized he'd only put on his headphones. He was showing some consideration— and cutting her out at the same time.

Billy and Jesse left the next morning. Prudence saw them off, kneeling on the porch to get a last hug from Jesse. He wrapped his little arms around her neck and she breathed in his sweet nearly-a-baby smell and the breakfast Cheerios on his breath. When she kissed him, she closed her eyes so the feel of his downy-soft skin against her lips would be what she remembered. Later.

''We've gotta go.'' Billy was standing over them.

She pulled back from Jesse, straightened the collar of his shirt. ''You have a nice trip.''

Jesse gurgled, a happy, agreeable sound, then reached out and hugged her once more. ''Woo.'' A baby giggle in her ear. She kissed him one more time.

At last, there was no way to stretch the goodbye one bit further. She stood, relinquishing the child that she had once almost dared to think of as her own.

Billy said, "Good luck." His eyes were open, but everything in them was closed to her.

"Thank you. You, too."

"You'll be in touch, right?"

"I will. We'll settle everything, eventually. But I'll need to get established first, if that's all right."

"Whatever. You let me know."

"Yes." Huge spaces, she thought. Empty holes. "I'll let you know." *He's standing right next to me, but neither of us is really here.*

A flash of memory went off in her mind, blinding in its brightness. The first night they had made love. She had tossed the boxes of condoms in his lap. And he hadn't been able to look at her. He had taken her hand. Finally he had dared to look, to smile. Such stunned desire there, in his eyes.

Now there was nothing in his eyes.

"Okay, then." He took Jesse's hand and they went down the walk and out under the gray early-December sky. She followed at a distance, standing back a little, as Billy put his son in the car seat in back, closed the door, went around to the driver's side and got in.

Jesse waved at her through the window, grinning broadly, mouthing "Bye-bye." She pasted on a bright smile and waved back until the Jeep pulled away from the curb. And then she turned, wrapped her arms tightly around her middle and headed up the walk to the empty house.

The next morning, Prudence said goodbye to Eden. They had coffee at Eden's house one last time.

Eden said, "I honestly believe that Billy does love you. I know these Jones men. They don't give in to loving gracefully, but when it's all said and done, I swear to you, Prudence. They're worth the pain. If you would only give Billy a little time, give him a chance to—"

"Please, Eden."

And Eden sighed. "All right."

On the way home from Eden's, Prudence stopped in at Nellie's house and told the older woman she would not be able to help out with the Christmas Carnival after all, as Billy would be taking care of Jesse from now on, and Prudence intended to move to Sacramento.

An I-told-you-so look flashed in Nellie's eyes. But Prudence had to give her credit. She didn't say a word beyond, "We will miss you. Greatly. Are you sure you won't consider staying in town?"

Prudence made regretful noises—and said she really did have to go.

Once she left Nellie's house, she had planned to go over and say goodbye to Oggie.

But she just couldn't bring herself to do it. She didn't know how he would react to her news. He was so different now. The old Oggie, she liked to think, would have yelled at her. The old Oggie wouldn't have wanted her to leave his town, because he thought of her as part of his family and he wanted his family nearby. Of course, she would have stood firm in her determination to move on. But something inside her would have been nourished and uplifted by his obvious desire to have her stay.

The new Oggie, she feared, would do little more than wish her well. She didn't think she could bear that, so she took the coward's way. She decided she would visit him in a few weeks, when she came back to work out all those details that she and Billy would ultimately have to handle.

Prudence returned to the house on Prospect Street. She finished the last of her packing. Then she called a nice hotel in Sacramento and got herself a reservation for that night.

At five that afternoon, she put her bags in her car and headed out of town.

Everything went smoothly for Billy in Van Nuys. It turned out that Alexis's oldest daughter, Sheilah, was getting a degree in child development. She worked at a day-care center about six blocks from Bad Billy's. For a certain price, Billy could drop Jesse off there anytime. Sheilah gave him a list of trustworthy baby-sitters, so if he needed someone to help out at night, he only had to make a few calls.

On Wednesday and Thursday, Billy left Jesse at day care. He spent from ten in the morning until two in the afternoon listening to a succession of bands. After that, he closeted himself with Alexis.

"Sounds like you want a partner now, more than a manager," Alexis said, when he explained that he intended to start living in North Magdalene most of the time.

"Yeah, I think you're right."

"I'll buy in."

"What? You got rich managing this place? Should I look closer at the books?"

"You know the books are solid." Alexis seemed very pleased with herself. "And I have been saving, I admit it, hoping someday you'd be ready for this. I can get a good-size loan, too. And since I'm going to be doing most of the work, I figure you should give me a deal on my share of the buy-in."

Billy looked around his cramped, dusty office. Once,

he had lived for the place. "Getting Bad Billy's off the ground was the only time I ever worked hard in my life."

Alexis leaned back in the extra chair, whipped out her nail board and started filing away. "But you haven't had the interest, the last couple of years."

He knew she was right. "I guess it's time I moved on."

She stopped filing. "Partners, that's what I want. You come down a few days, once or twice a month. Book the bands, go over the money situation. Maybe agree to get out your guitar now and then. What do you say?"

"Sounds good."

By late Thursday afternoon, they had worked out a basic agreement. Alexis said she'd get a hold of the lawyer they always used, have him put it all down in writing.

Friday, Billy went to see his agent. The news was good there, too. Waverly had done a brisk business with Billy's most recent songs. A top country-western singer would use "Never To See You Again" as the title cut on her next album.

Billy should have been on top of the damn world. He had his son, and a family he hadn't even realized he needed. His music was making him lots of money. The club he'd grown a little tired of would run along just fine with Alexis in charge. He could book the bands and cash the checks Alexis sent him. And live in the mountains most of the time, teaching Jesse the things he needed to know: how to hit the urinal, how to dress himself, how to move back and then up on a fly ball.

What the hell more could he ask for?

As soon as the question took shape, the answer followed: Prue.

But he couldn't have Prue.

Hell, he *wouldn't* have Prue. Not if she showed up at his door and begged him to take her back, on his terms, for as long as he wanted her.

For the past few days now, that had become a fantasy of his—adolescent, yes, but nonetheless gratifying.

A knock at the door. And when he opened it, Prue. Standing in a driving rainstorm—for some reason, in this fantasy, it was always raining hard. And Prue was shivering, her hands stuffed into the pockets of a dripping wet trench coat. Over her hair she'd tied a scarf, all soggy and drooping now, from the rain. Behind her water-spotted glasses, her eyes were fixed on him in abject appeal.

"Oh, Billy. I can't live without you. Just give me one more chance. I'll do anything you want...."

Of course, he would be tempted. Prue willing to do *anything*—that would be something.

But he would hold firm. He would look her over good, from head to toe and back again. And then he'd shake his head.

"Forget it, Prue. You blew your chance." And he'd close the door in her face.

Unfortunately, after that fantasy, he'd always find himself remembering things he shouldn't let himself remember. Dancing with Prue in the living room of the house on Prospect Street. Or taking her hand at Sam's Thanksgiving dinner. Or the sight of her at the kitchen table in the morning, bending over her coffee cup, her fiery hair falling across her pale cheek. Or her blind look, with her glasses off, her face all soft and bewildered just before he would kiss her....

It all went in a circle. The wanting. And the infantile fantasy of rejecting her—and the sweet, aching memories that rose up when the fantasy was through.

It got him nowhere, he knew. The hard fact was, he didn't have her. And he had damn well better get used to not having her, because she wasn't coming back.

Wednesday night and Thursday night, he stayed home, with Jesse. It was kind of a habit he'd acquired lately: staying home. And since he'd left Jesse in other people's care most of the day, it seemed important to give the kid his evenings, at least.

His bungalow in Studio City had hardwood floors, perfect for toy trucks. They'd get down on the floor together, he and Jesse, and roll the trucks around. Funny, how quick those *vroom-vroom* sounds came back to a man. He and Jesse would *vroom* the trucks around and crash them into each other and laugh. They'd sing songs. And read stories. And by eight o'clock, Jesse would be off in dreamland.

And Billy would be going nuts, trying not to think about Prue. Wanting to call the house in North Magdalene, just to see if she would answer, just to see if she was still there.

By Friday night at eight-thirty, he gave in. He called. The phone rang four times. And the damn machine picked up. He heard her voice. "Hello, you have reached…" He listened to the mundane words, something dark and hungry moving inside him, something violent. Something lonely. When the beep came, he slammed the phone down.

And then he picked it up and punched redial. He listened a second time to the message, to the sound of her that wasn't really her. Just an echo, captured on a machine.

And this time, when the beep came, he said, "Prue. Damn you, Prue. Pick up."

Silence. Endless. Maddening.

He punched the disconnect button. Then he called Sheilah. She answered on the second ring. He told her he wanted to go over to the club for a few hours and asked which of the people on her baby-sitting list he should call first.

She said what he'd hoped she might. That she had a mountain of studying to do and there was no reason she couldn't do it at his place and keep an eye on Jesse at the same time.

The band that night was glad to let Billy sit in. He played three sets with them, joining them at their table in between, laughing too loud at bad jokes, drinking a little more than he should have, maybe, trying to tell himself he was having a good time.

He saw Sharlee, sashaying by in her red cowboy boots. She held her drink tray high and looked as happy as a heifer in an alfalfa field. She caught his eye and winked at him.

Surprisingly, according to Alexis, Sharlee was working out just fine. "Bakes cookies for the bartenders, can you believe it?" Alexis had told him. "And if someone's feeling low, she'll go and sit with them on her break, listen to their tale of woe. Everybody loves her. And she's always right on time for her shift...."

Little Loretta was still around, too. And up to her old tricks, licking her lips and flashing her gorgeous teeth, rubbing those plump breasts against him when she served him his drinks. Maybe he played up to her a little more than he should have, because he'd had a few too many and he was here to forget a certain bossy, bug-eyed redhead.

At one point, when things had started to get pleasantly hazy, he put his arm around Loretta and asked her how the world was treating her. She smiled up at him, dreamy-eyed, the way a woman ought to look at a man. "The world is treating me just fine, Billy. Just…spectacular."

"Glad to hear it." He bent his head a little and she lifted hers and all of a sudden, he was kissing her.

The girl really went all out. When he came up for air, the guys at the table were applauding. With a mock bow, he dropped into his chair and wiped the lipstick off his mouth. Then he picked up the shot of Black Jack she'd brought him and knocked it back. He squinted against the heat of it, going down.

When he opened his eyes again, Loretta had moved off to bring more drinks—and Sharlee was standing over near the platform stairs that went down to the dance floor, glaring at him. He frowned back at her, wondering what the hell she thought she should be giving him dirty looks about.

"Women," he muttered under his breath.

Soon enough, Loretta was back. "Dance with me, Billy."

Now, how could he refuse a sweet request like that? He went down the platform stairs with her and took her in his arms. They danced two jukebox numbers, close and slow. She rubbed herself against him, making sure he got the message just in case he'd missed it so far.

He pulled her closer, fitting her up and into him. She was pretty and she smelled good, even if she didn't smell like Prue.

Too young, though, he knew that.

But hell. Lately he was breaking all his own rules anyway. He'd gone and said he'd marry Prue. Stone sober, he had offered her marriage.

Not that it mattered, since Prue had turned him down.

The second song ended. But Loretta hung on, offering up her full, soft little mouth.

Some shred of sense must have remained with him, because he stepped back, and said, "Thank you, darlin'," and headed the hell away from her.

Either he dodged through the crowd faster than she could keep up, or she got wise and decided not to follow him. Whichever it was, when he came up the stairs beside the main bar and ducked into the door that would take him back to the safety of his office, she was nowhere around.

He strode on, through the relative quiet of the deserted storeroom, shoving through the door to his office at last and dropping into his desk chair without even bothering to turn on the light. He slumped down in the chair, low.

With the door partway open, he could hear the music from the main part of the club, not loud enough for his taste, but pretty clear. The band was starting in again. Their final set. They had a hell of a fiddle player, name of Charlie Parvenu. Damned if old Charlie couldn't make those strings scream.

Billy swung his boots up on the desk, leaned back and closed his eyes.

"Billy." The soft voice came from the doorway.

He glanced over. Sure enough.

"Billy, you shouldn't have just left me there."

He told her, slow and clear, "You go on now, Loretta, get on out of here."

The light from the storeroom shone on her hair. Dark red hair. Longing sliced through him, sharp and singing, like a knife. Like Charlie Parvenu whipping that bow over those strings.

The girl came on, into the darkness with him, carefully closing the door behind her, shutting out the light.

"I told you to go," he said one more time.

"But I don't want to go." She was leaning against the door. He could see the shadow of her there.

Loneliness. All through him.

He heard her moving, the soft tread of her boots on the floor, coming toward him. Farther away now, that singing fiddle, the noise from the club.

Things sliding on the desk as she pushed them out of her way. And then she hoisted herself up, so she was sitting there, on the desktop, her thigh against his legs. He rocked back, dropped his booted feet to the floor.

She laughed, low. Knowing. And then she was bending forward, the unfamiliar scent of her all around him, her mouth opening on his, her hands fanning out against his chest.

He wondered in a distant way if he might possibly be able to get it up with her. After all, she did have red hair and he had an imagination. Maybe it would be like him and Jesse and the toy trucks, like the *vroom-vroom* sound that came right back to a man, even if it had been over thirty years since he did it last. Because that's what he felt like. Like he was playing some game he'd grown out of long ago.

Her mouth sucked his and her hungry, seeking hands moved downward. In a minute, she was going to find

out that he wasn't as involved as he should have been.
He wondered how the hell he was going to handle that.

But he didn't have time to wonder long, because
right then the door swung back and the overhead light
burst on, blinding him.

Chapter 19

Loretta gasped and jerked back, bumping the desk, and then dropping with an undignified, *"Oof!"* to the floor.

"Billy Jones, I am ashamed of you." Sharlee was standing in the doorway.

Billy rubbed his blinded eyes. "What the hell?"

Sharlee wasn't finished. "Didn't you learn a darn thing from what happened to me?"

"Huh?"

"It's a pity. It's a crying shame. What you are doing here tonight is only going to make things worse."

Loretta came up then, spitting mad. "You nosy little bitch. Get out of here. Now."

Sharlee planted her hands on her hips. "Don't you get nasty with me, Loretta. Don't you even try it."

"Why, you..." Loretta started toward Sharlee.

Billy stood. "Loretta."

Loretta turned and looked at him, her eyes a little

wild, her lipstick smeared down to her chin. "I'm getting rid of her. Now."

He wiped his own mouth. "No."

Loretta frowned. "What?"

"You'd better go." His palm was greasy pink. "Take the night off, if you want to."

"But, Billy—"

He put up that lipstick-smeared hand. "It wasn't a good idea, Loretta."

"But I thought you—"

"Let it go, Loretta. Sharlee did you a favor, I promise you."

She stared at him, caught now between fury and incredulity. He shook his head.

"Fine," she said. "Just fine." And she whirled on her heel and marched for the door. Sharlee slid to the side as she flounced out.

There was a smashed-looking box of tissues on the corner of his desk. Billy yanked one out and wiped the lipstick off his hand, hoping that Sharlee would follow Loretta and get lost. But he might as well have whistled for the moon.

"You love Prudence," Sharlee said. "How can you let some other woman crawl all over you?"

Billy dropped to his chair again.

Sharlee demanded, "How can you do that? It's revolting, is what it is."

All at once he was weary, right down to his bones. "Sharlee, leave me be. I've had enough for one night."

"But I was there. I saw what was happening between you and Prudence. I thought it was so beautiful, you and her and little Jesse. Didn't it work out, is that it?" Her round Kewpie-doll eyes brimmed with honest concern.

"Sharlee…"

"Well. Didn't it?"

"No. It didn't work out."

"Oh. Oh, how sad.…" She took a step toward him. "Maybe you want to talk about it?"

"No, thanks."

"You listened to me for a week straight. Now I've learned to listen. I'm not so bad at it. And I really don't mind."

"Sharlee. Thanks. But no thanks."

"You're sure?"

"I'm sure."

Still, she wouldn't go. "Maybe it will work out, after all. They say true love always finds a way."

He shook his head.

Sharlee let out a heartfelt sigh. "Oh, Billy. Life can be so…disappointing."

"Good night, Sharlee."

Her cute rosebud of a mouth quivered at the corners. "I'm…sorry, Billy."

He said nothing more, just sat there, waiting for her to give up and go. When she finally did, he went over and turned off the light again. Then he sat back down in the dark, swung his feet onto the desk and listened to that screaming, far-off fiddle until the last note died.

At his house, he gave Sheilah a fifty and thanked her for helping out. Then he went to the room he'd put Jesse in, just to see that his son was all right.

He found Jesse dreaming. His feet moved and so did his little mouth. Billy bent closer, wondering what a one-year-old would dream about.

He caught one word, "Woo."

That was enough. He turned and went quietly out the way he had come.

* * *

Billy and Jesse returned to North Magdalene the next day. They got in around dinnertime. On Main Street they were closing up the booths for something called the Christmas Carnival, that had evidently taken place that day. Billy was hungry, so he stopped to get a hot dog from a booth that hadn't closed yet.

Marnie Jones waited on him. As she squirted mustard on the bun, she reminded him of the kids' Christmas show at the town hall.

"Seven sharp," she said. "But you need to get there by six-thirty, to get a good seat."

"I don't think I'll make it. Sorry." He handed her the money and she passed him the hot dog.

"Tell Prudence, then, okay?"

He just looked at her.

She made a face. "Oh. I forgot. She left town, right?"

"Right." Jesse started grabbing for the hot dog. "Gotta go," Billy said.

"Sure. Okay." She made the words sound like an expression of sympathy.

He turned and walked away.

The house was cold, the air in there icy and strange. Billy built a fire and turned on the heater, which helped a little.

There was a message on the machine from Prue, giving the name and room number of a hotel in Sacramento. "I'll probably just stay here for a week or so, maybe longer, until I find a house or a condo. Something. I'm not sure what. Call me—if there's anything about Jesse, I mean."

He played the message three times, Jesse standing

beside him, sucking on a teething ring, his green eyes wide.

"Woo?" he asked.

Billy knelt and got himself nose-to-nose with the kid. "Yeah. Woo is fine. She'll be back to see you soon." You. Not me.

Jesse gave him a sweet, drooly smile and then turned and toddled away, still munching that teething ring.

Once Jesse was asleep, Billy wandered into Prue's room. He stood over that white cloud of a bed, staring down at it, remembering the first night they'd made love. The twenty-four condoms. The red stain on all that white.

Where was that damn stain, anyway? He pushed aside a pillow—and there it was. She'd gotten most of it out, but not all.

He turned and sat down. Pure self-indulgence, to be there, he knew it. But somehow, he couldn't stop himself. Just as he couldn't stop himself from thinking of the things they'd done there, couldn't stop himself from remembering what she'd said to him at the last.

You don't think about what's right. You don't think about the future. You don't think about the consequences to both of us....

He supposed she had him nailed, as usual. He supposed he hadn't thought about the things that mattered. Until now. When it was too late.

He ended up pulling open the bed stand drawer. One last condom waited there. He picked it up, turned it over, regret sluicing through him, burning like acid. Then he fell back on the bed and closed his eyes.

He woke to someone ringing the doorbell downstairs. He rolled his head and looked at the clock.

Three a.m., for God's sake. Who in hell would be ringing the doorbell at three in the damn a.m.?

Then he thought, *Prue,* and his stupid heart started beating like the drums in those jungle movies, when the cannibals are getting ready to boil up the missionaries for lunch.

But it couldn't be Prue. She had her own key. And anyway, she wasn't a woman to come ringing doorbells at three in the morning. She'd wait till a more decent hour. Decent. That was Prue.

The bell rang again. If he didn't get down there soon, the noise would wake Jesse. He pushed himself off the bed and staggered out to the upper hall.

When he pulled open the front door, he found Oggie, leaning on his cane, grinning as if it were three in the afternoon instead of the middle of the night.

"Don't just stand there, boy. Let me in. It's colder than the smile on a dead snake out here."

Still half-asleep, Billy ran a hand down his face. "You just called me boy."

"Damn tootin'." The old man hobbled forward. "Stand back. I'm comin' in."

Billy stepped aside. Oggie stumped over the threshold, turned and shoved the door shut. He grinned at Billy. "Coffee. I want me some coffee. Dark and sweet."

"At three in the morning?"

"Indulge me. I'm an old man."

They went into the kitchen. Billy brewed the coffee, while Oggie sat at the table, smiling in the way he used to smile—as if he knew something no one else knew and he wasn't telling what. It was a smile that had always made Billy feel edgy.

Just as Billy set the full cup and the sugar bowl in

front of the old coot, the phone rang. Billy picked it up.

"Yeah?"

"Billy, it's me. Jared. Is my dad there?"

"You bet. You want to talk to him?"

"Hell, no. This is more in the way of a warning. He left the Hole in the Wall about ten minutes ago. And I had a feeling he was headed your way."

"What gave you the feeling?" Billy watched the grinning Oggie, who would end up in a diabetic coma if he piled much more sugar into that coffee of his.

"He's not happy about you letting Prudence go. He's been blabbing about it all night, whupping everybody at five-card draw and moanin' how Prudence took off without even sayin' goodbye to him."

Billy glared at the old man, who winked back. "It's none of his damn business."

"Like that's gonna shut him up. Look, you want me to come and drag him out of there?"

"Thanks anyway, but I'll handle this." Billy hung the phone back on the wall.

The old man stirred his coffee and let out a cackling laugh.

Billy said, "I thought you turned over a new leaf."

Oggie set his spoon down, picked up the cup, guzzled a big sip and smacked his lips. "To hell with a new leaf. Our Prudence didn't even come and say goodbye to me. I was mightily injured, I gotta tell you. What the hell is goin' on, I want to know? I mind my own damn business for a few days, and everything goes to hell in a handbasket."

Billy dropped into the chair nearest the phone. "You finish your coffee. And then go on home."

"You love our Prudence."

"Stay out of it."

"You ain't never gonna find no peace, until you go and track her down."

Billy got up, went to the coffeepot, poured himself a cup, then plunked it, untouched, on the counter and whirled on the old man. "I'm fine. I got no problems."

"Yeah, and I never played poker in my life." He squinted at Billy, tipping his grizzled head sideways. "Did you tell her you love her?"

Billy folded his arms across his chest and said nothing.

"Right. I didn't think so." Oggie slurped more coffee. "You go to her. You get down on your knees. You beg. You plead. You do whatever you have to do. But you don't come back without her."

"You finished that coffee yet?"

"Maybe you're still tryin' to tell yourself you're gonna get over her. Wrong. This is the one for you. I knew it that day you came to the Bel Air mansion and set eyes on your son in the flesh for the very first time. I knew it from the way you shouted and swore when you stomped out of there, from the look on Prudence's face a few minutes later." He faked a woman's voice. "'Billy certainly is a volatile person,' she said to me. Her eyes said a lot more. Those eyes of hers said she was afraid of you, but not in the way she *thought* she was afraid of you."

"This is the most convoluted line of bull you have ever dished out," Billy said.

Oggie chortled. "You listen to me, boy. You do what I tell you. That woman loves you and you love her."

Billy had heard about enough. He advanced on the

old man, took his elbow and his cane and hustled him toward the front door.

Oggie jabbered the whole way. "I warn you, your wild days are through. It's over and done for you, that life. And you know it, too, boy. You know it in your heart. There ain't gonna be no savor in any of that no more. There ain't gonna be a bit of fun. Not without Prudence. So you go to her. You give in to her. That's what a man does in the end, and you know it now. He gives in to a woman. He gives in and they get on with their lives."

Billy pulled open the door, handed the old man his cane and guided him over the threshold.

"Three little words, boy. 'I love you.' Spoken sincerely, right from the heart. It ain't gonna kill you to say them. In fact, you're gonna find that sayin' 'em will give you the life you really want."

"Good night, Oggie."

The old geezer was still babbling away when Billy shut the door.

The rest of that night, the next day and that night, too, Billy found he couldn't get the old rascal's crazy words off his mind.

Around ten on Monday morning, a woman called from a Dr. Anselmo's office in Grass Valley. "Ms. Wilding's new glasses are ready," the woman said. "We are so sorry it's taken such a long time, but the lenses came in scratched at first. And we had to send them back. Please tell her she can drop by anytime during office hours to have them fitted."

"I'll do that." As he hung up the phone, Billy knew what he would do.

He packed up Jesse and took him to Eden's. "I know

it's a lot to ask, but could you watch him for four or five hours, do you think?'' He reconsidered. ''Hell. Maybe more than that, I'm not sure. I'll call you by six or so, if I'm not back. Okay?''

A hint of a smile tugged at the corner of Eden's mouth. ''Where are you going, Billy?''

''I've got business to take care of.''

''Business in Sacramento?'' He didn't answer and Eden's smile grew wider. ''You go on. We'll look out for Jesse.''

He thanked her and left.

At Dr. Anselmo's office, they didn't want to give him the glasses. The Nellie Anderson type behind the reception desk pursed her mouth at him. ''This is highly irregular. She'll need them fitted. And who *are* you, anyway?''

He lied like a rug. ''I'm a business associate and dear friend. And she has to have those glasses right away. She'll be back in to take care of the fitting within a day or two, I swear to you. How much do I owe you?''

The woman cleared her throat, looked away—and finally named a figure. He gave her the money, she handed him the glasses and he was out of there.

He got to the hotel at a little after one in the afternoon. Probably Prue wouldn't be there. Probably she was out finding a place to live or a job or something. But he went straight to her room anyway, running on pure hope.

And damned if she didn't answer his knock.

She pulled back the door and gasped, ''Billy!'' those bug eyes wider than ever. He looked at her and he knew that he was going to grab her soon, and when he did, he would never let her go.

"Wh...what's happened? Is it Jesse?"

"No." He stepped toward her. She fell back. "Jesse's fine. He misses you. Eden's taking care of him right now."

"Then what are you doing here?"

He shoved the door closed behind him. "Your glasses are ready." She was wearing a fluffy white terry-cloth robe and, in his expert opinion, not much else. Her hair was wet. "Just got out of the shower, huh?"

She clutched the facings of the robe at her throat and demanded a second time, "What are you doing here?"

It was a suite, with a sitting room in front and a bedroom beyond. He spotted a television in the corner—and a remote control on the coffee table a few feet away. He scooped up the remote.

"Don't," she commanded, anger replacing shock. "Don't even start..."

He pointed the remote at the television. A war movie popped on. The room came alive with the *rat-tat-tat* of machine-gun fire, the whistling of rockets through smoky air. "There. Better." He tossed the remote down and smiled at Prue.

She shook her head slowly. "Billy. Billy, no..."

"You never told me you went and got new glasses."

"I...um..."

"Don't you want your new glasses?" He started toward her.

She backed up, watching him warily. "Oh, well. Yes. I'll...drive up to Grass Valley soon, to get them."

"No need." He whipped them from his breast pocket and held them up.

She kept backing away. "I... Don't they have to be fitted? I don't understand...." She reached the wall. There was nowhere else to go. She let out a whimper.

He moved right up close. Carefully, to the accompaniment of several sharp bursts of machine-gun fire, he took her old glasses away and stuck them into the pocket where he'd carried the new ones.

"Billy." She was shaking. She smelled like shampoo. Like Prue. The best smell in the damn world. "Oh, Billy, no..."

"Yes, Prue. Yes," he whispered. He put the new glasses on her. Rockets went off on the TV battlefield. "Nice," he said. "Very nice. A little crooked, but they can fix that."

The tears came then, overflowing her eyes, trailing under those new glasses and down her soft cheeks. "Why are you doing this?"

He touched her hair. Wet. Wet silk. And then he tipped up her chin. "Did you find a job?"

She sniffed, straightened her shoulders. "Not yet. I...I've got some prospects, though."

He saw the truth in her eyes. She'd been holed up here, licking her wounds—wounds he had inflicted.

"Prospects, huh?" He smoothed her hair, brushed a tear away with a thumb.

"Yes. Prospects." She swiped at her nose with the back of her hand. "Excellent...prospects."

All he wanted was to kiss her. He tried. She turned away.

He whispered, "I love you," against her wet cheek.

"Oh, no." She sniffed some more. "You don't."

"I do."

"You can't. What's to love?"

"You, Prue. Just you."

"I'm quiet and boring and drab and shy."

"...and beautiful and brave and damn sexy when you want to be."

"You'll get tired of me."

"The hell I will."

She looked at him then. "You'll break my heart."

"No. I'll love you forever."

She gasped. "You? *You?* Bad Billy Jones?"

"Yeah. Me. Bad Billy Jones. Listen. I've done a lot of things you don't want to know about. But I swear to you, I never told a woman I loved her in my whole life until now...at least not when I was sober."

She let out a small moan that was almost a giggle.

"Look. I know I'm a loser. I know I don't have a clue how to love. I haven't done it enough, I've been one self-absorbed S.O.B. as a rule. But Jesse's been helping me with it. And you'll help me, too, won't you, Prue? You'll help me do it, help me learn how to love you like you deserve to be loved?" He could feel her trembling, see himself in her eyes. He knew his crazy old uncle had told the truth. "You love me, too. Don't you, Prue?"

"No. I..."

"Yes."

"Billy, I..."

"Take a chance on me, Prue. Marry me, Prue. Make an honest man of me, for once in my damn life."

"I can't..."

"To hell with all this talk." He captured her face between his hands and put his mouth on hers.

She stiffened—and then she melted. He knew then that everything would be all right, so he scooped her up and carried her to the bed in the other room.

On the TV, land mines exploded and cannons fired.

Tenderly he slid off her new glasses. With great care, he set them on the bed stand. Then he bent close to her again. "Say you love me, Prue."

Prudence could hold back no longer. Staring blindly at the blurred outline of his beloved face, she confessed, "Oh, Billy. I do. Heaven help me, I do...."

They were married the following Saturday at the white church across from their house in North Magdalene. Outside, the first snow was falling. And inside there was a little boy who needed them both. And a whole churchful of Joneses.

* * * * *

MORE MacGREGORS ARE COMING!

In November 1998, *New York Times* bestselling author

NORA ROBERTS

Brings you...

THE MacGREGOR GROOMS

Daniel MacGregor will stop at nothing to see his three determinedly single grandsons married—he'll tempt them all the way to the altar.

Coming soon in Silhouette Special Edition:

March 1999:
THE PERFECT NEIGHBOR
(SE#1232)

Also, watch for the MacGregor stories where it all began!

December 1998: THE MacGREGORS: Serena—Caine

February 1999: THE MacGREGORS: Alan—Grant

April 1999: THE MacGREGORS: Daniel—Ian

Available at your favorite retail outlet, only from

Silhouette®

Look us up on-line at: http://www.romance.net   PSNRMACS

Take 2 bestselling love stories FREE

Plus get a FREE surprise gift!

Special Limited-Time Offer

Mail to Silhouette Reader Service™

P.O. Box 609
Fort Erie, Ontario
L2A 5X3

YES! Please send me 2 free Silhouette Desire® novels and my free surprise gift. Then send me 6 brand-new novels every month, which I will receive months before they appear in bookstores. Bill me at the low price of $3.49 each plus 25¢ delivery and GST*. That's the complete price, and a saving of over 10% off the cover prices—quite a bargain! I understand that accepting the books and gift places me under no obligation ever to buy any books. I can always return a shipment and cancel at any time. Even if I never buy another book from Silhouette, the 2 free books and the surprise gift are mine to keep forever.

326 SEN CH7V

Name _____ (PLEASE PRINT)

Address _____ Apt. No. _____

City _____ Province _____ Postal Code _____

This offer is limited to one order per household and not valid to present Silhouette Desire® subscribers. *Terms and prices are subject to change without notice. Canadian residents will be charged applicable provincial taxes and GST.

CDES-98   ©1990 Harlequin Enterprises Limited

We, the undersigned, having barely survived four years of nursing school, do hereby vow to meet at Granetti's at least once a week, not to do anything drastic to our hair without consulting each other first and never, _ever_—no matter how rich, how cute, how funny, how smart, or how good in bed—marry a doctor.

Dana Rowan, R.N.
Lee Murphy, R.N.
Katie Sheppard, R.N.

Christine Flynn
Susan Mallery
Christine Rimmer

prescribe a massive dose of heart-stopping romance in their scintillating new series, **PRESCRIPTION: MARRIAGE**. Three nurses are determined *not* to wed doctors— only to discover the men of their dreams come with a medical degree!

Look for this unforgettable series in fall 1998:

October 1998: **FROM HOUSE CALLS TO HUSBAND** by Christine Flynn

November 1998: **PRINCE CHARMING, M.D.** by Susan Mallery

December 1998: **DR. DEVASTATING** by Christine Rimmer

Only from

Silhouette®SPECIAL EDITION®

Available at your favorite retail outlet.

Look us up on-line at: http://www.romance.net   SSEPMAR

**Don't miss
an exciting opportunity
to save on the purchase of
Harlequin and Silhouette books!**

Buy any two Harlequin or
Silhouette books and save
$10.00 off future Harlequin and
Silhouette purchases
OR
buy any three
Harlequin or Silhouette books
and save **$20.00 off** future
Harlequin and Silhouette purchases.

**Watch for details
coming in November 1998!**

PHQ498

Coming in December 1998
from Silhouette Books...

The BIG BAD WOLFE family is back!

by bestselling author

Joan Hohl

Officer Matilda Wolfe had followed in her family's law-
enforcement footsteps. But the tough beauty swore she
wouldn't fall in love as easily as the rest of the Wolfe pack.

Not this Christmas, not during this case...
and not with an ex-mercenary turned minister whose
sexy grin haunted her dreams.

Don't miss the brand-new single-title release
WOLFE WINTER this December 1998...
only from Silhouette Books.

Available at your favorite retail outlet.

Look us up on-line at: http://www.romance.net

PSWINWOLF

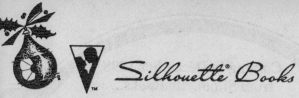

Silhouette® Books

**invites you to celebrate the joys
of the season December 1998 with
the Fortune Family in...**

A FORTUNE'S CHILDREN CHRISTMAS

Three Fortune cousins are given exactly one year to
fulfill the family traditions of wealth and power. And in
the process these bachelors receive a Christmas gift more
precious than mere riches from three very special
women.

**Don't miss this original collection of
three brand-new, heartwarming stories
by favorite authors:**

Lisa Jackson
Barbara Boswell
Linda Turner

Look for **A FORTUNE'S CHILDREN CHRISTMAS** this
December at your favorite retail outlet. And watch for more
Fortune's Children titles coming to Silhouette Desire,
beginning in January 1999.

Look us up on-line at: http://www.romance.net   PSFORTUNE